The Tick Tock Man

Terence Strong

POCKET BOOKS

LONDON • SYDNEY • NEW YORK • TORONTO

First published in Great Britain by William Heinemann, 1994
This edition published by Pocket Books, 2006
An imprint of Simon & Schuster UK Ltd
A CBS COMPANY

5 7 9 10 8 6 4

Simon & Schuster UK Ltd
Africa House
64–78 Kingsway
London WC2B 6AH

www.simonsays.co.uk

Simon & Schuster Australia
Sydney

A CIP catalogue record for this book is available from the British Library

ISBN-13: 978-1-4165-2205-8
ISBN-10: 1-4165-2205-0

Printed and bound in Great Britain by
Cox & Wyman Ltd, Reading, Berks

For Felix

The men and women of 321 EOD Squadron
and the Explosives Section of the Metropolitan Police.

And for those innocent survivors of
terrorist bombs who have to carry on
when the rest of the world so soon forgets.

Author's Note

It's called the most dangerous job in the world.

Seventeen bomb-disposal operators and three team members of 321 Explosives Ordnance Disposal Squadron (Royal Logistics Corps) have been killed in Northern Ireland since the unit was formed in 1971.

Twenty-six have been injured, many seriously; two such incidents occurred while this book was being written.

As often as not these men have been the deliberate target of terrorist booby traps; or else time and their luck ran out.

Yet in that time well over five thousand devices have been neutralised by EOD teams, saving an estimated bill for damages of some £500 million; the saving of innocent life and limb has been inestimable.

Between them, those teams have received two George Cross medals, 16 OBEs, 22 MBEs, 19 BEMs, 33 George Medals and 65 Queen's Gallantry Medals, with 115 Mentions in Dispatches. Probably that says it all.

Therefore it is a privilege to have written probably the first thriller ever to go deep into the bomb man's closed and frightening world.

Achieving this has been due in no small part to the kind co-operation of the British Army and in particular to members of 'Felix' (the traditional EOD call sign) in Northern Ireland and in mainland Britain.

I am particularly indebted to CATO ('Top Cat') for a tour of front-line bases and for allowing me to witness the incredibly realistic training procedures. My thanks to all those I met, for the warmth of their welcome, for sharing their experiences and some of their most private fears, and for their patient explanations. This could not have been written without them.

Thanks also to the Metropolitan Police. Although their equally courageous Explosives Section (all former EOD operators) were more reticent, I have attempted to portray their rôle and methods accurately.

The bombs in this book are my own invention; I felt it fair to ask the experts *only* how to dismantle them. For obvious reasons, some data and other information have been made deliberately vague.

Incidentally readers may be interested to know that Trafalgar House (unrelated to the company of the same name) really does exist. At the time this book is set it was empty and up for sale.

Finally I should like to give an extra special thanks to those who have been my guides in this unfamiliar world: Hugh, Gary, Andy and Kevin Callaghan GM OGM (the author of *A Price On My Head* from Owl Books).

These are the people who have really made this book possible.

Terence Strong
London 1994

Many others have contributed time and expertise which have assisted in the writing of this story:

The staff of the London Evening Standard, *including managing editor Craig Orr; editor Stewart Steven for allowing me to sit in on conference; news editor Steve Clackson and my good friend Steve Pryer. They've all promised not to sue for any unintentionally unethical behaviour by my fictitious characters!*

In Northern Ireland I was grateful for the hospitality, advice and observations of Pauline Reynolds; Richard Crawford, new author of a cracking thriller called Fall When Hit; *writer and journalist Eamonn Mallie, and Mike and Brad at Lisburn for smoothing the way.*

On the medical front I thank my long-term adviser Major Janice Perkins (long overdue a credit) and Lieutenant Colonel Roddy MacDonald and Lieutenant Colonel Graham Hopkins and staff of the Cambridge Military Hospital, Aldershot.

Those close to both sides of the paramilitary divide in Northern Ireland were kind enough to explain their political beliefs both eloquently and passionately: Ken (for Sinn Fein) and Steve and Charlie (for the Loyalists), which I hope will go some way to explaining what so many of us have failed to understand fully.

Other 'regulars' on my team have again done sterling work with technical advice: Neil, Robin and Leslie, and on the editorial production front I thank my wife Lindy, my editor Carolyn Caughey and typist Judy Coombes for performing another minor miracle.

And, of course, to those who have inspired but cannot be named. They know who they are.

Prologue

The soldier had died instantly.

A single sniper round had shattered his skull without warning. One moment he was a bright and friendly nineteen-year-old on his first tour of Belfast, an entire lifetime stretching ahead of him; the next he was a corpse who would never grow old. A crumpled sack of camouflaged combat fatigues, virtually indistinguishable from the weeds and rubbish on the overgrown patch of wasteland.

Virtually trapped on the open plot and fearing another unerringly accurate shot, the dead man's foot patrol had been obliged to seek what little cover they could find for almost ten minutes. They couldn't fire because there was nothing to shoot at, and they couldn't manoeuvre because they were sitting ducks.

At last reinforcements of 1 Light Infantry moved in to surround the row of derelict houses from which the shot was believed to have come.

The body of the dead soldier had only just been retrieved when the Ammunition Technical Officer, Captain Tom Harrison, arrived.

The two Humber 'Pigs' and Saracen of 321 Explosives Ordnance Disposal Squadron, which had been tasked to the incident, pulled in behind the ambulance. Armoured Land-Rovers of the British Army and Royal Ulster Constabulary had already gathered.

Harrison jumped down from the cab to be met by the first subaltern to have arrived on the scene. With him was the Light Infantry sergeant who had been leading the patrol.

'Another shoot, ATO, I'm afraid,' the infantry officer confirmed. Despite his confident manner, he looked ridiculously young for the job, the down of fair hair above his upper lip hardly looking as though it had need of a razor. 'Paddy is playing with his new toy again. That's the third time this month.'

Harrison watched the dead man being zipped into the body bag. 'The Tikka?'

'I think so, sir.' It was the NCO who spoke. Unlike the junior officer by his side, the sergeant looked a decade older than his twenty-five years, an age he shared with Harrison. The eyes amid the cam cream were wary and red-rimmed with fatigue as he introduced himself. 'Sarn't Copes, sir. I was leading the patrol when we heard the crack and the thump. Next thing we knew, Bates was down. Poor bleeder didn't stand a chance. Took half his fucking head off.'

Certainly sounds like the Tikka, Harrison thought.

According to 'Whiz', the Weapons Intelligence Section, it had been used in this Ballymurphy ghetto area on the two previous 'shoots' that month. A deadly new toy indeed for the terrorists. The Finnish-made bolt-action rifle capable of throwing a hollow point 7mm cartridge five hundred and fifty metres with deadly accuracy. As the veteran sergeant had said, the dead soldier hadn't stood a chance.

Harrison viewed the stretch of wasteland with its weeds, wind-strewn rubbish and abandoned household appliances. Each side of the redevelopment area was flanked by the gable-end walls of terraced housing. They were adorned with elaborate and sinister pro-Republican graffiti. The far side was denoted by the next parallel street and a row of derelict houses like rotten teeth awaiting extraction.

Car bombs and derelicts. They were Harrison's very private fears. Fears that he never shared with another human soul. And on which he didn't even allow his own mind to dwell. Yet those fears were always lurking at the back of his mind like the proverbial black dog. Because the truth was that a car or a derelict building was never necessarily what it seemed. Even if a vehicle had been subjected to a controlled explosion, there was never any guarantee that there wasn't something very nasty lying in wait for the unsuspecting ATO. There were a hundred hidden recesses in which something could be secreted. Likewise with an empty house. Plenty of time for a terrorist to plan his deadly trap and even more places to hide a device.

That's exactly what had happened after the first sniper shooting. During their attempt to flush out the assassin, an unwary infantryman from the Unit Search Team had tripped a wire in an upstairs room. The blast from the hidden explosive device had taken off his right arm and left him blinded.

But the soldiers had been swift to learn their lesson. After the next sniper killing in similar circumstances, they had radioed 'Felix' – call sign of the bomb-disposal team – for an ATO expert to clear the sniper's eyrie.

Tasked to the scene, that time Harrison had found by a window some hand-rolled cigarette ends and a tin of Golden Virginia tobacco. Inviting inspection.

Harrison had declined the invitation. Having learned that you could never be overcautious, he had fitted a hook and line to the tin before giving it a tug from a safe distance. The tin had only contained an ounce of plastic explosive fitted to a trembler switch, but it would have been enough to destroy eyesight and remove the careless pair of hands that had touched it.

Now here he was again, faced with almost exactly the same scenario. And that black dog was right behind him.

It didn't help that there was a name being mentioned. Knowing a bomber's name just made it that much more personal. Harrison's friend Don Trenchard had told him of the man's suspected identity a few days earlier.

Harrison had known Trenchard, who was a few years older than himself but didn't look it, since his Sandhurst days when his friend was lecturing on the rôle of intelligence in Northern Ireland. Trenchard's groomed good looks and boyish charm were not what one associated with the murky world of covert warfare, but as a prankster and dedicated womaniser he was a welcome companion. Always to be relied on to bring more than one pretty girl to a party.

Although a major, Trenchard never introduced himself by rank and was rarely to be seen in uniform. Working as he did with 14

3

Intelligence Company under the Intelligence and Security Group, he was privy to many of the Province's secrets.

Hughie Dougan, he had told Harrison. That was the name that 14 Int and 'Whiz' thought was behind the latest rash of booby-trapped bombings in Belfast. Dougan was a 'Sixty-niner' who had joined the IRA after the August riots of that year. As a former REME technician in the British Army, his professional knowledge was soon put to good use by the fledgling Provisionals. He was finally arrested and imprisoned for nine years on a charge of conspiring to cause explosions.

According to Trenchard, Dougan had been released earlier that year before going 'on the gallop', in Provisional IRA slang, disappearing over the border to help plan the bombings and make the devices.

Harrison had gone back over the Dougan files from nine years earlier. There were, he had to admit, distinct similarities. The most glaring was the inevitable use of one or more antihandling devices and deliberate 'come-ons' to lure troops or ATOs.

After all, Trenchard pointed out, the Provos were currently paying a thirteen thousand-pound bounty to their members for a dead bomb-disposal operator. Thirteen. It had been unlucky for several of Harrison's oppos. But did it help having a name?

Not really. You still couldn't take anything for granted. Or assume you knew how the bomber's mind worked. Familiarity and contempt were dangerous one-way streets. If anything, having a name just added to the tension. Encouraged the black dog.

He became aware that the subaltern was talking: 'We've cordoned off this whole area down to those derelicts and around the back of them. We appear to have identified the building that the sniper used.'

'Yes?'

The officer shrugged. 'Three witnesses, kids who were playing behind the derelicts. Swore they saw a man jumping over the back-yard wall and running away. Said he was carrying what looked like a long canvas case.'

Harrison narrowed his eyes. 'Don't tell me, the kids were under fourteen?'

4

The inexperienced officer looked puzzled.

'Unsafe evidence, sir,' the sergeant explained with weary patience.

'Kids in the Ballymurphy aren't usually that keen to assist the security forces,' Harrison said. Probably recruited from the *Na Fianna Eireann*, the Republican boy scout movement, he thought. 'They've been put up to it. My guess is it's a come-on and we'll find your sniper actually fired from someplace else.' He looked up at the shabby concrete monolith beyond the line of derelicts. 'Maybe that block of flats.'

The officer looked suitably chastened. He'd learn, and fast too, if he wanted to survive for a second tour.

Harrison made two decisions. The first was to wait for another ninety minutes 'soak time', as the delays most commonly used by the Provisional IRA were one- or two-hour – although, of course, nothing was ever certain. Only then would he task in a specialist High-Risk Search Team of Royal Engineers to scour all the other derelicts in the row before he alone approached the suspect house.

His second decision was on the siting of the Incident Control Point. 'I don't like it here,' he said. 'It's too exposed and over-looked. There could be a command-controlled device anywhere on this wasteland and it would take a month to find it.' He consulted his large-scale map. 'I'll set up the ICP down nearer the derelicts on the next street intersection. We can't so easily be watched from there.'

The officer nodded, seeing the sense in that.

'Just one thing, sir,' the sergeant said. 'The stairways in those derelicts are very narrow with a tight bend on the landing. So if you need to go up I don't think you'll be able to send a Wheel-barrow in.'

Harrison smiled grimly. 'Anything else I ought to know?'

The sergeant grinned for the first time since the shooting. 'And I think it's about to rain.'

He was right on both counts. The Royal Engineers confirmed the restricted access on the stairways as well as the structural unreliability of the upper floors. And when Harrison was finally ready to be fitted with the armoured khaki bombsuit, the air had been filled with a warm drizzle for over an hour. He stood at the new Incident Control Point with his arms outstretched as though beseeching the gods for good fortune as his Number Two – an earnest and moustacheoed corporal called Marsh – expertly strapped together the back of the jacket and slid the Kevlar armour chest and crotch plates into their respective pouches. Now he resembled a rather dowdy medieval knight, an impression completed by the bomb helmet with its thick Plexiglas visor.

A total weight of some seventy pounds reduced Harrison's forward movement to a waddling gait and turned the slightest action into a sweaty, exhausting effort. But that was the Army rule. Bombsuits to be worn until the threat was evaluated and neutralised unless it was judged directly prejudicial to the operator's safety.

'Let's at least get the Wheelbarrow up outside the house, Corporal,' Harrison said. 'See if we can't get a look-see inside.'

'Boss,' Marsh acknowledged. Harrison wasn't one for formality, but like many soldiers the corporal felt uneasy with undue familiarity. He liked to know exactly where he stood.

Returning to the back of the Pig, Marsh sat opposite the TV monitor which relayed from the video camera on board the little tracked vehicle that resembled a miniature tank some three feet in height. He picked up the separate control console. Then at the press of a button, the Wheelbarrow robot began its familiar defiant whir, trundling down the deserted street with the command-cable playing out from the coils beside the first Pig.

Harrison perched beside the corporal and studied the fuzzy TV picture from the boom-mounted camera. 'Give the door a miss, Corporal. Let's see if there's a way in through the window.'

Marsh nodded, slowing the 'barrow and executing a neat turn to bring it at right angles to the kerbstone. From that position they had a midget's eye view of the window. It had been barricaded with a sheet of corrugated iron held in place by cross-spars of timber nailed to the rotten frame.

The corporal began extending the telescopic boom to which a small metal attachment was fixed. Known as a 'door opener', its usual function was to open the doors or boots of suspect cars. But now, with the front tracks of the 'barrow jammed against the kerb for leverage, Marsh was hooking the attachment under the cross-spars. There was little resistance as the boom retracted, yanking the nails free. Two minutes later the iron sheet flapped and crashed noisily to the pavement, revealing a gaping black hole.

With an energetic wheeze, the tracked robot struggled over the kerbstone and edged closer to the window. Nothing but darkness showed on the screen from the boom camera. Marsh switched on the mini-floodlight and Harrison involuntarily winced. Light-sensitive switches had been used recently to trigger hidden bombs in derelict buildings, just waiting for an unwary ATO to switch on his torch.

But this time nothing happened and the monitor showed only the dusty shell of a building as the circle of light traversed the one-time parlour. Plaster had crumbled from the walls and lay on dried-up yellowing newspapers; a door hung from a single hinge where vandals or vagrants had tried to remove it; festoons of lighting cable protruded from a hole in the ceiling like a hernia.

Harrison made his decision. 'I'll take a look now.'

Marsh avoided his eyes, perhaps not wanting to show that he feared for the officer's life. 'What you want to take with you, boss?'

'Just a Pigstick,' Harrison replied, smiling with a confidence he didn't feel. 'And a Jack-in-a-Box, so you can see what's going on.'

He didn't need to add 'in case things go pear-shaped'. Marsh knew.

While the corporal located the steel carrying case and plugged in the extension cable, Harrison took one last look at the dilapidated and empty street before snapping down his visor.

At once he was alone in another world. Outside sounds became instantly muted and he was aware only of the rasp of his own breathing. Through the thick scratched lens of the visor he could see the Wheelbarrow waiting patiently by the window fifty metres away; Light Infantry soldiers crouched at each end of the waste-land that flanked the left-hand side of the street, ready to retaliate should the sniper still be lying in wait.

Marsh handed over the carrying case and the long walk began. A mere fifty metres but, as always, it seemed to take for ever.

Each footstep was laboured, his breath harsh in his own ears as he shuffled under the weight of the bombsuit and the portable camera.

He tried not to hold his breath, but that was never easy. However much rational thought reassured him that he was not in danger, the truth was that you could never be sure. Because the only man who knew the truth was the bomber, and he would be the very last person on earth to tell you.

The first few footsteps were the easiest because if a device went off where you expected it to be, then your face and body were well enough protected. But as you began to halve the distance you began to remember previous bomb blasts you had seen and the damage they had inflicted on their victims. The destructive power of explosives on soft body tissue was awesome, especially when nails and shipyard bolts had been added for good measure. At twenty-five metres it was impossible not to feel increasingly vulnerable, aware that the protective suit would probably keep you alive, but that the shockwave would invariably tear the limbs from your torso. However calm you might appear, you were aware of the increasing tempo of your heartbeat and the hot flush of fear that caused the sweat to gather in the small of your back.

He thought of his wife Pippa then, and her breathless voice on the telephone the previous night. Her hardly suppressed excitement and his impatience as she deliberately taunted him with her news, keeping it to herself for as long as she could before she finally admitted, Yes, she was pregnant. The doctor had confirmed it. About two months gone, so Harrison could expect to be a father before Christmas.

And then the image had flashed unbidden through his mind. Pippa pushing the cripple in the wheelchair. The child staring at the man who could neither see nor hear, who had no hands with which to hold his own child.

Harrison paused. The trailing cable from the carrying case had snagged and as he turned in slow motion like an astronaut, Marsh was already jinking it free. Thumbs-up signs were exchanged.

The walk began again.

There are only three types of bomb, Harrison reminded

himself, once more going back over his earlier threat assessment in order to quell his unreasoned feeling of panic. To shake off the black dog. There was the time bomb which logic dictated was no longer likely in this situation. Then there was the command-controlled device, perhaps detonated by wire or radio signal. That required an observer and no terrorist who valued his freedom was likely to be hanging around after a snipe; besides which the few occupied buildings that now overlooked him had already been searched by the infantry.

That left the third type of bomb: victim-operated. Cold military parlance for the booby trap.

To an outsider that might seem like a poor comfort. But for Harrison the rerun of his earlier mental process of elimination and his reaffirmation of the nature of the threat steadied his nerves. Whatever might lie in wait for him was not under someone else's control. Whether he lived or died would be up to him alone. His skill, his decisions, his mind against that of the unknown bomber.

He stopped beside the deactivated Wheelbarrow, feeling calmer now.

Ever aware of the possibility of light-sensitive devices, he extracted an Allen cold lamp from the equipment pouch in the tail of his bombsuit and shone the diffused beam into the dark interior. It gave poor definition but was at least preferable to a surprise explosion.

Inside he could see nothing to arouse his suspicions and, after checking the perimeter of the windowframe for wires, he climbed awkwardly over the sill. With his feet planted firmly on the bare floorboards, he flipped up his visor to improve his vision. If the cool flow of air on his face was welcome, the smell of mildew and dog faeces was not.

It took several minutes of playing the beam around the room before he was satisfied that there were no tell-tale electrical leads or tripwires.

So far so good. But then he was painfully aware that he couldn't double-guess everything. Every day more and more electronic sensors of one type or another were coming onto the domestic market. From infrared anti-burglar alarms to acoustic keyrings.

9

It was only a matter of time before such things were adapted by the bombers. And a derelict like this would be the perfect place to try them out. But at least not, it would seem, today.

Feeling more comfortable, he lowered his visor and edged towards the front door. Nothing appeared to be fixed to it. No wires, nothing.

He crossed the hallway to the foot of the stairs. Before attempting to climb, he tugged through more slack on the portable television cable. Each step creaked unnervingly underfoot. He tested his weight gingerly every time he moved until at last he could view the upper landing.

All the doors were missing here, no doubt taken for second-hand resale by the workers who had boarded up the place. He was thankful for that, because every closed door was a potential deathtrap.

He took another step up, then he saw it. From the top of the stairs he had a clear view across the short landing to where a wedge of daylight filtered through a gap in the boarding of the front bedroom window. It glinted on the half-dozen spent brass cartridge cases lying on the bare boards. Very possibly 7mm rounds.

Suddenly the doubts crowded in on him. Had he been wrong? Had this indeed been the sniper's nest? Had the Catholic kids really seen the assassin legging it away before the Light Infantry closed their net?

There was a discarded chocolate-bar wrapper and a can of Tango orange drink beneath the window where the gap in the boarding would have been sufficient to view the army patrol.

Carefully he placed the Jack-in-a-Box case on the floor and squeezed the carrying handle so that it opened, the pop-up legs lifting the closed-circuit camera automatically into position. Whatever he did now, Corporal Marsh would be able to observe from the monitors in their vehicle.

He moved forward cautiously, looking around for anything out of the usual, probing with his tripwire feeler. Only when he saw it would he know what he was looking for. A near-invisible length of monofilament wire, some exposed firing cable . . .?

At the doorway of the bedroom he dropped to a crouch and

stared across the bare boards to the collection of cartridge cases. Then suddenly a thought occurred. Only one shot had been fired, that was the name of the sniper's game. One spent case only, normally retrieved by the sniper as a matter of routine. One, not six. He thrust up his visor and sniffed the musty air. Not a hint of cordite, a smell that normally lingered about in a confined space like this.

Was this a come-on? Should he exit now, take time to think it over? Hell, no, he'd only have to come back again eventually. So keep going and get it over with.

Once more he played his lamp across the floorboards, the ceiling and along the walls. At the light switch by the door, an edge of floral wallpaper had come adrift from the wall. Damp seeping in from missing roof tiles? Probably, yet there were no tell-tale watermarks and elsewhere the wallpaper appeared sound.

It was nothing, yet somehow it niggled him. A growing sense of edginess prevented him from putting a foot inside the bedroom. Something purely instinctive persuaded him to use the tripwire feeler.

He extended the end of it forward towards the light switch and pulled a length of wallpaper free. As it flapped down he saw the slightly darker patch amid the white friable plaster of the wall.

His heart began to pound; his hand trembled. Another hour or so and the patch would have dried and become virtually indistinguishable.

Had something been wired to the light switch? Surely the electricity was cut off to these derelicts? Dammit, he really should have checked that. Stupid! His eyes travelled down to the floorboards. He shone the Allen lamp. It was then he saw that the nails were loose, that there were scratch marks on the old dry timber. Frayed, fibrous scars where something like a screwdriver had been used as a lever.

Extracting a light chisel from his tool pouch, he tackled the board closest to the wall skirting, easing the thin blade into the gap and gently prising it free.

Although he'd been half expecting it, the sight of the white twinflex wire still came as a shock. His mouth was suddenly dry, his heart beginning to palpitate.

Now he knew. He thumbed up his visor to see clearer, the effect of the air on his face helping to clear his brain.

Sitting back on his haunches, he went to work again with his chisel, easing out the two adjoining floorboards.

And there it was, a simple pressure mat. It was old and scuffed and had probably been taken from the front door of a grocer's shop. But instead of ringing a bell to warn that a customer had entered, it had been connected by a wire channelled into the wall to a home-made directional mine at chest level. The wall had then been thinly replastered and the wallpaper restuck with Copydex adhesive.

Now certain that he wouldn't be cutting into a collapsing circuit – a favourite Provo trick – he turned back to the wire leading to the mat. Flat twinflex, with positive and negative currents running side by side, could be lethal if carelessly cut. It was so easy for bare strands of copper to touch each other and complete the circuit accidentally. That's why he always used a small pair of needle-pointed garden secateurs, first snipping one line of the double-stranded flex with absolute accuracy, then moving an inch farther along before snipping the second half so that there was no possibility of the two arcing together.

That done, he cautiously scraped away the hardening plaster in the wall and removed the detonator from the explosive. It had been placed in a lidless rectangular biscuit tin set on its side, the open top facing into the room with four ounces of Gelamex kept in place by two layers of insulation tape between which was held a row of four-inch galvanised nails.

He felt his stomach turn to liquid and the nauseous bile rise up into his throat causing his eyes to smart.

It had been meant for him. Just like the last two come-ons after a snipe. The PIRA bomber, whoever he was, would be perfectly aware that an ATO would be tasked to clear a suspect house. It would be an ATO who took the first tentative step into the bedroom, momentarily overcome by the sight of the spent cartridges and the opportunity to seize crucial forensic evidence.

12

Harrison would not be the first bomb-disposal operator to become paranoid. To believe that a bomber was after him and him alone. That he had become a personal target. It had happened to several brave, rational men. They rarely returned for another tour.

Looking down at the pressure mat, he could understand how it could happen, how imagination could start to take over from logical thought.

The feeling of unease was still with him when he emerged from the gloom of the derelict ten minutes later and squinted at the watery sunlight squeezing out from behind the rain clouds.

As he retraced his footsteps towards the ICP, he saw that a few additional and familiar figures had gathered by the 'bomb wagons'. One was his immediate commander, the Senior Ammunition Technical Officer.

'Well done, Tom. Heard you had an interesting box of tricks down here. Mind if we have a look over it together when you're ready?'

'My pleasure, boss.'

The second onlooker was a fellow EOD operator out of Girdwood Park, Al Pritchard.

A warrant officer first class, Pritchard was a tall man with thinning black hair and a cultivated expression of gloom. Although the two men maintained a professional tolerance of each other, theirs had always been an instinctive mismatch of chemistry. This wasn't helped by the fact that, as ten years Harrison's senior, Pritchard had vastly more experience, although in the past Harrison had been required to discipline the older man on two occasions when he had been a senior NCO under his command. And Pritchard's was not a naturally forgiving nature.

Harrison couldn't resist a good-natured jibe. 'Come to see how it's done, Al?'

For once Pritchard responded with one of his severely rationed sardonic smiles. 'We were called out on a rubber duck. Thought this shout might be entertaining.' He indicated the TV monitor at the rear of the Pig. 'Better than an episode of *Coronation Street*.'

13

Harrison knew this was as near to a compliment as he was likely to receive from his rival. 'That exciting, eh, Al?'

'Good enough for me, sir.' Another smile. Was this a record? 'Another happy little memory for when I've got my feet up in London.'

The SATO overheard. 'What Mr Pritchard means, Tom, is that we're going to be losing him. Landed himself a cosy little number with the Met's Explosives Section at twice his army salary.'

So that's it, you smug bastard, Harrison thought as he offered his hand. 'I'd like to say how much I'm going to miss you.'

Pritchard's hooded eyes smouldered back resentfully, unsure how to take the words.

But Harrison only grinned and turned away just as a car pulled up beyond the cordon and he recognised Don Trenchard at the wheel.

'I understand double congratulations are in order, Tom?' he said, as he was escorted in by Corporal Marsh. 'A bun in the oven and a bomb in the bag.'

Harrison laughed, now beginning to enjoy the steady release of tension that was fast becoming a flood of euphoria. 'Make it a treble, I've just heard that Al's leaving us.'

But Trenchard was clearly in a hurry. 'Listen, Tom, just popped by on my way to XMG. The Regiment have pulled in a Provo unit crossing the border. One of them was that name I gave you. Hughie Dougan. Probably responsible for that thing you've just defused. Thought you'd like to know.'

The news was almost uncanny. The man who had just tried to kill him was already sitting in a cell at Crossmaglen while he had been dismantling the device. 'I'll see if I can't save you a nice set of fingerprints for the trial.'

As Trenchard drove away, Harrison joined Corporal Marsh to be helped in the removal of his bombsuit.

'By the way, Tom,' the SATO said. 'I've just had the results of the Pre-Ops course. Three got by on a seventy-five per cent pass, so I can relieve you at the end of the week. How would that suit?'

The perfect end to a perfect task. That Friday – ten years earlier – just couldn't come damn quick enough.

1

'Don't kiss him.'

The rusted orange Datsun slowed at the junction before turning right out of Harry's Road towards the Maze Prison set in rural isolation on the outskirts of Hillsborough in the province of Northern Ireland.

'I don't understand,' Caitlin Dougan murmured.

'You don't have to,' her older sister Clodagh replied evenly, changing gear. 'It's what our da wants.'

Caitlin stared out of the passenger window, glimpsing the green steel security fence through the roadside shrubbery.

She was apprehensive, confused and hurt. In all her nineteen years she had never once been permitted to visit her father, who had first been sent down three months before she was born.

The first time she saw him was when he was released in 1982. She was nine years old and they had been strangers. Even now she remembered vividly how she had pulled away as he tried to hug her to him. The hurt and the tears in his eyes.

And then he was gone again, doing a runner to the south and resuming his work for the Provies. Just six months later he was rearrested and sentenced for a further nine years. Again he refused to let her visit.

It had been his wish apparently, but she had never understood why. To her it seemed the only real proof of his existence were the faded black-and-white prints in the family album. A tall, handsome young man with black hair and a charming smile. Not the middle-aged man, the stranger who had hugged her. As she grew up she felt increasingly rejected by his continued refusal to allow her to visit. At one stage she even denied that he was her father to her school friends, only to

15

become a laughing stock because they all knew the truth.

Their parents had told them that Caitlin's father was a fêted freedom fighter of the Provisional IRA in its struggle against the British occupation. A local hero whose exploits had entered the boozy ballads sung in the pubs and clubs of west Belfast. Hughie Dougan was a champion of the cause, and she was the daughter he had never wanted to see.

She sighed. 'It doesn't make sense.'

Clodagh half smiled, applying the brakes as they approached the security ramp in the road. 'Everything our da says and does makes sense. Hasn't it been his way of protecting you all these years?'

'That's easy for you to say. You're the one he sees, the one he's always seen. You're the one he cares about.'

Clodagh glanced sideways. How easy it was to forget that her baby sister was ten years her junior. So young and naive, having been sent away to the quiet backwater town of Magherafelt to stay with relatives after their mother died, educated at the Rainey Endowed with its tradition of religious integration. Caitlin Dougan was an innocent, having been allowed to grow up relatively unaffected and untainted by the turmoil of the troubles – just as her father had intended.

'Believe me, Da loves you,' she reassured. 'Sure didn't he send you a card every birthday and Christmas.'

'But no letters.'

'Think on, Cait. What could he write to you about? Life at the Kesh?'

Her younger sister stared straight ahead, still sullen. 'And now he doesn't want me to kiss him.'

'Either of us, not just you. He has his reasons.' She gestured forward to the video cameras poised on gantries above the road by the entrance of the prison. 'Remember, Cait, the bastards are always watching.'

She signalled, slowed and pulled into the small lay-by in front of the gates. 'One more thing, wee sister, don't tell him about that. Not yet.'

Caitlin glanced down at her seat belt where it emphasised the slight swell of her belly. Three months gone and fathered by a good-looking young Protestant lad who was a reservist in the Royal Irish Regiment, formerly the UDR. 'You think our da will be mad at me?'

Clodagh smiled uncertainly. 'Just give him a little time, eh?'

The gates swung open to admit them to the car park that was already full with families waiting to collect relatives due for release. Despite the oppressive presence of the razor-wired security fence and the watch-towers, there was almost a carnival atmosphere amongst those who waited. Much banter and jokes with strangers. For most it was a day of optimism, of a new start and better things to come.

Caitlin watched her sister pace beside their car, hands clasped behind the neat waist of her beige linen business suit as she kicked gently at the dust with the points of her high-heeled shoes. How smart and self-assured Clodagh looked, she thought. A university graduate like herself and now a research scientist with one of Ulster's leading manufacturers of electronic components. A career that she too had hoped to follow before the news of the baby. Still, not bad for two girls from the Catholic ghettos of the Lower Falls.

He was the last to come out through the security turnstile gate.

Caitlin saw immediately that it wasn't her father. A tall, thin man of about the right age, but his shoulders were stooped and his curling grey hair had receded to show the polished skin of his crown. The grey suit was crumpled, limp with age and sported wide lapels that had been all the fashion in the 1970s. His shirt was frayed at the open collar and he clutched a pathetic leather suitcase of the type that had been issued to servicemen in the Second World War.

The man paused to look around at the unfamiliar surroundings, momentarily closing his eyes. He drew a deep, deep breath.

'Da,' Clodagh said.

The eyes opened again and Caitlin could see how dark and alert they were beneath the black beetle brows that were now feathered with silver. She suppressed the small gasp of recognition in her throat. His eyes were the only clue, the only feature she could recognise from the family snaps and her memory of ten years before.

He dropped the case by his feet and reached forward with arms outstretched to embrace her sister. But, as his lips went to brush her cheek, Clodagh stepped back suddenly as though irritated by the display of emotion.

Caitlin thought she caught the quick, knowing wink in her father's eye before his attention turned to her.

'Cait.' His voice was thick.

She didn't move, staying beside the car, unable to smile and not knowing what to say or feel.

His eyes didn't leave her, but he made no attempt to close the distance. 'You're looking grand, Cait. Your photos don't do you justice.' There was a ghost of a smile on his lips. 'Sure you've put on some weight.'

Clodagh said: 'Da always wants to see the latest photographs of you. He must have enough to fill that suitcase.'

Caitlin still didn't move, but found herself pulling a tight little smile in response. Yes, the photographs. Clodagh's frantic searches for the latest snaps each time she set off to visit the prison. Hugh Dougan wanted to see every one ever taken of his daughter, but still never wanted to meet her in the flesh.

'We ought to be going,' Clodagh said, dumping her father's suitcase in the boot.

Caitlin sat in a back seat, allowing Dougan to take his place in the front. An uneasy silence settled between them, Dougan immersed in his own thoughts and memories as Clodagh drove back along the narrow road. He was absorbing the colour and smell of the countryside, as though seeing grass and leaves for the first time. Viewed from inside prison, everything was seen in just a million shades of grey.

They turned off down Harry's Road. Sight of the simple sign triggered something in his head. How long was it since he had last passed down Harry's Road? Nine years, and even then he had not actually seen it, incarcerated in the armoured prison van. At first he had not understood the expression by other inmates: 'When I took the trip down Harry's Road.' And, anyway, who the hell was Harry?

18

Apart from six months spent 'on the gallop', mostly in Eire, he'd been away for eighteen years. Eighteen springtimes and summers missed. Eighteen Christmases. He looked down at the hands on his lap and splayed his fingers and thumbs over his knees. He clenched his fists and spread them again, this time with his thumbs folded in. Counting like that made you realise just how long it was. Each finger a year. Each year twelve long months with never a visit to a pub or a home-cooked meal. With never the taste of a woman's lips unless it was under the scrutiny of the screws. Certainly never feeling the warmth of a woman's body beneath the sheets. Eighteen years. A generation, a lifetime.

A lifetime that had begun when the Maze was called Long Kesh – the name by which it was still referred to by Republicans. The days when convicted Provos like Dougan still enjoyed political status under a loose and easy regime when they were housed in Nissen huts of the former wartime airbase.

Days of not waking until eight thirty or nine, education classes in Irish history and language and freedom to read, watch television or play records, with a mug of illicit poteen always on hand to lift the spirits. Before the prisoners burnt them down in a trivial dispute with warders and the notorious H-Blocks were built and the prisoners' 'special category' privileges were withdrawn under a tough new policy from Whitehall.

Then had followed the turbulent years when the inmates refused to wear uniforms, draped themselves in blankets, refusing to leave their cells. The infamous 'dirty protest' had begun; the ordeal was to last five years before the death of Bobby won them back their dignity. Even after all this time, Dougan only had to think of those times for the remembered nauseous stench of the excreta-smeared cells to fill his nostrils again.

They joined the dual carriageway at the A1, speeding north to join the M1 at Lisburn, which would carry them back to Belfast. Even the traffic was of a different age. Boxy Cortinas and Maxis had been replaced by wind-resistant jellymoulds and sleek fuel-injected racers bearing unfamiliar Japanese names.

'They're behind us,' Clodagh announced flatly, adjusting her rear-view mirror. 'The bastards.'

19

Caitlin turned in the back. Just cars and lorries. 'Who?'

'The Brits,' Clodagh hissed. 'The army, RUC or Special Branch – what does it matter?'

Dougan sighed resignedly. 'It's to be expected. The peelers don't leave you alone until they're sure you're not going back to old ways.'

Clodagh laughed bitterly. 'You're going soft, Da.'

'I don't think so. After eighteen years of waiting, I've learned to bide my time.'

'Eighteen years or not, Da, I can tell you some things haven't changed . . .'

And her prophecy was proved correct even sooner than she had anticipated. As the M1 ran into the outskirts of south Belfast and she slowed at the roundabout with Grosvenor Road, she saw it. A vehicle checkpoint manned by helmeted troops of the RIR. Khaki armoured Land-Rovers parked in the middle of the street and a soldier with an SA80 Bullpup across his chest flagging down each car. His mates hidden at the roadside beneath the towering wall mural of the Madonna and Child that marked the entrance to the Falls.

'Welcome home, Da,' she muttered beneath her breath and wound down the window.

The camo-streaked face peered in. 'Driving licence, please.' A harsh Ulster accent.

Clodagh deliberately took time to fish in her handbag, waiting until the soldier showed signs of impatience. Then she thrust it at him.

'Clodagh Dougan,' he said aloud and she saw the stiffening of the muscles in his face. He stepped back and looked disdainfully at the rusty door sills. 'Your car, is it?'

'Yes.'

'Can you tell me the registration number?'

She told him.

'And your passengers?'

'My sister and my father.'

A smile, or it could have been a sneer, appeared on the soldier's face. 'So Hughie Dougan's coming home?'

20

'As if you didn't know.'

'Meaning?'

'Ask your friends in the blue Mondeo two cars back. Don't tell me they haven't been in radio contact with you. I wouldn't be surprised if you're not here just for our benefit.'

The soldier handed back the licence. 'Don't flatter yourself. We're not interested in geriatrics.' He stepped back and waved them on.

'Bastards!' Clodagh spat as she accelerated away from the checkpoint.

'Don't let them get to you, Clodie,' her father soothed. 'Sure that's just letting them win.'

But she was still seething when she turned off into the narrow back street of packed terraced houses where a small knot of neighbours and children waited expectantly. Strung between two windows, a makeshift banner made from old bed sheets bore the message in huge handwritten letters: WELCOME BACK HUGHIE.

And as Hugh Dougan peered through the fly-smeared windscreen he felt the prickling sensation intensify behind his eyes.

This had been his street, his home. Now he was back at the two-up two-down house he had not seen for nine years. And eighteen years since he had been taken from his bed in a dawn raid on an icy December morning. Three years before his beloved Mary had died, and his house was sold to Uncle Tommy, his daughters moving to the countryside.

Everything had changed and yet nothing had changed. From the Victorian brickwork and peeling blue paintwork and the yellowing net curtains. No, he corrected himself, Mary would never have stood for those. They'd have been bleached, the holes neatly sewn and then rehung. But, of course, Uncle Tommy's hands were too rheumatic to hold a needle and thread.

He emerged from the car to a ragged chorus of cheers and handclaps, the people pressing in on him, grinning and slapping his back and reaching out to shake his hand. As Clodagh cleared a passage across the pavement, the line of faces passed in a blur, some vaguely familiar, but most completely alien.

Then he found himself in the small front parlour with its wartime utility furniture and the coloured plaster cast of the Infant of Prague. Uncle Tommy, clutching his walking stick, sat in the big armchair and more well-wishers gathered around the sideboard set with bottles of drink.

More smiling faces, cheeks flushed with alcohol; more backslaps and handshakes; the room seeming to spin with unreality, the hubbub of excited, chattering voices rising like a wall. Dougan felt unsteady.

'Black Bush, is it, Da?' Clodagh asked.

Dougan grimaced, shook his head to clear it. 'A wee drop of water, Clodie, that's all.'

A loud voice boomed in his ear. 'Water! What they done to you in the Kesh? Sure this isn't the Hughie we know and love!'

Who the hell was this prat? Who *were* all these people? He didn't feel he knew any of them. Even those he thought he recognised had changed beyond measure in the eighteen years he had been away. At least two women, he knew, had been neighbours. Handsome women in their mid-thirties then, who had flirted with him after too much drink in the clubs – now pushing sixty with flabby bodies and fat faces. Young nephews and nieces, whose identities he could only guess at, had been playing hopscotch with Clodagh then, but now had homes and growing families of their own. And despite their welcoming words and cheerful familiarity, he sensed he was as much a stranger to them as each of them was to him. Even Uncle Tommy, already well pissed at the rare opportunity to drink like he used to, clearly had trouble in recognising him.

Dougan sought refuge in a corner and found, in confirmation of his suspicions, that the well-wishers soon drifted away into huddled, laughing groups, their duty done. And, in truth, he found it a blessed relief.

It was then that the man in the black suit, which he wore with a blue V-neck and tie, moved across to his side. Dougan had seen him earlier, standing back, nursing his drink and observing the proceedings in an aloof, detached sort of way. Very much the outsider, as indeed he himself was beginning to feel.

'Welcome home, Hughie.'

Dougan looked up at the swarthy, bespectacled face. Mid-thirties with black wavy hair, strong eyebrows and piercing eyes. A mirror image of himself eighteen years earlier. 'Do I know you?'

'Tierney. Kilian Tierney. I know you, but I doubt you remember me.'

Dougan frowned. 'Killy Tierney. Sure I remember you. A wee tearaway teenager on the barricades.'

Killy grinned. 'In the good old days. You were my hero, Hughie.'

'And they didn't put you away?'

'I did some time in the Crum. But then I got married and settled down in Andytown. Now I'm a councillor with Sinn Fein.'

Dougan raised an eyebrow. 'You didn't waste any time.'

'It's important for our people not to feel forgotten or neglected. So if there's any problems, anything you need, I'm your man.' He handed over a neatly printed card.

'That's not what I meant, Killy. After eighteen years in the Kesh, there's nothing I can't handle.'

'Getting a job might be difficult. There's rules now about any firm over twelve people employing a proportion of Catholics, but with your record –'

'I'm not talking about a job, Killy!' Dougan hissed. 'I've been making plans. You can make a lot of plans in eighteen years. I need to talk to someone in the movement. Someone who's connected, someone in authority.'

Killy stared down at his glass, swilled its contents in slow circles as he chose his words carefully. 'If you mean what I think you mean, then I suggest you forget it. You've done your whack. You're no longer a young man, so enjoy your retirement.'

Dougan couldn't believe his ears. He glared around the room. 'And end up like this lot, you mean? Forget it, I didn't serve eighteen years for the good of my health. Have you all gone soft while I was away?'

The other man sighed. 'Things have changed. The movement operates in tight cells nowadays. The big battalions have long

23

gone, as I'm sure you know. Now it's maybe two or three hundred active lads at most. There's no room for old-timers.'

'I'm the best.'

'Sure you are, Hughie. But for a start the authorities have got your card marked. You won't be able to fart without them knowing about it.'

'I know that!' Dougan snapped back. 'I told you – I got plans.'

The smile was sincere, but patronising. 'And the movement, Hughie, they'd want to be sure of you, too. A lot of the lads have been turned stag by Special Branch after they've been inside.' He saw the anger in the old bomber's face. 'Maybe, after a decent period, when you've been fully debriefed by the Sweenies, sure you could do a wee spot of lecturing for the up-and-coming. Tell 'em how it was in the old days.'

Dougan's explosion of indignation was defused by Clodagh's timely appearance at his side. Killy took the opportunity to make his excuses and move away.

'What's the matter, Da?'

'They think I'm finished,' he said hoarsely, holding her hand and seeking comfort in its warmth.

'They don't know anything.'

He forced a thin smile. 'No, of course not. Now, tell me, where's your man?'

'You haven't spotted him?'

'It's been a long time.'

'Over there by the door. Sweet-talking those two tarts from the Divis.'

It was the man with the loud voice who had spoken to him earlier when he asked for water. Jimmy Coyle. A big man with a mouth to match. Thirty-eight and married to a timid wife who'd borne him six children, kept house, and steadfastly ignored the numerous legovers about which he boasted to anyone who would listen. A self-professed Provie hero who in truth the organisation only used when it wanted a cheap thug to add muscle to its 'compulsory insurance' schemes.

'Have you told him?'

'Not yet.'

24

'Do it now. We have to go soon.'

Clodagh drained her glass to steel herself before she approached the man, took his hand and led him out of the front door to the empty street.

'Jimmy, I need to speak.'

'I thought you were ignoring me,' he chuckled, his voice slurred, his breath reeking of drink. 'Don't tell me you're pregnant, I won't fall for that one.'

She shook her head. 'Don't be silly, of course not. It's just that I'm going away with Da and Cait for a couple of weeks. Over the border, away from all this. A guesthouse in Sligo. Some peace and quiet for him to adjust.' She hesitated, forcing herself to go on as he slipped his arm around her waist and pressed himself against her. 'Look, Jimmy, we've hardly had any time together . . . There's a pub near the guesthouse that lets rooms. If you could get down there, I could get away. Spend some nights with you . . .'

She noticed how his chest swelled and the grin spread across his face. There was little doubt he'd take the bait; for months she'd been leading him a dance and now he thought he'd cracked it. 'I'm sure I could manage that.'

'Your wife?'

The smirk deepened. 'I'm a travelling salesman, Clodagh, always on the move. Sure Patty never knows where I am and knows better than to ask. Just give me the address.'

She handed him a scrap of paper. 'But it must be our secret, Jimmy. If I hear you've been bragging, it's off. Understand?'

'My lips are sealed,' he promised mockingly.

Just then they heard the whistle. It was the youth in jeans who had been leaning against the lamppost on the corner.

Clodagh's head turned in anticipation, her heart skipping a beat. It was only to be expected and yet she still felt her bile rise as the two grey Land-Rovers rounded the corner at speed. She had no doubt as to their destination.

They pulled up outside, the doors swinging open and the officers of the Royal Ulster Constabulary were out even before the vehicles were fully stopped. Pinched faces beneath their peaked caps, blue flak jackets and M1 carbines.

'What's this about?' she demanded.

The tall, middle-aged sergeant with white hair gave her a quizzical look. 'Hello, Clodagh. There's been a tip-off, that's all.'

'Tip-off about what, a family party?'

His men bustled past, shouldering their way through the people gathered at the front door. 'Hidden arms and explosives.'

'This is harassment.'

'This is crime-prevention,' the officer retorted.

An army patrol vehicle had now pulled up at the end of the street to provide any backup that might be required. High above, almost invisible in the cloud, an observation helicopter hovered.

'You know my da got out today, don't you?'

The sergeant's face was deadpan. 'Someone might have mentioned it. So this will be a good opportunity to pay my respects.' He turned abruptly and followed his men inside.

Within minutes the gathering had broken up, the guests returning to their homes.

Hugh Dougan appeared at the door with Caitlin, shielding his eyes against the sun that was breaking through the cloud to gild the surrounding hills.

He found himself standing next to Killy Tierney. In a low voice he said: 'One day the movement will need me. And when that day comes, I'll be waiting for the call.'

Tierney just smiled, polite.

'Time to be going,' Clodagh said.

He glanced back through the window at the RUC policemen riffling through the cupboards and drawers of Uncle Tommy's furniture.

Eighteen years and nothing had changed. Absolutely nothing.

'I can never forgive you for what you did, Da. Never!' Clodagh's voice rose above the hushed conversation in the crowded dining room of the Sligo guesthouse. Heads turned, mouths gaped. Cutlery poised above the plates of meat and two veg.

Caitlin could not believe her ears, had no idea her sister felt this way.

26

'Your actions brought shame on our family,' Clodagh continued, her words intense with suppressed anger. 'It killed our ma and destroyed our lives, ruined Cait's and my childhood! Damn you and your cause, I want no part of it. None, do you hear!' She shoved back her chair and stood up while her father just looked at her, stunned, and said nothing. 'We came here out of a sense of duty to you, but God only knows why! There's nothing left between us. Nothing. *You* destroyed it all!'

She threw down her napkin, turned on her heel and stalked from the dining room.

Slowly, very slowly, a murmur of whispered conversation rose to fill the shocked vacuum of silence, speculation and rumour abounding amongst their fellow diners.

Even now, as Caitlin lay on her bed, she could hardly believe what had happened earlier that evening. Could not believe that Clodagh had stormed out and taken their car, accelerating away angrily up the gravel drive. It was late when her sister returned, almost two when Caitlin heard the door slam. Not that her father would have known, not after the drink he had consumed that night, morose and silent in the guesthouse bar.

Still Caitlin could not sleep. The luminous hands of her watch told her it was now four o'clock and outside she could hear the first birds heralding the pre-dawn light.

Climbing out of the unfamiliar bed, she pulled on her dressing gown and drew aside the curtain. Below her she could see the dark figure swaggering towards the orange Datsun, still parked where Clodagh had left it on her return.

'Da!' she cried, but he could not hear and she could only watch helplessly as the engine started and the car weaved drunkenly up the drive and away.

She was still awake half-an-hour later when she heard the dull distant thud of the explosion.

Although it was late afternoon the blackened wreckage was still smouldering when the Irish Special Branch detective took his visitor from Belfast to the scene of the accident.

'Just took the bend too fast,' the detective explained. 'It's steep, you see. Went smack into the dry-stone wall. One hell of an explosion.'

'A fitting way for him to go,' Don Trenchard said.

'Hugh Dougan – yes, I gather he'd only been out of prison a week. As soon as we realised who he was we thought your people would like to be informed. Some of us really do believe in cross-border co-operation, you know.'

'We're grateful for that.' He watched the crane of the recovery vehicle begin to lift the wreckage. 'And you say his daughters have identified the body?'

A sombre nod of the head. 'Not that there was much to identify. At least there was a signet and a wedding ring.' He held out his palm, in it a clear plastic bag containing a plain gold band and a ring featuring the interlaced Celtic birds from the *Book of Kells*. 'If it was suicide, he made a good job of it.'

'Suicide?'

'Too much booze, an accident, suicide, sure who knows? Apparently there was a terrible Holy Mother of a row with the daughters last night – a lot of witnesses at the guesthouse. They say the oldest daughter virtually disowned him.'

Trenchard sniffed the air. Despite the thin summer drizzle that was beginning to fall, he could still detect the cloying sweet odour of human remains amid the more pungent stench of burnt rubber and fabric. He was all too familiar with the smell in the aftermath of past bombings back in the north.

He said coldly: 'Then the murdering bastard will be no great loss to anyone.'

It was six months later, on a chill and damp December morning, that the body of Sean Shevlin was fished out of the River Liffey in Dublin from under O'Connell Bridge.

The fifty-two-year-old senior civil servant had been missing for three days. When he did not arrive home on the first night of his disappearance his wife was not unduly concerned. Shevlin had been working exceptionally long hours for several weeks, evidently involved in a series of high-powered meetings at Leinster House, about which he had told her little. But then he had always prided

28

himself on his discretion and ability to keep the secrets of high office to himself.

She had become used to dinners spoiled in the oven, his late evening phone calls apologising for conferences that had overrun. Sometimes, to her surprise, he would be calling from another town or city, or a country house miles off the beaten track. Sometimes from another country, from Belfast, Liverpool or London.

She was mildly irritated that first night when the telephone didn't ring as she expected. But she only began to sense alarm the next morning when his office rang asking where he was. Then at noon a plain-clothes officer of the Garda arrived at her front door.

Sean Shevlin's car had been found abandoned in the car park of the Royal Dublin Golf Course on North Bull Island. According to witnesses, her husband had last been seen at lunch time the previous day talking to three unknown men outside the clubhouse; he had left with them in their car.

There was no mention of his disappearance in the newspapers or on television. For that his wife was grateful, but she considered it mildly unusual because he was an important and well-known establishment figure.

When his corpse was retrieved, the same officer returned to break the sad news with carefully chosen words of sympathy. Her husband had apparently committed suicide; he had lately been under great pressure of work. Eventually the coroner would confirm the cause of death. But no mention was made of how Sean Shevlin had managed to shoot himself in the back of his head, or why he should have torn out his own toenails before he did so.

As the detective left the grieving widow, three men drove north out of Dublin towards County Leitrim. They were members of the All Ireland Philately Society which met irregularly at different venues around the country to exchange rare stamps. This day they were to meet in the back room of a run-down motel.

Two members had already arrived, made a discreet security check of the surrounding countryside and electronically swept the bare and cheerless meeting room for listening devices. They were armed with automatic pistols and only opened the door on hearing the password 'Penny Black'.

Inside, the curtains were drawn at the high, cell-like strip of window and the bleak fluorescent tube light switched on although it was midday. The three men from Dublin sat on plastic chairs at the peeling Formica-topped table and waited impatiently, smoking and drinking coffee from paper cups.

It was to be another ten minutes before Donny Fitzpatrick arrived; the Chief of Staff of the Provisional IRA had driven down from his home in Scotstown, County Monaghan.

Next to appear was the organisation's Quartermaster General, Maedoc Mallally, known to all as Q, from Black Rock in Dundalk. Two more Army Council executives arrived before the final member's car pulled up in the car park.

Pat McGirl, commander of Northern Brigade had farthest to come. He shared his home in Bundoran, County Donegal, with a former bank clerk who had planted numerous bombs at her lover's behest.

Travelling with McGirl was Killy Tierney of the 'Sweenies' – the movement's notorious security section which dealt with suspect agents and informers within their ranks.

The only people absent were Martin McGuinness from Londonderry and Sinn Fein president, Gerry Adams. Representing between them the Armalite and ballot box strategy of PIRA, they had become important figureheads but were now too high profile to attend planning meetings of this nature. Nevertheless their views were well known and it was the trusty Killy's job to see that both were kept fully informed.

As soon as McGirl took his seat, Chief of Staff Fitzpatrick opened the meeting; there was only one item on the agenda. The talks.

He addressed the three men from Dublin. 'Have you got the tape?'

A machine was placed on the table. 'It goes on some. I think the last hour is the most relevant.'

'We've got all the time it takes.'

'It's not – er – let's say it's not for the squeamish.'

30

Fitzpatrick's eyes were unblinking. 'Just play it.'

They listened in silence watching the recorder with its irritating scratch of cassette cogs, the rasping whisper of words extracted syllable by syllable from the unwilling speaker. Words that nevertheless seemed to fill the room along with the accumulation of cigarette smoke, their significance as shocking and awesome as anything the men around the table could have imagined in their worst nightmares.

When the dialogue was punctuated by a series of sickening screams, Fitzpatrick lifted his cup and sipped cold coffee. Q scratched at his nose, studied his fingernails. McGirl leaned back in his chair and closed his eyes as though listening to his favourite Sinead O'Connor number on his Sony Walkman.

The final, single slam of the gunshot came as a relief, breaking the spell. Someone switched off the tape.

Silence continued, heavy, until Fitzpatrick cleared his throat. 'Do they know that we know yet?'

'His body was found at first light this morning. We heard it on the radio on the drive up. They made it sound like it was suicide.'

McGirl gave a mirthless chuckle. 'They would.'

'The thing is,' Fitzpatrick said slowly, 'do we believe it?'

A Dublin man said: 'Sean Shevlin believed it. With his dying breath.'

'Then we have a problem.'

'It's a load of crap,' McGirl intervened, 'whatever Shevlin believed. Dublin is never going to change Articles Two and Three in the constitution and remove its claim to the Six Counties. Never! They just hint at it when it suits them. They've watched the North tear the heart and soul out of itself for over twenty years and haven't conceded, so why should they now? Any more than they'd agree to internment this side of the border. What would Dublin get out of that – except alienate its own people and betray its own historical rights?'

The leader of the Dublin men said: 'Shevlin said it's all part of the secret protocol that's *already* been agreed by both governments. That and internment on both sides of the border, including the Orange paramilitaries, is the cornerstone on which

31

everything else will be agreed. You heard him say it, the Americans are insisting that everything else is on the table. And he quoted that Yank – "There must be a big solution or no solution." It's all up for grabs, open negotiations on a constitutional settlement between all parties.'

McGirl angrily stubbed out his cigarette end in the foil ashtray. 'And us left with our noses pressed up against the window. That'll be the Brits, insisting we're excluded.'

'I know what Brownie would say,' Killy Tierney interjected, referring to Gerry Adams by his old *Republican News* pen name. 'We have elected politicians who've done things the democratic way and yet their words still cannot be heard directly by the people. Banned from visiting England. We should expect nothing better from Whitehall.'

Fitzpatrick asked: 'Do we know anything more about this secret protocol?'

The Dublin man shook his head. 'Shevlin told us *everything* of what little he knew, believe me.'

The Chief of Staff was inclined to. 'Look, these talks have got to be stopped unless we are part of them. With us and the UDA excluded there is *every* chance of an agreement. And almost certainly that will leave us marginalised, rebels without a cause. They *can* do it. They set a precedent with the Anglo-Irish Agreement. The door was opening, we thought then. Just one more long, hard push . . . But we were wrong. Now we know just how wrong.'

'You make it sound hopeless,' Q observed disapprovingly.

'There's something I'm sure Brownie would point out if he was here,' Killy Tierney said. 'That is Dublin's insistence that nothing will be agreed until everything is agreed. I read that as meaning the secret protocol – whatever that really is – may be *already* signed, but it cannot be implemented until the whole final package is agreed by all sides. And that is going to take some time.'

The Dublin man agreed. 'Shevlin anticipated the talks would continue for a year or more. Obviously there will be no quick fix.'

Fitzpatrick smiled gently. 'Then thank the Lord that there are still some sane heads at Leinster House. They may have given us the breathing space we need.'

Q said abruptly: 'We should interrupt the talks – a fucken great bomb, that'll stop 'em talken.'

The leader of the Dublin men leaned forward over the table, his voice low and earnest. 'First we have to know *where*. They move the talks down here in the South around like we do. The Garda Special Branch vets all the locations and they're chosen at random just one day before. Even if we find out, it's hardly enough time.'

'Hit Dublin,' McGirl urged. 'It's time they tasted blood in their mouth. They'll buckle soon enough.'

'Shit on our own doorstep?' Fitzpatrick sneered. 'That's very clever. It's something we've never done and never will.'

McGirl said: 'Then it has to be London. Teach them it's just not worth carrying on unless we're included. The Brits can't take that. Campaigns in England are always what got things moving, one way or the other. Nothing like the blood of voters on the pavement to concentrate their minds.'

'I'm not sure Brownie will approve of this,' Killy Tierney said.

'He doesn't have to,' McGirl replied darkly. 'He's had his chance to try his way and it hasn't worked. It's our turn now.'

The faces around the table were impassive. They all knew it was easy to agree, but much more difficult to put into effect. Their men on English soil would be operating in hostile territory. They could not go near the enclaves of their fellow countrymen, because that was where the enemy would be watching. However successful they might be – and in the recent past they had been spectacularly successful – there was a sacrifice to be made. Namely the men themselves. Inevitably they would end up dead or behind the wire. No one around the table doubted the effort and resources the British Government would throw into the fray if its capital was under serious and prolonged threat.

At length Fitzpatrick broke the silence. 'We would have to start afresh. For all we know our active service units currently in England could already be compromised. They've been running successfully for some time, perhaps nearing the end of their natural life. Any new campaign cannot be allowed to fail. For that we will require the very highest security, a new controlling unit and a new team. The best planning brains and the best bomb makers, because they'll have to be able to outthink and outwit the very top experts the Brits will set against them.'

'We could do with some of the old hands from the seventies,' Q said wistfully. 'Those boys really knew a trick or two . . . What about Willie MacEoin, what's he doing now?'

Kilian Tierney, whose Sweenies also had responsibility for keeping tabs on ex-cons, knew the answer to that. 'Willie wouldn't want to know. Sure he's a broken man, just sits and weeps by his dying ma's bedside all day.'

Q looked despondent. 'It's a pity they've buried Hughie Dougan, he'd have been your man. No one ever had a brain like him. Bright as sixpence. Completed *The Times* crossword every day in twenty minutes, a member of Mensa. What a mind!'

McGirl said testily: 'He'd be senile by now, for Christsakes. This calls for new blood, new thinking.'

Fitzpatrick sniffed heavily; this was no time for discussing the dead. 'There is still no substitute for experience, Pat, and that's what the old boys had. Anyway, that's by the by. We'll have a think and talk around, discreet like. Next meeting in five days, venue to be advised. Each of you put together a list of names of people who would be best suited to do the job.'

The meeting broke up, each member picking up his briefcase that contained a stamp album before leaving for the cars.

Donny Fitzpatrick lingered, deep in thought, reaching up to open the curtains and allowing a shaft of smoky sunlight to penetrate the stale air. As he turned back into the room, he saw that Kilian Tierney had returned.

'What is it, Killy?'

'I didn't want to say anything in front of the others.'

'Well?'

'I had a visit the other day from Clodie Dougan, Hughie's oldest girl.'

'So?'

'Hughie isn't dead.'

Rain dripped steadily from a cold and sodden sky. A crocodile of schoolchildren were the only other visitors to Belfast Zoo, lost in the dank mist that clung to the mountainside site.

Donny Fitzpatrick climbed the winding leafy path that led up from the entrance, the four-year-old boy clutching his hand. By the time they reached the rocky pool where the blind Californian seals swam, the man was out of breath. Nevertheless he felt compelled to light a cigarette, cupping cold pinched fingers against the hard drizzle. The boy hung over the railings, mesmerised by the circling mammals, puzzling why if they were blind they did not collide. He did not notice the woman approach.

'Your boy?'

She stood a short distance away, a turquoise umbrella shielding her long black hair and trench coat from the rain. A good-looking woman, Fitzpatrick thought, with nice legs and dark steady eyes.

He moved towards her, away from the child. 'I borrowed him for the day.'

'You don't have a son of your own then?'

He noticed the shaped arch of her eyebrows as she appraised him, approved of the fullness of her lips. 'My own boy's a wee bit older, serving seven in the Kesh.'

'Perhaps he knows my father.'

'Everyone knew Hughie Dougan.' It sounded like a compliment, a recognition.

'You turned him away when he came out. He didn't like that.'

'It's policy. People get turned inside.'

'Not my father. You must know that.'

'Perhaps.'

She looked past him to the boy and the man saw the strange expression in those deep, dark eyes. A sadness perhaps and, just for a moment, vulnerability. 'My father knew his time would come again. He'd made plans, just waiting for when he'd be needed. I told Killy Tierney that, told him to pass it on.'

Fitzpatrick put the cigarette stub to his lips and drew heavily, but the rain, running in rivulets down his face, dampened the paper. He tossed the remains over the rail into the seal pool. 'Faking his own death, was that part of the plan?'

'The RUC won't hunt for a dead man.'

'How did you do it?'

'It doesn't matter.'

Fitzpatrick stared up at the mist coiling around the mountainside. There was a distant barking sound from the gorilla compound. 'Jimmy Coyle went missing at about the same time Hughie was supposed to have died. Is that how you did it?'

She averted her eyes. 'It was easy enough. The explosion made a mess of the body, but I'd put Da's rings on his fingers first. I was asked to do the identification.'

'You killed Jimmy Coyle?' He couldn't keep the surprise from his voice.

Clodagh's eyes met his again, dark and fathomless. 'He was so eager to get his leg over, it wasn't difficult. A hammer, that's all it took.' There was an accusation in her expression. 'I was only doing your job for you. Jimmy Coyle fingered Da nine years ago, everyone knew that. The dog should have been put down then.'

He didn't like being told what he should or shouldn't have done by a woman, least of all one he'd only just met. 'That was speculation. I think you'll find it was the evidence of the bomb-disposal and forensic-science boys that put your da away.'

'Well, he's not going away again, we're all determined about that.'

'Where is Hughie now?'

'Only I know that. You reach him through me. Phone me at work, never at home.'

'What about your sister?'

Her eyes narrowed. Was there a sneer on his face? Did he know that Caitlin was living with the part-time soldier in the Royal Irish Regiment, who was the father of the child she carried? 'She knows nothing about all this.'

Fitzpatrick looked down at the grunting, bewhiskered torpedo flapping smoothly through the chill water. 'One thing worries us.

Your father was good in his time, but he's no longer a young man. Time has moved on, technology has changed.'

She leaned her back against the railing. 'I studied hard at school and made sure of a place at the Poly. CDT. Craft, Design and Technology. It went into the whole manufacturing process of electronics, vac-forming, PC boards, the lot. I'm a highly paid electronics expert. In fact I expect I earn more than you. And none of it was an accident, it was Da's idea for keeping abreast of developments. We've both waited eighteen years for this. We'll be working together.'

'I'm impressed.' He meant it.

'But I'll warn you of one thing. Any operations will be run our way, that's a precondition. And you can't expect my father to get involved unless it's for a good reason, an important campaign.'

Fitzpatrick's voice was low, earnest. 'There's never been a more important campaign.'

'What do you want done?'

'A short campaign here first. To be sure you're up to it, to iron out any problems.'

'And then?'

'We want you to set London ablaze. We want the capital and the government brought to its knees.'

Five minutes later he watched the slender figure retreating down the pathway, disappearing into the mist and rain.

The man walked on towards the penguin pool, the little boy skipping at his side.

2

It was December and all the transatlantic flights were delayed.

That suited Hal Hoskins as he crouched over his camera case at the edge of the Heathrow terminal concourse and selected the best lens for the job. More time for Casey to squeeze something original out of the interview, more time for him to get the lighting right. And tomorrow their exclusive on Mandy Righteous – superstar singer, actress and self-proclaimed sex goddess – would hit the London streets in the *Evening Standard*. With accolades all round.

He draped the Pentax strap over his shoulder, locked his case and looked around at the milling crowd of hot and anxious travellers. No sign of Casey, she'd left for the VIP lounge twenty minutes ago. He looked at his watch. At this rate they'd lose the time advantage they'd gained.

Then he saw her.

Casey Mullins was not easy to miss. She was slim and tall. Too tall, she said, any taller and she'd be in a zoo. That was a typical self-deprecating one-liner from the thirty-five-year-old American. You had to get in quick with your jibes about Yanks if you wanted to get there first. It was a quality which had quickly endeared her to the staff, along with her buoyant humour and the ready smile that brightened the cream-and-freckles face. Probably it would go some way to ensure that she was taken on permanently when her three-month trial was up.

But there was no sign of that good nature now as she stomped angrily towards the photographer, high heels snapping and her amber hair swinging.

'I do not *believe* that woman!'

38

'What's up, Case?'

Casey glared as passers-by gawped at her obvious show of rage. 'She's changed her mind, that's what's up. Mandy Righteous changed her frigging mind. She won't give the interview now because she says she's got a migraine.'

Hal shrugged. A born fatalist, nothing ever perturbed him. 'Perhaps she has. It can be pretty painful.'

Casey delivered a withering scowl. 'Hal, she was eating a cheese sandwich. Migraine sufferers do not eat cheese sandwiches.'

'At least you've discovered something. The exotic Mandy Righteous eats plain old cheese sandwiches.'

'She was also sitting next to that awful Australian TV soap star. No, not *him*, his *female* co-star. But I can hardly base a two-page exclusive feature on those two facts.' She looked around at the milling crowds, all heading home for Christmas and a good time. And all she had to look forward to was a bollocking – that cute English expression – from the editor and an insufferable Yuletide with her second husband's business contacts over for meals and drinks. The only consolation would be her daughter's shared sense of fun. 'All this time wasted, Hal. Wasted.'

'If Eddie was here he'd say you look magnificent when you're angry.'

She almost smiled at the name of the veteran reporter who made no secret of the fact that he fancied her rotten. 'Don't talk dirty, Hal. I'm nearly old enough to be your mother.'

They began walking. 'I'll buy you a drink when we get back to London, Case. Anyway, who needs an interview with a singer who can't sing and an actress who can't act. Just because she's told the world she doesn't wear knickers.'

Suddenly she stopped still as though she'd seen a ghost. 'Isn't that him?'

'Who?'

She pushed forward, threading through a line of passengers with their luggage. 'Abe what's-his-name? Senator Powers?'

'Wouldn't know about that.'

'That's because you're not an American,' she replied tartly.

Now she was sure. He was a big man, probably six-five, with

huge shoulders encased in an expensive Gianni Versace suit. He made light work of the trolley piled high with suitcases, his huge knuckles gripping with the same determination as the set of his chin. He was heading for the exit and no one was going to slow him down. And the two soberly dressed minders, one on each side of him like outriders in a fast presidential cavalcade, were making sure that no one did.

'Who is he?' Hoskins asked, trotting to keep up with Casey's lengthening stride.

'Senator Abe Powers,' she replied. 'The third, I think. Like one of your English monarchs.'

'Delusions of grandeur?'

'Wouldn't be surprised. His family is close to the Kennedys, but always in their shadow. He's made quite a name for himself in Washington recently as a peace-broker. Played quite a rôle in the Palestinian talks and in the Bosnian efforts . . .' She'd outflanked Senator Abe Powers III now, overtaking him behind a queue of passengers and then sweeping around in a path across his bows.

The trolley struck her hard in the thigh, bringing Powers to a shuddering and apologetic stop.

Her smile as she winced through the pain was just short of angelic. 'Gee, I'm sorry too, it was my fault for not looking.' She feigned a sudden recognition. 'It's Senator Powers, isn't it?'

The man looked embarrassed, ran one of his hambone hands through the lush thicket of silvery hair. 'Yes, I am.' The voice rich baritone.

Behind him the burly minders hovering, uncertain, awaiting instructions.

'I'm Casey Mullins of the London *Evening Standard*. A fellow American. I'm a great fan of yours,' she babbled, throwing in everything she could think of to make him respond.

'That's most kind, Miss Mullins. An honour to meet you,' he said, attempting to push his trolley past her.

She resisted. 'We met last year.'

'Oh, really, where?' His eyes were searching for a route through.

'Washington,' she guessed. 'At a party, but of course you wouldn't remember me.'

'I'm sure I do.' Terse and getting terser.

That melting smile again. 'Then you remember that interview you promised me?'

He looked perplexed.

'But you had to rush out of town,' she explained, letting him off the hook. 'On government business.' I know you are an important man, she implied, who wouldn't break a promise to a lady. She added: 'Can I ask what you're doing here? There's been no media release from Grosvenor Square.'

The full, handsome lips twitched. 'That's because this is a personal visit. Family, you know.'

'I don't see your wife and kids,' she said, tiptoeing to look between the senator and his guardians.

'They're in Aspen, skiing. Now, please, if you'll excuse me, I really *am* in a hurry.'

'That interview, Senator Powers, perhaps we could have it while you're in London?'

'I'm sorry, my schedule's much too tight.'

'Just half-an-hour? Fifteen minutes even?'

'I don't think so.'

The bright light dazzled as Hal Hoskins, down on one knee, took a superb undershot of Abe Powers' jutting chin and nostrils flared in defiance.

Before she or the hapless photographer were aware of what was happening, the two minders moved into action. Hoskins's camera was gently but firmly prised from his grip, the back opened and the stripped roll of film sent spinning to the floor. A powerful forearm swept behind Casey's back, an irresistible force carrying her away to allow the trolley to move on.

By the time she and Hoskins had recovered, they were watching Senator Powers' broad shoulders disappear through the exit doors.

'Guess he's shy,' Hoskins observed ruefully.

'C'mon, Hal, he *loves* publicity. He can't ever get enough. Back home he's always inviting the press to his home to photograph

41

him with the wife and their all-American sons. Pillar of traditional family values and all that pap.' She glared after her quarry. 'So why's he in London for Christmas and they're in Aspen?'

'Perhaps they've fallen out.'

'Don't be stupid. He'd never *allow* her to do that.'

'Maybe he's got a secret assignation with Mandy Righteous.' She grinned at the thought. 'I'll tell the ed to hold the front page.'

The initial plans were ready and approved within a week.

Donny Fitzpatrick found that Clodagh Dougan and her father had been as good as their word. The Chief of Staff suspected that Hughie had drawn up a plan for an attack on London years before while languishing in the Kesh which had virtually become a university of terrorism. Irish history and *Gaoltacht* – a play on the *Gaeltacht* Gaelic language, taught in jail – were two of the more innocent subjects studied.

To see Dougan's proposal was like peering into a time warp, so many things had changed. Small, insignificant things like the recommended makes of vehicle to use, references to buildings and locations that had since been redeveloped, roads that had been altered to become one-way traffic systems or had disappeared completely.

But the genius and thinking that had gone into each device and its careful placement for maximum effect and damage was as bright and fresh as the day it had been first conjured in the bomber's mind.

Significant new funding would be required and an intermediary was dispatched to the stud farm in Curragh owned by 'Big Tom' O'Grady who managed PIRA's funds. Money as such was not a problem, but liquidity was. Rackets and extortion on both sides of the border, and contributions from supporters in the Irish communities of the United States, covered day-to-day operations, token salaries and modest benefits to widows and wives of men serving time in the cages.

The big money for arms, mainland operations and the political fund, plus a contingency account were allocated annually and more than covered by the most secret and darkest of the Provisionals' revenue-raising efforts, the importation of narcotics. Originally cannabis in the seventies, then heroin which had created a nightmare problem on the streets for the authorities in Dublin. Eventually they had graduated to cocaine, co-operating with the cartels of South America which were always on the lookout for new markets.

These vast profits were laundered through a number of legitimate businesses, one of which was the Moylan Construction Group which operated out of Southampton in the south of England.

It was fortunate that the Group had recently been sold – the PIRA Army Council were concerned that the firm's activities were under scrutiny by MI5 – to a large public company. As a result there were ample cash deposits in various offshore bank accounts awaiting reinvestment. Finance would not be a problem.

As Quartermaster General, Maedoc Mallally had much to organise. He told a law firm in Dublin to instruct solicitors in Liverpool to appoint estate agents to search for a suitable smallholding somewhere in the Home Counties. There was an abundance of farms on the market; the lunacy of the EC's Common Agricultural Policy and a recession prolonged by the Exchange Rate Mechanism had resulted in a crash in land prices, widespread bankruptcies and a soaring level of suicide amongst farmers. A ten-acre arable plot was found near Henley-on-Thames at a snip. It would provide the necessary cover and facilities to receive large deliveries of ammonium nitrate-based fertiliser without raising suspicions. The site was within easy driving distance of the M40, M4 and M3 main artery routes into London. Two large barns were included, one of which would be made fully secure. This would become the main workshop where larger vehicle bombs would be constructed.

A 'virgin' PIRA member from Cork, who had been brought up in England and therefore had an acceptably neutral accent, would go through the motions of running the farm and keep everything looking normal. A local lad would be hired two days a week to do whatever had to be done in the fields with a tractor for the sake of appearances. This was a deliberate policy to allay the suspicions of nearby villagers; the farmer would make a point of befriending the youth to ensure that he knew enough about the fake cover story to satisfy the inevitable local gossip. The farmhouse and barns would be railed off and topped with razor wire, infrared sensors installed and four ferocious guard dogs kept to deter nosy neighbours.

A nearby house with a large integral garage and secluded gardens was rented on a one-year let from the owners who were working on contract in Bahrain. Two more basement flats were rented, one in Reading and another in Slough, to act as safe houses as and when required. These were in addition to other premises already in use by active service units operating on the mainland.

Rather than plunder PIRA's stockpile of Czech-made detonators, originally obtained through Libya, supplies were provided through the movement's new contacts within the Russian mafia. These were smuggled into the country via Dover in a family saloon car.

A one-room office was rented, cash down, for a month in the seedy back streets of Southampton; a small plaque on the door read Solent Electronics Manufacturing. Others in the building would rarely see the owner, an untalkative nondescript individual who would occasionally take in postal and road courier deliveries of what appeared to be component parts. No one was surprised when the For Rent sign reappeared on the door.

Meanwhile Pat McGirl had been appointed operational commander.

McGirl, not currently on the British wanted list, travelled on a false American passport from Shannon to Paris, before making his way by rail and ferry to Oslo. From there he travelled by train to Bergen where he caught the North Sea ferry to Newcastle. This had long proved to be the safest way of entering Britain undetected. The simple expedient of growing a beard and dying his blond hair dark brown was all that was needed by way of disguise.

After taking the Inter-City to London, he booked in at a cheap hotel and spent the next two weeks checking over Hughie

Dougan's plans. Where necessary he updated them after visiting the various locations, taking photographs and making notes on a portable tape-recorder. Sometimes he added ideas of his own. He also hired a car for three days which he spent inspecting various road tunnels and the capital's outer motorway network that Dougan had only been able to assess from maps and atlases.

Before returning to Ireland by the route he had come, McGirl packaged the undeveloped film and voice cassettes in three large Jiffy bags and posted them to an address in Cork. In the unlikely event of his being apprehended for any reason, he had no intention of being caught with *prima facie* evidence in his possession.

When McGirl arrived back in Eire, the first face-to-face meeting was set up with Hughie Dougan himself and Donny Fitzpatrick. Clodagh arranged to pick them up in her car at a deserted lay-by in County Roscommon, far away from the troubled border areas.

As she drove towards Mayo she brought them up to date with her plans. 'I've quit my job as electronics consultant in Belfast. As far as the company, my friends and anyone else is concerned, I've landed a job in Canada. I intend to fly there, set up a mail-forwarding address, then return to Ireland under an assumed name. Can you supply a passport?'

Fitzpatrick nodded. 'That shouldn't be a problem, for you or your father. But not Canadian, their vetting procedures make it almost impossible. Anyway, you just supply the necessary photographs. We've friends who can make false applications for us in several countries, like the States or Australia. Of course the Free State is easiest for us, but in this case I think maybe American would be best. Less suspicious and it's an easy accent for someone Irish to adopt. Worth the extra time delay. Even so, the passports should be through within a month.'

Everyone appeared satisfied with the arrangements and they drove on in silence, Fitzpatrick with a growing admiration for the woman at his side as she drove fast and confidently down the winding country lanes.

The rented cottage was set in a remote copse of trees reached by a long, unmarked cart track that fed off the main road. Strains of Beethoven reached their ears as Clodagh stopped the car in the muddy yard of the slate-roofed building. She led the way to the open frame-and-brace door, chickens scurrying noisily from their path.

It was an incongruous sight. Hughie Dougan, in old corduroy slacks and shirtsleeves, was seated at the huge refectory table, warmed by the wood-fired kitchen range. He was oblivious to their presence, humming happily to the overture blasting from a portable CD player on the windowsill, the whole paraphernalia of the bomb maker spread out before him. There was a pile of neatly glued plywood boxes to house the time and power units, known as TPUs, a hot glue gun and soldering iron, cardboard boxes full of Memo Park timers used in the manufacture of parking meters, tilt switches, microswitches, batteries, tremblers, universal counters, thyristors and printed-circuit boards.

He looked up, suddenly aware of their presence. Fitzpatrick was struck by how much older he looked than the most recent photograph he had seen. The man's past nine years in the Kesh had taken their toll; the thick hair on his crown had all but gone, leaving just wisps of grey on the freckled pate, the skin of his jowls slack and wrinkled. But his eyes were dark and bright like those of a young man.

Clodagh said: 'Our friends have arrived, Da.'

Dougan smiled, climbing quickly to his feet and wiping his hands on his trousers before greeting the two men. 'Sure you'll be wanting a wee wetty after your journey. Put the kettle on, Clodie, there's a sweet.'

As she went to the sink, McGirl said: 'I see you haven't been wasting your time, Hughie.'

The bomber shrugged. 'I've had a long time to think about this. Eighteen years designing things in my head. I can't tell you how it feels to be putting my ideas into practice. To smell the glue and the soldering iron again.' He laughed nervously, embarrassed that these hard men at the top wouldn't understand. Then he indicated the pile of completed TPUs. 'These are my masters. Clodie and I have been working together – she knows so *much*! New developments and techniques, it's all changed so much. We've been experimenting, making sure all the ideas work. The best of the old and the best of the new.'

'That's why we wanted you, Hughie,' Fitzpatrick assured quietly.

The Chief of Staff was impressed, even more so when they took out the maps and the plans and the revisions that McGirl had made following his reconnaissance trip to London. He could almost hear the crackle and fizzle of Hughie Dougan's brain cells as the man studied the details, grasping even insignificant points instantly, making countersuggestions and improvements that he and McGirl hadn't even begun to consider. There was no doubt about it, the man was a genius.

Before the two Provisional officers left, details of the experimental 'dry run' campaign in Ulster were agreed. After test explosions of ANS mix south of the border in rural County Leitrim, devices would be tried out in Ulster. While serving its own purpose, it would enable them to refine ideas and technology and to gauge the amounts of explosive required to achieve certain results before the mainland campaign began.

From past experience both Fitzpatrick and McGirl realised that targeting innocent civilians like the Guildford and Birmingham pub bombings and later Harrods, even if in error, could prove counterproductive. Nevertheless, the creation of a degree of 'terror' would be necessary in order to stir public opinion and force the British Government's hand.

Dougan and his daughter clearly appreciated that fact. Their proposals were twofold. To disrupt the daily lives of as many ordinary people as possible in a spectacular and visible way, but without casualties if possible. And secondly to create fear and public paranoia by aiming specifically at the police and other emergency-service personnel. This included London's bomb-disposal officers from the Metropolitan Police Explosives Section. Dougan appeared to have a particular appetite for this aspect of the campaign, because he had heard that they were all ex-army bomb-disposal operators – the very people he seemed to hold responsible for his last nine years in confinement.

Neither Fitzpatrick nor McGirl were in any doubt that, despite their intentions, there would be innocent civilian casualties. It was always the case, because mistakes inevitably happened, however carefully one planned. Nevertheless neither man thought to point this out. They all knew the facts of life and death.

When his daughter drove the two men away back to their car, Dougan was overwhelmed by his sense of elation. His head was spinning with new ideas and he saw vividly in his mind the flashes of explosive and the chaos and destruction he would take to London. Only then might he play a part in achieving a just peace, the cause to which he had devoted and sacrificed so much of his life.

He poured himself a straight Black Bush and thought how much he loved his daughter, how much he owed her.

Even now he remembered that particular day. It must have been 1967, two years before the latest troubles began. Having retired from the British Army, he had been working as an electrician for a house-building contractor in England. It was his first time at home on a twelfth of July for years. He was dozing in his armchair after a lunch-time drink when he was awakened by the drum and Clodagh's scream of terror.

He found the petrified three-year-old clutching at his legs, crying, inconsolable, the pitch of her yells rising with each exploding thud of the gigantic Lambeg wardrum.

The Loyal Lodges were on their annual march, full of grim and righteous wrath, with sash and bowler and gilded banners flying to the triumphant call of the flute bands.

To this day Dougan could recall how he'd hugged the child in his arms until, slowly, the noise had faded away. All that day she remained unsettled and tearful, frightened of what was going on outside. Yet she knew nothing of the pompous prayers, the raging bonfires, the frenzied crowds and the burning effigies of the Pope. But Hughie Dougan did. Then it all came back.

Of course, by the time she was ten years old, Clodagh did know what was going on. That was when she had made her pledge to him, when they had made their pact. Even now he could see that small angelic face, those cute pigtails, those innocent eyes filled with so much dark anger that it broke his heart to see it in one so young. Her voice so full of hatred as she whispered to him on visiting day: 'I'll help you get back at them, Da, honest I will. However long it takes. I promise you.'

He thought little more of it at first. Only gradually had he come to realise that she had meant every word. Never very academically minded as a child, she began to study hard. And before her death, Dougan's wife had proudly told him how their daughter had come top of her class in almost every subject. By the time she was eighteen and at the Jordanstown Campus at the University of Ulster, he finally realised she had no other ambition in life than to fulfil her pledge to him.

A year later he was released from the Maze. That time his homecoming had been a quiet affair at his own request. Uncle Tommy had gone to visit his sister so that Dougan could spend his first weekend in peaceful readjustment. Young Caitlin was still in Magherafelt with her aunt and, with his wife long dead – a result of depression, too many tranquillisers and alcohol – it had fallen to Clodagh to prepare the house for his homecoming. On the first night they had sat on the rug in front of the two-bar electric fire in the front parlour, laughing together and sharing a bottle of Bushmills. He had listened as she eagerly told him how she wanted to join with her father in the fight against the British, to help him make bombs. He could recall every word, see the tears of happiness in her eyes.

Then, with the bottle nearly empty, she had done something that unnerved him. Taking his hand, she placed it on her left breast. 'Da, if you have need of a woman, you don't have to go looking for a whore. I am a woman and I am here.'

It had taken a second for him to realise what she was doing, what she was saying. Through the fog of euphoria and alcohol it had been like a bizarre dream. But as he began to withdraw his hand, she had clutched it with her own, pushing his fingers hard against her soft flesh. 'It's all right, Da. I understand about men's needs. And I know about prison, what it can do to a man. I know it might be difficult for you to do it, I understand. With me, it won't matter.' She had reached out and stroked his hair with her

49

other hand, her eyes dark and limpid. 'You can take all the time in the world.'

His voice was hoarse, touched by her tenderness, yet confused and angered at what the world had done to her, how it had distorted her innocent mind. 'Clodie, you are my daughter.'

But she had held his hand fast. 'Yes, Da, and I love you.' He felt the stiffening of her nipple against his palm through the material of her dress. 'See, some things cannot lie.'

Then he watched her expression of dismay, the disappointed pout of her mouth as he pulled his hand free and climbed, unsteadily, to his feet. 'We will never speak of this again. Do you understand?'

And he had closed the door, aware that she was quietly sobbing. By the morning he had gone, spirited away during the night by his old friends in the Provisionals. Six months later he was arrested while crossing the border on a raid to bomb an RUC police station.

Only later, back in the Maze, did he have time to reflect on the incident with his daughter that had unsettled him so much. To Clodagh, he decided, he had become the personification of the fight against those forces that had destroyed her family and her childhood. He was more than a father, he was a hero; yet a hero whom she knew, could trust, could touch. It was a bonding of blood. The natural love of a daughter had become grotesquely distorted into a passionate obsession. And she, in her confused devotion, had attempted to replace her own dead mother in the only way she knew how.

Even now, as he sat in the isolated cottage awaiting her return, he could still remember the burning passion of that moment. For one split second, caught up in the stupidity of drink, he had been tempted and he could never forgive himself for that. How different would be their relationship now, he wondered, if he had succumbed? And he thanked God that he hadn't. It just made him more determined than ever to rid his country of the British scourge that had ruined his and his daughters' lives. To this day he had never heard Clodagh mention that there was a man in her life; it was his belief that there never had been.

He heard the car pull up and moments later she entered the cottage, a smile of triumph on her face. She reached across and kissed his cheek. 'We've done it, Da. They really liked what they saw.'

'You did it, Clodie. You did it all.'

She sat in an upright chair, stretched her legs and kicked off her high heels before reaching for the bottle to pour a glass. Then she noticed what he had been working on. 'You shouldn't solder when you're drunk. It could be dangerous.'

He laughed. 'I'm not drunk. You forget, daughter, that I'm not as young as I was. My eyesight's not so good and my hand tends to shake – and I can't get on with those surgeon's gloves.'

She shook her head. 'I've told you, you should let me do the tricky stuff. Your work might be good, but it's untidy.'

'Sure you have your mother's tongue on you, girl. Now let me be.'

Her laugh was a relief from the day's tensions. 'Whatever you say, you're the boss, Aidan.'

He didn't understand. 'Aidan?'

'That's the codename they've decided to give you. AIDAN. Anglicised as Hugh, from the old Celtic god of sun and fire. It was my idea – they thought it doubly suitable.'

'AIDAN,' he repeated, thoughtfully.

It was late May – with AIDAN's experimental campaign still creating havoc across Northern Ireland – when Hugh Dougan and his daughter completed their final briefing and personal firearms training at Colloney Strand in County Sligo. They then flew separately to Paris from Shannon, following the route used earlier by McGirl. A few days later they were on the same ferry as it crossed a mirror-smooth North Sea to dock in Newcastle.

A small fleet of second-hand vehicles had been purchased at auction by PIRA's so-called 'flying column', its logistical wing on the mainland which supported individual active service units. Each vehicle was fitted with false number plates of identical legitimate models that had been spotted on the streets of major cities. Some vans and cars would be used as mobile bombs; others, including three motorcycles, would be used as transport for the new AIDAN active service unit. One such car was waiting with a driver at the docks, ready to take them to the newly rented house near the Henley farm.

The stocks of fertiliser were already mounting in the secure barn together with catering supplies of icing sugar. McGirl's farm manager was well advanced in his programme of grinding and refining vast quantities of the home-made explosive mixture.

In early June the campaign began.

It started simply enough. A time-delay device containing incendiary powder and lighter-fuel capsules was left in the soft furnishings department of an Oxford Street store. A vague thirty-minute warning was issued at noon, but with no recognised codeword. With an accuracy that was to become an AIDAN hallmark, a photo flashbulb triggered the device at the predicted time while police were trying to find it amongst hundreds of rolls of curtain and dressmaking fabric. The store was still only partially evacuated.

Only when the initially small blaze activated the automatic sprinkler system did London witness the first example of AIDAN's trickery. Attached to the incendiary was a secondary device containing a sodium base. The more water that poured from the ceiling, the fiercer became the blaze. In seconds the entire floor had developed into a raging fireball that swept through two entire floors before it was brought under control.

It was a mirror incident of what had happened to a Londonderry store just four weeks earlier.

Twenty Oxford Street shoppers were hurt in the scramble to escape, three suffering serious injuries. Several policemen and fire crew were treated for smoke inhalation. That evening's television news carried graphic eyewitness reports of the terror and panic in the crowds as they had rushed for the escalators and stairs.

Two days later, following an uncoded tip-off to the Samaritans, an explosive device was found in a lamppost in Hammersmith. After it had been dismantled by hand, its positioning such that it was impossible to use a remote 'disrupter', the bomb was found to be made up of a dummy Semtex charge. That afternoon an identical charge was found in the Fulham Road. An officer from the police Explosives Section had just confirmed that it was another dummy device when a nearby Keep Left bollard exploded. Two policemen attending the scene were seriously injured.

A further two days elapsed before a black briefcase was found abandoned at a bus stop a quarter of a mile from Paddington Green, home of London's top-security police station to which all terrorist suspects are taken. An alert member of the public informed a young police constable on traffic duty.

Aware of the recent incidents, the officer radioed the duty inspector and the area was sealed off. A bomb-disposal expert from the Met's Explosives Section was called in to examine the briefcase: it was found to contain innocuous business papers and a round of chicken sandwiches wrapped in cellophane. Nervous laughs all round and merciless leg-pulls from the constable's mates.

The cleared briefcase was taken to the regular front office of Paddington Green where the desk sergeant arranged for the lost property to be deposited in store.

At four in the afternoon the thin slab of Semtex concealed in the lining exploded. One civilian storekeeper was killed outright and a policeman lost his arm. There was severe structural damage to the building.

No one claimed responsibility.

However the Anti-Terrorist Branch of the Metropolitan Police had no doubt that it was also part of a new campaign by the Provisional IRA. Each was virtually a repeat incident of an occurrence in Northern Ireland during the preceding three months. And all of those had followed warnings with the codeword AIDAN.

There was no doubt now. Unannounced or not, AIDAN had come to mainland Britain.

3

The news editor covered the mouthpiece of the telephone. 'It's a fucking bomb warning.'

Immediately his deputy turned away from the story he was scanning on the Apple Mac's VDU.

Had he heard right? Was his boss taking the piss or was he pissed? Despite the popular misconception that bombers phoned newspapers, that happened rarely nowadays. Modern X-system exchanges automatically logged the source numbers of all incoming calls and the terrorists knew that. Even in the old days, warnings were made to the switchboard, not a bloody person-to-person to the news editor. And that's what this call had been. The deputy knew because he'd taken it initially as the news editor was sauntering back from the toilets.

Now his boss was scribbling frantically on his pad. '*Where* was that?' he was asking.

But the caller wasn't falling for delaying tactics. Instead he continued with his message, if anything talking faster so that the newsman needed all his rusty shorthand skills to keep up.

Christ, the deputy thought, this is genuine.

He snatched up the handset of his own phone. Who were you supposed to call? Special Branch, the Anti-Terrorist Squad, the Bomb Squad? He didn't have the numbers of any to hand. It would have to be 999 and all round the sodding houses.

The dramatic effect of the bomber's call spread like a ripple on a pond through the first-floor editorial offices of the London *Evening Standard* overlooking Kensington High Street. Unlike the newspaper offices of old Fleet Street, the fully computerised nerve centre exuded the air of activity and suppressed tension of a merchant bank. Ringing telephones and crashing typewriters had been replaced by electronic bleeps and the muted clack of terminal keyboards. Even what little noise there was now fell away to a hushed silence as the whispered word passed from the editorial hierarchy on the so-called Back Bench. It spread through the work stations of the reporters and copy-takers on one side of the vast carpeted floor and the features and diary desks on the other.

By the time the news editor replaced his receiver it seemed that everyone on the floor knew.

Casey Mullins, the American features writer, had been passing the news editor's desk and had just sweet-talked veteran Fleet Street reporter Eddie Mercs into parting with one of his bacon sandwiches when the call came through.

'Is this for real?' she asked incredulously, her hunger pangs suddenly forgotten.

Mercs shrugged. 'Looks like Steve thinks so,' he replied through a mouthful of bread as the news editor switched to the deputy's line and repeated details of the bomb warning to the police.

When the conversation ended, Mercs asked: 'Genuine threat you reckon, Steve?' His bulky presence, reinforced by the inevitable combination of rolled shirtsleeves, askew tie and voluminous trousers supported by garish braces was not easy to ignore.

'Seemed so, Eddie,' the news editor replied quietly. By contrast to the reporter, the man was reed-thin and swarthily handsome with a thick mane of black hair. Despite the absurdly long shifts that he worked, he looked much younger than his forty-eight years. 'Something about it being a protest by the IRA against some secret talks now being organised by the Americans.'

'Yeah, I've heard that rumour. Mind you, when aren't there rumours about secret talks? What did the police say to that?'

The news editor grinned as the executive and picture editors rushed to join them. 'Nothing, of course. Told me to mind my own fucking business. I think he was pissed off 'cos it was too late for an instant trace on the call.'

'Where's this bomb supposed to be?' Mercs asked, determined to be first in the queue when the job was allocated.

The news editor glanced at his scrawled hieroglyphics. 'Tower Street, off Shaftesbury Avenue.'

'I know it, just off Seven Dials.'

'In a blue rented van – actually gave the registration number.'

Mercs grunted. 'That's thoughtful of the buggers.'

'And unusual, I think. They gave a sixty-minute warning.'

As unflappable as ever, the exec ed was consulting his watch. It was eleven o'clock and they'd just cleared a second slip of the City Prices edition. 'If there's anything in it, it'll be too tight for Late Prices, but we should make the West End Final, even if we have to go for an extra slip.'

That gave them until two in the afternoon to clear. Just three hours.

'Do you want me to take it, Steve?' Mercs offered.

'You free?'

'Nothing that can't wait.'

The decision was made. 'Then get yourself down to Seven Dials. Like pronto!'

'And take Hal Hoskins with you,' the pics ed added.

It was the second reference to the location that triggered Casey Mullins's recognition of the name. She had been watching on, bemused to find herself caught up in the middle of one of the numerous bomb scares of recent weeks. Mostly, like everyone else, her experience was second-hand through television and newspaper reports.

'Oh, my God, did you say Seven Dials?'

Eddie Mercs turned. The tall American had been sitting on the edge of an adjacent desk, long legs outstretched as she munched idly on his hijacked sandwich. Now the muscles in the face framed by wavy, pale copper hair had frozen, her blue eyes wide.

'Seven Dials,' Mercs confirmed.

'Near Covent Garden?'

'That's the one.'

'My daughter's there at dance school.'

'You sure?'

She smiled weakly. 'It's called the Seven Dials Academy, how sure do you want me to be? Jesus!'

56

'She'll be all right,' Mercs said. 'If it's not a hoax the police will evacuate . . .'

But Casey had gone, sandwich dumped on the nearest desk as she sprinted back to her own telephone.

Mercs and the news editor exchanged amused glances. Americans!

It took Casey two misdials before she got through to the office of her estranged English husband whose legal practice was in sumptuous offices in Pall Mall.

Then she hit the usual brick wall. 'Randall Thurlow and Partners, how can I help you?' That disdainful nasal voice.

'May I speak to Mr Thurlow, please, it's urgent.'

'Who is that calling?' Condescending.

Cow! You know bloody well who it is, I've spoken to you enough times over the past six years. 'It's his wife.'

Not a flicker of recognition, not an iota of humanity. Just – 'I'm afraid Mr Thurlow is in conference with an important client at the moment –'

'I don't care if he's in conference with God Almighty, this is a matter of life and death – just *put* him on!'

That did the trick, but it was still several minutes before she recognised her husband's voice on the telephone. The irritation in his impatient silence managed to convey itself down the line as he listened to her garbled story.

'Listen, Casey, I'm with a client, I can't just leave.'

She glared at the handset. 'For God's sake, Randall, your office is just down the road from the studio – can't you get someone to just jump in a cab and collect her?'

'Everyone's up to their neck, Casey. It's the High Court case tomorrow –'

'Dammit, Randall, this is *our* daughter's life we're talking about.'

'Candy is not technically mine,' Thurlow reminded icily.

'Well, she has been for the past six years as far as *I'm* concerned, you callous bastard.'

Thurlow's voice cracked. 'Don't be so melodramatic. You say there's been an hour's warning, the police will get the area cleared –'

Casey was exasperated. 'I could be there myself while I'm standing here arguing with you.'

'Then why don't you do that.' Cold.

'Stuff you, Randall!' she said and slammed down the telephone.

God, whatever had she seen in that bastard? How could she ever have been fooled by that smooth, supercilious English voice and all the rich trappings of inherited wealth.

She snatched her handbag, checked for her car keys and raced across the news floor to the glass lift. It descended to the vast beige marble arboretum that formed the reception area of Northcliffe House. Once outside the doors, she found it was raining heavily, the forecast July showers having turned into a prolonged torrential monsoon. Eddie Mercs was still standing on the corner of Derry Street with Hal Hoskins, the young leather-jacketed photographer.

Both men were trying in vain to flag down an empty taxi.

'EDDIE! D'YOU WANNA LIFT?!'

A smile of relief broke over the veined and florid face, rain flattening what was left of his curly grey hair.

By the time they caught up with her, Casey had already reached her meter space and had the engine of the red Porsche purring eagerly. The photographer scrambled in through the passenger seat to the rear squab while Mercs dumped himself beside the driver, water forming a pool by his feet.

'Nice motor, Case,' the photographer observed appreciatively. 'First time I've been on a job in a Porsche. Yours?'

'My late husband's,' she replied, peering through the thrashing motion of the wipers, the windows already fugging with condensation.

'I'm sorry,' Hoskins said.

Mercs explained helpfully: 'She means late as in former – or else it's just her wishful thinking.'

'We're separating,' Casey added. 'Halfway between nisi and absolute – there must be a word for it. We're getting separate new homes but the Porsche goes back to his side of the asset sheet. Guess I must make some concession to growing up – just don't ask me to give up tap-dancing.'

The Porsche swung across Kensington High Street to join the eastward flow of traffic streaming towards the West End.

'You could do worse than marry me,' Mercs offered, wiping the rain specks from his glasses with a handkerchief.

'I couldn't afford the liquor bills.'

'But I'd let you keep up the tap-dancing.'

She grinned without taking her eyes off the road. From the moment she had met Mercs in Jimmies Wine Bar after her first shift on the *Standard*, they had hit it off instantly. Considered dour by those who did not know him, Mercs had found that his own dry wit was triggered by Casey's quick-fire one-liners. She had also used them to good effect in an occasional humorist column called 'A Yank in London' which the editor had grudgingly trialed. Too much of her day, she was aware, was spent replying to Mercs's romantic proposals which were invariably sent via their VDUs after he had imbibed an extended liquid lunch. But at least it proved a welcome antidote to her troubled personal life.

'How long you been living here now?' Hal asked.

'Six years. Since I married Randall.'

'Worked on other national papers, have you?'

'No, this is my first proper job now Candy's grown-up. Randall insisted I stayed at home so I'd been confined to freelancing features for the women's mags. But I used to be a real journalist for a time back in the States. My first husband wasn't so stuffy about that sort of thing. I did some good investigative jobs – only local, mind – but I helped to get a corrupt local police chief fired. It's my only claim to fame.'

'Perhaps you can do some of that here,' Hal suggested.

She smiled. 'I don't think so. They're keeping me a million miles from any real in-depth work. It's all leisure and life style for me. We Yanks may be cute, but we're not to be taken seriously.'

'Besides which, you can't spell,' Mercs added for good measure.

They were through Knightsbridge now, Casey deftly changing gear and overtaking whenever an opportunity presented itself. Using the car's power to full advantage, she shot through the underpass beneath Hyde Park Corner and into Piccadilly. From there Mercs gave directions enabling them to miss the hold-ups at Piccadilly Circus by cutting up through lower Mayfair, crossing Old Bond Street and Regent Street to Soho. When they reached Old Compton Street, he advised her to pull in and park.

It was to prove a wise move. Because continuing on foot, they discovered that the traffic had become grid-locked. Police had sealed off the entire length of Charing Cross Road and Shaftesbury Avenue, which would normally carry motorists past Tower Street where the bomb had supposedly been planted.

Until this time Casey had been persuaded by the assurances of her husband and Eddie Mercs that Candy was in no danger. But now the sight of so many blue uniforms, flashing lights and tape cordons holding back masses of pedestrians set her heart racing again.

She glanced at her watch. It was forty minutes since the bomb warning had been received. 'Eddie, where do we go now?'

'We'll drop south around the cordon and get to Seven Dials via Upper St Martin's.'

Then they were on the move again, crossing Shaftesbury Avenue to take the back streets to Leicester Square station before turning into Cranbourne Street. Along Upper St Martin's Lane, past Stringfellow's nightclub and Peppermint Park to Monmouth Street, one of the seven roads that fed into the Dials circus like the spokes of a wheel. They had been moving fast, Casey particularly surprised at Eddie Mercs's remarkable energy. For someone so overweight, who smoked and drank too much, he nevertheless managed to keep at the front. Now, however, their progress was slowed as they found themselves struggling against the crush of people coming in the opposite direction. Evacuated office workers, shoppers and tourists were advancing across the full width of the narrow street. There was no sign of panic, in fact many were laughing and joking, probably shop assistants welcoming the enforced break from boring routine.

Casey glanced around at the bobbing mass of heads. Candy could have been anywhere in the crowd and she could have unknowingly missed her by a matter of feet. Suddenly this didn't seem like a very good idea.

The scene at Seven Dials was one of total chaos. It had been selected as the rendezvous point for the emergency services. Being close to the suspect vehicle bomb, it was also large enough to allow police cars, fire engines and ambulances to gather together. Yet it was clearly far from an ideal site. The circular traffic circus, with its central modern sculpture, was crammed with official vehicles and overrun with evacuating civilians. The west end of Earlham Street, which ran into Tower Street where the bomb was reportedly placed, had been cordoned off with police tape. Guests from the Mountbatten Hotel and restaurant were being directed away from the star-shaped junction up Mercer Street and north Monmouth to the safety of Shaftesbury Avenue theatreland. Meanwhile the Cambridge Theatre matinée audience and drinkers from the Crown pub were being guided south and east towards Covent Garden.

Under a prematurely dark sky, the rain-drenched spectacle was bizarrely lit by the pulsing blue strobes of the emergency vehicles.

A middle-aged police sergeant, rain dripping from the peak of his cap, spotted the three of them moving against the flow of humanity.

'Sorry, folks, you're going the wrong way! A bomb scare, no sightseers, I'm afraid.'

Mercs showed his press pass. '*Standard*, Sergeant. Okay if our photographer takes some pics?'

The policeman grunted. 'Just keep out from under our feet – and don't try sneaking through to Tower Street. Don't want you ending up like that *News of the World* photographer at the Bishopsgate bomb.'

The reporter nodded. 'And this lady's trying to find her daughter.'

'Lost is she?'

Casey anxiously wiped the rain-lank hair from her face. 'She's at the Seven Dials Dance Academy.'

'Ah, we've just cleared that. Over there, behind that squad car . . .'

Without waiting, she rushed off, struggling through the throng to where a group of teenage children were emerging from stairs that led up to the over-the-shop studio.

'Have you found the device yet?' Mercs asked.

The sergeant nodded. 'I believe so. The Bomb Squad boys are around there now. We can expect a controlled explosion at any moment.' He consulted his watch. 'I just hope those bastard Irish were telling the truth – if so we've got four minutes. I wouldn't want that job for all the tea in China.'

His last word was smothered by the sudden dull thud of explosive from the next block. It was followed by a musical tinkling of glass as a few nearby windows shattered.

'Thank God for that,' the sergeant said with feeling.

Hardly had the words escaped his mouth when a uniformed inspector crossed from one of the police Range-Rovers. 'Sergeant, I've just been talking to Explosives Section. They say there's a strong chance of a secondary. Something to do with the codeword they used. So get this whole area cleared fast, right down to Long Acre and Endell Street – we've had enough excitement for one day.'

Meanwhile Casey had found her daughter in the stream of young dance hopefuls emerging from the glass doorway. The tall slender sixteen-year-old, a raincoat draped over her leotard, was surprised to see her mother.

'What are you doing here, Mum?'

'We got the bomb warning at the paper, so I came straight over.'

'Jeez, that was quick, we've only just been told ourselves.'

Momentarily Casey's anger flared at the delay of almost an hour, until she reasoned it would have taken time to get forces in place, to find the bomb and confirm it wasn't a stupid hoax. And, of course, the evacuation of so many people would take time, naturally starting with Tower Street itself and the immediate vicinity. She realised then that a sixty-minute warning was hardly as considerate as it first appeared.

She said: 'Don't worry, sweetheart. Someone said the bomb-disposal people have destroyed it.'

Candy looked pained. 'I'm *not* worried, Mum. Don't make such a fuss. We heard the controlled explosion. One of the girls knew what it was, she heard a *real* bomb a couple of years ago. She said you'd know the difference.'

'Turning into a proper little Londoner, aren't we? You'll be talking about the Blitz next.'

'The what?'

Casey was suddenly aware of someone standing beside her, holding an umbrella with a clear plastic canopy. The woman was thin and pale with an anxious expression on her face. 'Casey, isn't it? Remember me? Gwen. We met when our daughters did the Christmas show . . .'

Recognition dawned. 'Yes, of course . . . Isn't this a terrible business?'

'Oh, yes. I'm so glad I decided to pick Shirley up today. I don't usually but she's got this tummy bug, you see.' She glanced around at the group of young dancers walking away towards Shaftesbury Avenue. 'You haven't seen her, have you?'

A frown creased Candy's forehead beneath the tightly pinned hair. 'I expect she's in the loo upstairs. She was having a terrible time.'

'Alone?' Gwen's face was aghast.

'No, I think the teacher's still up there with her.'

Gwen smiled her flustered apologies. 'Please excuse me, I must find her.' She turned and disappeared into the doorway.

As she did so the harsh metallic voice of the bullhorn cut above the hiss of unrelenting rain: 'PLEASE CLEAR THE AREA! WE ARE EXTENDING THE CORDON BECAUSE THERE MAY BE ANOTHER DEVICE IN THE VICINITY! PLEASE CLEAR THE AREA! DO NOT STOP TO PICK UP POSSESSIONS . . .'

'Oh, God,' Casey breathed, 'not another one.'

'Don't panic, Mum, you're embarrassing me.'

It seemed that Seven Dials and the six open streets were more filled with people than ever, a fresh wave having emptied from the Cambridge Theatre.

Casey gathered her arm around her daughter and urged her forward towards the sergeant she'd spoken to earlier. 'Do you know where this other bomb might be? I mean, which is the safest way to go?'

The sergeant shrugged grimly. 'Your guess is as good as mine, love, just be quick about it.'

She glanced around. There was no sign of Eddie Mercs or Hal Hoskins. Each of the exit streets running north and south were filled with people, some now starting to run as the voice on the bullhorn repeated its warning. She flicked the wet hair from her face, trying to focus through sheeting rain. Somewhere distant thunder rumbled in the prematurely black sky. Still the blue strobes flashed dizzily around the walls of Seven Dials.

God, which way, she wondered? The south stretch of Earlham Street was packed, probably with people heading for the tube station and an unexpectedly early journey home.

'Mum, this way,' Candy urged.

They stepped past the green-tiled frontage of the Boxfresh men's clothing shop to the mouth of Shorts Gardens. The last of the evacuees were halfway down the straight recobbled street which was some hundred metres long. Following behind them were two uniformed policemen who were checking the few remaining vehicles which hadn't been driven away by their owners. Litter bins and refuse bags were being prodded and probed.

'They're looking for more bombs,' Candy observed matter-of-factly.

Casey swallowed hard, placed her arm firmly around her daughter's shoulders and started walking. They passed the brown-tiled walls of the Crown pub, the pretty window boxes of evergreens unnoticed above the elegant shop fronts of the Andrew Chan and Elinor Lamond boutiques.

Before them stretched the long rendered facade of residential flats on the left and the hanging blue banners of a shopping arcade on the right. Then abruptly the street ahead was clear of people; Casey realised that they must have decided to run. She began to feel uneasy. There was a tightening in her chest. She felt giddy. They were left behind. Everyone had gone. The pace of her footsteps quickened with the pounding of her heart. She was aware of the crack of her heels on the cobbles rising above the sound of rainwater gurgling along the gutters.

Lightning spat and fizzled from the sky somewhere above the Thames, momentarily brightening the underbelly of the dark cloudbase. The rain-lacquered street shone with the bizarre patterns of refracted light thrown from the thrashing strobes in Seven Dials.

An instinctive sense of self-preservation was taking over. Deep, base and animal. Raw fear. They began to run, breath catching in their throats, the rain whipping at their faces. All pretence of calm was now abandoned, replaced by stark panic, unaware of sodden clothes and squelching shoes. The towering street walls seemed to be closing in, tottering above them.

Near the end of the street a policeman was standing beside a parked car. Casey saw his hand, a white blur, waving frantically. Urging them on. He was shouting something but she couldn't hear above the drumming of the rain and the sound of her own blood rushing in her ears.

The constable was still waving. They were last. He must have been warned of something on his radio, she thought. He appeared frantic.

'MUM!' Candy yelled.

Casey stopped suddenly, lungs heaving. Oh, Christ, she'd misunderstood! He wasn't hurrying them up, he was trying to tell them to go back.

She hesitated as he came racing towards them, the ridiculous bell-shaped helmet clasped in one hand, his short black hair plastered flat against his scalp by the rain.

He looked so young, his face pinched and anxious. 'Better not come down here, miss. There's a suspect package in that car. We'll get the Expos to have a look.'

Casey didn't understand. 'Expos?'

'Sorry, Explosives Officers. Now if you just walk quickly back up to Seven Dials and take another route.'

'What about you?'

He grinned an uneasy boyish grin. 'A policeman's lot, as they say.'

She returned the smile. 'Take care.'

They turned, leaving the young constable to his unenviable task, and began walking briskly back the way they had come. Candy seemed to be taking it in her stride and Casey felt increasing relief as they put more distance between themselves and the suspect car. At least now they knew where it was, knew they would be safe –

The scorching white core of the blast seared into their retinas. Up ahead the scene at Seven Dials pulsed in a flux of blinding light. The dark outlines of police cars and fire engines were lifted off the ground, bodies hurtling like limp dolls against the background of flame. The images were drilled into the backs of their eyes as the fireball erupted. But the split fraction of a second in which it happened appeared to run in slow motion, their confused brains absorbing every microsecond of detail in a single instant. Feeling the cobbles quake and tremble beneath their feet, even registering the advance of the invisible shockwave as it came towards them like a mighty juggernaut, tossing parked cars into collapsing shop fronts, contemptuously wrenching lampposts from the pavement . . .

And then it hit. With the power of an Atlantic breaker and an awesome explosion of sound that pierced the eardrums and stunned the senses. Casey was swept helplessly backwards by the tumultuous hurricane of displaced air. Felt herself flying through the red mists of space, her hand ripped from her daughter's grip. Spinning through space, endless, blind and deaf.

Then she landed, her body thrown against one of the decorative metal stanchions that lined the pavement. Pain! Her ribs throbbed where they had been struck, the agony of it seeming to consume her whole body. But she knew she must be alive. Alive!

Candy?

She tried to open her eyes before realising that they were already open. The blinding flash of the explosion was still etched in her vision, the moment of horror frozen for all time. The vehicles lifting under the force of the blast, the flying bodies, the great tongues of flame. That nightmare would be in front of her eyes for ever. She shook her head, trying to erase the image, but it wouldn't go. To be blind in total darkness would be a blessing, it occurred to her, compared with spending the rest of her life before this picture of hell.

Slowly, very slowly the brightness began to subside, the details of the carnage began to lose their definition and the brilliance of the explosion began melting away. At last she could focus on the debris-strewn cobbles on which she lay.

Silence. Absolute silence. There was not a single noise. Nothing. Just an awesome, eerie silence. And flowers. Blue flowers scattered amongst the shards of glass that glistened like jewels on the cobbles. And in the air. The air was filled with petals; it was raining petals, floating down like feathers.

Then she realised. The flowers had been tossed skyward from the window boxes and hanging baskets at the pub. And the street wasn't silent; she was deaf, her eardrums shattered by the explosion.

Gradually reorientating, she pulled herself into a sitting position and drew up her legs. Her tights were in ladders, covered in tiny starbursts of blood from flying glass fragments.

She looked around for Candy, but the first sight to catch her eye was the young constable farther down the street. He was picking himself off the pavement, nursing his arm where his tunic was torn. Even from that distance, she could see the blood dripping through his fingers, mingling with the rain.

'M-mum?' The sound was muted, distorted.

Her daughter was standing, trembling, clutching her arms around herself. She was paralysed with fear, the raincoat she had been wearing over her shoulders now metres down the street. A pathetic and incongruous sight in her brightly coloured leotard. Her eyes were wide, questioning, but she was unable to move. Again she tried to speak but this time no sound escaped. Then Casey noticed the urine stain dribbling down the inside of her daughter's leggings.

'Darling, darling!' Casey could scarcely distinguish her own muffled words as she found her balance, hobbled across the pavement and drew Candy into her arms. The girl collapsed against her, the slender body heaving as she began to sob. Tenderly Casey ran one hand over the tightly banded hair in slow and reassuring strokes. The last time she had needed to do this had been on the eve of her marriage to Randall Thurlow.

For the first time she allowed her eyes to return to the grim aftermath of the explosion at Seven Dials. How long ago had it happened? One minute, two at the most. Now it was a scene of total devastation. The sleek white patrol cars and sturdy red fire brigade tenders were just raging pyres, the trees now leafless and broken, black skeletal fingers reaching to the sky in supplication against a background of leaping flame. Every now and again there was a sudden eruption as a fuel tank ignited or upholstery caught fire. Some of the surrounding buildings in the circus were alight and great stalactites of broken glass dropped free as of their own volition to smash down on the street below.

'Oh, my God,' she thought aloud. 'Eddie and Hal.' Both were certain to have been there, somewhere, probably talking to the police. She had to go, but couldn't. Couldn't leave Candy in such distress. Moisture began welling in her eyes.

'Fucking bastards!' She turned. It was the young constable, his own cheeks wet with tears. 'My mates are up there. I don't *believe* this is happening.' He looked like a child himself, barely more than a teenager.

She touched his shoulder. 'I'm so sorry. Are you all right?'

He nodded. 'And you? The girl?'

'My daughter.' Neither seemed to know what to say. Words were so inadequate. 'Perhaps I can lend a hand?'

He shook his head and took a deep breath to steel himself. 'No, it's too dangerous. Petrol tanks are going off and there could be another device . . .'

'But we can't go the other way,' she protested, 'You said that car . . .'

'I know, I know. You'd best stay here till I sort something out.' He tried to raise someone on his radio but only the hiss and crackle of static came from the set on his lapel. Nothing. He pointed to the shallow arched doorway that surrounded an emergency exit from the Thomas Neal shopping complex. 'Shelter in there until someone gets back to you – just in case.' She nodded numbly; there was no other choice. They huddled together against the locked door, Candy still crying on her mother's shoulder while Casey peered around the edge of the brickwork, watching the policeman make his way nervously back towards the scene of the disaster.

Shortly afterwards the fires began to subside. Casey could see the outline shapes of people moving about in the sizzling wreckage and hear the distorted sound of ambulances reverberating in her ears. The rain had eased to a drizzle, but it did nothing to dampen the acrid smell of burning. Ashes floated in the air like the macabre confetti of death.

Then she saw the two white Range-Rovers arrive; they parked nose to nose in V-formation, pointing towards her and so cutting off her view of the carnage.

Candy's hysterical sobbing finally subsided. She sniffed heavily to staunch her tears, following her mother's gaze towards Seven Dials.

'M-mum, who's that?'

Now a solitary figure had appeared from behind the vehicles and was walking steadily towards them. As he neared she could see that he wore a helmet and visor and what appeared to be a flak jacket over police-blue clothing. In one hand he carried a black metal object that resembled a crude sort of shotgun from which a line of cable trailed back to the Range-Rover; his other hand held a multijointed length of angle iron.

He crossed deliberately to them and stopped, dropping one of his loads and tilting up his visor with his free hand.

'Afternoon, ladies.' The voice was unbelievably calm and the accent unmistakably Scottish; his shrewd eyes smiled with easy reassurance. 'Are either of you hurt?'

Casey shook her head. 'Just a few cuts and bruises, I think – and shock.'

'Aye.' He nodded in sympathy. 'Well, we'll soon have you out of here. Guess you two lassies really are in the wrong place at the wrong time. Now, I can't let you walk back to Seven Dials because if that is a car bomb down there, it's almost certainly on a timer. That puts us in the crucial danger period when we'd normally leave it well alone. But we've got you here and other buildings in Neal Street haven't yet been evacuated.' He tried the emergency exit behind them, but it was firmly barred. He grimaced, then inspected the shallow brick arch in which they were sheltering. 'Och, you'll be okay here if you huddle tight in the corner. There's no glass to fall on you and that's the biggest danger.'

'Are you the bomb-disposal man?' Candy asked incredulously.

He nodded. 'Aye, Jock Murray, I'm an Explosives Officer with the Met.'

'You're going up to the car?' Casey asked.

'That's my job,' he answered unhurriedly. 'And I'll tell you exactly what's going to happen. I've got to check out the car, there's something in the front seat footwell. If it is a bomb then I've got some equipment here that can deal with the timer unit.' He lifted up the disrupter which looked like a crude sort of shotgun fitted to a multijointed length of metal. 'I'll need to break a window to get at the TPU – sorry, the timer and power unit – just in case they've wired the courtesy lights. When I've positioned my kit, I'll join you here while I radio my partner to carry out the controlled explosion. Bet you've heard that phrase before.' Again the blue eyes smiled. 'And we can all go home for tea – or something stronger – and you can forget all about this. Okay?'

Candy nodded eagerly and her mother shared her sense of relief, thankful the man had taken the trouble to soothe their fears. He made it all seem so normal and routine.

'Five or ten minutes at most,' he said and snapped down his visor.

Then he was gone, walking steadily towards the car, loaded with his bits of gadgetry, the cable trailing behind him.

Casey made her daughter crouch in the corner of the archway, while she positioned her own body as a shield. After a few moments, curiosity overcame her and she looked cautiously round the vertical brick line until one eye could see the Expo peering through the driver's window of the car. Presumably he was attempting to confirm the policeman's report of the device's location. She saw him raise the spring-loaded centrepunch to the side window before she instinctively drew back to safety.

A short, sharp crack echoed down the deserted street.

It was followed by an expectant silence, the intensity of her concentration blotting out the extraneous noise of more emergency service vehicles arriving in Seven Dials. She was aware only of the sound of rainwater gurgling down a nearby drain and the rising tom-tom thud of her own heartbeat.

Seconds dragged by like hours. Any sense of real time was lost.

Again she was tempted and moved towards the edge of the arch, finding the indentation of mortar between two lines of bricks from which to see.

The Expo was picking carefully away at the spider's web of frosted glass, then reaching in his hand.

Just then the car exploded.

Instinctively Casey threw herself over her daughter, her mind's eye filled with the vision of that split second when the vehicle blew apart. The bursting white star of the blast. A fleeting impression of distorted metal panels spiralling skyward like bats taking flight from hell's inferno. The earth-shaking roar and the sudden shower of warm blood amid the drizzling rain. The abrupt and stunning silence that followed was ended as something heavy landed just feet from the archway where they sheltered. Its force of impact buried the object in the cobbles. An axle, a gearbox or even the engine? It was impossible to tell from the burnt and tortured shape. Instantaneously the air was filled with flying debris and glass, clattering and shattering all along the street.

Slowly, grudgingly, a final blanket of silence smothered the wrecked street. Casey eased herself from her daughter's shivering body and forced herself to look towards the car.

The scorched banners of the shopping complex hung like tattered flags at the height of battle; below them, having shifted several feet, was the flaming, mangled framework of the car.

There was no sign of Jock Murray.

She had scarcely time to absorb the awful sight of devastation – burning shop fronts, hundreds of shattered windows and the sky filled with floating papers sucked out of surrounding offices – before the deserted street was suddenly filled with people from the emergency services. Paramedics and policemen were everywhere.

The young constable returned with an ambulance woman who quickly draped space blankets around the shoulders of both Casey and her daughter. There were words of sympathy and reassurance, helping hands and sad, gentle smiles.

Slowly the small group retraced their steps over the

71

debris-strewn cobbles of Shorts Gardens to Seven Dials. Newly arrived ambulances and police cars were parked, bright and white beside the blackened hulks of those vehicles caught in the earlier blast. Even now wreckage still hissed and sizzled in the fine rain, such had been the heat of the explosion.

'Casey!'

It was Eddie Mercs, threading his way anxiously past stretcher-bearing paramedics and policemen who were helping their less seriously injured colleagues from the scene.

'Eddie, thank God!' she gasped, throwing her arms around his neck and kissing his cheek. 'I thought you and Hal had been caught in all this.'

He gave her an embarrassed hug. 'I might have been but for that silly bugger Hal. Wanted to get a shot of the controlled explosion, so we slipped the cordon. It saved our lives.' As he stepped back from her she saw the haunted look in his eyes. 'It was you and Candy I thought were goners. Some young copper said a bird with an American accent was trapped down there with her daughter. I thought it might be you.'

She pulled a tight smile. 'Then I guess this is the luckiest day of both our lives.'

'So you saw what happened at the car?'

'I saw.'

'What happened to the Expo?'

She looked at Mercs and tried to find the words. But they stuck in her throat.

He understood, nodding grimly as he surveyed the chaos around them. 'I've never known anything like this in all my years.'

There was a sudden flash of light to one side of her and she jumped, her nerves frayed. She saw then that it was Hal, using a zoom lens to photograph a teenage girl being lifted onto a stretcher. The blast had ripped away most of her clothing and rain pattered on her damp, blood-drained flesh until the blanket was drawn over her.

Hal turned, saw Casey and steered her to one side. He kept his voice low, so that Candy could not hear. 'Someone said she's your daughter's friend. I'm sorry.'

The shock of his words hit her like a punch to the stomach. 'Shirley! Oh, God, no . . .'

He grasped her arm to stop her moving. 'There's nothing you can do. She's dead.'

She stared at him in angry disbelief as though it were his fault. 'That can't be, Hal.' She hesitated, allowing the words to sink into her befuddled mind. Little Shirley, dead? 'And her mother – Gwen – is she . . .?'

'I checked for you, they've taken her to the Middlesex.'

'I must go.'

'Leave it, Casey. She lost half her face in the blast and God knows what other injuries. My guess is she'll be in theatre for most of the night. Sorry.'

She stared back across the circus as the young dancer's stretcher disappeared into the ambulance and the doors slammed shut. It was all so final. Her eyes prickled with tears that for some obscure reason refused to flow. Instead she felt the tight knot of anger expand in her chest until it threatened to suffocate her.

She only half heard Eddie Mercs's words in her ear. 'You saw it all, Casey, I didn't. This is your story.'

'What?'

His eyes were fierce slits. 'You've got to write this one. For that girl and her mother. For that Expo . . .'

'Don't be ridiculous, Eddie!' she retorted, angry that he could even think of the newspaper at a time like this.

He shook his head. 'That man died to save you and Candy. You owe it to all of them to tell the world how it was, Casey. You owe it to yourself.'

She stared at him as though he were mad.

Mercs said softly: 'Remember, a reporter first, a human being second.'

His words left her stunned and reeling, grasping for reality. But as she looked around her, she could already see the words of rage forming into sentences in her head. An inner voice was dictating in her brain. A power that was out of her control. She felt a sudden urge, a need to get them down on paper. To capture them before the moment was lost.

More ambulances were arriving to ferry away the injured; it was now the turn of those who had been less seriously hurt.

'I'll have to go with Candy,' she murmured.

Her daughter had been listening to what Mercs had said. With a serious expression on her face, she said: 'He's right, Mum, you're a journalist. You must write about what happened, about that nice man.'

Hal had emptied the film from his camera and now held it out to Casey. 'If you want, I'll go with your daughter and see she's okay. I've got a good bedside manner.' He winked at Candy who blushed; she would clearly have no objections to a good-looking escort. 'You can take my film back with you.'

At that moment a paramedic approached. 'Excuse me, will you come along with me please . . .'

Casey looked to Mercs and Hal Hoskins, then at her daughter for confirmation. Candy smiled tightly and nodded.

Her mother turned to the paramedic. 'Sorry, I'll have to come along later. I've got a story to file.'

The telephone call came out of the blue.

Peter Rawlings was sitting down to a TV supper with his wife and two daughters in the Belmont suburb of east Belfast when the Ulster Unionist Party headquarters rang.

'Dove,' was the codeword the caller used.

'Where?'

'The Europa. Ask for Mr Montgomery.'

'When?'

'Now.'

Damn. Rawlings, a senior political adviser to the party, was beginning to understand how the American worked. He recognised the need for secrecy and for security, but such summons, at short notice without warning, were still inconvenient and sometimes irksome.

He telephoned his friend, Ian Findlay, a similar adviser to the hard-line Democratic Unionists, and passed on the news. Findlay, who lived farther out of town, agreed to pick up his colleague from his home on his way into the city centre.

While he waited, Rawlings made his excuses to his wife and went upstairs to the bedroom where he changed back into his suit. Then he slid the steel security box from under the bed, pressed the coded combination and removed the documents. They had been there, ready and completed, awaiting this call for two weeks.

Findlay arrived and the two Protestant political advisers drove off towards the Europa Hotel in Great Victoria Street.

Rawlings's friend was in a bad mood. 'I thought seriously about wearing my bowler and Orange sash.' He was a staunch 'no-surrender' Paisleyite; he didn't like the American or appreciate the man's interference in Northern Ireland's affairs.

'Not very diplomatic.'

'I don't feel very diplomatic, Peter. We're being crushed between a rock and a hard place. Since '69 we've given the Papists everything they want. Disbanded the B Specials, surrendered Stormont, changed the voting system and introduced positive discrimination in housing and jobs. And still it isn't enough! Goddammit, Peter, we've got nothing left to give.'

Except our surrender, Rawlings thought, but said nothing more to deepen Findlay's depression.

The Europa was busy, its public bar and restaurant bustling with revellers, and they went unnoticed to reception and had the dour desk clerk call the man they had come to see.

'Mr Montgomery says go up, someone will meet you at the lift.'

An American in a grey-flannel suit was waiting for them on the second floor. He was wary and uncommunicative with alert eyes and close-cropped hair.

Bald eagle, thought Rawlings mischievously as the man escorted them to one of the small syndicate meeting rooms. It was opened by another bodyguard of almost identical, mean-mannered appearance.

Senator Abe Powers III was seated at the head of the table, his shirtsleeves rolled and the colourful floral tie loose at his neck. A bottle of mineral water was open in front of him.

It was too stagey, Rawlings decided at once. This was American can-do, will-do bravado. An extension of the breakfast business meeting and solve-the-problem-before-nine corporate philosophy.

'Nice to see you again, gentlemen.' Powers rose from his seat, towering above them and offering a handshake of bone-crushing sincerity. But he was not one to dwell on pleasantries and, as soon as they had taken their seats on either side of him, he launched into the fray. 'I hope you have some positive answers to my first proposals?'

Rawlings dipped into his briefcase and dropped the papers on the table. 'We had no problem with that.'

The American's bleak grey eyes switched to Findlay. 'And the Democratic Unionists?'

'We agree,' he replied grudgingly, slapping his document down with undisguised contempt. 'With such trivia we could hardly do otherwise.'

There was a ghost of a smile on Powers' face, or was it just a tic of mild irritation? 'Much of the world's problems stem from trivial matters. And, trivial or not, you may be interested to know that we now have full and *unanimous* agreement between all parties on the following points.'

He perched a pair of gold-rimmed, half-moon reading glasses on his nose before consulting his notes. 'That the philosophy and spirit of these talks shall be – quote – "to put the past behind us, to live with and recognise present practicalities and resolve our differences in the interests of our children's future".'

Findlay almost yawned. 'Rhetoric.'

Abe Powers shook his head. 'Not rhetoric. I assure you I intend to keep *firmly* to the letter and spirit of Clause One in all negotiations. It was a similar preliminary agreement that paved the way for the Israeli–Palestinian accord. So if you have an attitude problem, Mr Findlay?'

A shake of the head.

'Then, the other clauses agreed,' Powers continued, 'are for a new Bill of Rights for Northern Ireland, incorporating the European Convention on Human Rights. A new cross-border economic and trade institution to be formed between Ulster and Dublin and a new scheme to encourage integrated housing with subsidised rates or mortgages . . .'

'Which won't work in practice,' Findlay pointed out. Rawlings agreed, but kept a judicial silence.

Powers removed his spectacles. 'Perhaps not. But the point is, it's been *agreed*. By your party, the Ulster Unionists, the Catholic SDLP and seconded by *both* governments.'

'But it's trivia,' Findlay repeated.

'These are building blocks,' Powers countered. 'Keep building and before you know it, we'll have a complete wall. Let's first agree what we can, rather than what we can't.' He took a deep and weary breath. 'But if you want to look at one architect's plan of a finished house . . .? Let me tell you, I had private meetings in London last week with the Prime Minister and Opposition leader, as well as several academics. I received broad agreement in principle. I have since been to Dublin. In fact, I have only just got back from there . . .'

Findlay's exasperation finally broke. 'Why Dublin, for heaven's sake? It's a foreign country. You might just as well talk to Japan or India!'

Powers' voice was deep with dramatic gravitas. 'Clause One, Mr Findlay, "To live with and recognise present *practicalities*".'

Bloody smart arse! Findlay fumed inwardly, but could not contain his indignation. 'And just what gives you the right, Senator-Abraham-Patrick-Know-It-All-Powers-the-Third to come here and meddle in another sovereign state's internal affairs? What qualification do you have for that? Tell me that, will you?'

For a long moment the two men glared in mutual hostility, rutting stags with antlers locked. Then Powers relaxed back into his armchair. Quietly he said: 'Because I am one of forty million Americans who are descended from Irish families dispossessed by British indifference and landlordism after the Potato Famine of 1845. One of the million families who fled to America in order to survive certain death by hunger. Is that qualification enough?'

There was a faint, sardonic smile on Findlay's face. 'Then there's no doubt where your sympathies lie.'

You've made your point, Rawlings thought. None of us like meddlers in our affairs. But at least Abe Powers was making progress, even if it was inch by inch. To prevent the antipathy from growing, he said: 'Then you'd better tell us, Senator, just what is your proposal that so charmed London and Dublin.'

Powers signalled his appreciation with a brief smile. 'In general terms, it is this. The introduction of Voting Registration, whereby all subjects of Northern Ireland will be required to register as either Irish or British citizens. They retain all rights, including voting in local council elections. But those who register as Irish will only be able to vote for a parliamentary member of the Dáil in Dublin. Only those registering as British will be able to vote for an MP at Westminster. Of course, it would mean acts in

Parliament and the Dáil to end dual nationality and Irish rights to vote in the UK.'

Rawlings frowned. 'And exactly what do you see as the benefit of this to us Protestant Unionists?'

Powers turned his palms upward. 'For you it is a permanent safeguard against the inevitable day when there is a Catholic majority in the Province – one of your greatest fears. And, if mainstream Irish political parties are encouraged north to win the Catholic-British vote, then Sinn Fein will be fatally undermined.'

'And the Anglo-Irish Agreement?' Findlay asked.

'It would go. Redundant, you see.' Powers looked smug.

'No, Senator, it would be a Trojan horse. For a start every Catholic in County Londonderry, Fermanagh and Tyrone would be voting for a member of the Dáil – it would be untenable. Just how long before the Six Counties were reduced to the Three?'

Powers said: 'I'll remind you of the Secret Protocol. Dublin is to renounce all claims on the Province. It will not be an issue.'

Findlay shook his head. 'Regardless of Dublin's promises, the issue would not go away under your proposals.'

Something had been bothering Rawlings for a while now. 'Tell me, Senator, there's more to this Secret Protocol than you've told us, isn't there? It doesn't make sense, Dublin doing all the giving. I mean, what's in it for them?'

Powers pursed his lips in long and careful consideration of what he should say. 'I will tell you this in private, but I shall deny it if ever I am challenged in public.' The faces of the two Protestant politicians were impassive masks, only the intense look in their eyes signified their interest in how Powers had pulled it off. 'As you know, Eire is virtually a bankrupt state. On the face of it, the worst thing that could happen would be for its dream of a United Ireland to come true – with Ulster's unemployment added to its own. So, in return for dropping Articles Two and Three and co-operating with mutual selective internment, the British Government has pledged full support to Irish demands on the Regional Support Fund, the Social Fund and the Common Agricultural Policy through the European Community.' Powers smiled. 'Do I have to spell it out? Money will flood in. For once,

Ireland will not need to raise taxes and, for once, the current Irish Government will not lose its next election.'

Rawlings and Findlay looked at each other; they'd been friends long enough to know what the other was thinking. Their expressions of stunned surprise said it all. Powers had the major players already sewn up. It was up to the rest of the ragtag politicians to grab whatever they could.

At that point the conversation was interrupted by a heavy knock at the door.

Clearly irritated at the intrusion, Abe Powers called for the bodyguard to enter. 'Yes, what is it?'

'Sorry to disturb you, Senator –'

'Yes?'

'I'm afraid there's been a bomb threat.'

Major Tom Harrison had just turned in for the night at British Army Headquarters, Lisburn in Northern Ireland, when the call came through from the watchkeeper.

It was the Europa again. Considered to be a symbol of successful commerce and business in Belfast, the hotel had been a regular target of the Provisional IRA over the years. Probably, Harrison reflected, the most bombed building in the world.

A sixty-minute warning given in a phone call made to Ulster Television. That had been just five minutes earlier.

As Senior Ammunition Technical Officer in day-to-day command of 321 Explosive Ordnance Disposal Squadron, he would not normally expect to be called out to a routine task. The section leader – a captain, warrant officer or sergeant – would be more than experienced and competent to deal with every usual eventuality. But being an hotel this was a high-priority threat due to the possibility of considerable loss of human life. And, secondly, the warning message had been codesigned AIDAN.

Several weeks earlier, after discussions with his colonel, the Chief ATO, or 'Top Cat', as he was still nicknamed from the days of insecure radio when that was the most senior ATO's call sign – it was decided that the SATO would put in a discreet appearance whenever the name AIDAN was associated with a threat. So far they had lost one ATO and had two injured since this apparently new bomber had come on the scene. It was the worst casualty record since the early seventies before new techniques had been perfected. And that was not to mention the write-off of two Wheelbarrow robots.

Harrison replaced the receiver of the bedside telephone and switched on the light. No amount of travel posters affixed to the bare painted walls, or homely ornaments and books could disguise the fact that his mess quarters were no more than a cell in an open prison for well-behaved inmates. Still, it was infinitely preferable to 'Cardboard City', the flimsy-walled annexe in which most junior officers had to endure many a disturbed night; it was said that if just one man broke wind the entire block woke up.

He turned on the shaving-mirror light over the basin and spun the cold water tap. A drawn face reflected back at him, the humorous brown eyes bloodshot with fatigue and the result of two beers too many in the bar earlier. That had been a mistake, breaking his own rules. But then it wasn't every day you heard that the best man at your wedding had been blown to smithereens on the streets of London. Les Appleyard had phoned to break the news, his voice choked with emotion. Although Les and Jock were older, they'd been close friends for almost fifteen years – in Germany and then in Northern Ireland. All in all, it had been a bad end to a bastard week.

As he cupped his hands and sluiced his face, it occurred to him that he'd aged visibly during this tour-of-duty. Only thirty-six, but the responsibility of one of the toughest jobs in the army was taking its toll. Lines etched a little deeper in his skin, wisps of grey starting to show at his temples and his tan fading. There had been little opportunity for hillwalking or playing rugby in recent months; too many hours spent in the office. He had even allowed his regular regime of running and weight-training to slip, although it didn't yet show – the slim body in the mirror was still taut and well-muscled.

He turned away, pulled on a casual shirt and corduroy slacks, then grabbed his tweed sports jacket before making his way down to where his driver and the civilian Rover waited on the forecourt.

There were said to be seventeen routes out of Lisburn, but Harrison's army driver, a local lad called Corporal Craggs, appeared to know even more than that. Each time they left the safety of the heavily fortified camp, a different way would be chosen. In Northern Ireland, any routine, any developing pattern would be noted. There was always someone watching, waiting for a slip-up. The word would be passed down the line, and then a culvert bomb or a horizontally fired Mark 12 anti-vehicle mortar would be lying in wait. Or even something as unelaborate as an ambush and a car full of PIRA gunmen. Over the years it had all happened at different times.

Harrison carried a Heckler and Koch sub-machine-gun beneath his seat, his driver a 9mm Browning automatic. While Craggs settled on his route, his boss followed it with a finger on the map. If anything unexpected happened, he would know immediately where they were and what options they could take. All the time the radio frequencies were adjusted to maintain contact with local friendly forces.

After a while they were on the M1 motorway for the thirteen-minute drive to Belfast centre. Following the bomb warning, the RUC and Royal Irish Regiment patrols were out in force, the vehicle checkpoints sealing off all routes in and out of the city, hoping against hope to catch the terrorists responsible.

Now Harrison flipped down the flashing blue strobe lights attached to the sun visor and the vehicle was transformed instantly into a police car to be waved past the traffic queues by soldiers with faces screwed against the dark Belfast rain.

The Incident Control Point had been set up in Amelia Street by the Quality Plaza Hotel to which the Europa's residents had been evacuated. The modern leafy piazza for pedestrians provided ample space for emergency-service vehicles and was out of line-of-sight from the bomb in the next street. Harrison parked and strolled the short distance to the junction with Great Victoria Street. There, two recently introduced Tactica trucks of the bomb-disposal team were parked nose to nose in V-formation just back from the corner, using the Crown pub as a shield from any blast. The ornate turn-of-the-century building with its green tiles and magnificently engraved glass had suffered much over the years due to the close proximity of its towering modern neighbour across the street. Rumour had it that the Crown's owners kept a secret store of replacement glass and filigree woodwork in anticipation of the next Europa explosion, whenever it might come.

Helmeted drivers, infantry escorts and other specialists were standing around at the ICP. There were a few nods and 'sirs' of acknowledgement. All low key.

In the back of the first vehicle, Corporal Clarke, the ATO's overweight Number Two, who wore thick pebble spectacles, was studying a couple of colour-television monitors. In his hand he held the remote-control unit of the tracked Wheelbarrow robot.

To one side stood the twenty-four-year-old operator, Captain Peter Heathcote, with his arms outstretched as another soldier loaded the chest and crotch plates into the bulky brown bombsuit. Harrison had come to know the man and his corporal well. Both had been in Bravo Troop of 821 EOD Squadron, which he had commanded before his promotion and appointment as SATO. Formally P Company, the unit specialised in working with the SAS and SBS.

'Any problems, Peter?' Harrison asked.

Heathcote looked round. 'Hallo, boss.' He wiped a hand across his forehead, already starting to sweat under the weight. 'No problem. The fire-alarm evacuation went smoothly except for the usual bonking couple who thought it was a practice drill. I sent in the Unit Search Team and they've found an abandoned suitcase in the lobby.'

'That's all?' the SATO asked.

Heathcote nodded. 'We're just about to Hotrod it.'

As if in confirmation he heard the stoical whir of the Mk8 Wheelbarrow as Corporal Clarke steered it by remote radio-control across the street towards the foyer and atrium of the hotel.

Harrison nodded. 'Carry on, Peter. Mind if I stick around?'

The captain grinned. 'No poaching, sir?'

'No poaching,' Harrison assured.

'Then it's my pleasure.'

83

Harrison was pleased to see how quickly Heathcote had got on top of the task, but he was hardly surprised. Those ATOs with the fastest reaction times were often posted to Belfast or Londonderry, whilst those operators who were deployed in rural areas, particularly border 'bandit country', would need different qualities – especially the experience to tackle more cunning and deadly devices in remote regions where the bomber could plot and plan undisturbed. But at least in the countryside time was also on the ATO's side. By contrast, the city fathers of Belfast did not appreciate their streets being grid-locked for hours on end just because of some Provo bomb, real or hoax. If the ATOs didn't clear them fast and efficiently, Harrison would soon receive a phone call from on high demanding to know the reason why.

Heathcote had indeed moved quickly, getting in with the Wheelbarrow before the standard cut-off point after a warning had been issued. Then it would be left for a statutory 'soak time' following the expiry of the deadline before the operator would risk an approach. That was to allow for any discrepancy in the timing mechanism, deliberate or accidental. The latter most usually occurred when the bomber used a watch-face timer, relying on an hour hand alone, which could prove notoriously inaccurate. In fact, more recently PIRA warnings had shortened to half-an-hour to allow less opportunity for the ATOs to get a result. For some reason best known to the bombers, AIDAN devices had so far come with a full sixty minutes' grace.

Moving across to the primary vehicle, Harrison joined the captain to watch the television picture transmitted from the camera on the Morfax Wheelbarrow as Corporal Clarke trundled it towards the suitcase beside the foyer wall.

The item began to fill the screen before Heathcote said solemnly: 'That'll do.'

Clarke duly released the drive buttons, switched to the downward-facing camera and began extending the Wheelbarrow's mechanical boom with the deftness of a school kid with a radio-controlled tank. Perspiration was beginning to bead the corpulent soldier's chubby cheeks. His tongue appeared between his lips as his concentration deepened while he extended the boom over the suitcase, then hovered.

The Hotrod – a larger version of the Pigstick disrupter – was now poised to shoot its high-velocity water jet, the effect of which was so powerful that the plastic plug it fired could kill anyone standing in its path.

'In position,' Clarke reported.

'Okay, Nobby.'

Clarke bellowed out his one-minute warning with relish, then selected the circuit and uncovered the firing switch on the control box.

'STANDBY! FIRING NOW!'

Even across the street they heard the virtually simultaneous crack of the charging explosive and sound of the Hotrod ripping through the suitcase to shatter the circuitry of the bomb before it could close. There was a brief moment of anticipation as each man waited for the earth-shaking roar that would tell them that they had failed.

Nothing.

'Well done, Nobby,' Heathcote said. Together they viewed the results of their handiwork through the Wheelbarrow's colour cameras and identified the critical components of the shattered bomb. After waiting for the mandatory 'soak time', the captain made his decision. 'I'd better go take a look-see now.'

Clarke scrambled down from his perch, hoisted up his baggy DPMs and helped the operator on with his helmet. Harrison watched on with a curious mixture of envy and gratitude that it was no longer his job to take that lonely walk. The suitcase device may have been 'disrupted', but there was never one hundred per cent certainty until it had been eyeballed at close quarters.

Involuntarily his mind flashed back to the sniper in Ballymurphy in '82. The derelict and the pressure-mat booby trap . . . He was older and wiser now. Perhaps he really should learn to be happy living without the daily adrenalin rush.

'Tom.'

He turned.

It was Don Trenchard. Harrison was somewhat taken by

surprise because he had hardly seen his friend during the past year. Now a half-colonel, Trenchard recently seemed to spend most of his time in London.

'Good grief, Don, what are you doing here?'

Trenchard smiled tersely and drew him to one side. 'A bit embarrassing actually. I'm not here and you haven't seen me, right?'

Harrison was well used to his friend's mysterious operational rôle, although he sometimes suspected that the melodramatics were as much cultivated for effect as actual. 'What's the problem?'

'The Europa bomb. Get your lads to tread extra warily.'

Harrison nodded. 'You don't need to tell me that, Don. They used the AIDAN codeword. We've learned our lesson.'

Trenchard was impatient. 'There's more to it than that. There was a secret meeting going on tonight. High-powered political stuff – sorry, can't go into details. It could be merely circumstantial, but then again PIRA might have been trying to kill those taking part.'

'Where was this meeting taking place?'

'One of the syndicate rooms on the second floor.'

Harrison considered for a moment. 'Then there's not much point in leaving a device of that size in the foyer.'

'Precisely.'

'You're saying that there could be a secondary, perhaps a bit better placed?'

'I'm guessing, but you should be warned. Don't make a big fuss about it, Tom, but maybe you could take a discreet look around without alerting the whole team. These talks are secret and we'd like to keep it that way.'

Harrison was irritated. 'If these talks are likely to attract PIRA's attention, why the hell hold them in a *public* place, just inviting innocent casualties?'

Trenchard shrugged. 'They're *unofficial*, I suppose that's why. There have been enough higher-profile talks going on in the last year to satisfy the media and the pundits. But *these* are the really important ones, the ones that count.' He gave a sympathetic smile. 'All I can tell you is that this venue wasn't decided on until this morning, if that helps. Okay?'

'I suppose it will have to be.'

'There's a chum.' He told Harrison which syndicate room had been used. 'Forgive me, Tom, but I have to scoot now.'

And then he left Harrison alone to watch as Heathcote plodded his way back from the Europa. The ATO looked bemused.

'Done the trick, Peter?' the SATO asked.

'Yes, boss. But then it wouldn't have gone off anyway. Come and see for yourself.'

Together they returned to the foyer where the suitcase now lay in two pieces on the floor, the disrupter having burst open the lid and left the component parts scattered over a wide area.

Heathcote picked up the remnants of a Memo Park timer. 'This bit's genuine, but it was an elaborate hoax. The det was a dummy and the Semtex is coloured modelling clay.' He held out a piece of yellow substance for the SATO's inspection. 'Someone's idea of a joke.'

'At our expense,' Harrison murmured.

'As this is one of AIDAN's stunts, boss, I think I ought to call in a High-Risk Search Team before Scene-of-Crime and the forensic boys take over, just in case. What do you think?'

'Sounds a wise precaution. And while you're organising that, I'll have a quick snoop round myself, if you don't mind?'

'Course not, boss.'

'Put someone on the reception telephone, but keep everyone else *outside* the building until I get back.'

Heathcote looked suspicious. 'Have you got something in mind, boss?'

'Just a hunch. Have you got a set of pass keys?'

Heathcote nodded and called across to Corporal Clarke who was now entering the foyer. 'Nobby, give SATO the master keys will you – and look sharp!'

Harrison took them and headed for the main staircase that would lead him up to the complex of business conference and syndicate rooms on the second floor. He located the room in which Trenchard said the secret meeting had taken place. Apart from chairs left askew around the table the place was totally empty, every scrap of paper having been removed. It was in direct contrast to the two adjoining rooms: in one a cocktail party had been abandoned in midflow, bottles and glasses everywhere; in the other, documents relating to a trade-union branch meeting had been left behind when the fire alarm sounded. But there was nothing suspicious in either room.

His eyes wandered to the ceiling. If he were placing a device, he would go for the floor above. Bring the whole lot down on top of them.

Being reasonably familiar with the Europa, he knew that the bedrooms began on the third floor. He left swiftly, making his way towards the fire-escape stairs, taking them three at a time. At the next floor he hesitated, drawing breath before pushing open the door.

He was at one end of the carpeted corridor, bedroom doors to the left and right. From where he stood, he could see clearly to the first fire door. Beyond it, he knew, were the two side-by-side elevators and then, farther along, another fire door.

The place was uncannily hushed, the only noise to reach his ears was the background murmur of the air-conditioning and, somewhere, the faint hiss of running water. He advanced quickly, desperately trying to relate the layout of this floor to the one below. Which rooms might be above where the secret talks took place? It was impossible to be certain without studying the architect's plans. No doubt the manager would have a copy in his office, but Harrison wasn't sure he had that much time. Indeed he wasn't sure he had *any* time.

He glanced up at one of the fire-extinguishers, then dismissed the notion. Trenchard had said the venue had only been decided that morning. Therefore any device would have to be compact and portable, easy to smuggle in. Maybe hidden in some bedroom furniture or inside a bath panel.

With some trepidation he examined a laundry trolley that had been left by the fire door. It was close to what he judged was the right area . . . But no, there was nothing.

As he eased open the fire door, the sound of rushing water became louder. He was close to the source.

The bedroom door stood open, inviting, the urgent hiss and

splutter of a fully open tap roaring in his ears. Cautiously he peered inside: the light still on, a dressing table littered with cosmetics, a brassière lying on the crumpled cover of the bed, a pair of trousers discarded on the carpet. His heart began to thud as he edged open the bathroom door – only to be immediately engulfed in steam. With a gasp of surprise he stepped back to regain his breath. The noise was like a waterfall in full torrent. Taking a lungful of air, he plunged back into the billowing damp fog and blindly sought the hot tap with his fingers. Suddenly he hesitated, his hand poised. What if . . .? Then, his decision made, he spun the tap hard until the rush of water subsided, the sound replaced by an expectant silence.

He was aware of his heartbeat slowing as he straightened his back. What the hell was the matter with him? Who'd ever heard of a device triggered by a water tap? As he checked out the room he found himself assessing how it could be done – then forced himself to stop. Paranoia was not a luxury he could afford. Christ, the bastard AIDAN really was starting to get to him. He couldn't remember such a profound sense of foreboding since . . . When? Memories of the booby-trapped devices of the early eighties flooded back into his mind. A feeling of *déjà-vu*.

Still chiding himself, he completed his search of the furniture, checked the toilet cistern and the bath panel. Now satisfied, he stepped back into the corridor. It was still eerily silent. Deserted, empty. He looked left towards the elevator doors. Then right, back the way he had come. Then he saw it. His eyes seemed to zoom in on the object that stood beside the corridor fire door. In his eagerness to get to the bedroom, he must have walked right past the thing. Could so easily have kicked it. A case tucked carefully against the wall.

He took a step towards it. A silvery aluminium photography case, a name label attached. It looked innocuous enough. Discarded when the firebell rang. In fact the Unit Search Team had probably overlooked it. Just a piece of luggage – the one thing that never looked out of place in an hotel. The one item that could be taken in and out without a second glance. And it wasn't as though it was in an obvious position to do any specific damage . . . Yet its positioning could well place it above the syndicate room on the floor below.

What had Trenchard said? That the venue had only been confirmed that morning. And therefore it would have been virtually impossible for a terrorist planting a bomb to book the exact bedroom he wanted, even if he knew which one was best. Therefore this might be the closest he could get.

Treading lightly, Harrison retraced his footsteps and crouched down beside the case. It looked solid. Expensive with combination locks. The leather name tag read: *Mrs J Maher, 27 Rose Gardens, Bangor, Co. Down.* A nice, respectable Protestant seaside town.

It occurred to him that, without the benefit of Trenchard's warning, he too might have thought little of it. How many other suitcases had the Unit Search Team found in the twelve storeys of hotel corridor. Probably several.

He glanced at his watch. Paranoia or not, timewise he was on a knife edge. Returning quickly to the bedroom he had just left, he picked up the telephone handset and dialled reception.

Heathcote answered.

'Peter, I've got a suspect IED up here in the corridor on the third floor. Looks like a photographer's case –'

'Aluminium, boss?'

'Yes.'

'It was reported by the Unit Search Team. Belongs to a Mrs Maher – in fact she told us she left it behind, too heavy.'

'Where is she now?'

'She was evacuated to the Quality Plaza with the other residents. Want me to find her?'

Harrison's mind was racing. Was he making a fool of himself? He only had Trenchard's warning to go on. Yet a secondary device would explain the elaborate hoax in reception. Let them think they'd got it, then take out members of the follow-up search teams, police or ATOs. No civilian casualties, just security forces. Point made and good publicity. Not killing the members of the meeting, but letting the British government know that PIRA knew. Not much doubt about that when the ceiling of the secret meeting room had collapsed.

He said: 'Yes, Peter, find the woman. But meanwhile I intend to destroy the case.'

'Boss?' The ATO's voice betrayed his scepticism. His SATO had lost touch with reality.

'You heard,' Harrison rebuked, 'and I don't have time to argue. And, look, this case could be a tough nut. I don't want to chance a Pigstick, it might not be man enough for the job. Can you get a Mini-Flatsword up here pronto?'

'Wilco, boss, but it'll take some time to get up the stairs.'

Heathcote was correct. Lifts were never used during a bomb scare, and the ATO was right to remind him about the ticking minutes. In his mind's eye Harrison imagined the circular face of a Memo Park timer edging remorselessly towards zero, the attached nail just a fraction of an inch from the contact point. And it would take a good ten minutes for laden troops to sweat and lumber their way up the flights of stairs.

He said: 'Just throw all the kit I need in the lift and send it to the third.'

Heathcote acknowledged briskly and hung up, leaving Harrison to await the lift's arrival. It was an unnerving five minutes that felt like an eternity as he sheltered out of line-of-sight in a bedroom doorway. When he returned to the lift his eyes were drawn magnetically to the aluminium case, at any moment anticipating the blinding flash and the instant avalanche of masonry from above and the floor collapsing beneath his feet.

He watched, mesmerised, as the floor numbers blinked above the elevator door, deliberately delaying its arrival to annoy him. Finally the doors slid reluctantly open with a pneumatic wheeze. Quickly he pulled the load clear. As well as the Mini-Flatsword, Heathcote had thrown in a bomb helmet and an improved-body-armour flak vest.

Harrison took one glance at his wristwatch and decided that the extra time spent struggling into one wasn't worth the risk. The delay might mean he'd be standing over the case when it blew.

His decision made, he carried the Mini-Flatsword across to the case and assembled the steel firing-frame. Encased in green plastic, the charge itself comprised a flat rectangular slab of PE4 plastic explosive from which protruded a tempered steel blade at right angles. Like a symmetrical shark's fin. It fitted horizontally to the firing-frame so that, when detonated, the cutting edge would be blasted sideways in a guillotine motion, slicing through the main body of the bomb. It had originally been designed to disarm devices packed into fire-extinguisher cylinders; there was a large version for use against milk churns or steel beer kegs.

Taking a deep breath, he positioned the erected Mini-Flatsword alongside the aluminium case. It seemed to have grown in size and menace. Big, silver and smugly evil. Playing a game with him. Am I or aren't I? Will I explode or won't I? He could almost believe he could hear the damn thing ticking.

While he worked, checking the electrical connections, his awareness that time was inexorably running out began to build up the mental pressure. It slowed the function of his brain. He felt as though he were in a trance, drugged, his actions slow and ponderous like a man freezing to death. It took a deliberate effort to clear his head, to focus his attention. At last, clumsily he thought, he completed his task. Unaware then that he had done the job in record time.

He played out the firing cable, ran it under the fire door and back along the corridor to the relative safety of the emergency exit staircase he had climbed earlier. As he began fitting the wires to the Shrike exploder box, he heard the sound of hurried footsteps from below.

Heathcote came bounding up the stairs, his face perspiring with exertion; Corporal Clarke, ruddy-cheeked and wheezing, was just a few feet behind.

'Boss?' the captain asked, too breathless to put a sentence together.

'All set,' Harrison replied. 'We'll see if this is a threat or if I'm just being an old woman. Want to push the tit?'

Heathcote gave an exhausted, lop-sided grin. 'Your honour, I think, boss.' Clearly he meant all the egg was going to be on the SATO's face when this turned out to be a rubber duck.

Harrison thumbed the circuit button and the light showed green to confirm that the firing circuit was complete. His thumb shifted to the prime button, holding it down for the two or three seconds it took for the internal capacitor to charge. Yet it seemed like for ever before the red confirmation light began to flash. His thumb released its pressure and moved to the fire button.

'FIRING!'

The thumb of each hand came down simultaneously on the circuit and fire buttons.

There was an instant whipcrack of sound as the Mini-Flatsword's explosive baseplate blew and unsheathed the blade. Immediately it was swallowed by a second, muffled blast that shook the floor and walls. But instead of a deafening roar, the noise was uncertain, the containment spoiled, a furious grumbling that spluttered to nothing.

Heathcote blinked. 'Shit!' Slowly he added: 'I think I owe you an apology, boss. And a beer.'

The SATO stood up. 'Two at least.'

Corporal Clarke was clearly impressed by their chief's near-clairvoyant power for sniffing out a bomb; it would be the talk of the mess that night.

He followed Harrison and Heathcote into the corridor to see how well the Mini-Flatsword had done its job. The dense and stinking smoke parted to reveal that the unleashed blade had been propelled straight through the aluminium case until it embedded in the corridor wall. Although the bomb had ignited under impact, it had done little damage as the explosive mix was already tumbling out of the case as it blew, burning and fizzling onto the carpet. With the essential compression gone, the bomb's force had been spent uselessly along the scorched corridor walls.

'Let's see what we've got,' Harrison said.

As they approached, he found the detonator on the carpet. Closer to, the three men expertly ran their eyes over the array of burnt-out components. It looked like an ounce of Semtex as a booster charge and maybe twenty pounds of ANS mix now spilled and smouldering on the carpet. The plywood timer-and-power unit lay shattered. Harrison examined the baseplate to which the Memo Park timer was fitted. He swallowed hard and felt the small hairs crawl on the back of his neck. There had been just two minutes left to run. Two bloody minutes.

He said: 'Somehow I doubt you'll find Mrs Maher is still hanging around to collect her case. Better give her details to SOCO.'

'The brazen cow,' Heathcote muttered.

'What's that, sir?' Clarke asked, hunkering down beside them, his pebble glasses steaming up with his body heat after all the excitement.

It took a moment for Harrison to distinguish the buckled tin box at the bottom of the case. There was little remaining to show what it had contained, but logic dictated that it had been a separate antihandling charge. Either a trembler or a mercury tilt switch, only forensics at Carrickfergus would be able to say for certain now.

What was without doubt was that it had been designed to kill any unfortunate member of a search party. Probably a soldier or a policeman, but it could have been one of the hotel staff. Assuming it to have been abandoned during the evacuation, it would have been the simplest mistake in the world for someone to have picked it up with the idea of reuniting it with the owner.

In fact he could have so very nearly kicked it over himself or knocked it as he opened the corridor fire door earlier.

Suddenly he felt weary, tiredness dragging at his eyelids. He straightened up and thrust his hands deep into his trouser pockets.

He really didn't want either Peter Heathcote or Corporal Clarke to realise that they were trembling.

5

The day shift at the Explosives Section headquarters on Victoria Embankment started at eight o'clock. And thirty minutes later Jock Murray's desk had been cleared.

There was not much to show for a lifetime's work in the bomb-disposal business. A small pile of paperwork: two draft reports on likely future trends in the technology of illegal explosive devices and some notes for a lecture that would never now be given. And on top, a tasking form for the Tower Street callout that would never be completed.

Les Appleyard tried to busy himself with work, but it was hopeless. Just when he succeeded in taking his mind off the previous day's events, he would find himself about to speak to the man with whom he had shared an office for so many years.

Again he stared across at the empty desk. At the pile of papers and the pathetic collection of personal possessions in a polythene bag. And still he could not accept it. There was more of Jock Murray here than they'd been able to scrape off the London streets . . .

He shoved back his seat and stood up. For over three hours now he'd kept up the pretence of normality. Well, to hell with it! Angrily he snatched the pack of cigarettes from his desk. Empty. Sod it, he'd smoked forty already since Jock's death the previous afternoon. The Scotsman would have seen the funny side of that. Not much point in giving up smoking when you dismantle bombs for a living. And if a device doesn't get you, then the ciggies will.

Appleyard grinned at the memory of his friend's sardonic wit. It was a sense of black humour they'd shared since they'd first met as two nineteen-year-old volunteers during their basic

95

army training at Blackdown. Two naive and happy-go-lucky lads from similar backgrounds in deprived inner-city areas. Appleyard from Manchester and Murray from Glasgow. Both with bleak prospects of employment and both with a thirst for excitement and adventure. This was noted by the army recruitment officer who duly offered them the then Royal Army Ordnance Corps.

Being sent for technical ammunition training was not *exactly* what either had in mind at the time. But then such was their youthful bravado that neither friend was going to admit to the other that he didn't have the taste for handling lethal high explosives for a living.

Yet by one of the strange paradoxes of life, both Murray and Appleyard found they had stumbled into an occupation that was more demanding and fulfilling than they could ever have dared hope. It was quickly to become a vocation rather than a job. And their reward for doing what the newspapers were fond of calling 'the most dangerous job in the world' was to enjoy an immensely strong and unique camaraderie within a small élite who were held in something resembling awe by fellow soldiers and public alike.

To be a bomb-disposal man was to exude an air of mystery and danger – that meant that there was never any shortage of female admirers. And the two young soldiers were never slow to exploit the amorous perks of the job in their various postings around the world – postings that were to take them to Germany, Hong Kong and Cyprus as well as secondments to several African and Middle Eastern countries.

At the age of twenty-five both friends were promoted to sergeant, having completed their advanced training, and both settled down to married life after a double wedding. Later, as warrant officers, they were to serve as operators in Northern Ireland where their paths first crossed with Tom Harrison, now the Senior ATO in the Province. The three of them had become the closest of friends.

Then, five years earlier, Appleyard and Murray had left the army and were recruited to join the Explosives Section of the Anti-Terrorist Branch within three months of each other.

Now all that was at an end and Appleyard felt an aching emptiness in the pit of his stomach. Losing Jock was like losing a brother. Worse. It was as though he had lost part of himself. And that was now, when he still hadn't fully accepted the fact that Murray was dead. The grief, he knew, would become deeper before it got better.

He looked down at his friend's desk and saw Brenda smiling up at him from the silver photograph frame in the polythene bag. Large bashful eyes and flyaway blonde hair, just like the nine-year-old son who stood beside her and Jock. It was their daughter, just seven, who had her dead father's dark hair and determined facial features.

If Appleyard was feeling the pain of his friend's loss so much, then God only knew what anguish Brenda must be suffering. His boss had broken the news. As Senior Explosives Officer, it had fallen to Al Pritchard to telephone her shortly after the incident. With more deliberate hoaxes that night he didn't even have time to pay a visit. Instead he had to endure the stunned silence at the other end of the line and then her sudden outburst of hysterical disbelief. Slowly, very slowly, she began to calm until she finally murmured: 'We always knew it could happen, I suppose. But we never really talked about it.'

That evening Appleyard had driven down to the Murrays' house near Dorking. He found Brenda alone, the children sobbing quietly in their bedrooms, as she waited for her parents to make the long journey down from their home in Perth.

He held her hand and they had sat talking and remembering together until almost midnight, drawing strength from each other's presence. The two glasses of brandy were left virtually untouched.

Appleyard was shaken from his thoughts by the sudden trilling of the telephone. It was Al Pritchard. 'Would you come over to my office, Les. I've got the Chief Super coming down to talk about that business at Seven Dials.'

That business? What a euphemism for a monumental cock-up. 'On my way.'

In truth he welcomed the opportunity to leave the confines

of his office. As he couldn't drag his mind away from Jock, then it wouldn't hurt to go over the previous day's events yet again. It might even help as a sort of therapy. At least it would stop him smoking for a while; Pritchard was a fervant born-again nonsmoker who at one time had consumed three packs a day.

Appleyard shut the door on his memories and walked along the corridor to his chief's office. As Civil Service rather than police employees, members of the Explosives Section were granted furniture and furnishings according to status. Therefore Pritchard enjoyed the benefits of a large room, well-appointed with a leather swivel chair, teak desk and sideboard with the obligatory coffee table and sofa.

It was on this sofa that he found Pritchard seated when he entered. Sitting next to him was another Expo, a Yorkshireman called 'Midge' Midgely. At barely over five feet in his socks, Midgely was a typically no-nonsense Bradford man with a dust-dry sense of humour. His to-the-point wit would be delivered with a deadpan expression on his florid face, the colour of which always reminded Appleyard of uncooked gammon.

Both men looked up from the newspapers they were reading.

'Fancy a coffee?' Pritchard offered. The cheerful tone hit a false note; Appleyard's chief, stocky and prematurely balding with dark appraising eyes, was never the most jocular of souls. Normally his manner was sullen and forbidding, an image that appeared to have been cultivated with some deliberation. Nevertheless Appleyard appreciated his chief making the effort to lift his spirits.

'Have you read last night's *Standard*?' Pritchard asked conversationally as he handed over the mug.

'I wasn't exactly in the mood to read the papers, Al.'

Pritchard gave one of his vinegary smiles. ' 'Course not, Les. But it's a good piece.'

'Written by some American reporter,' Midge added. 'Seems like she and her daughter got caught between Seven Dials and the bomb that killed Jock. Saw the whole thing.'

'I know. I was there, remember?' Appleyard replied. In fact he'd been watching it all through his binoculars from the relative safety of the Section's Range-Rovers. Waiting for Jock's message while Seven Dials was in flames all around him. 'But I didn't know she was a reporter. Just our luck.' He had a military man's instinctive distrust of the media.

Midge shrugged. 'It's a fitting epitaph for old Jock. Reckons if he hadn't stopped to reassure her and her daughter he wouldn't have run out of time. Says what a hero he was. Reckon old Jock would have liked that.'

Something snapped in Appleyard's head. 'How the fuck would you know what Jock would like? I tell you what Jock would like. He'd like to have gone home to Brenda and the kids last night. He'd like to be sitting with us here now, longing to get the meeting over so he could have a smoke . . .'

'Steady, Les,' Pritchard chided.

Appleyard made himself stop. Determinedly he relaxed his shoulders and forced a sheepish smile. 'Sorry, Midge, that was out of order.'

There was a knock on the door and Pritchard looked up. 'Come.'

It was Detective Chief Superintendent Jim Maitland. A man in his mid-forties, he was the deputy head of SO13 Anti-Terrorist Branch. There was something reassuringly solid about him. The stout frame and plain dark suit inspired confidence in the same way that the genial face suggested that he was a man to trust.

'Is this a private row, or can anyone join in?' he asked. Bright blue eyes enlivened a complexion that obviously didn't see enough daylight.

Pritchard beckoned him in. 'We're just letting off some steam, Jim. It's a few years since we've lost one of our own.'

'Terrible business,' Maitland agreed, acknowledging Appleyard and Midgely. 'My commiserations to all of you, it can't be an easy time. Specially as it seems we could be at the start of a new bombing campaign. Yesterday may have been the first time the AIDAN codeword was given, but we've reason to believe the same active service unit has been behind the other recent attacks.' He accepted the coffee that Midgely handed him. 'And I can tell you the ripples have been felt all the way up to Number Ten. The PM is fully aware of the havoc this AIDAN group has caused in the Province over the past months. Our masters are already getting nervous. You've seen the papers. Front page on the *Standard* last night and all over the nationals this morning. In fact, the Commander and I have got an appointment with the Home Secretary himself this afternoon. We're looking forward to it like a proverbial hole in the head.'

'I can imagine,' Pritchard sympathised.

Maitland settled himself on the arm of the sofa. 'Seven dead and two dozen injured is not good news for the government, especially when most of the casualties were police and emergency-service workers. Apart from a very real sense of horror, politicians start to get twitchy about their own survival. Start demanding instant results, however unrealistic.'

'Can you give them any?' Pritchard asked.

'Hardly, that's why I'm here. I've got your reports, but I want to get the situation clear in my own mind. Now I understand that after you neutralised the first bomb in Tower Street someone here got the idea it might be a come-on. That there could be other devices we hadn't been told about. All too right as it turned out.'

Pritchard nodded. 'That happened back here. As soon as we received a copy of the warning PIRA sent to the *Standard*, AP and Reuters, we were suspicious. As you know most real warnings come via the Samaritans so they can't be traced. Most papers and newsagencies automatically record the caller's number. Then we ran the codeword through the computer.' He spelt it out. 'It's never been used over here before, but it's turned up a number of times recently in Northern Ireland. A combination of particularly tricky devices and situations. Well-thought out by some scrote with a very cunning and nasty mind. Caused a number of deaths, troops and RUC as well as civilians.'

'Is there any pattern?'

'That's what gave me the clue that there might be more trouble in store at Tower Street. Over in the Province, this AIDAN cell has always made a point of giving fairly precise locations and times in their warnings. All good public relations for the Provos. What they've neglected to say is that they've been deviously booby-trapped and that there are secondary devices they *haven't* told us about. Tends to make the authorities, the RUC and the army look like incompetent chumps.'

'So as soon as you recognised the significance of the codeword, you contacted your Expos at Seven Dials, right? And in fact there were four bombs in total?'

Appleyard answered. 'There was the one Jock and I cleared first in Tower Street. It was in a van with an antihandling device wired to the courtesy-light system. That was actuated by a one-hour Memo Park timer in the TPU. We overcame the problem with standard window-entry procedure. Fragments showed that the main microchip timer was operating on an eleven-hour fifteen-minute delay. Due to go off at five past midday.'

Maitland frowned. 'And when did the Seven Dials bomb go off.'

'About five minutes later,' Appleyard replied. 'It had been placed in a street manhole. My guess is several sacks of ANS with a Semtex booster. Judging by the damage, maybe four hundred pounds.'

The detective nodded grimly. 'We're trying to establish how it was put there. Some local shopkeepers said a couple of local council workers appeared to be inspecting the drains yesterday evening. Apparently they looked the part – orange overalls and a van with council livery. At any rate they aroused no suspicions. Inquiries are at an early stage, but that would seem to be our best lead so far.'

'Seven Dials had never been used as an emergency rendezvous before?' Maitland asked.

'No,' Pritchard confirmed. 'That's one reason why it was chosen. We often can't get local police inspectors to understand the need to vary RV sites. Keep using the same one in a given area and you're asking to be set up.'

This time Midgely added: 'I think PIRA was trying to

double-guess where the RV might be. While all that was going on down at Seven Dials, I was working on another device in a car next to the Palace Theatre at Cambridge Circus due to go off at twelve fifteen. That was the most likely RV, but it was considered too close to Tower Street for safety.'

'That's the one bomb you haven't made public, right?' Maitland asked.

'Not us,' Pritchard replied tartly. 'It's what the Home Office decided in its infinite wisdom. Thought three bombs in an area at once was quite enough for the public to contend with. Said they didn't want a major panic in future. People would start to expect a bomb on every corner next time there's a scare.' He obliged with one of his icy smiles. 'Which I expect is PIRA's exact intention.'

'And when was this Palace Theatre bomb timed to go off?'

'Ten after noon,' Midgely answered. 'And it also had an antihandling circuit wired to the courtesy light.'

'So apart from the under-road device at Seven Dials, all three vehicle bombs had the same type of booby trap which you overcame by not touching the doors?' The detective looked round the room for confirmation. 'So poor old Jock Murray just ran out of time, is that it?'

Al Pritchard nodded his concurrence. 'It would seem so, unless there was a different sort of antihandling mechanism. That would fit in with AIDAN's method in the Province. Two or three identical devices to create a degree of complacency, then the last one with a subtle difference. Anyway, we'll not know till we get forensics back from Fort Halstead.'

'I understand,' Maitland said, glancing at his watch. 'Look, I must be going. Just wanted to double-check all the facts before we see the Home Secretary. The Commander wants to be able to give the minister some reassurance that we're taking all necessary measures to get on top of this business.'

'What do you have in mind?' Pritchard asked.

Maitland shifted his stance uneasily; this could be prickly. 'The Commander thinks we should get someone over from Northern Ireland. Someone who's had direct experience with the AIDAN bombings over there. Cover ourselves politically in case this joker continues to make his presence felt here in London. Purely in a liaison capacity of course.'

The air in the office seemed to freeze. Reactions on the faces of the Expos confirmed exactly what Maitland had anticipated. To these men, who were asked to risk their lives every day, the suggestion sounded like a breach of faith.

'We can handle it,' Al Pritchard said darkly.

'Of course you can, Alan. This is mostly a cosmetic exercise, although I'd have thought two heads would be better than one, so to speak. Get a top army ATO over here for a week or so, just so we can be *seen* to be doing something.'

Pritchard was not one to hide his wounded pride. 'It's a knee-jerk reaction, Jim. Do I have to accept it?'

'It's an official recommendation by the Commander.' The detective looked sympathetic. 'And I'm sure it'll receive the Home Secretary's sanction.'

'I'd like it to be known that I do not consider it necessary.'

'Then I'll pass your comments on.'

'You do that, Jim.'

Maitland stepped towards the door, then turned. 'I'll tell you something, Al. As this AIDAN cell is now operating on the mainland, we could be in for a long hot summer.'

Pritchard's hooded eyes were half closed, predatory. 'Is this all to do with these secret talks PIRA mentioned in their warning?'

'Don't even ask, Al, don't even ask. I can tell you officially that I have no knowledge of the existence of any such discussions.'

'Thank you for sharing that with us, Jim,' Pritchard replied with heavy irony.

The morning news conference at the London *Evening Standard* was its usual low-key affair.

At the head of the long mahogany table sat the editor. Resplendent in bright blue braces and tie to match, he listened as the news editor went through the day's running order. Only occasionally he interrupted the steady monologue with a query or a topical wisecrack. Sometimes the deputy news editor, or one of the other editors or department heads, would expand on the ideas behind proposed items.

'So what are we splashing with, Steve?' the editor asked.

'It's got to be the aftermath of the Seven Dials bombs.'

'Just the front page?'

'Plus one and two,' the news editor replied. 'We've got more of Hal's pics we didn't use yesterday, plus a lot of good eyewitness accounts.'

The editor's thick eyebrows rose behind his heavy black spectacles. 'We're not in danger of giving this too much coverage? The oxygen of publicity to the terrorists, and all that.'

'I don't think so. It's more than justified seeing as it's the biggest single attack since the City bombs. Or the seventies if you consider the casualties caused. And the first time they've used car bombs for about nine years. Besides, I think there could be more behind this latest campaign. I took the bombers' warning call yesterday and they mentioned secret talks between the British and Irish Governments. They're demanding a seat at the table. Now, as we've been told nothing about this, I've asked Eddie Mercs to do a little digging.'

The editor said: 'I know. I had a telephone call this morning from the secretary of the Defence Advisory Committee,' the editor explained. 'Charming chap. He pointed out – rather unnecessarily, I thought – that we were legally prevented from repeating the bombers' demands. He also said it had been brought to his attention that Eddie was asking questions of the Northern Ireland Office and Dublin about rumours of secret talks. Said he hoped we weren't going into print on the subject as it would almost certainly be contravening an unsung new subparagraph to Code Six that slipped quietly into being last year.'

The news editor's nostrils flared with the scent of a good story. Someone somewhere was manipulating the good old D-Notice system to suit his own purpose. 'This isn't the rumoured Humes-Adams talks. It's something altogether bigger. And we're being muzzled.'

'Possibly, Steve, but anyway I'm not sure this is for us. People are sick of hearing about peace talks recently – this is just one more.'

'Even when their bombs are devastating our city?' came the rather tart reply.

But the editor was unmoved. 'I'm not certain revelations by us about any secret peace talks or whatever are going to help the situation. Rather the reverse, I'd have thought.'

'You're asking me to drop it?'

There was a shake of the head. 'Just be a bit discreet. Put it on the back burner so we don't get left behind if the story breaks. But for the time being if there's going to be a first move, leave it to the nationals.'

The news editor drew a large dagger through the doodled sketch on his pad.

'By the way, the decision to lead with the Mullins girl's piece on Seven Dials yesterday was a masterstroke,' the editor said in an effort to lighten the atmosphere. 'Wonderful spot of first-hand feature reporting. Not a dry eye in the house.'

It was the turn of Billy Billingham, the jocular and flamboyant features editor, to bask in some reflected glory. He was never more pleased than when scoring points off the news desk. 'My pleasure to oblige. Just remember us next time you need some *real* talent, Steve.'

The news editor ignored the barb. 'I was wondering whether we ought to get some coverage of the bomb-disposal man's funeral. After Casey's story he's being treated as something of a national hero. Television and this morning's papers are going overboard.'

The editor grimaced. 'We must be the only nation in the world that celebrates failure more than success – Dunkirk, Arnhem, Bravo Two Zero – Was he a Londoner?'

'No, Scottish. He lived near Dorking. I imagine that's where the funeral will be.'

'Well, about time we had a hero, failed or not. It'll be a nice tribute, but no doorstepping the widow or telephoto pictures of weeping kids –'

'Of course not.' And get bollocked if another paper gets better shots, he thought.

'Tell you what, Steve, why not let the Mullins girl cover it.'

Billy Billingham grinned.

The news editor sighed. 'She's features.'

The editor said decisively. 'But she was *personally* involved. Nice touch that.' He placed both hands firmly on the table in front of him, a sure sign that the meeting was concluded. 'Anyway, give it some thought.'

The news editor shoved back his chair in a fit of pique, more certain now than ever that Eddie Mercs had an unlikely rival for the affections of Casey Mullins in the editor. It really would not do at all, he decided.

As he left the conference room he found himself passing Mercs in the corridor and updated him on the editorial decisions.

'Sorry about the funeral, Eddie. I had you earmarked for that.'

Mercs shrugged. 'Not bothered, old son. I'm sure Casey can handle it. It's this business about the talks that peeves me. Defence Advisory Committee, I ask you. There's something big in the air and it's not going to go away.'

'What do you mean?'

Mercs drew to a halt. 'Look, there's been a sudden rash of London bombings over the past three weeks. This is the first time we've been on the inside track and heard about secret talks. Even if this is the first time the Provisionals have mentioned it, then no doubt other papers have been called.'

'And presumably have also had deputations from the Defence Advisory Committee.'

'But people will talk, Steve, especially if the bombing campaign continues and they know it's connected with these mystery talks. They won't be able to keep the lid on if it's that important. If it doesn't break here, it'll appear in one of the European papers for sure. It's the best potential scoop since I've joined you and now I'm told I can't run with it.'

'Perhaps you should have joined one of the rags, Eddie.'

The reporter grimaced. 'You were the only one who'd have me.'

'Yeah, I prefer spotting talent on the way up, not pissheads on the way down. Anyway, don't back off completely. Keep digging, but gently. If the story does blow, then we might not be first, but at least we could be the best informed.'

That was of little consolation to Mercs. He wandered off towards the coffee machine to drown his sorrows in caffeine and sugar.

Meanwhile Billy Billingham was breaking the good news to Casey Mullins. 'Looks like your star's in the ascendant, my little Yankeedoodle.'

Casey cringed at the excruciating nickname he insisted on giving her and glanced up from the article on Herbal Remedies for Hayfever she was tapping into her terminal. 'Pardon me, BB?'

The permanent grin was wide on his freckled face. With his unruly mop of red hair, he always reminded her of a sort of bloated carrot. 'The editor was much impressed with your feature yesterday.'

'Really?' She wasn't sure whether to be flattered or irritated. Under the tragic circumstances, it seemed like a hollow victory.

'So much so he wants you to cover that poor bomb man's funeral.'

'Oh, I see.' Her eyes flickered with uncertainty. 'Well, I'm not sure about that . . .'

'It's quite an accolade,' BB assured. 'Not often the big white chief interferes with editorial decisions at this lowly level. You should grab it with both hands.'

'You think so?'

'Your second byline in a week.'

That was a thought. Establishing her byline with a big story had always seemed so important, yet she'd forgotten the significance of it in the trauma of the past twenty-four hours. 'Do you know when and where the funeral's being held?'

'No, but then you always told me you wanted to be an investigative journalist –'

Casey beat him to it. 'So investigate!' As he turned to go, she said: 'By the way, BB, I wonder if I could take the rest of the afternoon off. I'd like to visit a friend of mine injured in yesterday's bombing. And I'm anxious not to leave my daughter alone too long, she's still very upset.'

'Of course, I take it you're clear on anything urgent?'

She nodded towards the calendar. 'Unless you'd like me to write something on the Fourth of July?'

He looked momentarily bewildered.

With a smile she said: 'But then you folk don't seem to celebrate that holiday, do you?'

'A signal from London,' CATO said. 'The Home Office is requesting assistance from us over the new bombing campaign that's started there. I thought you were the best man for the job.'

Tom Harrison stared at the GO AWAY! sign pinned to the front of Colonel Gareth Lloyd-Williams's desk. Perversely its message of bluff humour made 'Top Cat' all the more approachable to his staff. Harrison's own relationship with 'Taff' Lloyd-Williams was excellent, each man willingly standing in for the other as situations demanded. It was a mutual trust and respect as well as friendship. 'That's a bit unusual, Colonel. What's the Met's Explosives Section going to say about it?'

The Chief ATO allowed himself a sly smile. 'The initial request came from Al Pritchard, if you can believe that.'

'I can't.'

'Under pressure from on high, I imagine, after the Seven Dials fiasco.'

'Ah,' Harrison said, 'that's more like it.'

'Have you heard the latest from London?'

'I haven't been into the office yet.'

The Welshman linked his fingers over the desk top. 'The Seven Dials bombings appear to be the handiwork of our old friends AIDAN.'

It was like a douche of cold water; suddenly Harrison felt wide awake. 'You're joking.'

'Wish I was, Tom. It was confirmed in the warnings. Seems

like our bomber is putting himself about a bit. That's why they want someone over there who's had some experience of how AIDAN works. See into his mind, so to speak.'

'I'm not sure I can do that, and I'm not sure I'd want to, the evil bastard.' He almost spat the words, giving vent to his rising anger. So it had been the same AIDAN cell who'd killed Jock Murray and had come within a whisker of catching himself at the Europa the previous night. 'I mean we still don't know if the AIDAN codeword signifies a particular active service unit, a new strategy or an individual bomb maker. I don't suppose "Whiz" has been able to shed any light on the matter?'

The colonel shook his head; the Weapons Intelligence Section had been working overtime to get a lead on the bomb maker's identity or some common pattern that might give them a clue. 'What we can guess, Tom, is that the situation on the mainland can only get worse. The warnings have made it quite clear that the campaign is a protest by the Provisionals at being left out of the latest peace process.'

'I'm sorry?' he said, recalling what Trenchard had said to him outside the Europa.

'It must be the world's worst kept secret. Protracted talks between Dublin, London and the major political parties in Ulster. They started last winter and the prevailing wisdom is they're likely to continue throughout this summer. Politicians on both sides are determined to get a result. Quite far-reaching and controversial proposals apparently. But, the official line is strictly no comment and no knowledge of any such talks. I imagine the Defence Advisory Committee and any Irish equivalent have got their hands full keeping it out of the media.' He held Harrison in a steady gaze. 'So you can see that PIRA thinks it's got nothing to lose. My guess is that's why they've let AIDAN – whoever or whatever that is – loose on the mainland. To bomb its way to the conference table. So, can I confirm you'll be giving London a hand?'

London in summer. The warm dusty streets, the leafy parks, the pubs, restaurants and theatres, pavement cafés – what humble squaddie in his cramped billet wouldn't willingly give up a month's pay for such a comfortable posting?

Was he really the only soldier in Belfast who would prefer to stay where he was? But, despite his misgivings, he knew he couldn't let CATO down. 'If that's what you want, Colonel, of course I'll go.'

He read the relief in the colonel's gentle smile; although he had the authority to order such things, he was a man who liked to rule by consent. 'I thought I'd pull in Meredith from the mainland to replace you. Meanwhile, of course, you'll be walking on eggshells. You'll need to be the model of diplomacy not to upset Al Pritchard's wounded pride.'

'I know Al well – we used to work together some years back when he was still with us. I think I can handle it.'

'Not the easiest of men to get on with.'

Harrison thought for a moment. 'I was wondering if I'd be able to get over. At least it'll give me a chance to visit Jock's wife and pay my respects.'

'Jock was best man at your wedding, wasn't he?'

'We were good friends.'

CATO nodded sympathetically. 'Then I expect Pippa must be pretty upset too.'

The sudden use of his wife's name had a profound effect. It hadn't even occurred to him to telephone her and break the sad news. Hadn't occurred to him? Did he really mean that? Or was it the sure knowledge that he'd just be handing her a stick to beat him with? Although Pippa came from an army family herself, she'd always hated the work he did in bomb disposal. Pippa had never been able to accept it any more than he could bring himself to think of any other life. Perhaps it had been more convenient to drown his own personal sorrow in the mess last night before the Europa bomb. After all, it wouldn't have taken much to have picked up the telephone.

He realised too late that he'd allowed his concentration to lapse and that CATO was watching him carefully, waiting for the reply. Harrison tried to sound casual. 'Yes, I'm sure she'll be shocked. We've both known Jock a long time.'

'You haven't spoken to her yet?' Mild surprise registered in his tone. The colonel took a particularly keen interest in the social wellbeing of his men and their families on the basis that a happy ship was an efficient ship, with no unnecessary mental distractions from the dangerous job they did. Usually Harrison welcomed Top Cat's concern, but not at the moment. Not until he'd sorted out things in his own way.

'She was away on business when I called yesterday,' he lied.

CATO nodded in his usual understanding way. The way he did when he didn't believe a word of what he was being told. 'Still doing well is she? What's her father's business? Publishing?'

'Public relations,' Harrison corrected. 'And she's enjoying it, keeping busy anyway.'

'So still no chance she might come and join you over here?'

Harrison had to laugh at that. 'She feels she's had to wait long enough since Archie was born to resume her career. She hated life over here behind the wire and I can't say I blame her for that.'

'So you're both happy with the arrangement?'

'That's the bonus with not seeing much of each other, we have some great reunions!' Harrison laughed as he said it, but even to his own ears the words had a hollow ring to them. And he was sure the point wasn't lost on CATO.

But then they were interrupted by the commander's aide, informing him that the party of Members of Parliament from London had arrived for a briefing by him.

As the door closed he raised his eyebrows in an expression of absolute despair. 'That's the trouble with this job, Tom. Seem to spend all my time wet-nursing politicians and journalists.'

Harrison sympathised. He said: 'I think I'd prefer to defuse a bomb any day.' But he wasn't sure he really meant it.

CATO stood up. 'By all accounts the politicians are getting pretty anxious in London. Meredith will be over here on Wednesday morning so, allowing for a handover session, you could take the shuttle out that evening and report to Al Pritchard on Thursday. In fact, you'll probably see him at Jock Murray's funeral in the morning.'

Funeral. That single word was so cold and final. Clods of earth clumping onto a coffin roof. Dead and buried. Gone for ever, but not forgotten. Memories of laughter shared in the mess, Jock's wicked sense of humour, their celebration in Cyprus when he heard that Brenda had given birth to their first.

Harrison felt the emotion rising in his chest, the choking claw at his throat. CATO may have sensed it, for he indicated for his 2IC to leave with an understanding smile.

He was outside the door before the moisture came to his eyes and dampened the skin of his cheeks. Roughly he rubbed it aside with the back of his hand.

Jock, you old bastard, stop taking the piss.

6

The press hounds were out in force. The pack had descended on the small village in the Surrey hills. They doorstepped Brenda Murray's modern detached house on the outskirts until she made a brief appearance at the front door. She wore dark glasses to hide her grief; her hair was lank and dishevelled. The cameramen with their probing telephoto lenses had the picture they wanted.

It made all the tabloid front pages the next day, although the dark glasses made her look slightly sinister, more like the wife of a serial killer than that of an innocent national hero. Because that was what Jock Murray had become.

Casey Mullins had started it with her poignant first-hand account, but by the next morning it had been taken over by the national big boys, her original contribution lost in a welter of column inches and big pictures with headlines screaming for the blood of the IRA terrorists who had killed their new-found hero.

One reporter wheedled his way into the household in the guise of a representative of Jock's life insurance company; after gleaning what he could about the family's finances, he stole a photograph of Jock, his wife and children.

A police constable was put on the door of the Murray house, so the hounds resorted to telephoning at all hours of the day and night until the receiver had to be left permanently off the hook. They took over the local pub and quizzed neighbours for snippets of gossip. Then, getting bored the day before the funeral, some hacks began asking if Jock had been having an affair? Was that why his mind wasn't fully on the job at Seven Dials? It was splashed by one paper on the morning of the funeral.

When Casey arrived at the village with Eddie Mercs and Hal

Hoskins, she had difficulty in finding a place to park, finally abandoning her Porsche at the edge of the village. It was difficult walking in the black high heels that matched her flared skirt, jacket and wide-brimmed hat. Nevertheless she turned down offers to carry the simple wreath.

'You look good in black,' Mercs remarked. 'I always think widows look sexy.'

'Don't be vulgar, Eddie.'

'*And* brides. Widows and brides.'

'I'm neither, Eddie.'

'Just an observation.'

Cars were parked all along the grass verge that bordered the churchyard, many with photographers standing on the bonnets, trying to peer beyond the trimmed hawthorn hedge. A small knot of reporters and villagers were gathered at the lych gate where a police sergeant stood with a clipboard of names.

'Sorry, folks, *only* those on my list.'

'This is supposed to be a place of public worship,' one hack complained.

'Not today, it isn't,' the policeman countered. 'There's a security aspect to this, the IRA and all. And if we catch any of you scaling the walls or hedges . . .'

'Trespass isn't criminal, Sergeant, it's a civil matter.'

'. . . then you'll be charged with causing a breach of the peace. Now, please give Mrs Murray a break, eh? You'll get your chance when she leaves.'

Casey turned to Mercs. 'There's no way he's going to let me in.'

'Bluff it out, sweetheart,' he urged. 'You're dressed for the occasion, these oiks aren't. And put your sunglasses on in case anyone recognises you.' As she fumbled in her handbag, Mercs pushed her forward through the bystanders. 'Step aside, gents, let the lady through.'

'Hello, Eddie,' someone said. 'Long time no see.'

He ignored the man. 'Morning, officer. Can't you control this rabble? The lady here will miss the service.'

The policeman did a double-take at the sight of the tall, elegant woman, the sunlight on her coppery hair in striking contrast to the charcoal material of her hat and jacket.

'It's all right, miss, you're in good time. Can I have your name please?'

She was aware of the hot, perspiring faces of the hacks all around her, their ears straining and pencils poised. Another relative? A mystery blonde, or would you call her a redhead? Jock Murray's phantom lover? Now that would be a turn-up . . .

'Casey –' she began, her voice hoarse with embarrassment.

'Pardon me?' the policeman couldn't hear.

'That's Eddie Mercs! What's he doing with that bird?'

She cleared her throat and grabbed at a name. 'Tracey Collins.' The policeman consulted his list.

'What's your game, Eddie, you old reprobate?'

'I'm afraid I don't see the name here,' the sergeant said, realising now that Mercs was a reporter. 'Are you with the press, miss?'

'Hardly, officer. I'm a friend of the family and I've come a *long* way to get here.' She thrust her wreath towards him.

'Ah, an American,' he said, now picking up her accent. He looked awkward. 'It's a bit difficult, see. Your name's not here and I've got my instructions . . .'

'Is there a problem, officer?' The new voice came from behind her shoulder, resonant and with a natural authority. As she turned she caught sight of him. He stood a couple of inches taller than her own five foot eleven in heels and his shoulders looked solid beneath the navy blazer. She was distracted by his tie – green with the repeated motif of an orange hand and a cartoon cat – before she noticed his face. It was full and serious with dark brows and steady brown eyes that had the bright glint of someone enjoying a private joke. She noticed the small cleft in his chin and the bluish sheen to his skin that suggested he needed to shave twice a day.

'And you, sir?' the policeman asked.

'Harrison. Major and Mrs Harrison.' He added: 'And son.'

Casey twisted round to see the woman who stood by his side. She looked doll-like beside her husband, a pale and delicately

115

boned face with wide and wary eyes beneath the upturned brim of her hat. A young boy clutched nervously at her hand.

'That's fine, sir,' the policeman ticked his list.

'And the lady?' Harrison pressed, smiling at Casey to let her know she wasn't forgotten.

'I'm afraid I've no Miss Collins here.'

Casey said: 'I'm not really expected. I didn't think I could get away. Mrs Murray wouldn't have put my name down.'

'Brenda didn't think you'd be able to come?' Harrison asked. 'You're from America?'

'California.'

Harrison turned to the policeman. 'We can't have a family friend come all the way from California to be turned away at the funeral, Sergeant. It's okay, she can come in with us . . .'

The policeman was pleased to have his dilemma solved and stepped aside to allow the four of them to pass.

Casey breathed a sigh of relief, despite the insistent voice of a reporter calling after her. 'Miss Collins! What's your connection with the Murrays? Miss Collins!'

Ahead, an old flagged path meandered beneath brooding dark cedars, lichen-stained gravestones on either side. The mourners were gathering by the porch of the church; many wore police or army uniforms.

'Looks as though they've managed to keep the gutter press out,' Harrison observed.

'It's really disgusting,' Pippa said. Her voice was cultivated and perfectly pitched in the traditional BBC announcer's manner. Casey imagined Harrison's wife always had that slightly affronted tone whatever she was saying; it was the kind of voice she'd grown to associate with Ascot, Henley and the Peter Jones store in Chelsea. 'Usually I don't give them the satisfaction of reading their rags. In fact it was some time before I learned that Jock was dead. I usually just read the features – being in PR, I have to really. But as for what they rate as news nowadays.' She made a vague gesture towards the gate. 'You'd think they'd leave poor Brenda in peace for today at least. After all, she is burying her husband.'

Casey was irritated by the woman's superior attitude and felt an instinctive urge to defend the indefensible. 'I suppose they're just doing their jobs.'

'It strikes me,' Pippa responded, 'that they just like to build people up in order to be able to knock them down. It's just a game to them. I just hope they don't try to do that to Jock's memory. I mean, did you read what one of those scandal sheets said today?'

'Forget it, Pippa,' Harrison chided. 'They're not worth your breath.'

They stopped on the fringe of the gathering. 'You're right, Tom, of course.' She looked at Casey directly for the first time. 'You're a friend of Brenda's? I didn't quite catch your name? Tracey –?'

'Casey. Casey Mullins. It's a bit complicated, but I sort of knew Jock.'

Pippa's long eyelashes fluttered in a bewildered sort of way. 'Oh, really.'

Harrison frowned. 'I thought you said . . .'

Casey smiled demurely and removed her glasses. 'Actually I think you jumped to a couple of conclusions. But thanks anyway for sorting out that confusion with the policeman.'

Pippa had taken a step back. Rather stiffly she said, 'Well, anyway, we ought to introduce ourselves properly. I'm Philippa Harrison and this is my husband Tom.'

'Major, is that right?' Casey asked.

He nodded.

'You're not in uniform.'

'No, I'm not with the pallbearers or in the guard of honour. We don't wear uniforms off duty nowadays.'

'I see.'

'Best not to advertise to terrorists.'

'That's awful,' Casey said. 'And how long had you known Jock?'

'A long time. He was the best man at our wedding. Served with me in 321 EOD.'

'Pardon me?'

He smiled at the very American intonation. 'Explosives Ordnance Disposal Squadron in Northern Ireland.'

'You're a bomb man, too?'

117

Pippa looked pained, but Harrison just laughed lightly. 'We're called ATOs. Ammunition Technical Officers.'

'That makes it sound very dull.'

His wife began to feel excluded, so she placed her hands on her son's shoulders and propelled him forward. 'This is our offspring, Archie. Say hello to Miss Mullins.'

He offered his hand shyly and bowed stiffly at the waist. 'I'm very pleased to meet you, Miss Mullins.'

She smiled at his Victorian formality and impeccable manners. 'And I'm very pleased to meet you too, Archie. But please call me Casey and we'll get on fine. How old are you?'

'I'm ten. Nearly eleven.'

'And tell me, do you intend to be a bomb man when you grow up, like your daddy?'

'Over my dead body,' Pippa intervened. 'It's bad enough with one of them in the family.'

Again Casey felt an unreasonable irritation at Philippa Harrison's manner. Ignoring her, she said; 'And what do *you* think, Archie?'

He glanced sideways at his mother. 'Actually, I think I might like to, but I'm not sure I'd be brave enough.'

Casey couldn't help herself, she laughed brightly and loudly enough to prompt several heads to turn. 'How sweet! Oh, Archie, I'm sure you'd be quite brave enough.'

And while Pippa scowled, Casey noticed that his father gave his son a tight, proud hug around his small shoulders.

It was then that Brenda Murray extricated herself from the gathering of mourners and approached them. She had dark features like Pippa, although she was considerably taller and the ringlets of hair beneath her hat were distinctly grey.

'Pippa – Tom – little Archie – I'm so glad you could come.' Her accent was so heavily Glaswegian that even Casey had no trouble in placing it. Through the veil she could see that Jock's widow had a wide and generous mouth, managing to smile despite the sad look in her eyes.

'We're so, so sorry, Brenda,' Pippa said as the two women embraced and exchanged kisses on the cheek.

118

Brenda nodded, clearly finding it difficult to talk beyond perfunctory greetings.

Harrison said: 'This is Casey Mullins. I believe she was a friend of Jock's.'

She looked towards the tall American, an expression of puzzlement on her face as she extended her hand.

Casey felt her cheeks colour. 'This suddenly seems like a great impertinence, Mrs Murray. I had no idea it would be so – so busy.' She gestured vaguely at the sizeable gathering and the pressmen beyond the gate. 'I just wanted to sit quietly at the back of the church and pay my respects.'

'How did you know Jock?'

'Well, I didn't really. My daughter and I were caught in Seven Dials on the day of the bombing. Your husband came and spoke to us, reassured us. I was very grateful. We were right next to the car, you see.'

Brenda Murray's features seemed to freeze for a moment. Then she reached out for Casey's arm. 'My dear, you were actually *there* when it went off?'

Casey nodded, not sure what else to say.

'Then you were probably the last person to see Jock alive.'

She found her voice. 'He was very kind.'

Brenda noticed the wreath. 'And you've brought this – I'll put it with the others. Silly really, but Jock used to get terrible hayfever from flowers.' Her voice quavered for a second, then she regained her composure. 'It was good of you to come. But you won't know anyone. Perhaps Pippa and Tom will be kind enough to look after you.'

'Of course,' Harrison said.

'We'd best go in now,' Brenda said, adding: 'Do come back to the house afterwards, Miss Mullins. It's just sherry and a few snacks.'

Then she was gone and Casey stayed with the Harrisons, joining the end of the queue of mourners as they were swallowed up into the 17th-century church.

Despite Brenda's warm reception, Casey couldn't help feeling like an intruder. A gatecrasher into others' very private grief. For it became clear that this was a family in more than the usual sense of the word.

Almost all the men in the packed church were bound together in the brotherhood of the bomb. Harrison seemed to be known to almost all of them. It marked them out as men apart, men who alone knew what it meant to take the long walk that Jock Murray had taken. Theirs was an élite, a closed order in which it was not possible for the outside world to share, let alone begin to understand. Their work, their language and their jargon and their secret world of private fears were scarcely understood even by fellow soldiers and policemen. So how could someone like Casey begin to comprehend? Men from the British Army and the Explosives Section of New Scotland Yard stood shoulder to shoulder, heads bent in silent prayer. For Jock and his family, she wondered, or for themselves the next time a bomb warning was received?

And the women, too, were set apart. Who but they would know what it meant to be the wife or lover of a bomb-disposal man? Their private, silently screaming agony whenever they saw a newsflash on the television. Did they hush the kids and turn up the sound? Or did they look away and pretend that the real sordid world didn't exist? Did they just say Daddy will be home this weekend and leave it at that? A bomb in Northern Ireland or an explosion in the West End. What did it mean to them? All the time knowing that of all the places in all the world, that was exactly where their men were expected to be.

The service lasted half-an-hour; the lesson was read by a man called Les Appleyard, who Harrison explained had been Jock's closest friend, and a tribute was paid by a Yorkshireman called Midgely from the Explosives Section. He told the congregation that he was standing in for his chief who'd been delayed in London because of the current terrorist campaign.

Apparently at Jock's own request, when he was still very much alive and full of mischief, it concluded with the melancholy lament of a kilted piper.

There was a burning sensation in Casey's throat and her eyes were stinging as the pallbearers, police officers to which the Explosives Section was attached, stepped forward and manhandled the coffin onto their shoulders. Brenda Murray with her children fell in behind the silent procession, Jock's former colleagues, senior police and army officers following. Casey joined the Harrisons at the rear, passing the guard of honour formed by policemen and men in the white belts and peaked caps of the Royal Logistics Corps, on the way to the churchyard where the freshly dug grave waited.

She drew back then, distancing herself physically and mentally from the others who shared Jock Murray's strange world. Watching each solemn face in turn until she came to Brenda, a handkerchief pressed beneath her veil. Her children staring down at the lowered coffin, their eyes looking puzzled, almost frightened. Perhaps not understanding or perhaps just beginning to.

And Gwen. She thought of Gwen, lying as she had last seen her, and how she would carry the legacy of that day with her for ever if she managed to survive. Her punishment for being in the wrong place at the wrong time. Cruelly maimed and disfigured, her daughter taken from her.

And how many others were there like Gwen, she wondered, quietly struggling through the rest of their lives in Northern Ireland or in some suburb of London? Some without limbs, some with horrendous internal injuries but patched together with the wondrous technology of steel and plastic, or in a world of permanent darkness. Forgotten by the press who reported the events at the time, their stories giving way to the next day's news.

And what of the bombers? What of the men who planted the Seven Dials bombs, what were they doing this bright but chill July morning? At home with their own families? Or hiding up somewhere? Or were they laughing and drinking in some pub in Eire or Ulster? Perhaps even watching the television set above the bar as it relayed the pictures from the news cameras outside this very church in the Surrey hills?

Who were they? What drove them to such monstrous actions? Did they have a conscience or a soul?

The first handful of dry earth rattled on the coffin lid. Then others followed, splashes of soil spreading out to obscure the polished oak. Earth to earth, ashes to ashes, dust to dust.

Then it was over and the relief was tangible in the air. The crowd began to move away, allowing the sunlight to fall on the grave and the black marble headstone. Amongst the wreaths one in particular caught her attention – again it was the cartoon cat set in flowers against the orange hand of Ulster. A cooling breeze picked up, rustling the cedars and breaking the spell; someone made a joke and someone else laughed.

Hugh Dougan and Clodagh had planned it. Pat McGirl was responsible for the operational details.

The final briefing had been held the night before at the rented house near Henley-on-Thames where the bomb maker and his daughter were staying. McGirl and Dougan hit it off well enough, but an unspoken antagonism existed between the Northern Brigade commander and the girl. Nothing specific, just bad chemistry which resulted in silent friction. An unspoken hostility. He sensed her lack of respect for his authority and was irked by her constant questioning of his decisions. She considered him uncouth and ill-educated, he was sure. But then he could live with that. What made it worse was that he found her disturbingly attractive and, much as he tried to hide the fact, he was damn sure she knew it.

He had left the house at midnight, driven out of the integral garage and taken the road to the farm a few miles away.

The others were waiting, anxious to be going. Moira Lock was a farmer's daughter from Fermanagh and Leo Muldoon had been born and brought up in Derry's Catholic Bogside area. Liam Doran was a Dubliner and Joe Houlihan was of London-Irish stock. None had a record for terrorist activity.

Four Transit vans were lined up in the barn, each the same colour and bearing false number plates identical to those of legitimate vehicles spotted in the London area. Inside each one was loaded ten heavy-duty plastic sacks containing one thousand pounds of ANS-milled fertiliser and icing sugar mix.

The vans left at twenty-minute intervals, slipping quietly out of the yard and onto the dark and deserted country road. McGirl left in the last vehicle with Moira Lock. Their destinations were four separate lock-up garages that had been rented, cash down, by the Provisionals' mainland 'flying column' months earlier. Once safely under lock and key, the Transits were left until the following day.

Such was the size of the operation that McGirl had to draw in two other mainland active service units which had been operating in the UK for some time. One was a London-based reconnaissance unit which would place getaway vehicles close to the four target areas, each one legally parked, the keys given to McGirl for redistribution.

The second ASU was brought down from Humberside. This comprised six 'trainees' who had been cutting their teeth on low-grade economic targets. As such they were considered to be more 'expendable' than the two other seasoned cells operating in England at the time. Now would be the chance for the youngsters to prove their mettle, mounting the co-ordinated diversionary attacks.

At midday McGirl and Moira Lock returned to the garage in Willesden from the safe house where they had stayed overnight. They drove towards Kew Bridge until, nearing their destination, McGirl pulled up alongside the parked getaway car to let Moira climb out.

Then he drove on alone until he reached the Chiswick flyover which carried the heavy flow of M4 traffic in and out of central London. As he passed beneath the enormous canopy of reinforced concrete, he switched on the van's hazard lights and pulled over. With cars speeding past, he reached for the TPU beneath the passenger seat and pulled the two dowel pins: each released the pressure on a Memo Park mechanical timer, one set at thirty minutes to arm the antihandling devices, the second to set the main charge for sixty minutes.

He stepped onto the road, tugging up his jacket collar and pulling down the peak of his flat cap to obscure his face, before he propped open the bonnet to peer at the engine.

Later a motorist would recall how he saw the broken-down

Transit with its hazard flashers blinking and noticed the driver, hunch-shouldered and with hands in pockets, walking away. Presumably the unfortunate man was going off to telephone one of the breakdown services.

The motorist thought no more about it at the time. He was not to know that an identical incident had occurred at three other locations around London. All at exactly the same time.

'Casey!' She turned; it was Harrison. 'I thought we'd lost you. C'mon, I'll give you a lift to Brenda's.'

'Where's your wife?'

'Pippa and Archie have gone in one of the official cars with Brenda.'

She fell into step beside him. 'It was a lovely service.'

'Jock would have liked it. He always said his final vengeance on all of us would be to have a piper at his funeral.'

'I thought it was very moving.'

Harrison smiled. 'That's not what any of his mates would ever admit. Love of the pipes is a very Scottish thing. He always said it would be his last laugh on us for all the leg-pulls. That and the sweetest revenge of all – beating the life insurance company.'

She glanced sideways at him. 'You're being very flippant.'

He looked surprised, almost apologetic. 'I'm sorry, I didn't mean to offend you. If you'd known Jock for any time, you'd understand. You can't afford to be sentimental in our game.'

'I suppose not.'

They had reached the lych gate and Casey replaced her sunglasses.

'Afraid of being recognised?' Harrison joked.

'My mascara's run.'

The press pack that had been clamouring for a quote and the best picture of the grieving widow and her children had lost interest now that the crowds had dwindled. She saw no sign of Eddie Mercs or Hal Hoskins.

Harrison's car was parked in a side street alongside a rose-pink thatched cottage. Without a word he dropped down beside the rather battered blue Vauxhall Cavalier, checking the chassis and wheelarch on the driver's side.

'What are you doing?' she asked, but even as she spoke she realised with a small sense of shock that she already knew the answer.

'Just checking,' he replied lightly, opening his door and reaching across to open hers.

'You don't really expect a bomb, do you?' she asked as she took her seat.

He started the engine. 'You can't be too careful. This funeral's been a high-profile affair and PIRA are always watching.'

'Here?' She was incredulous. In the Surrey hills?

'We're only thirty miles from the centre of London, and I'd be considered a good catch by PIRA. The Senior ATO in Northern Ireland.'

'That's your job?'

'Running all the EOD sections in Northern Ireland, yes. Above me is the Colonel or Chief ATO. I'm in day-to-day command while he attends all the meetings with the top brass, looks after overall strategy and all that. Or in theory. The reality is rather less formal. Many of our duties are really shared and we stand in for each other as the need arises.'

She frowned. 'Is he the one I've heard referred to as Top Cat?'

Harrison drove past the church, the crowds now dispersed. 'That can be him or me, but the term's a bit old hat now. It used to be our radio call sign in the old days. And "Felix" for any bomb-disposal operator. The nimble cat with nine lives.'

She shivered involuntarily, remembering Jock Murray at Seven Dials. 'No wonder your wife isn't happy with what you do.'

The major smiled gently. 'She's never really understood and I doubt that many wives do. There is the odd – let's say dramatic – moment, but mostly it's just routine. It's rarely hands-on stuff, that's strictly for the movies.'

'But you've had casualties?'

He nodded, studying the road as it opened up beyond the congested high street. 'We've lost twenty in Northern Ireland since the troubles began and twenty-four injured. The majority were in the early days while our techniques were being developed, but you still can't eliminate all the risks.'

She was intrigued, trying to imagine what his service life was like. 'Are you ever at risk, Tom?'

'Only from dying of boredom with all the paperwork,' he laughed. 'My job's to supervise. I've done my bit – being a born coward I'm quite happy for the youngsters to have their turn now.'

Somehow she didn't quite believe his reply. It came a little too easily; too glib and well-practised.

Pippa had said as much to him the previous night when he'd returned to the family home in Pimlico, a house that his wife's father had bought for them.

Harrison had made the mistake of mentioning his involvement with the Europa suitcase bomb. It was still fresh in his mind, his nerves still raw and he'd wanted to talk to someone about it. Pippa was not the wisest choice.

'What is it with you, Tom?' she'd challenged. 'You're always trying to convince me you don't get involved any more and now you come up with this one. How many other times do you do this and don't tell me? For God's sake, you've done your share over the years – God knows how many weeks' sleep I've lost with the nightmares – so why? So you happened to be there and the ATO wasn't. Who cares if the bloody Europa blows up?'

He had poured himself a drink at the Louis Quatorze cabinet – another gift from Pippa's father. 'It's my job. Blowing up the Europa has always been one of the Provos' big dreams and it would be the biggest possible propaganda victory for them. I took all necessary precautions, minimised the risk and did the business. It's what I'm paid for.'

'I'm not your bloody colonel, Tom!' she had almost shrieked. 'Don't give me your bloody official sitrep or whatever your jargon is. It's me you're talking to, your wife. Jock died last week and I expect he gave Brenda exactly the same bullshit. Oh, darling, there's nothing to worry about, it's all remote nowadays – and now he's dead and it could have been you the other night in friggin' bloody Belfast!'

He had downed his double finger of whisky hard, enjoying the

126

burning rasp in his throat. 'So what do you expect me to do about it?'

She stood across the room from him and glared. 'What do I *want* you to do, or what do I *expect* you to do? I want you to jack it in, Tom, like I've always wanted. I want you to put me and Archie fucking well first for once.' She was small and beautiful and magnificent in her rage. Her slightly plummy voice excited him when she resorted to gutter language; in bed she would sometimes use words he would hardly have guessed she knew. 'You know there's a place for you in the company, on the board.'

'Daddy's company,' he mimicked unkindly. But he knew really that he meant it and so did Pippa. 'I know nothing about public relations and I've no time for the press – that hardly qualifies me.'

She placed her hands on her hips. 'Yes, Tom, that is what I *expected* you to do. Bloody nothing. This silly thing you've got about Daddy. You resent this house and you resent his offer of a board position in his company. Why? He was a major once, just like you. He comes from a military family. So what is it? Is it this damn I'll-stand-on-my-own-two-feet thing, resenting a helping hand from your wife's rich family –'

'Don't be crass, Pippa,' he said, but he knew she wasn't too far from the truth. Her father had risen to the rank of brigadier in the Brigade of Guards and never tired of letting Harrison know that he didn't consider technical 'blue-collar' arms of the services, like ordnance disposal, to be 'proper soldierin' ', as he liked to put it. Without saying so directly, he made it perfectly plain that he would have considered a cavalry officer to have made a far more suitable husband for his daughter. 'I'm staying with bomb disposal because it's what I know and what I'm good at. And I happen to enjoy it.'

'Even though it means living apart from me?' she challenged.

'That was your decision.'

She didn't like that; it edged her onto the defensive. 'I've played the dutiful wife, Tom. I spent nine years living behind the wire while Archie was growing up. It's my turn now. I've got my career to think of.'

'I know that.' He meant it. 'And so have I.'

Pippa shook her head slowly as though in exasperation at an irascible child. 'But it means we continue living apart, Tom, and that's not good for our marriage. You can't always expect me to be waiting with a warm bed for your nine days' R and R every six months.'

If it had been a warning, or a hint of things to come, then Harrison had missed it. After three months of enforced celibacy in Lisburn, Pippa looked more dark and delicious than ever, a sheen of perspiration on her face after a long summer's day in her hectic office, her silk blouse and the hip-flaring business skirt looking fetchingly tired and crumpled.

Hoarsely he said: 'Let's go to bed.'

She had given a small, tight smile, but had not resisted.

Now Casey Mullins was saying: 'I can sympathise with your wife,' as he approached the driveway to the Murrays' mock-Georgian home. 'Especially having seen what happened to Jock. But at the same time I'd be very proud of you.'

He glanced sideways at her and caught her smile; it was wide and infectious and it lifted his spirits as he turned into the driveway and parked.

'Just one thing, Casey,' he said as he switched off the engine. 'Can you remember if Jock opened the door of that car?'

She shook her head emphatically. 'Definitely not. He actually told me he'd break through the window in case the bomb had been wired to the courtesy light or something.'

'That's good. Running out of time is one thing, I hate to think of Jock getting caught out by that old trick.'

She walked with him towards the house, puzzled that such an academic point could mean so much to him. After all, Jock Murray was dead – did it really matter how?

The front door was ajar and they were almost bowled over by two of the mourners' children playing tag, the funeral forgotten and their lives to lead. People were standing in the hall, chatting and trying to balance plates of tiny sausage rolls and glasses. Their relief at the return to normality was obvious. But the good humour was a little forced, the laughter too loud. Even Brenda was making

128

a determined effort, talking articulately in the packed chaos of the front lounge, her hat and veil abandoned.

Followed by Casey, Harrison made his way to the kitchen where bottles and cans had been laid out in readiness for the invasion of mourners.

'To Jock,' Midge Midgely, the Yorkshireman, was saying. He toasted the lager can with Les Appleyard. 'To Jock.' Then he saw Harrison: 'Hello, Tom. Sorry I didn't get a chance to speak earlier.'

'A lot of people.'

Appleyard nodded. He was a tall, thin man with swept-back hair that emphasised his angular features and prominent beaked nose. 'Jock was well liked. A good send-off, nothing more than he deserved.' He noticed Casey and grinned enthusiastically. 'What can I get you? Seems I'm the unpaid bar staff. Looks like lager or sherry.'

'A lager, please.'

A wink. 'American? No root beer, I'm afraid.'

'Lager's fine.'

Harrison took two cans; they were out of glasses. 'This is Casey –'

'A sort of family friend,' she said quickly. If these were Jock's working colleagues she didn't want to end up talking about the events at Seven Dials. She wondered if Harrison might tell them, but something in his eyes when he looked at her made her think he wouldn't. That he would understand her reticence to talk about it.

Midgely said: 'Al's not too happy about this turn of events, Tom. You might as well be warned if you hadn't already guessed.'

Harrison took a swig of the beer. 'I'm not too chuffed about it either, Midge.'

'Al's like a bear with a sore head at the best of times.' Appleyard added. 'At the moment it's like working with a cocktail shaker full of nitroglycerine. If you squint you can almost see the old black dog trailing round after him.'

'That bad, eh?'

'Moody sod,' Midgely agreed. 'Mind you, this new campaign

is getting us all down. It feels sort of personal – and I've never felt that before. Like someone's deliberately trying to catch us out and make us look chumps into the bargain.'

'Whoever's behind it, is good,' Appleyard said with an air of professional detachment. 'After all, he or they got old Jock.' He looked at Harrison. 'But you'd know all about AIDAN, Tom.'

A vision of the third-floor corridor in the Europa flashed through Harrison's mind, the silvery photographer's case seeming to beckon him like a siren's song. He took another draught of lager. 'Sure, we've had that codeword in Belfast for – what? – two months now. I think that's about when it began. One ATO dead and two injured – the first in a long while. Not to mention two 'barrows destroyed.'

'Then that's two lives saved,' Appleyard mused. 'Our bomber's been a busy little bugger then, hasn't he?'

Midgely was about to respond when his bleeper went.

'Use the wall phone,' Appleyard suggested.

The Yorkshireman picked up the extension receiver and punched in a central London number. 'Al, it's Midgely here. What gives?' He listened intently, his inscrutable flat features giving nothing away. But his knuckles turned white as he slowly crushed the lager can in his left fist. He tossed it into the waste bin. 'Okay, Al, we'll be waiting – Listen, Al, Tom Harrison's here at the funeral. Shall I – ?' His lips clamped shut as he continued to listen to the voice at the other end. Midgely said nothing more before replacing the receiver.

'Well?' Appleyard asked.

Midgely was grim. 'All hands to the pump. There've been bomb warnings coming in from all over London. Four vans left abandoned under the Chiswick flyover, the A40(M) flyover into Marylebone, the M25/M4 junction and the Blackfriars Bridge underpass – all with our friend AIDAN's calling card. Then, just for good measure, there's a suspect package at Clapham Junction and a threat of firebombs in Oxford Street – the greatest time-wasters of all.'

'Are those AIDAN-coded too?' Appleyard asked.

Midgely shook his head. 'Apparently not, but why make life

simple for us? Al reckons it's all part of the same setup, otherwise it would be too much of a coincidence. Anyway there's a squad car on its way from Dorking police station.'

Appleyard glanced at his watch. 'If the driver's good we can make it in twenty minutes.'

7

Harrison said: 'Did I hear you ask if I could come along, Midge?'

The Yorkshireman looked uncomfortable. 'I'm afraid I got a dusty reply, Tom. The boss is having apoplexy at the moment and says your presence in England is due to an official Home Office request. Therefore, according to protocol, you should report first to Chief Super Jim Maitland. He'll bring you down to us and you'll be allocated a desk.'

'For God's sake, Midge!' Harrison retorted with a rare display of anger, 'that's hardly the right attitude.'

Midgely shrugged. 'I know that, but it's the one Al Pritchard's got. He's a prickly bugger at the best of times. And this is *not* the best of times, as you can gather.'

'But you can give me a lift in the car, can't you? At least I can report in and be on-scene . . .'

The Yorkshireman was shaking his head. 'I'm afraid he was quite specific, Tom. You're British Army, not police, and until you've reported in you're on your own.'

Harrison drew a deep breath. He just could not believe what he was hearing. But then it had been a long time since he had served with Al Pritchard. He'd forgotten what the man could be like. There was no doubting the man's personal courage – as testified by the MBE and QGM – but other people's sensibilities had never been high on his list of priorities. He ran a tight ship and you did things his way or not at all. Already he was sending out the warning signals loud and clear: he resented the request for outside help and considered it an affront to his leadership of the Explosives Section.

At that moment Brenda Murray appeared at the kitchen door

with Pippa. 'There's a policeman at the front door, Midge, asking for you. A car to London, he says. Is something wrong?'

'A spot of bother, I'm afraid. We've been called back to London.' He didn't elaborate. 'No rest for the wicked.'

As he and Appleyard moved into the hallway, Harrison turned to his wife. 'I've got to go too and I'll need the car.'

'Can't you go with them?'

He shook his head. 'It's a formality thing.'

'That's ridiculous, Tom. How are Archie and I going to get back home tonight?'

Before he could respond, Casey interrupted: 'Look, I ought to be going back now. My car's in the village and you're welcome to a lift.'

Pippa grinned triumphantly. 'There you are, that's solved then.'

She drove her husband and Casey back past the church to where the Porsche was parked. There was no sign of Eddie Mercs or Hal Hoskins; Casey assumed they'd made their own way back to the city.

Harrison found himself distracted by the American's long tanned legs as she hiked her black dress up to her thighs for freedom of movement before engaging first gear. It had been an unconscious action and he found it beguiling how seemingly oblivious this woman was of the power of her own sexuality, apparently unaware of his admiring glances. He also realised for the first time how tall she was. She drove with skill and confidence, unafraid to use the car's unbridled acceleration, changing through the gears with a deft economy of movement, her overtaking fast and decisive. There was no sense that she was intimidated by the presence of a male stranger as passenger, or that she was trying to impress; he had the distinct feeling that this was how she always drove. Had he been driven this hard at this speed with most male colleagues he knew, he'd have been holding his breath. With Casey Mullins at the wheel, he felt in surprisingly safe hands.

'I wasn't expecting a Porsche,' he ventured as they raced along the country road towards the A3.

She smiled. 'I guess I'm what's known as a fast woman. But come back next week and it'll be a Number 9 bus.'

'I'm sorry?'

'My divorce settlement. He gets the car – unless I prang it.' Another half-laugh, half-giggle. 'That's a thought, it might almost be worth it. Just to see the look on his face.'

'Not while I'm on board, thank you.'

'I would have thought you thrived on danger.'

'Sorry to disappoint. I'm a natural coward, which is how I've survived in this game. I like the odds heavily stacked in my favour.'

Again she laughed and he found himself watching her with an amused half-smile on his face. He felt remarkably relaxed and good-humoured in her company. Yet he hardly knew her. He recalled then what she had said at the church. How she and her daughter had almost fallen victim to the Seven Dials bomb. The thought made him both angry and genuinely relieved that she'd escaped injury.

He said: 'I think Brenda was very pleased you came. It was a lot of trouble to go to and a very nice gesture.'

That made Casey feel awkward. She had been *directed* to go and had welcomed the opportunity to show her gratitude to the man who had died, but it had not been the other way round. 'It was nothing,' she replied more curtly than she had intended.

'Do you work in London?'

Oh, God, here it comes. She winced inwardly as she imagined his reaction to the revelation that she was a journalist. 'Yep,' she said, adding quickly, 'in publishing.'

He nodded. 'Is that books or magazines?'

'Look, Tom, would you mind getting that road atlas from the glove box, I don't want to get us lost . . .'

She successfully deflected his line of questioning and for the next ten minutes they concentrated on finding their way to the A3 carriageway which swept towards the suburban sprawl of south London.

By that time she had decided that attack was the best form of defence and began asking a welter of questions about his work and his private life. He was, she learned, the same age as herself, thirty-six. In fact he was one month younger and a different star sign; he was Capricorn while she was Sagittarius.

'I might be older,' she said as they thundered along the Kingston bypass, 'but I bet you weigh more.'

Things military were an almost total mystery to her, but she learned that Harrison was the son of a Hampshire doctor and had excelled at mathematics and chemistry at school before going on to Sussex University. After graduating and with a job lined up with the ICI chemical giant, he had been persuaded by a friend to take a six-month working holiday with a safari adventure company in Kenya run by the boy's uncle. It had been exciting and fun, living most of the time in the bush, close to African wildlife and meeting people from many different walks of life. After that, the prospect of life as a laboratory technician lost its appeal. On the very last safari, he met Philippa Maddox and her father. Harrison recounted that, strange as it seemed now, the then retiring brigadier had inspired him with his anecdotes of army life. On his return to England, Harrison had abandoned his future life as a chemist in favour of a commission in the army. Given his qualifications, the Royal Army Ordnance Corps appeared to be the perfect choice. Plenty of opportunities to travel while inspecting ammunition-storage depots wherever Britain still retained a base. And none of the risks run by the poor bloody infantry in dangerous places like Northern Ireland.

Casey was as surprised as he had been at the time to learn that he was directed to take a psychometric test to assess his suitability for bomb-disposal work. Not unexpectedly, it appeared that there were few, if any, volunteers for the work.

From the School of Ordnance he had proceeded to the ATO or Ammunition Technical Officer course, comprising six months at the all-services Royal Military College of Science at Shrivenham, followed by six months at the Army School of Ammunition near Kineton in Warwickshire, which culminated with the Intermediate IEDD course. IEDD sounded deceptively innocuous. Improvised Explosive Device Disposal. The terrorist bomb.

During his first two-year posting as a section commander he met Jock Murray and Les Appleyard who were to become his closest friends. He had known Al Pritchard too, but the man had never really been one of their circle. Harrison had gone on in 1982 to serve with them on his first four-month tour in Northern Ireland as an 'operator'. More jargon – hardly a befitting term for what the general public called the bomb-disposal man, the quiet hero of hundreds of television news and press reports from the savage terrorist war in Ulster.

Casey was curious. 'And are there any special qualities needed to become – what is it, SATO?'

He laughed, catching her mood. 'They say to qualify you must have a wife, two point five children, drive a Volvo estate and have a dog.'

'But you've just got Archie and drive a Cavalier.'

'Ah, but until last year I had a dog. A failed bomb dog.'

'Failed?'

'He was a great sniffer-out of explosives. Problem was he was a retriever. Rather an unfortunate trait for a bomb dog really. He was dishonourably discharged after bringing back a live device to Top Cat himself.'

They were now crawling through the Wandsworth traffic south of the Thames. Casey had switched on the radio and the local news was warning of considerable hold-ups on the western approaches to the city due to bomb alerts.

Harrison noticed the car phone. 'Okay if I make a call?'

'Why not, my ex will be paying the bill.'

He took a notebook from his jacket pocket. 'You're a hard woman, Casey.'

She giggled. 'You'd better believe it, bomb man.'

After dialling he got a feeble line through to the Explosives Section. A terse Yorkshire voice answered.

'Midge, it's Tom here, I've just hit London. I wondered what gives?'

There was a grunt at the other end. 'We do. We're giving like knicker elastic at full stretch. We're coping, but just. Even got one Expo being helicoptered in from his camping holiday in Wales.' He took a deep breath. 'At least nothing's gone off yet.'

'Well, if there's anything I can do?'

'Thanks, but I don't think . . .' There was a hesitation. 'Well, there *is* something. The chief will probably shoot me for it, but

I've got to hold the fort here. There's a suspect letter bomb been delivered to some visiting American senator at his hotel in London. It's low priority, but I can't see us getting around to it for hours. Ought not to leave it, though. Would you mind?'

' 'Course not.'

'It's been received by Senator Abe Powers the Third. Got to be a Yank with a name like that really. He's at Dukes Hotel in St James's Place. Expensive, but discreet, if you know it?'

He didn't, but Casey did. She didn't mention her reason for being there had been to interview a visiting Booker author. 'Did you say Abe Powers?' she asked.

'D'you know him?'

'He ran into me at the airport last Christmas – literally. A staunch Democratic who's a leading light in the Irish lobby. In bed with the Kennedy clan – but then who isn't nowadays? Before President Clinton was inaugurated there was a lot of speculation that Abe Powers would be sent to Belfast to bang heads together and sort out the troubles. But then your Prime Minister had a meeting with the President and I guess *real* politics took over and the idea was quietly shelved.'

Harrison thought aloud. 'But it could be someone's motive for a letter bomb.'

She almost recounted how the senator had brusquely rejected her request for an interview. Instead she decided to keep her mouth firmly shut and concentrate on her driving.

They arrived at the hotel off St James's at two thirty.

To Harrison's surprise there was not a policeman in sight. Only the anxious manager waited for him at the head of the steps, together with an elegant, familiar figure with a brown felt fedora and a Crombie coat worn over his shoulders like a cloak.

'Don! What are you doing here?'

Trenchard laughed. 'Yes, we really must stop meeting like this. I know, I was surprised when the Expos said you'd be coming. Sort of exchange thing, is it?'

Harrison nodded, taking in his friend's usual sartorial dash: the Tommy Nutter suit and gold pin at the knot of the regimental tie. 'So as I was here, I offered to lend a hand. And you?'

'I was called in when they found the suspect package.'

'And where is it now?'

'Still in the American gent's suite – in the bedroom.' He appeared very relaxed about the whole business.

Harrison noticed that hotel guests were milling in the lobby. 'The place should have been evacuated, Don.'

'That's what I said,' the manager interjected.

Trenchard ignored him. 'It's small, Tom. 'Can't contain more than a few ounces.'

'There's always the risk of fire,' Harrison began.

'I know, Tom, and the hotel staff are ready to act. But I talked it over with the manager and we decided a lot of fuss and unnecessary panic wouldn't be good for the hotel's reputation.' Harrison had the distinct impression that Trenchard had done all the persuading. 'By the way, a police car delivered some kit for you a few minutes before you arrived.'

Harrison said: 'Then I'll take a look.'

Casey tapped him on the shoulder. 'Tom –'

As he turned, Trenchard noticed her for the first time. 'A new woman in your life, Tom?'

Harrison felt his cheeks colour, yet he wasn't quite sure why. He stumbled over his words. 'A friend of mine. She's just given me a lift back from Jock Murray's funeral.'

Trenchard's smile turned down. 'Poor Jock.'

'Casey Mullins,' Harrison introduced. 'And an old pal of mine from way back, Don Trenchard.'

'Casey Mullins,' Trenchard repeated. He said it slowly and thoughtfully, extending the vowels smoothly as though savouring a particularly fine vintage claret. His friend hadn't changed, Harrison thought. The full head of crinkly hair still gold blond and the same winsome smile that had charmed so many girls into his bed. Once that had almost included Pippa – almost but not quite. Now the cobalt-blue eyes fixed Casey's as he took her hand and pressed it briefly to his lips. 'Enchanted to meet you, Miss Mullins.'

An uncertain expression showed on her face and a nervous tic flickered at the corner of her mouth. She withdrew her hand rather quickly. 'I'm so glad you've already eaten, Mr Trenchard.'

Trenchard's smile faded as Harrison tried to suppress his laugh.

Casey turned to him. 'Look, Tom, I really must fly. I have to be back at my office. Perhaps I can give you a ring?'

Again he felt the blood flush his cheeks; he put it down to Trenchard's appraising eyes and his knowing smirk.

'Of course,' Harrison said, and jotted down the number of the Explosives Section on a spare page of his notepad before tearing it out. 'I might be busy while I'm here, but leave a message.'

'*Ciao*,' she said, then caught him by surprise with a kiss on the cheek before she strode towards the door. The hotel manager looked on, bemused. Somehow he hadn't imagined that the arrival of a bomb–disposal expert would be quite like this. At the door Casey turned. 'And, Tom, *please* take care.' Then she was gone.

Don Trenchard said nothing more until they were climbing the stairs, carrying between them the kit sent over by Midgely. ' 'Course, Tom, you know why she was in such a rush?'

'Casey? No, she didn't say.'

'It'll be to file her story for the West End Final edition.'

'What?' He didn't understand what Trenchard was on about.

'Wake up, Tom. She's a journalist on the London *Evening Standard*.'

Harrison stopped dead in his tracks; he felt as though he had been struck a physical blow. 'You're joking!'

'It's no joke.'

'She said she and her daughter had been caught up in the Seven Dials bombing. And she told me she was in publishing . . .' His voice trailed off as he realised what he was saying.

'Not exactly a lie, was it? And she was at the bombing which she wrote about in the *Standard*. Presumably that didn't reach Northern Ireland?'

Harrison shook his head.

'Did you discuss anything about this current bombing campaign with her?'

He hardly registered the question, still shocked at how easily he'd been conned. How he had even helped her through the police cordon at the funeral. 'No, I don't think so, I'm not sure. To be honest there's not too much to tell.'

'Presumably she knows all about this suspect package?'

'Of course, I phoned the Section from her car. And she knows about Senator Powers.'

Trenchard gave one of his disarming half-smiles. 'Bound to, I suppose, being an American.' He continued walking. 'Never mind, it can't be helped. I just wanted to keep the lid on, that's all. The same reason I didn't want to evacuate the hotel.'

'What the hell's going on, Don? Are you still with 14 Int?'

Trenchard was evasive, but with his usual charm. 'Not really. I'm transferred to the Security Service with a sort of open liaison remit with 14 Int.'

It was a garbled answer that suggested to Harrison that Don Trenchard might not be exactly answerable to either in a strictly official capacity. That could be useful if anyone started asking awkward questions; it made things simpler to deny if someone like Trenchard could just conveniently disappear in the gap between the two organisations. Or perhaps he just meant he was paid by both; he'd always had expensive tastes.

'And what about this senator?'

Trenchard shrugged. 'Just a private visit, Tom.'

Bullshit, Harrison thought. 'So why are you involved?'

'MI5 – counter-terrorism and all that. Senator Powers has connections with the US administration, Tom. A personal friend of the President. Can't have anything untoward happening to him.'

Harrison drew to a halt outside the door to Powers' suite. 'Look Don, I'm just about to go in there with a possible IED. If it goes wrong I could lose my hands and my face. You owe it to me to tell me if there's anything else I should know.'

Trenchard lifted his arms, his palms turned up in a gesture of innocence. 'Nothing I can think of, Tom.' He pointed to the portable Inspector X-ray machine and toolbag in the SATO's hands. 'Besides, you've got your box of magic tricks. You'll be all right.'

Without waiting further Trenchard rapped on the door. There was a brief wait while someone peered through the tiny fisheye security lens before opening the door.

The minder from Special Branch was a slim but powerfully built man in his late thirties. He had alert mistrusting eyes, a bushy but neatly trimmed moustache and wore a well-made suit of inconspicuous charcoal-grey material. As he allowed them in, he resheathed his revolver in its rear waistband holster.

It was a large, well-appointed room with two doors opening off, presumably to the bathroom and the bedroom where the suspect parcel had been left. The television was on and a large man in fawn slacks and a lemon cashmere sweater was slumped in an armchair watching it. He seemed unaware of the arrival of the two men.

'Did the package come by post?' Harrison asked the minder.

'No, sir, by motorcycle courier. I answered the door, of course, and signed for it. It's one of those large padded Jiffy bags and feels like there's a book inside. I checked the docket and it was sent by a bloke calling himself J. Smith.' He gave a sheepish smile. 'The senator said he wasn't expecting anything and couldn't think of anyone of that name – apart from the Labour Party leader. And I didn't like those waxy stains on the package. So I phoned the courier's office. Apparently this Mr Smith walked straight in off the street *and* he had an Irish accent. He gave an address which I'm having checked out . . . I hope I'm not wasting your time.'

Trenchard raised an eyebrow. 'I hope you *are*, Sergeant.'

The big American in the armchair suddenly became aware of their conversation and levered himself to his feet. He had a broad, determined-looking face and thick silver hair with that glamorous tint of purple favoured by middle-aged stars in American soap operas. Harrison suspected that the colour was as artificial as the sun-lamp tan.

'Who is this guy?' he demanded of his minder. His manner was impatient and superior, the words spoken as though Harrison wasn't actually there himself.

'He's from bomb disposal, sir.'

A grunt. 'He's taken his time. I thought you Brits were supposed to be experts. Just as well it's not the real thing.'

Harrison said: 'What makes you think that, Senator?'

The man spared him a sideways glance. 'Because no one knows I'm here, for a start.'

'This Mr Smith does.'

He didn't like that, clearly he wasn't used to smart backchat from those he considered his inferiors. 'And anyway, who the hell's gonna want to blow me up?'

Your minder for a start, Harrison thought. But he said: 'PIRA perhaps. The Provisional IRA.'

The cold grey eyes stared. 'If you'd done your homework, you'd know I'm renowned as a sympathiser of the Republican cause. But then I guess paranoia about the IRA's pretty endemic over here.' He added dismissively: 'Why don't you just get on with your work and let me relax before my car arrives for the heliport.'

As the American returned to his chair, Harrison spoke to Trenchard. 'As this package has been handled by the courier and the senator's minder, it should be stable enough for me to carry outside.' He lifted a coil of Cordtex explosive cable from the toolbag. 'I'll lean it against a wall and use a strip of this as a cutting charge. You won't want the bits spread all over. So if you can clear me a route down, get all the guests out of the lobby and cordon off the street . . .'

Trenchard looked incredulous. 'This isn't Belfast, Tom. I've told you, this needs to be handled discreetly. You've got an X-ray machine, so why not do it *in situ*? My people would rather you cut it open and save any evidence in preference to blowing the thing up.'

Harrison was irritated at his friend's willingness to compromise safety. 'I told you earlier. There's a risk of damage and fire if it goes wrong.'

'We've already agreed to compensate the hotel.'

'And the surgeon's bill for sewing my hands back on?'

Trenchard grinned. 'You don't mean that, Tom. Look, you've got the X-ray, so take a dekko and if you don't think you can handle it, we'll do it your way. That fair?'

Reluctantly persuaded by the compromise, Harrison donned his flak jacket and helmet, picked up the toolbag and the Inspector, and headed for the bedroom. He felt mildly irritated, aware that the Explosives Section would have had no problem in complying with Trenchard's wishes, whereas his was the army's way.

Don't sit on top of a bomb when you can open it up at a distance. He knew whose philosophy he shared.

Once inside the room it was like shutting off the outside world. It was uncannily still and quiet, just the muted sound of London traffic beyond the window and the soft burble of the television set from the next room. Crumpled sheets lay on the bed, waiting for the chambermaid to be allowed in to do her work.

The package had been left on the dressing table. Harrison approached and drew the curtains closed at the window behind it. He didn't want glass showering the street below if there was an accident. He then went down on his haunches to examine the package. Senator Powers' name and the hotel had been written directly onto the brown paper in felt-tip pen, the end of the padded envelope stapled. When he moved his head slightly, he could detect the sheen of the wax or grease stains on the surface. Probably marks from someone's fingers.

Satisfied, he placed a film cassette under the envelope, then picked up the Inspector X-ray machine by the handle and took an overhead shot. Transferring the plate to the small processing unit which resembled a single-sheet desk-top photocopier, he waited impatiently for the minute to elapse until the positive-image picture was ejected.

He knew exactly what he was looking for and there it was. A fat hardback book, possibly some type of dictionary, a recess having been cut into the pages with a craft knife. The thin wafer of plastic explosive was difficult to distinguish, showing up as a grey film. Its presence was better indicated by the positioning of the detonator cap and the short twist of wires that led from it to the two slim 1.5-volt batteries positioned underneath.

He searched for the expected spring-loaded microswitch, the small metal arm of which would be held closed by the front cover of the book – nothing. Then, it must be – Yes, there it was. Two strips of foil paper, one adhered to the inside front cover of the book, the other glued to the first page. Between them, just standing proud, was a piece of cardboard. It looked like an official invitation with smoothly rounded corners.

In his mind's eye he could visualise Senator Abe Powers tearing open the envelope, glancing at the book, puzzled, then seeing the invitation card protruding. Intrigued, the American would have pulled it out and the two separated strips of foil would have touched. The circuit would have completed instantly.

He double-checked the X-ray print of the wiring until he was satisfied that he could account for every intended function.

Rummaging in the toolbag, he selected a scalpel with a pristine razor blade, then lowered his visor before returning to the package. Concentrating hard, and aware of the steady thud of his heart, he made the first incision. That was always the worst. Rapidly he cut away an entire end of the envelope. Then, clasping the book firmly closed between the fingers of his left hand, he slid it completely clear.

The next part was easy, but irrational fear made it the hardest. Leaving the invitation card in place, he flipped open the front cover of the book. Nothing, of course, happened. There in front of him on the inside of the cover was one strip of foil with its attached wire. He clipped it, breaking the contact and rendering it safe.

He removed the card, placing it to one side, then snipped the wire attached to the foil on the first page, just to be doubly sure before removing the detonator from the explosive.

Only then did he become aware that he had been holding his breath for several seconds. Now he relaxed sufficiently to allow himself a small, smug grin of satisfaction.

Idly he picked up the invitation card. It was black-edged and properly printed in a copperplate typeface. It invited Senator Abe Powers III to attend a funeral. His. And there was a signature in blue ink. AIDAN.

Harrison froze, dropping the card as though the thing itself was capable of inflicting injury, and glared down at the book on the dressing table.

AIDAN. If it was AIDAN, then he couldn't take *anything* for granted. Nothing was as it seemed.

Suddenly he made his decision. Picking up the X-ray machine, he took a second, cross-section, shot from the side and waited anxiously for the processor to deliver up its verdict.

144

The seconds dragged by. Then, grudgingly, the print was ejected. And there it was. Another component beneath the small explosive slab and the batteries. It had been missed when viewed solely from the top. He cursed himself for almost being tempted to take short cuts, for making assumptions. Familiarity bred complacency and complacency with IEDs could eventually have only one consequence. Sometimes, he thought perversely, it was better not to have experience in this game, better to be suspicious of absolutely everything.

He stared hard at the print, then took another X-ray from a different angle. Neither picture was clear, something obstructing the camera's view of the small component beneath the explosive. Some sort of container, maybe five-and-a-half by three inches. Half-an-inch deep. A cigar tin?

Although he was confident that no wires connected it to the slab of explosive, it clearly had to have some purpose. And he didn't intend lifting out the Semtex to find out what it was.

A microswitch or pressure plate perhaps? Triggered when the weight of the explosive was lifted? He returned to the X-rays, but could detect no clue. Now he really was annoyed with himself for agreeing to Trenchard's request. If he'd dealt with it in the street, using a simple cutting charge, it would all have been over by now. As it was, with the device half dismantled, it was dangerous even to touch it.

After considering for a moment, he hunted in the toolbag for a hook-and-line, rigging the small pulley to the overhead central light. Then, keeping finger pressure on the explosive in the book, he attached one end of the line to the stiff clayish substance using a drawing pin.

He retreated to the door and picked up the other end of the line. A deep breath. One, two, three . . . He gave a quick tug on the line. The slab of Semtex was whipped into the air. Instantaneously there was a short, sharp crack and a flash as the book disintegrated on the dressing table. The mirror glass shattered and burning pages fluttered unhurriedly down to the carpet. In the middle of the room the Semtex swayed harmlessly to and fro from the overhead lampshade.

Quickly he stepped forward and stamped on the smouldering paper before kneeling to examine the pieces. A wafer layer of lead solder had been glued to the cigar box lid to defeat the X-ray machine. Assuming the device to have been rendered safe, any bomb-disposal expert could be expected to lift the explosive and expose . . . he picked up the shattered remnants of a photoelectric cell. As soon as light fell on the mechanism, the little device would have been ignited. Probably just a charge of a few grams, but sufficient to have taken off his fingers.

Heads the bomber won and killed Senator Abe Powers, or tails he injured the expert sent to defuse it. And either way AIDAN's jokey little invitation would be found afterwards on the floor.

Quite ingenious, Harrison had to admit, a perfectly contained little minibomb.

There was a movement behind him and he turned to see three anxious faces in the doorway.

'It's all over,' he assured, and picked up the invitation card from the dressing table before crossing to the American senator.

'What's this?' Powers asked, ashen-faced.

'An invitation from your friends in the Provisional IRA,' Harrison replied. 'Maybe they don't like you quite as much as you thought.'

8

'Not a very auspicious start, was it?' Al Pritchard challenged. 'Getting that journalist woman in to the funeral. Then giving her all this personal stuff.'

It was the following morning and Detective Chief Superintendent Jim Maitland had only just left the office of the Explosive Section's chief having formally introduced Major Harrison to his special attachment.

Harrison could see that the Sexpo was on edge, his eyes sunken and his face haggard through lack of sleep. While he had no desire to exacerbate Pritchard's understandable tetchiness after the events of the previous day, it was not his intention to give him the upper hand at their very first meeting.

'I hardly gave away any state secrets, Al. It's all harmless, anecdotal stuff. Besides which, I think we've more important things to concern ourselves with this morning, don't you?'

Midgely and Appleyard, who were on the sofa nursing mugs of coffee, exchanged glances. It was indeed no more of an inauspicious start than they had anticipated.

The Yorkshireman said: 'With respect, Al, both Les and I also met the lass. Neither of us quite realised who she was either – and *we'd* read her articles.'

Pritchard snatched up a copy of the previous night's *Standard* final edition and aimed it accurately at his wastebin. Then he glared back across his desk top. 'Let me make it perfectly clear and remind you all of my long-standing rule. Unless specifically ordered to do so, we don't talk to the press. Ever, period.'

Appleyard nodded his agreement. 'But at least her funeral coverage was sympathetic, unlike that other rag . . .'

'Mawkish crap,' Pritchard snapped back. 'I guess we can be thankful she didn't name all the members of this squad.'

Harrison remembered the conversations they had had in her car, her easy laugh and quick-fire humour. He felt an overwhelming urge to defend her. 'I think she's more responsible than that, Al, and she had a genuine personal reason to attend the funeral. Besides which, it was she who gave me a lift to Dukes Hotel.'

The hooded lids half closed over Pritchard's eyes. 'And don't remind me about that, Tom. Midgely's already had a bollocking. Just how would it have looked if they'd scraped you – a bloody army officer – off the bloody ceiling, had you missed that secondary?'

Harrison stood his ground. 'I found it because I've had more experience of this AIDAN character's handiwork than anyone else. That's why I'm here.'

The Sexpo saw his opportunity and pounced. 'Wrong, Tom, you're not here to defuse *our* devices. That's what we're paid to do. You can observe, advise, liaise and write reports until you're blue in the face, but you are *not* operational. You are a soldier, not a civil servant or a police officer. This is *our* patch. Remember that and we'll get on fine.' He took a deep breath, reached for the jar of indigestion tablets on his desk and began munching on one of them as he continued: 'Thankfully it's been decided from above that the letter-bomb incident never occurred, so I won't have to justify your presence. MI5 wants it all kept hushed. Don't want to alarm the Americans into thinking we can't protect their diplomats over here.'

Harrison frowned. 'But Senator Powers was there, Al, he knew what happened. So I don't really understand that reasoning.'

Pritchard stared for a moment, then allowed himself a sour smile, traces of white chalk at the corners of his mouth. 'God you're in an argumentative mood this morning. We don't have to *understand,* we just defuse bombs and leave the politics to those who think they know what they're doing.' Believing that he had succeeded in crushing all rebellion, he sat more easily behind his desk. 'After yesterday's events in London, the commander of the Anti-Terrorist Branch is holding a press conference at eleven this

148

morning. Mostly it's to show the flag and assure the dear general public and the tabloids that we're on top of things and that there's no need to panic.'

'Can you bring me up to date with what happened?' Harrison asked. 'Yesterday Midge said there were four identical van bombs and incendiaries in Oxford Street. This morning's papers talk about a store fire and just one van bomb going off.'

Pritchard nodded. 'Well, let's start with the incendiaries. Four were found in time, but one went off. They used their trick again of using a sodium base, so the more water that fell from the sprinkler, the greater the blaze. It was a bloody great fireball. The entire floor was gutted. Luckily the fire brigade were exceptionally quick to react, realised what was happening and shut down the sprinklers. But it was still a damn close thing, the entire store could easily have burned down.' He looked towards the Yorkshireman. 'Midge can tell you about the vans.'

'There were four,' Midgely confirmed. 'The warnings came in one after the other within seven or eight minutes. A similar setup in each case. Vans abandoned under flyovers and in the Blackfriars underpass, apparently broken down. The drivers propped open the bonnets, left the hazard lights flashing, then just walked off as calm as you like. Anyway, our first Expo was tasked to Blackfriars Bridge. He approached from the rear, knocked out a window and threw in a Candle charge for a controlled explosion. Afterwards we found an antihandling mechanism had been fitted to the courtesy-light system, just like the cars at Seven Dials.

'By that time the Chiswick flyover bomb had gone off – well within the warning time. What a mess! Bloody great crater and serious cracks to the bridging span. Over traffic's been reduced to one lane each way and all heavy vehicles are being diverted. Odds are the surveyors will say the whole thing has to come down and be rebuilt.'

'What about the M4 Marylebone flyover?' Harrison asked.

'It was the same setup as Blackfriars, only afterwards Al realised he'd had a bloody lucky escape. They'd only added an additional pressure switch in the front-axle spring, hadn't they? Just the movement as he climbed aboard should have set it off. It's got to be confirmed yet, but it can only have been a poor electrical contact that prevented it from blowing.'

'And the M25 junction at West Drayton?' Harrison asked. 'Was that a controlled explosion too?'

Midgely shook his head. 'No, that's just what was put out to the press. You see, we'd just got back to London from the funeral then and Les was tasked to it.'

Appleyard took up the story. 'By all accounts it was the same as the other two. Same vehicle type and similar location. But remember, they were going off at ten-minute intervals, so information was pretty sketchy at the time. I was just about to make my initial approach, when at – what? – thirty metres the thing blew up. Thought I was a goner, I can tell you. I'm still half deaf.'

Harrison nodded. 'It had been fitted with infrared detectors?'

Appleyard's jaw dropped. 'How did you know?'

'The AIDAN cell used a three-van ploy about five weeks ago in Belfast. One of them was parked under a new flyover. We called it Find the Lady. It cost us a Wheelbarrow.'

The Expo pursed his lips and blew softly as he recalled the narrow escape of the previous day. 'I just saw them mounted above the rear doors a second before I set them off. They were like the type used for automatic household porch lights. Luckily I had on a helmet and flak jacket, it threw me quite a distance.'

Al Pritchard said: 'It was one of those fluky things with that explosion. Although the van appeared to be positioned well to damage the flyover, afterwards the engineers reckoned there was no structural damage and the police were able to open up the road again. It was decided to claim that we'd successfully done a controlled explosion on a hoax. On the basis that the terrorists weren't going to hang around to see what happened, they'd be none the wiser. And on the other two bombs, it was decided to say they were false alarms, just to keep the buggers guessing what we're playing at.'

Harrison nodded. 'All part of the public relations war, I suppose.'

Pritchard began fiddling with his paperknife. 'What you've got to remember, Tom, is that there's a great deal of interest in this new campaign being shown by Whitehall. It's caused the biggest amount of damage in London since the City bombs and it's more ambitious than anything we've seen in the past. And I detect that the Provos are less interested in avoiding civilian casualties than previously – at least, as long as it appears to be due to police ineptitude rather than deliberate PIRA policy.'

'It was ever thus,' Harrison said.

That annoyed Pritchard. 'But more so, Tom. There's some new political dimension to this that we're not being told about. The Home Office is convinced the bombing is going to get worse over the summer. That's why you're here and that's why MI5 is co-ordinating the response on all of this. The Anti-Terrorist Branch and Special Branch are dancing to their tune. And, in their wisdom, MI5 has decided to put it about that there was only one van bomb at the Chiswick flyover and that the other three were hoaxes or false alarms. That's what's going to be confirmed at this morning's press conference.' For a moment he stared morosely at the paperknife in his hands as though it held some magic property which might help him understand the thinking of the Security Service. 'I suppose it helps to reduce the level of public hysteria. I mean one bomb's quite enough. No need to overalarm Joe Commuter with four of the blighters. But to be honest, I don't know what real good it does.'

Then the meeting was at an end, Midgely and Appleyard pitching their plastic mugs into the wastebin as they made their way to the door. Pritchard said: 'I suppose you're still smoking that awful pipe of yours, Tom?'

Harrison smiled. 'Wild Cherry tobacco. Taxi drivers are always saying how they like it.'

Only Pritchard's eyes showed he appreciated the SATO's swift comeback. 'I'm not a taxi driver, Tom. So I'll put you in with Les Appleyard at Jock's old desk. You can smoke each other to death.'

'Thanks, Al.'

As he went to follow Appleyard through the door, Pritchard called: 'Just a minute, Tom.' Harrison turned back to the desk. The Senior Explosives Officer had resumed his seat and his expression appeared a little more relaxed, his features almost softened by the first hint of a smile. 'Sorry if I've been a bit hard on you, Tom. I know I can be a miserable bugger at the best of times – comes from having too much male hormone –' Harrison assumed this was a vague reference to his bald crown as well as being a joke, a rarity in itself. At least the man was making an effort. 'The pressure's been pretty tough since this new campaign began. It's been round the clock and not a lot of sleep. I'll be frank, I don't appreciate your presence here. Nothing personal – when we were serving together, I always reckoned you were the best ATO we had.'

Harrison wasn't sure Pritchard really meant that, so said nothing.

'You've got your job to do,' the Sexpo continued, 'and I'm sure you'll do it, whether I co-operate or not. In fact I'm expected to attend this press conference later and I'd like you to come along too. Handling the media is all part of the overview, even if it's not the Section's direct responsibility.'

'Thanks, Al. Whatever you suggest.'

But Pritchard was staring into the middle distance as though apparently unaware that Harrison had spoken. 'Trouble is I can see where all this is going to lead.'

'Meaning?'

'You're going to be asked, you realise that? The Home Office is going to ask you for recommendations.'

'No one has yet.'

'They will. And you're going to give all the answers based on your experience in Belfast. You're going to say we're doing too much hands-on. That my lads should be making more use of Wheelbarrows, not sitting on top of bombs with a pair of pliers and a Stanley knife. Am I right or am I right?'

Harrison regarded him in silence for a moment. 'I admit the thought had crossed my mind.'

'Then it's time you understood a few home truths.' He gestured for Harrison to take a chair. 'This isn't Belfast and the Home Office doesn't want it to start looking like it. Over there you get dozens of real bomb alerts every week. Here, until recently, we could go months between major incidents. Plenty of hoaxes and small incidents – animal-rights activists, gangland killings – to keep us

152

busy. But imagine if we took Wheelbarrows on all of these shouts. Using them to search for suspect car bombs etc, it would take for ever. Half the streets of London could be closed down every time the Provos or some prankster made a malicious call. There'd be an outcry from the business and retailing community and as much demand for compensation as if the bloody thing had been for real. And that's another reason we still keep mostly to hands-on. We can move quicker, assess the threat and, if it is genuine, deal with it while your lot would still be trying to get a Wheelbarrow out the back of your truck. You know what the Criminal Compensation Act costs the taxpayer in a piddling city like Belfast – just imagine the scale of it when applied to London. The bill would run to billions. And even in Belfast or Londonderry you can't go round blowing up every suspect car, because you know damn well that every scrote who wants a newer model will be phoning up saying his old banger's been nicked by terrorists. So we certainly can't do that here. That's why we stick to the old-fashioned eyeball and hands-on approach.'

Harrison said: 'That approach killed Jock and nearly took you and Les Appleyard yesterday.' It was out before he could stop himself; it had been unthinking and unkind, however true it might be.

Al Pritchard regarded him with a long and steady gaze. When he spoke his voice was low and hoarse. 'That's why my lads get paid twice as much as yours. It's our job and, unlike the army, there's no one to tell us how to do it.' He picked up his paperknife and pointed it directly at Harrison. 'And now, because the politicians are running around like headless chickens, they'll listen to your recommendations and probably implement them in some knee-jerk reaction. Like they have in the past over guns after the Hungerford massacre and those unworkable dangerous-dog laws. If they insist we do things your way, they'll be playing right into the terrorists' hands. Because those Irish bastards will soon see what's happening. And all you'll have succeeded in doing will be to bring London to a standstill with a tab that'll have to be picked up by the hapless taxpayer.'

Quietly Harrison said: 'Al, no one has asked me yet. Until they do, let's just get on with working together.'

Pritchard lowered the accusing knife slowly. 'Okay, Tom, lecture over.' He hesitated, pausing to pick up a folder from his desk. 'Work together, you say? All right, let's talk about Seven Dials. A total of three car bombs, two we know about with antihandling devices fitted to the courtesy-light system. Then the one that killed Jock. What d'you think happened there?'

Harrison felt angry, as though Murray's death was somehow being used to test him in some obscure way. 'How the hell should I know, Al? Perhaps, he ran out of time, perhaps . . .'

Pritchard's eyes were steely. 'Perhaps what, Tom? You want us to work together. So, based on your much-vaunted knowledge of how AIDAN works, what do you think happened? Come on,' he goaded, 'give it your best shot. Just between you and me.'

The tension in the atmosphere of the office was suddenly electric. It was almost possible to smell the charged emotions of anger, resentment and sorrow. All simmering under the unrelenting practical and political pressures of the job.

Harrison said slowly: 'I don't think Jock Murray just ran out of time. He broke a window to avoid triggering any antihandling device wired to the courtesy light.' He paused. 'I think forensics will prove that the device that he initiated had been rigged to an infrared car burglar system placed on the dashboard. As it detected the movement of his hand inside the car . . .' He didn't finish the sentence.

Al Pritchard's face was immobile, as still and white as a waxwork. 'What makes you say . . .?'

His question was interrupted by a telephone call informing him that the press conference would be starting soon.

When he hung up, Harrison said: 'Because that's exactly what AIDAN did in Belfast three weeks ago.'

Pritchard slid the dossier marked Top Secret across the desk. 'The forensic evidence on Jock's bomb from Fort Halstead. You're absolutely right.'

The words flickered on the screen of Eddie Mercs's VDU: *Some mechanically romantic megabytes are amassing in the RAM of my hard drive.*

He leaned back in his chair and munched sensuously on his bacon and tomato roll; it was ten o'clock and unofficial breakfast time for the early shift at the *Standard* who had been in since seven. Sandwiches, yoghurt cartons and even bowls of cereal were much in evidence amongst the high-tech computer equipment – all strictly against the office rules.

After considering for a moment, Mercs tapped a reply into the keyboard of his Coyote 22: *What does this mean?* and punched it down the line to Casey Mullins on the far side of the editorial floor.

Seconds later her reply came up on his screen: *It means my Apple Mac is in love with yours. It doesn't mean they are bad computers. Let's meet up like responsible parents and discuss their future before we have the patter of tiny Laptops to contend with. How about you take me to lunch and we talk?*

He grinned and wiped a dribble of tomato from his chin. With genuine regret he responded: *Sorry nocando. Must attend Scot Yard Conf on bomb campaign then riteup.*

Can I come too?

No

Pleeeeeeeeeeeese

OK. U talked me into it. Reception in ½ hour.

They met in the vast arboretum lobby at the top of the escalators; as usual, Casey was several minutes late. 'Sorry, Eddie, I had to finish this stupid article on Starsign Lovers.' She grinned at him apologetically. 'I'm afraid it means we can never get married. We're air and fire – we'd burn out in no time.'

'What a way to go,' he said ruefully, and meant it.

Within minutes they were in Casey's Porsche and racing towards Westminster. 'Randall gets the car back tonight,' she said miserably. 'I'm getting a second-hand Mini, but I'm really too tall for it.'

'Let me buy you a bus.'

'Sweetie.'

'And why exactly do you want to come to this conference? It is definitely *not* features material, it's hard news. You'll be the ruin of me – you hijacked the funeral story yesterday.'

155

She spun the wheel to avoid a tourist coach that considered it had the right to pull out in front of her. 'Don't be greedy, Eddie, it was a shared byline. You know I need just one little Pulitzer Prize and I can name my own price. Don't stand in my way, you'll get trampled.'

'I don't know how you're getting away with this!'

'Because the editor's got the hots for me.'

'That I can believe.'

'And I'm the only one on the *Standard* who knows anything about bombs.'

'Since when?'

'Since yesterday, I gave a lift back to London to one of the bomb-disposal guys. A big shot over from Northern Ireland. SATO.'

'What?'

'Senior Ammunition Technical Officer. Your actual disposable bomb man, get it?'

'That's sick.'

'It was his joke. They don't take themselves too seriously.' They were nearing Broadway and she began looking for somewhere to park. 'Honestly, Eddie, I'm just interested in all this on a personal level since Seven Dials and I've got a few hours off.

'Randall and I are selling the flat and the estate agent's got some people coming to look at it later today. I hope they're taller than the couple who came yesterday. I hate the thought of short people living there. I mean, are only short people rich in this country?' She glared through the windscreen. 'Short people shouldn't have money.'

Even during the walk from the parking bay to New Scotland Yard, the heightened sense of security was evident even to the casual observer. There were officers on most corners around Parliament Square and stationed at intervals around the police headquarters building which took up the entire block.

Eddie nudged Casey as they walked and pointed to a police car stationed opposite the entrance. 'An armed response vehicle, see? I've spotted several on the road this morning. Everyone's expecting trouble, you can smell it.' As they showed their press passes at the door, he added in a conspiratorial whisper: 'I was talking to some copper mates of mine in the Albert last night. Apparently all leave's been cancelled in the Anti-Terrorist Branch. London's been flooded with plain-clothes cops, several hundred in fact.'

She knew what Mercs meant about the heightened atmosphere of expectation on the London streets. Bombs in the West End and at Chiswick, they were on everyone's mind. The previous night, alone over a TV supper with Candy, she'd been aware of the near and distant wail of police car sirens, seemingly crisscrossing the city into the small hours of the morning. Responding to raised alarms, false or otherwise, ever vigilant; just waiting, knowing that the next terrorist attack would come, it was just a question of when and where. It made her want to cuddle up with her daughter in front of the television, to draw the curtains and shut off the outside world in the optimistic belief that everything would be all right in the morning. Yet somehow she suspected that this was one storm that hadn't yet run its course.

By contrast the press conference was a very upbeat affair, a superlative example of mass media management. Or was it manipulation? Rows of hard plastic chairs filled the room, all facing the rostrum with its heraldic crest and cluster of microphones. The place was packed to capacity with Casey's flush-faced newspaper rivals, several of whom she recognised from the scrum outside the churchyard the previous day. Radio reporters checked their sound levels: 'Two, three, one, testing. I had bacon, eggs, sausages, coffee' and the television news crews fiddled with their lights, blinding some and just irritating others, demanding the best positions and tripping people up with their coils of cable. Meanwhile the sallow-faced young men and serious-looking women from the Met's public relations department put on plastic smiles to hide their exasperation with the unruly, jostling mob which was never satisfied and would never quite do what it was told.

In one corner by the door a number of senior officers with peaked caps and smart-suited civilians watched on with varying expressions of disdain. Clearly these official observers were not liking what they observed.

Mercs felt a nudge in his ribs.

'That's him,' Casey said. 'Look, right at the back.'

'Who?'

'Major Harrison. Tom Harrison.' She raised her hand and waved above the surrounding sea of heads. For a second she thought she'd caught his attention, but then he appeared not to have noticed. He looked to the man next to him. A man with a tanned face, easy smile and crinkly gold hair. The man who had been at Dukes Hotel, the man who had kissed her hand.

Then the Commander of the Anti-Terrorist Branch swept in with his entourage. A distinguished man in his early fifties, with an open face but wary eyes, he fiddled for a moment with the height of the microphones. Then he appeared to take a deep breath, like a man about to plunge into a pool full of sharks.

His speech was brisk, no-nonsense and well-rehearsed. He skimmed across the facts quickly, offering little detail that the gathered journalists didn't already know, and his words were riddled with clichés.

'This latest barbaric IRA campaign with scant regard to innocent life.' 'One real bomb of about one thousand pounds of home-made explosive at Chiswick flyover.' 'Warning totally inadequate.' 'Three other hoaxes swiftly dealt with by our bomb-disposal experts using controlled explosions.' 'All obviously intended to bring London traffic to a standstill and to cause maximum economic damage.' 'Eyewitness descriptions of people we'd like to eliminate from our inquiries . . .' Details followed, then: 'Need for continued vigilance.' 'Any questions?'

Hands flew up, waving for attention. Casey had to shout in Eddie Mercs's ear. 'There were four *real* bombs yesterday, not hoaxes. Tom said so on the way back from the funeral.'

'Your disposable bomb man?'

'Sure.'

'Maybe he didn't know all the details then.'

She didn't answer, instead slipping into deep thought, only half listening to the Commander fending off the barrage of questions, trying to introduce a note of cautious optimism.

As the proceedings ran their natural course and the Met public relations people began looking pointedly at their watches, she suddenly realised that no mention had been made of the Dukes Hotel parcel bomb. She raised her hand.

The Commander looked in her direction and smiled.

'Casey Mullins, sir, *Evening Standard*.' Many heads in the audience turned. Few knew her personally, but most had become familiar with the by-line in the past week. 'Can you confirm that a parcel bomb was sent to a guest at the Dukes Hotel in London yesterday?'

The smile on the Commander's face melted like butter in the sun. 'Er, I have no knowledge of such an incident.'

Casey frowned. 'Are you saying there was *no* such incident, sir?'

'Young lady, if there was such an incident I am certain I would have heard.' He looked at his senior PR officer and nodded. 'Thank you, ladies and gentlemen.'

That was it. Everyone started to move, the meeting breaking up, the gabble of conversation rising.

'What was that all about?' Mercs hissed. 'Who was sent a parcel bomb?'

She shook her head. 'Not here, Eddie, not in front of all these news vultures.' Then she noticed Major Tom Harrison moving towards the door, talking with his fellow observers. 'Just a minute, Eddie.'

The crowd was thinning and she elbowed her way through, clumsily upsetting several chairs. Ahead the observers had almost reached the door leading to the inner sanctum of New Scotland Yard. Tom Harrison was near the back, chatting to the man who had kissed her hand. The name came back to her. Don Trenchard.

'Major Harrison!'

He hesitated and turned, his face clouding as he recognised her.

'Hi, Major,' she was breathless. 'I didn't expect to see you here.'

He looked uncomfortable, almost angry. 'Miss Mullins,' he acknowledged stiffly. 'You didn't tell me you were a journalist.'

She shrugged, her cheeks colouring. 'I'm sorry, but when I realised all of you were so anti-press, I thought it best. I didn't want to cause a scene for Brenda Murray's sake. And I really didn't want you to be annoyed and upset.' Her laugh was forced and nervous. 'It was all a bit of a silly mistake really. Please forgive me.'

Under her winning smile and the earnest shine in her eyes, he felt his resistance crumble, but refused to show it. 'Forgiven, but I think you'll find that in life honesty is usually the best policy.'

The hurt flickered momentarily in her eyes; somehow she hadn't anticipated such a patronising put-down. Glancing round, she realised he had been separated from the rest of the group. Only the man she knew as Don Trenchard lingered at the door for his friend. She said quickly: 'I was worried stiff after I left you at Dukes Hotel yesterday.'

He looked uncomfortable. 'You shouldn't have been,' he countered quickly. 'It was a false alarm.'

'Your friend Trenchard seemed certain enough yesterday.'

'Don isn't an expert.'

'Is that why the Commander knew nothing about it?'

'Probably,' he replied irritably, edging towards the door. 'But I'm afraid I have nothing more to say to you, Miss Mullins.'

She reached out her hand as he moved away, catching his sleeve. 'I'll call.'

'Don't bother,' he replied coldly and was gone.

After telephoning over an article on the conference to the *Standard*'s copy-takers, Eddie Mercs took Casey to an hotel across the road from New Scotland Yard. On the way she told him about the parcel bomb sent to Senator Powers and Harrison's denial. St Ermin's was discreet and palatial, its verandah in the cul-de-sac entrance providing shade from the sun and shelter from the skittish northerly wind.

After ordering two beers from the waiter, Mercs observed: 'You're quiet. Just because your boyfriend gave you the old heave-ho?'

'It was my own fault. He suddenly realised I was a journalist. I think he hates us more than he does the bombers.'

Mercs flicked a match under his cigarette. 'The military don't

160

have much time for us until one of their precious regiments is about to get the chop in defence cuts.'

'He was quite rude,' she said, still smarting with disbelief. Then she seemed to take a grip on herself and smiled. 'I don't mind the blood, guts, violence and mayhem, Eddie, but I just hate having my feelings hurt.'

He grinned at her. 'So anyway, what's he doing here?'

'Pardon me?'

'Your friend. I thought you said he's the Senior ATO from Belfast. So what's he doing at a New Scotland Yard press conference? I thought he was just attending Murray's funeral?'

Casey shrugged. 'I don't know.' She hesitated. 'Wait a minute. They were talking yesterday at the house. There was some argument over the phone. Something about Harrison's presence being an official Home Office request. His presence here, I suppose, I wasn't really paying attention.'

Mercs let out a long low whistle and looked slightly embarrassed when the waiter arrived unexpectedly. The man gave the reporter a coy smile as he placed the drinks on the table. When he left, Mercs said: 'Those men were from the Met's bomb-disposal unit, the Explosives Section, right? Your boyfriend's been drafted in from Belfast by request of the government. That'll ruffle a few feathers, I'll be bound.'

Casey didn't understand, and told him so.

'Look, sweetheart, we all know this latest IRA campaign's been unusually active and successful. Maybe more so than we realise. Listen, what you said earlier at the conference, about you being certain there were *four* real bombs, which today they denied. Already Fleet Street has swallowed the story. But imagine, just imagine, that there *were* four and they'd all gone off. Three main artery routes into London from the west and another into the city. It would have caused chaos and choked the capital's roads for months. Millions of pounds in business losses that, one way or another, would have cost the taxpayer.'

'I don't know what to believe,' Casey said.

'Consider this,' said Mercs, sipping his beer and wiping the froth from his upper lip with the back of his hand. 'They, the

161

government and the police, might have been lying. Like this parcel bomb that was sent to Senator Powers.'

She stared gloomily and confused at her untouched glass. 'What does it mean, Eddie?'

'It means, sweetheart, that you might have got yourself a scoop.' He jerked his mobile phone from his pocket and flipped it open. 'Let's just verify a couple of points with an old oppo of mine in Belfast.'

Gerard Keefe, he explained, was an ex-staffer on the *Telegraph* who'd turned freelance some five years earlier. His contacts with terrorists – which he deferentially referred to as 'paramilitaries' – on both sides of the political divide were legendary, his sources impeccable. As many who read his work considered he was a secret supporter of the Provisional IRA as believed him to be in the pocket of the Protestant extremists. Which probably meant that he had his editorial balance just about right.

However, his notoriety for having contacts with the rival leaderships had led to his increasing paranoia about his own safety. And that concern seemed to worsen each time Mercs spoke to him. The reporter was one of the few people to be trusted with his home telephone number; even that method of contact was of intermittent value, as Keefe regularly changed it and neglected to inform Mercs of his new number.

Today they were in luck. Keefe answered with a gruff 'Yes' to the background noise of his children shouting and shrieking over their lunch. It was incongruous for someone who believed he was a marked man by two terrorist organisations as well as British Intelligence.

'Hallo, Gerry, it's Eddie here. How's life treating you?'

'Sure mustn't grumble, still strugglin' on,' came the unusually soft Ulster accent. 'Can I be doin' something for you, Eddie?'

'I'd like to run a couple of things across you, Gerry.'

The slow, disapproving intake of breath was unmistakable. 'Not over the phone, Eddie, you know how I feel about that.'

Keefe's paranoia focused particularly on the telephone ever since he'd unearthed a story that all calls across the Irish Channel were screened by computer to pick up key trigger words in order to track down terrorist active service units on the mainland. Although Mercs had no way of knowing the veracity of the story, he tended to be sceptical. 'Nothing sensitive, Gerry, and you don't have to answer me.'

'Go on then.' Reluctant.

'Can you confirm the name of the army's Senior ATO in the Province?'

'You mean Colonel Taffy Lloyd-Williams?'

'No, not the Chief, his 2IC.'

A short pause. 'Without referring to my files, a Major Harris, I think. Harris or Harrison. Tom Harris, I'm sure that's it. But Lloyd-Williams is Top Cat, the main spokesman.'

Mercs grinned at Casey and raised his thumb in a gesture of triumph. 'Would it strike you as odd, Gerry, if I told you this Harris or Harrison had been seconded to the Met's Explosives Section over here?'

There was a chuckle at the other end. 'Very odd, especially in mid-tour. Someone in Whitehall must be very worried about that latest bombing campaign over there. But it could make sense, what with the threat over these talks.'

Talks. Mercs was instantly on the alert, recalling the contents of AIDAN's warning to the paper and the subsequent request for silence from the Defence Advisory Committee. He played it dumb. 'What talks are these, Gerry?'

'Sure it's the worst kept secret in the Province. The place is alive with rumours about the talks.'

'What's this, another Sunningdale? Government talking to the terrorists?' Mercs asked. 'Presumably it's not to do with the Humes-Adams discussions?'

Keefe's voice laughed down the telephone again. 'More like a reworking of the Anglo-Irish Agreement. Strictly between Dublin and London to the exclusion of all the paramilitaries. The Provies have got wind that it will include internment of terrorists on *both* sides of the border, that's why they're creating such a stink. They want the talks torpedoed unless they're included.'

'Who told you that, Gerry?'

'A reliable source, Eddie.' A hard edge had crept back into his voice. 'That same source assures me the mainland campaign won't stop 'till the Provies get their way.'

'D'you know where these talks are being held?'

'If I did I could be a rich man!'

'Or at what level?'

'Sorry, Eddie. All I know is what my source said, that it's the result of a secret American initiative. What I can tell you is that some politically well-connected Yank has been reported doing a flying shuttle between Dublin, Stormont and London. You know, like old Henry Kissinger used to do.'

'Does this Yank have a name?'

'This'll cost you, Eddie.'

'Fifty?'

'A hundred.'

Mercs's lower lip puckered. But then his freelance friend had to earn a living and had a lot of mouths to feed. 'Okay, Gerry, the cheque's in the post. What's the name of this Yank?'

'Senator Abe Powers.'

On the drive back to the *Standard*'s offices, Mercs went over the new intro to his story with Casey, jotting his own indecipherable form of Pitman's into his notebook, oblivious of the jolting motion of the car.

They arrived at one thirty. Casey was taken over by Mercs's enthusiasm, although still not quite certain what she had discovered and what all the excitement was about. Amid the chaos of his work station, with overflowing ashtrays and dead plastic coffee cups, someone had left a proof of the front page. His earlier telephoned story had made the splashed lead:

YARD PLAYS DOWN BOMB CHAOS

'Gordon Bennett!' he groaned. 'Is that the best the subs could do? With headlines like that, I'm surprised all our readers aren't dead through boredom. At times like this I wouldn't mind working on the *Sun*. BOMB BUSTERS BEAT BRIDGE BLASTERS or some such.' He snatched up the telephone and punched in the news editor's extension. 'Steve, Eddie here, I've got an update on that bombing conference. New angle – and hopefully a new soddin' headline.'

Across the room the news editor was glancing at his watch. Twenty-five minutes to clear the West End Final. 'Run it up and let's see what it looks like.'

'Shall do,' Mercs snapped, hung up and looked at Casey. 'A shared by-line okay?'

She laughed. 'Here comes my Pulitzer.'

Eddie Mercs clamped a cigarette, unlit, between his teeth and called up the news 'basket' on his VDU, splitting the screen with his original story on the left, running his 'revise' down the blank right-hand side.

He began tapping: *One of the British Army's top bomb-disposal experts, Major Tom Harrison, has been called in from Northern Ireland to assist the Metropolitan Police in their fight against the latest terror-bombing campaign in London . . .*

While he worked Casey made three telephone calls in an attempt to get official confirmation of the story. The Home Office, the Ministry of Defence and the Northern Ireland Office all denied any knowledge, with varying degrees of hostility. But none, she noticed, categorically said that it was incorrect.

'No comment,' she said, replacing the receiver after the last call.

Mercs's eyes sparkled mischievously. 'Then it's true. Otherwise they'd have said.'

With the story complete, Mercs punched it down the line to the news editor.

A few minutes later the exec ed, who ran the production side, phoned to invite the reporter to join him at the Graphics Desk.

'C'mon,' Mercs said to Casey, 'this is a moment to cherish.'

Having seen thousands of his masterpieces decimated over the years by subs, news editors and production wallahs at various newspapers, he welcomed any chance to cross the jealously guarded divide between the editorial hierarchy and the humble news hounds.

Such occasions were rare, restricted to when a real rush was on and even then a reporter's presence was not only informal but barely tolerated.

The exec, news and picture editors as well as a senior sub were gathered behind Mandy Oates, a failed actress, who was operating the Display Mac.

'Nice one, Eddie,' she murmured, studying the full front page on the screen. Mercs's revise fitted the space to within a line.

'Cut out the second "and" on the third para,' advised the sub and Mandy dutifully cut and realigned the column. Perfect.

'The overall balance is all wrong now,' observed the exec ed. 'If we could ditch that caption story of the kid from Bosnia at the zoo and replace it with . . .'

'Nothing suitable,' the pics ed said glumly.

'How about a nice sexy pic of a bomb-disposal bloke from Northern Ireland,' Mercs suggested brightly.

The pics ed scowled; he hated library pictures on the front page; this was most definitely not a reporter's province. 'Like living dangerously, do you, Eddie? Just stick to your joined-up writing, there's a good lad.'

But the exec ed liked the idea. 'Let's see what we've got on file.'

While they waited for the photographs and Mandy began rearranging the layout, the news editor ran his eye over the story again.

'What's this tailpiece about a parcel bomb?' he asked Mercs. 'I haven't heard about that before.'

'Casey was there when it happened, Steve.'

'Senator Powers? Wasn't he the one who refused to give Casey an interview last Christmas? Said he was on a private visit?'

'Private, my arse, Steve. He's involved in those secret talks. That's obviously why he was sent the bomb.'

Steve's eyes were dark and suspicious as he glanced sideways at Mercs. 'You know we've been told not to mention them.'

The reporter appeared unconcerned. 'We haven't. It's just a pure statement of fact – that Scotland Yard denied any knowledge that Senator Powers was sent a bomb.'

'You know that implies we don't believe them,' the news editor warned.

Mercs allowed himself a sly smile. 'It might shake something nasty out of the woodwork.'

'You're a crafty bastard, Eddie.'

'They're making the rules, Steve, I'm just playing by them. Fair enough?'

The news editor nodded. 'Fair enough.'

A selection of photographs came down the old-fashioned air tubes from the Picture Library on the next floor. One was chosen, a dramatic scene of hellfire and damnation in Belfast with an ATO in a sinister-looking bombsuit emerging from the flames.

'Looks good,' the exec ed said.

The picture editor grunted. 'Gives the impression London's turning into a second Belfast.'

'Maybe it is,' Mercs replied, placing his arm around the sub's shoulder. 'And for God's sake, Reg, come up with a more imaginative headline this time.'

'And quickly,' the exec ed urged, tapping his watch. 'The time's ticking away. Five minutes.'

'Ah,' Reg said thoughtfully.

9

The meeting was held at the new Thames House head-quarters of CI5 – still more generally referred to as MI5 – immediately following the press conference.

John Nash, head of the Security Service's Counter-Terrorism Department, was in the chair. The personal protégé of Director General Clarissa Royston-Jones, he was a youthful-looking forty years old with baby-blue eyes and black hair that had yet to show signs of greying.

He greeted Harrison warmly. 'Please to have you aboard, Major. I understand you've hardly been wasting your time since you arrived. I'm referring, of course, to Dukes Hotel.'

'I was just helping out.'

'Well, it was appreciated.'

Harrison smiled. 'Perhaps not in all quarters, sir. But thanks anyway.'

Nash gave a knowing nod of the head, but made no further comment. 'Now I think you know Lieutenant Colonel Trenchard and Detective Chief Superintendent Jim Maitland of the Anti-Terrorist Branch . . .'

The SATO acknowledged the two men who were amongst a dozen gathered round the table.

'I'll introduce everyone else as we go,' Nash said easily. 'We have representatives here from Special Branch, GCHQ, SIS, the Home Office and the Northern Ireland Office, as well as others holding various watching briefs.'

'Not Al Pritchard, though,' Harrison pointed out.

'Ah,' Nash said, 'a slightly delicate matter.'

Jim Maitland intervened. 'As Senior Expo, Al has his work cut out right now, Tom. Besides, you have a much wider remit.

Rather than invite antagonism between you both at an early stage, we felt it best that we establish your liaison rôle with us. You can report back to him on this meeting. That way he starts to see your value as an independent adviser rather than develop the notion you're muscling in to take over the Section, so to speak.'

Nash motioned everyone to sit. 'Help yourselves to coffee,' he invited. As the insulated pot, milk jug and sugar bowl began the ritual hand-to-hand shuttle around the table, he began. 'Today we have one overriding concern. That is to identify the structure of PIRA's so-called AIDAN active service unit operating here on the mainland and to hunt down those concerned.

'Now, in broad terms, I can tell you that all security elements are putting pressure on the various agents and informers that they run in Northern Ireland. I have . . .' Pause for a knowing half-smile here '. . . the dubious honour of trying to co-ordinate our own efforts with those of the Field Research Unit, E3A of RUC Special Branch, and SIS south of the border – that's not to mention any low-grade sources run informally by the Regional Crime and Intelligence Units or the TCGs. In fact, if one lowly Provo courier blows his nose, we want to know about it.'

'Any luck so far?' Maitland asked.

'Only one strong possibility so far, but it is a good one. It's not new, but that makes the gentleman concerned a major contender. The commander of Northern Brigade, one Patrick Francis McGirl went on the gallop back in late May. There was a rumour that he flew from Shannon to Paris, but Irish Special Branch have been unable to verify this. Nevertheless he is very much the calibre of operator that PIRA would need to manage the current mainland campaign. Needless to say SIS is organising round-the-clock surveillance of his home in Bundoran – but, of course, a bit late now that the proverbial horse has bolted. And, unfortunately, he's not one of your new men who's likely to phone home nightly to his common-law wife.'

'If he does we'll be on to him,' the representative from GCHQ stated flatly. 'We've extended the code range and the NSA is co-operating fully.'

The man did not elaborate that the Government Communications Headquarters at Cheltenham was using four filial Cray computers routinely to scan all UK telephone conversations at a rate of 500 million characters per second, which was the equivalent of between 400 to 500 full-length novels. 'Key words', including many that might be used as open codes, would trigger automatic transcripts that would then be referred to experts at the Defence Communications Network. While the BT switching centre at Oswestry monitored line phones, American satellites thirty miles in space relayed conversations on mobiles to the US National Security Agency listening posts in York and Morwenstow in Cornwall.

'And, Jim,' Nash asked, 'what particular lines of inquiry are you following?'

'Apart from the usual co-operation with Immigration we're concentrating on the explosive mixture that was used at both Seven Dials and the flyover bombs yesterday. Huge amounts of ANS. As you know, that's a fertiliser and icing sugar mix. The stuff had to be purchased somewhere and we're in talks with manufacturers and suppliers to try and get a lead. But it's going to be a long plod.' Then he attempted to look more optimistic than he really felt. 'We might have more luck with some of the electronic parts. We're starting to get first forensic reports back from Fort Halstead and, again, we'll be working back with suppliers and manufacturers in order to identify batch numbers. That's worked before. Hopefully it'll work again.'

Nash turned to Harrison. 'What can you tell us about this AIDAN bomb cell, Major.'

Harrison considered for a moment. 'Well, the first time we received the AIDAN codeword in Belfast was at the tail end of March. And it wasn't long before we realised it was different from all the rest. Not that the bombs were necessarily bigger or better than any others. It was more the methodical planning that went behind their use, always designed to create maximum disruption. There'd be no hesitation in spending time and effort on elaborate hoaxes or in changing the antihandling devices on a series of apparently identical bombs. It became like a game of cat-and-mouse. As though someone was setting out to get us to lower our guard and make mistakes. The one thing we could be certain of was that there was something – real or hoax – where the warning said it would be. It became a sort of trademark. Of course, with AIDAN, that was never even half the story. We soon recognised the campaign as probably the most serious we'd faced in a decade.'

'And are we talking about the work of one active service unit?' Nash asked.

'Or even one bomb maker?' Maitland suggested.

Harrison shook his head. 'I really can't be sure. What you've got to remember is that few AIDAN devices have failed to go off. Those that have, or those we've got to in time, offer mixed clues. Some have been fastidiously neat and precise whilst others have been a bit shoddy. One that failed to go off had poor connections. On another, I remember, the soldering on the universal counter was messy. That could mean the bomb maker was a novice or was perhaps nervous. Or old and shaky. Maybe he was wearing dirty spectacles and didn't realise the poor job he'd done. Or he could just have sneezed in the middle of doing it. That could indicate the devices were made by the same man who's just getting more expert as time goes on. Or, more likely, one man who supervises two or three others who do the constructing.' Harrison gave a slight smile. 'Either way, a splash of solder in the wrong place could have been lethal to whoever planted the bomb.'

'That we should be so lucky,' Nash said wistfully. 'Unfortunately AIDAN hasn't yet obliged us with an own goal.'

'If it's any consolation,' Harrison said, 'the more complicated a bomb becomes – like anything else – the more there is to go wrong. Like any other equipment, civilian or military. For instance, compare old idiot-proof Eastern Bloc aircraft with American superfighters. Never mind the best, you know which ones are the most *reliable*.'

As he stopped talking a brooding silence fell over the table. Nash was staring at him as though he'd seen a ghost, a half-smile frozen on his face.

'Mr Nash?' Harrison asked.

The MI5 man appeared to shake himself out of a trance. 'Sorry, suddenly had a thought. Miles away. So, Major, what do you think we can expect next from our friend AIDAN? Apart, that is, from the unexpected?'

'That rather depends on what PIRA is trying to achieve . . .?' He deliberately let the question hang. The talks, he meant. These goddamn secret talks that no one would mention. He'd seen all the AIDAN warnings issued in Belfast and London. The Europa bomb. And now the parcel bomb sent to Abe Powers – according to Casey, the man whom the US President had at one time earmarked as a possible peace envoy to Ulster before the idea was shelved . . . The talks, they were the common thread. But clearly no one around this table was going to admit it in front of others. Feeling mildly irritated, he moved on: 'All I can tell you is that most things AIDAN has tried over here have already been tried out in Ulster.'

Maitland sighed gloomily. 'So they've had plenty of practice.'

The meeting ground on in tedious detail until lunch time.

As it broke up, Don Trenchard approached Harrison and Jim Maitland as they stood talking. 'Tom, Nash has asked me to go over the list of all known bomb makers with you. Narrow the field a bit, if that's possible?'

Harrison turned to the Anti-Terrorist Branch detective. 'Is the Section's computer linked to Lisburn, Jim?'

'No problem. We can do that this afternoon.'

'Fine,' Trenchard said, 'then why don't I treat you two to lunch at my club. I tell you, their spotted dick is beyond belief!'

They began walking down the corridor together.

'One more thing,' Trenchard added, addressing both men. 'Nash would also like Tom to make an independent assessment of the AIDAN threat on the mainland and put forward any considered recommendations to counter that threat.'

Harrison wasn't at all happy to hear Pritchard's words of prophecy come true so rapidly. 'Look, Al's in the thick of all this and, technically at least, he's got ten years' more experience than I have. Shouldn't this at least be a joint effort?'

Trenchard shook his head. 'This comes from the very top,

Tom. And when COBRA requests, it's an order from God Almighty.'

That was hardly an exaggeration, Harrison knew. The acronym for the Cabinet Office Briefing Room referred to the most powerful co-ordinating body in the land, put in place to counter specific terrorist threats and usually chaired by the Home Secretary himself.

Jim Maitland said: 'Look, Tom, I'm not one to speak against my own people, but we've got to face facts. Al doesn't like the idea of you being here. You know what he's like. Every change you wanted to make he'd see as a threat to undermine him. He'd subvert everything you wanted to suggest, if he hasn't done so already. He's a lovable, crusty old dinosaur who hates change and moving with the times. Never was happy with all the technology the army developed for Northern Ireland.'

Harrison remembered Pritchard's dark warning to him that he'd be asked to make recommendations, but he decided not to mention it. Something else was concerning him more.

But now was not the time. He waited until they had finished lunch and Jim Maitland had returned hurriedly to New Scotland Yard. Over brandy, he said to his friend: 'Look, Don, if I'm to prepare this risk assessment I need to know what's really going on.'

Trenchard raised a quizzical eyebrow. 'Meaning?'

'I'm beginning to know how mushrooms feel. Kept in the dark and fed on bullshit. Now forgive me if I'm putting two and two together and making five, but I know AIDAN bomb warnings have consistently referred to, I quote, "unconstitutional talks" between London and Dublin. Then there was that bomb incident at the Europa, followed by a parcel bomb sent to Senator Powers who, I understand, is a leading figure of the Irish lobby with close connections to the Clinton administration. So what gives?'

Trenchard leaned back expansively in his chair and linked his hands together in an attitude of considered thought. 'I'm impressed, Tom. Didn't know you were so au fait with American politics.'

'Don't patronise me, Don,' Harrison retorted. 'This might be a game to you, but to the likes of Al and me it's more than a job. Our lives and those of our men can be at stake, as we've already seen. We don't want any more disasters like Seven Dials. And there are thousands of innocents at risk out there on the pavements of London.'

'Okay,' Trenchard said suddenly. He leaned forward and lowered his voice. 'Just the bare bones, right? Enough for you to judge the situation fully. But it must go no further, not even to Al. Agreed?'

Harrison nodded.

'Before President Clinton was elected on the Democratic ticket last year, he'd made a great play about appointing a special envoy to look into the Northern Ireland situation. With some forty million voters of Irish descent, he had to really. He didn't even wait for the inauguration. As soon as he had the result in early November, he sent over Senator Powers on a private mission to start the ball rolling. That ruffled a lot of feathers in Whitehall, as you might imagine. We didn't want any interference from Americans meddling in our affairs – besides, Britain's own secret negotiations with Sinn Fein had reached a delicate stage. Clinton was told this, of course, but he was determined to push ahead. This was mostly due to the fact that he was pretty miffed with the Conservatives at the time for actively assisting the Republicans – to the extent of ordering Box to try and dig some dirt on his student days at Oxford.

'Things were stiffly polite between the White House and Downing Street – it was clear the old special relationship had cooled. Clinton refused to back down on the Irish issue, but a compromise was reached. Washington would quietly drop its peace envoy idea, but instead the State Department would continue its covert effort with Powers to try and seek some common ground to bring an end to the troubles.'

'Then maybe he's making some progress. Let's hope so.'

'I don't think Downing Street would agree with you.'

'Why?'

'The government is horrified at the prospect of an American solution being found to Britain's most intractable problem. If you ask me, they rather poisoned the chalice by insisting on one condition. That no terrorist organisation should be included in Powers' informal discussions. It's nonsense, of course, because *they* are the only people in the position to deliver peace.

'And what has Number Ten been doing in the meantime? While it's appeared to go along with Powers, it's been mounting a huge secret effort to reach a settlement of its own before Powers gets his. And they haven't hesitated to make contact with the terrorists, I can tell you.'

'So who's going to win the race?'

'I think the government underestimated Abe Powers' abilities as a negotiator. To show willing, they had to give him what he wanted from them at the start. Then he wrung a major concession out of Dublin on the strength of it. He held all the key cards before he even started talking to the smaller players.

'And, until Christmas, he'd managed to keep everything secret. It was then that PIRA got hold of a senior civil servant in Dublin called Sean Shevlin.'

Harrison frowned, the name was vaguely familiar. 'I remember reading about it. Didn't he drown in Dublin?'

His friend's laugh was bitter. 'Oh, he drowned all right. But when they dragged his body out of the Liffey, they found he had all his toenails missing and a bullet in the back of his head.'

'That wasn't in the press?'

'No, it certainly wasn't. Although there was considerable pressure from some elements in Whitehall to let the Yanks know, hopefully to frighten them off, although I don't think that would have worked. The point is, the fact that Sean Shevlin was killed after interrogation suggested that PIRA were satisfied he'd told them everything he knew, and that was a lot. And you don't float a body through central Dublin if you don't want it to be found. It was telling everyone that PIRA knew about the talks and didn't like what they heard. It was their first warning shot.'

Harrison drained the last of his brandy. 'That explains a lot, Don. The time frame fits. Just a few months after Christmas and the AIDAN campaign starts in the Province. And we can see now it was just a dry run for London.'

Trenchard's eyes had become hard and intense. 'They're determined to do it, I can tell you that. They'll either bomb their way to the conference table or destroy the talks completely, one way or another.'

'I suppose they reason they've got nothing left to lose.'

'Nothing at all,' Trenchard confirmed. 'And that means we can expect them to go for a campaign that really hurts. And this time I don't expect they'll be overconcerned about innocent casualties, as we've already seen.'

Harrison nodded. 'If the stakes are as high as you suggest, Don, then they won't stop until they bring London to its knees.'

'There's a cheerful thought,' Trenchard said.

Even outside, as they began their walk back to the Section office, Harrison could sense the anxious air of expectation. Nothing specific, just small pointers. The July sun was bright yet there was no heart in it and it failed to warm the streets. There seemed to be few people about and those who were, walked briskly about their business. No one sauntered, no one lingered. He noticed no tourists but an increased presence of blue serge uniforms. Almost one on every corner, he thought.

Trenchard put it into words. 'You can almost smell it, Tom. It's a city in fear. I haven't felt it so acutely since the mid-seventies. And I'm getting a queasy feeling of *déjà vu*.'

He stopped at the news stand to buy the latest edition of the *Evening Standard*. The paper's coverage of the morning's press conference would probably set the tone of that night's television news and the following day's nationals.

Harrison looked on, his expectation of an optimistic and upbeat story of how government and police were coping with the latest wave of terror shattered the moment he read the screaming front-page headline:

Government calls in 'The Tick Tock Man':
BELFAST
BOMB EXPERT
FOR LONDON

For Harrison the repercussions of the *Standard* article began immediately on his return to Section headquarters. He met with Al Pritchard's stony stare the moment he and Trenchard set foot in the place.

'Well, Tom, we all know who's running the show now, don't we? My phone hasn't stopped ringing for the past hour. The Home Office, the MOD and the Branch Commander have all been on demanding to know the source of the leak. And the Yard's entire public relations department has had a roasting for lousy news management. Anything to say?'

'Not really, Al. That woman put it all together herself.'

'With a little help from you.'

'She must have picked up all that stuff at Jock's funeral.'

Pritchard's eyes had become fierce slits. 'Do you deny you spoke to her at the conference this morning? I saw you with my own eyes, dammit.'

Harrison's jaw clenched as he checked his anger. 'I told her nothing, just gave her marching orders.'

The Section chief almost laughed. 'That's a good one. The only one around here who should be getting marching orders is standing in front of me.'

'Okay, Al, I ballsed up at the funeral, we already know that. And I'm sorry about it, truly. But I didn't know who she was then, now I do. End of story.'

Pritchard was trying to decide if he'd drawn enough blood. 'I'm not covering up for you any more.'

'Don't bother, Al. Any more calls and you can put them through direct to me. I'll take any flak there is.'

Trenchard intervened quickly. 'Listen, gents, far be it from me to spoil a good fight, but my boss is anxious to put together a list of any bomb makers who we think could be involved with the AIDAN campaign.'

Pritchard glared once more at Harrison for good measure, before turning to the MI5 man. He sounded weary. 'Yes, of course. Where do you want to start?'

'Well, we do know that the AIDAN cell has been set up recently for a specific purpose. Possibly an entirely new active service unit.

Maybe a new bomb maker, too. I understand there's a marked sophistication in the devices they've been using. It all points to new blood, I'd have thought.'

As they entered the main administration office, Al Pritchard said: 'In a way, you know, it's more like a throwback to the early days in Belfast. Of course, there wasn't the technology there is now, but nevertheless they were up to all sorts of tricks then. Developed a whole new range of antihandling devices. But then they got a little too cocksure. Scored a few own goals. We didn't shed any tears over that, of course, but they did.'

Harrison agreed. 'For a long time now PIRA's devices have kept mostly standard. Quite simple and idiot-proof. Virtually factory-made on someone's kitchen table, usually over the border. The bomb maker presets the timer, then all the man who's planting it has to do is pull out a wooden dowel plug which activates it. He then takes the dowel back to his unit commander to prove it's been set.'

'So in a way these AIDAN devices represent a return to the old days,' Pritchard said.

'It happens quite frequently in Northern Ireland nowadays,' Harrison added. 'As you probably know, no two men will construct a bomb the same way. The circuits will be slightly different and they'll choose alternative component makes. One might make use of superglue or another double-sided tape. Each bomb maker has his own signature.'

Trenchard nodded; he knew little about improvised devices, but it made sense. 'So what are you saying, Tom?'

'Only that we've come across several signatures in recent years that haven't been seen for a decade or more.'

'Ah,' Trenchard exclaimed, suddenly seeing the point.

Harrison said: 'Guys are coming out of the Maze after a nine- or eighteen-year stretch and going back to work.'

'And you think AIDAN might be one of them?'

'It's not impossible.'

The administration office, its walls lined with large-scale maps of London and the suburbs, contained the library, main computer, fax, copier and all the paraphernalia of modern communications. Les Appleyard was on the duty desk, talking to the librarian who was one of the three male administration-support staff.

'Anything happening?' Pritchard asked.

Appleyard shook his head. 'Just a run of false alarms. Hardly surprising after yesterday.'

'No hoaxes?'

'Amazingly not. As well really, we're at full stretch. In fact, I've had to put John and Dickie on standby.'

'That'll please their wives,' Pritchard said flatly. His own marriage had ended several years previously and Appleyard sensed that he secretly resented any of his Expos who managed to hold theirs together.

Trenchard said: 'In view of what you and Tom have been saying, I wondered if we ought to start with a look at which convicted bombers have been released from prison in the last year.'

There was a shrug from Pritchard. 'It's not an area that usually concerns us, but I think we have the necessary access. But I'm computer-illiterate, so you'll have to ask "Boffin",' he said, nodding towards the long-haired librarian. Despite the fact that he shampooed his locks regularly and was always smartly if casually turned out, Pritchard still considered the twenty-eight-year-old graduate as being little better than a New Age traveller.

Boffin bared his teeth in an unfriendly smile. 'My parents did give me a real name actually, chief.'

A smile almost cracked Pritchard's thin lips. 'Pity I can never remember it. If you had a haircut so I could see your face, it might help.'

'Prat,' Boffin muttered under his breath and took a seat by the terminal, deftly tapping in the password. 'Shall I go back eighteen months, gents, just so we don't miss anything?'

'Good idea,' Harrison said, standing at the librarian's shoulder.

The list sprang onto the screen.

Behan, M.	McCann, M.P.
Blaney, R.J.	MacEoin, W.M.
Colley, B.N.R.	MacGuire, B.S.
Daly, T.	O'Brien, R.
Dougan, H.	O'Shea, D.A.
Gallagher, O.D.	Ryan, F.J.
Lehane, J.	

Names, just names. As cold and impersonal as a telephone directory; as meaningless as names on headstones to a third generation. No hint of the real man behind each, their loves and fears, their hatreds. Like the bombs they built, unfeeling mechanisms that just did what they were designed to do, mostly. That was all that concerned men like Tom Harrison and Al Pritchard. Respond, locate and assess the threat, decide on counteraction, destroy. Then go home. Only Don Trenchard habitually looked beyond the guns and the bombs to the men behind them.

'Any name ring a bell?' the MI5 man asked. 'Of course, some will still be on working-out schemes or weekend release. Others might be under surveillance. I'll go through RUC Special Branch and get a fix on each. Either way I'll arrange to put some pressure on. See they're paid a visit.'

Pritchard jabbed a finger at the screen. 'I'd try McEoin, I remember him. He used to make some really tricky devices. Milk churns with a bomb within a bomb. You'd do a controlled explosion, walk up to it and then a separate secondary hidden in the base would go off. I lost two mates through him, the bastard. About 1975, I think.'

Boffin tapped in the follow-up code and waited for McEoin's details to swipe onto the screen.

'There you are,' Trenchard said. 'Living in retirement with his dying mum in Newtownhamilton. Last Int summary in late May.'

'Too late,' Harrison said. 'AIDAN was already active in Belfast by then.'

Trenchard fiddled with the brim of his fedora, feeding it through his long fingers in a circular motion. 'We can still give him a tug. Maybe something got overlooked.' He didn't sound convinced.

Harrison said: 'There was another name I thought I recognised.'

Obligingly Boffin returned to the menu list.

'Dougan, H.,' Harrison said. And even as he said the name an involuntary chill quivered down his spine. For a moment he was back there at the derelict on the Ballymurphy estate. Ten years earlier, then just a captain. Inching up the collapsing staircase, searching out the sniper's nest. The come-on of spent cartridges. The moment's hesitation that had saved his life. One footstep away from the pressure mat and the hidden bomb in the wall that would have cut his body in half.

'Dougan,' Harrison repeated dully. 'Oh, yes, Hughie Dougan. You must remember him, Don. He'd just come out of the Maze after serving a nine. Within a week he'd done a runner to the south and was back in business.' He turned to Trenchard. 'Didn't your lads in 14 Int pick him up?'

'Yes, we caught him crossing the border. But I'm afraid you're barking up the wrong tree there. Hughie Dougan is dead.'

Boffin had now punched up his details:

DOUGAN, Hugh, Joseph
Born:	Belfast, 2 April 1934 Married: Mary Florence McKearney (Deceased: 1978)
Daughters:	Clodagh, Maria (B 1964) Single. Currently working in Canada Caitlin, May (B. 1974) Married Currently resident in Belfast.
Occupation:	Electrician
Service Career:	Royal Electrical and Mechanical Engineers (1953-65) Rank: Sergeant
Served: Convictions:	Kenya (Mau Mau) and Cyprus (EOKA)

- Unlawful assembly 1969 (Conditional discharge)
- Riotous behaviour 1970 (Fined)
- Bomb making and conspiracy to cause explosions 1974 (Nine years – Maze) (Released 1983. Broke

181

probation and absconded to the Republic.
Recaptured Co Armagh 6 months later)
• Bomb making and conspiracy to cause explosions
1983 (Nine years – Maze) (Release 1992)
Killed in car accident Co Sligo in the Republic, June 1992
FILE CLOSED

'Well, that's one more bastard off the list,' Pritchard said dispassionately.

Harrison spent the remainder of the afternoon drafting his thoughts on the course the AIDAN campaign might take and his recommended plans to counter it. The more he wrote, the more it resembled a battle campaign for the streets of Belfast. As Pritchard had warned him, it was exactly what PIRA wanted. But what else could he do? The government needed answers and he'd been chosen to provide them.

It was seven thirty when he left the Section office, so absorbed in his work that he completely forgot about the supper party he was due to go to that night until he was heading home in the taxi. Pippa would be furious; she had their host, a wealthy industrialist who lived at Albany in Piccadilly, firmly in her sights as a prospective client.

But, as the cab arrived at the end of their street in Pimlico, he realised that his late return would be the least of their troubles that night.

'Looks like the ratpack's onto something,' the driver observed. 'Not your house, is it?'

Harrison peered through the glass partition with a sinking sensation in his stomach. He could see the cluster of journalists and photographers by the railings, the terraced Victorian town house floodlit by a television news team.

'Drive on,' he ordered.

Paying off the cab at the far end of the street, he entered an alleyway between the end-of-terrace house and the antique shop on the corner. It led behind the back-garden walls of the houses, the gates long ago nailed up for reasons of security. With the aid

182

of a dustbin, he scaled the wall. In the process he ripped his trousers on the broken bottle-glass embedded in the concrete capping before he dropped down into a dense bed of hydrangeas.

Cursing, he fought free of the shrub and made his way up the path and across the crazy-paved patio. The French doors were open and Pippa, dressed in blue satin finery, was standing by the fireplace which was filled with a display of dried flowers.

She turned sharply. 'Christ, Tom, you gave me a fright!' She took in his dishevelled state. 'What on earth have you been doing?'

'I thought I'd avoid that lot outside the front door.' He looked down at his torn and flapping trouser leg. 'Maybe it wasn't such a bright idea. Sorry I'm late, I got held up.'

'Never mind about that,' she snapped, her cheeks pink with anger. 'Why have we got the press camped on our pavement? They've been there for half-an-hour. What the hell happened at that press conference this morning? Have you read the *Standard*? Surely you didn't give them our address?'

'Don't be stupid. It's *you* who is listed in the telephone book. I expect they've been telephoning all the Harrisons in London since the paper came out.'

'No one phoned here, Tom, and I wouldn't say you lived here – I'm not that daft.'

There came an embarrassed cough from the corner. For the first time Harrison noticed his father-in-law sitting on the sofa in tuxedo and black tie. His collar was loose and he had a brandy glass in his hand. A nervous smile played on the broad, veined face. 'Ah, Pippa, my dear, that could have been my fault. Some-one phoned about an hour ago while you were upstairs getting changed. Asked to talk to Tom, so I said he'd be here any minute.'

'They didn't leave a name?' Pippa asked.

Brigadier Mervin Maddox looked suitably sheepish and ran a hand over his neatly raked silver hair. ' 'Fraid not. Can see why now.'

Her face softened. 'You weren't to know, Dad.' She turned to Harrison. 'It's all down to that damn Mullins woman. I didn't trust her the moment I set eyes on her. Anyway, it's too late now. I'm going to pack a bag.'

'What are you talking about?' Harrison asked. 'I didn't know we were staying over after supper.'

She stared at him in amazement. 'What supper, Tom? Apart from being an hour late, your American friend has blown that right out of the water – and my contract with it, I expect. We can hardly go with that lot trailing after us. And we can't stay here with half of Fleet Street outside – certainly not in the middle of this IRA blitz. It's an open invitation.' She paused to draw breath, just. 'We're going to have to stay with Dad while we put the house on the market.'

Harrison blinked. 'Don't be ridiculous, Pippa.'

Her eyes were afire with anger. 'That's what this means, Tom. If the press know where we live then those Irish bastards can find out. You can go swanning back to Belfast, but it's me who'll get the letter bomb or my car blown up. I don't trust those thickos to work out whether you're actually here or not. I'm not sure they'd even care. So why don't you just stop arguing and pack an overnight bag.' She spun on her heel and marched from the room.

It was suddenly very quiet as the two men remained in an awkward silence, listening to her high heels resounding angrily on the stairs. The noise of the mantelpiece clock seemed intrusively loud.

Harrison said: 'I need a drink.'

The brigadier studied him carefully from the sofa as the whisky was poured. 'You know she's having an affair, don't you?'

10

Harrison looked at Pippa's father sharply, not sure he'd heard the words correctly.

'It's true, Tom. She's having an affair with Jonathan Beazley, our managing director –'

'I know who Beazley is,' Harrison snapped.

Maddox appeared to be mesmerised by his brandy, swilling it slowly around the glass. 'It's been goin' on about three months now. Don't approve, of course. Beazley was in my regiment once, you know, a subaltern. Long time ago, though. But you can't blame Pippa, not with you away all the time, not knowing when you're going to get yourself blown up. Terrific strain on a marriage. A big city can be a lonely place, you know.'

Obviously not lonely enough, Harrison thought silently and savagely. He didn't doubt her father's words; the brigadier may have been warning him in order to save the marriage, but somehow Harrison doubted it. He suspected the old bastard was subtly, smugly gloating.

The brigadier was saying: 'Can't blame Jonathan either really, although it's damn bad form. His marriage has been on the rocks for years.' Then, as though it explained everything: 'And Pippa is a damn handsome woman, even if I say so myself.'

That's rich. Pippa not to blame. Beazley not to blame. Obviously there was only one person left to carry the can. Him.

Harrison swallowed his drink in one gulp, the harsh burning at the back of his throat helping to revive him. He felt exhausted and drained, his mind fully occupied with the AIDAN campaign. This in addition he could do without.

Before he was able to marshal his thoughts or come back with some suitably cutting reply, the telephone rang. He snatched up the receiver.

'Harrison household? Bill Rivers of the *Mirror* here. Wonder if I could speak to the major?'

The receiver crashed down. Harrison turned as Pippa struggled on the stairs, her cases thudding against the banisters.

'Don't say I told you,' Maddox breathed anxiously, as he raised himself from the sofa. 'She'd never forgive me.'

As Harrison stepped into the hall, Pippa looked him directly in the eyes. He could see only anger and fear in her expression, nothing else. Certainly not what he was hoping to see. 'Dad's going to take me now, Tom. I take it you'll follow over?'

Harrison shook his head. 'I'm not staying with him.'

For a moment anxiety clouded her eyes and she glanced over his shoulder as her father walked towards the hall. 'What has he been saying?'

Wearily Harrison shook his head. 'Only what *you* should have told me yourself. About you and Beazley.'

'Oh.' She was visibly shaken, stopped dead in her tracks.

'"Oh"? Is that the best you can do? Is that "Oh, I'm sorry, it was just one of those things, but now it's finished, please forgive me?" Or "Oh, God, I've been caught with my knickers round my ankles?"'

Anger flashed in her eyes. 'There's no need to be bloody vulgar, Tom.' Attack always had been Pippa's method of defence.

'Adultery's a pretty vulgar business,' he snapped back, 'as you must be all too aware.'

Now she was looking flustered. 'This really isn't the time or place, not with the press outside . . .'

'Sod the press, Pippa! This is our lives we're talking about. Ours and Archie's. What do you want me to do, make an appointment to discuss it?'

She saw her opening and went for it. 'Why not? That seems to be how we've been running our marriage for the past year or more. Everything deferred until you're home on leave. How the hell

186

d'you think it feels being a part-time wife? Sometimes I think a prostitute knows her clients better than I know you.'

'Now who's being vulgar?'

'I mean it, Tom. You've become like a stranger to me, and to Archie.'

That bit hurt. 'And what about Beazley? He's certainly no stranger, is he?'

Suddenly she seemed to calm down. With a look of resignation on her face, she said: 'You're right, it did just happen. Jonathan and I were working hard on a series of presentations to new clients. Late nights at the office and then a few drinks after. We got to know each other better. We found we had a lot in common.'

'Like both being married.'

She ignored the jibe. 'We liked the same things, spoke the same language. He can be very funny, you know.'

'I hadn't noticed.'

'And like me, he is very unhappy.'

'Meaning?'

'He's going to divorce Vanessa.'

Harrison's laugh was bitter. 'And don't tell me, you want a divorce too?'

Pippa took a deep breath. 'Yes.'

Of course he had half anticipated her reply, yet still didn't really expect it. Not like that. Its effect was shocking, leaving his mind in a spin, unable to grasp the full implication of her words – that his life and marriage had just crashed around him.

She was saying '. . . I was going to tell you, obviously. When Jonathan and I had sorted everything out.'

'So you already knew?'

'What?'

'When we made love the other night. You already knew.'

Her features hardened. 'When we screwed, Tom, not made love. I don't think we've made love for years.'

'But you knew?' Insistent.

There was a momentary flicker of warmth in her eyes. 'You're a very hard man to hate, Tom. And you can still stir something in me. But the love has gone.'

187

He felt sick, a nauseous churning deep within him. Not so much anger as an aching emptiness. A stunning sense of sadness and loss.

The brigadier gave an embarrassed cough. Harrison turned towards the living-room door. 'It's all right. It's safe for you to come out now.'

Pippa said: 'You can still come with us tonight, Tom.'

'I don't think so.'

She gave him the look she reserved for Archie when he was behaving at his most childishly obtuse. 'What will you do then?'

'I don't know. Hotel room or something.'

She'd put on her favourite Hermés headscarf to which she now added designer sunglasses to complete her disguise. 'Call me at the office tomorrow, tell me where you are.' Her lips brushed against his cheek. He thought how cold they felt.

The front door swung open to a bewildering array of popping flashguns and a babble of excited voices. 'Mrs Harrison! Mrs Harrison, look this way please!' 'When will your husband be home?' 'Mrs Harrison, what does it feel like to be married to a bomb-disposal man?' 'Aren't you afraid of being a target of the IRA, Mrs Harrison?' 'Mrs Harrison . . .?'

She was swallowed up in the mêlée, huddling close to her father as he struggled towards his parked BMW. As Harrison began to ease the door closed, the figure in trench coat and fedora hat slipped easily round behind the crowd and up the steps.

Don Trenchard grinned. 'Under siege, eh? Looks like you could do with some moral support.'

The door slammed, shutting out the noisy hubbub on the pavement. 'You can say that again. I've got that rabble outside and Pippa's off to stay with her father.'

'Not you?'

Harrison hesitated for a moment. 'Hell, Don, you may as well know. Pippa's just walked out on me.'

His friend frowned. 'Serious?'

'She wants a divorce and I think she means it.'

'Oh, shit, really? I am sorry.'

'Don't be. I think it's been on the cards for a long time.'

Trenchard considered for a moment. 'Look, Tom, why don't you stay at my place. Haven't seen it, have you? A bijou two-bedroom job in Knightsbridge. I'll lend you a shoulder to cry on.'

Harrison was relieved to find he still had at least one friend left. 'I'd appreciate that.'

'I'm sure you won't cramp my style. We'll have a ball.' Trenchard gave him a friendly slap on the back. 'And we can start with a nice bit of nosh at a little Italian bistro I know. Lovely waitress and great pasta. We can chat over a couple of things.'

Harrison realised that there had to have been a reason for the unexpected visit. 'Like what?'

Trenchard removed his fedora and ran a hand through his hair, loosening the crinkled waves. 'Look, I appreciate this isn't really the best time . . . It's about what you said at the meeting this morning. About the more complex a bomb, the more dangerous it is to the person who plants it.'

'So?' He wasn't really concentrating, his mind on Pippa and Archie.

'It got my boss, John Nash, thinking. He asked me to come and talk to you. He thinks that maybe it's something we could encourage.'

'We can hardly phone up PIRA and suggest it.'

Trenchard jerked his thumb towards the front door. 'No, but indirectly that lot can. They're baying for a story.'

'I wouldn't trust them. I'm in enough trouble with the press.'

'Not any more.' He tapped his nose with his finger. 'I've been pouring oil over troubled water. Before I left I phoned Al Pritchard, the Home Office and the rest and told them – confidentially – that it's all been part of our ploy. It wasn't when it happened, of course, but it is now.'

'What ploy?'

'To cultivate that Mullins woman.'

Harrison almost choked. 'Forget it!'

'It's been sanctioned by she who can do no wrong – Clarissa Royston-Jones herself, queen of the Security Service.'

189

'Look, Don, get this straight. If it involves Casey Mullins, then I am not interested.'

Eddie Mercs said: 'Wherever Casey Mullins goes, the others follow.'

She turned from the collection of morning newspapers spread across the desk of her work station and peered at him over the top of her reading specs. 'Don't wind me up, Eddie, I'm a black dan of the fifth belt or something equally lethal. Don't mess with my emotions.'

'He's right, though,' the photographer Hal Hoskins added, sipping at a plastic mug of coffee. 'I was down at his place last night. All the hacks reckon you're on the inside track, especially after that funeral story. Green with envy, they are.' He looked down at the large front-page picture of Philippa Harrison putting up a hand to shield herself from the prying cameras. 'Had to make do with a shot of his wife – looks like a bit of a dragon there – sort of faded film starlet.'

'You didn't see Major Harrison then?' she asked, removing her spectacles.

Hoskins wrinkled his nose. 'Nah, but a couple of blokes did a runner out of a side-alley later on. Odds are one of them was him.'

'Oh dear. I don't think he'll be very pleased about all this. I never thought the other papers might track him down in his home.'

'The qualities are all right,' Mercs sniffed. 'It's the pops who've been going overboard on the doorstepping.'

'But our own headline,' she protested. 'Where did that expression Tick Tock Man come from? Half the tabloids have copied it.'

'Reg in subs,' Mercs said. 'It was his brainwave.'

'I think that's rather good,' Hoskins observed, biting noisily into an apple. 'Sort of tick-tock, bang. Clever that. And catchy.'

'I'm sure Major Harrison won't like that,' Casey said, shaking her head. 'Makes him sound like a clockwork soldier.'

'Not your problem, sweetheart,' Mercs said. 'Serves the

190

government right for trying to manipulate the media. All this baloney about on top of the situation and everything being under control when any fool can see they're running shit-scared.'

'Don't want to panic Joe Public, I suppose,' Hoskins remarked absently.

Mercs gave a snort of derision. 'Panic is nature's answer to danger, airhead. You see a bomb sitting there ticking . . . you panic and run. Panic is what saves lives.'

The telephone trilled and Casey picked it up. 'Mullins speaking, features.'

'Miss Mullins?' The voice was deep, the tone crisp. 'Harrison here.'

She felt the blood flood into her cheeks. 'Oh . . . It's lovely to hear from you, Tom – er – Major . . .?'

'Tom will be fine,' he said, but there was no mistaking the hard edge to his voice.

'Look, Tom, if it's about what I wrote yesterday?'

'Forget it, that was yesterday. There's someone I'd like you to meet. I wondered if you might be free for lunch. It'll be a good opportunity to put this current PIRA campaign into perspective.'

'Let me check my diary, Tom.' She placed her hand over the mouthpiece and looked at Mercs. 'It's my Tick Tock Man. He wants me to go to lunch. What shall I do?'

Mercs smirked. 'Are you hungry?'

She poked out her tongue, but she knew he was right. 'Hello, Tom, yes I can make that. And who is it you want me to meet?'

'You'll see.' He gave her the address. 'See you at one o'clock.'

Senator Abe Powers knew it was a gamble. But it was a risk he was willing to take, bringing the three of them together at this stage. Ian Findlay, adviser to Paisley's hard-line Democratic Unionists, would be the most intransigent, the least willing to compromise. But persuade him, and the milder-mannered Peter Rawlings of the Ulster Unionists would be sure to follow.

However, the big question was, could there ever be any

common ground between these two staunch Protestants and little Fern Kelly of the Catholic SDLP?

Liverpool had been chosen as neutral ground. Certainly Powers had lost his appetite for venues across the water after the bomb attack at the Europa Hotel. And he had selected the Adelphi simply because he liked the faded opulence of the old railway hotel. Or was it really, he wondered, because the building seemed symbolic of the long slow death of a once great trading nation? Another fallen empire of which Ireland had been both its first and last long-suffering colony?

He turned away from the panoramic view of the city's rooftops as his American bodyguard opened the door of the suite to admit the diminutive Fern Kelly.

A bluestocking, he decided immediately. A bluestocking in blue stockings to be precise. At least they were feminine and sheer, blending elegantly with the smooth grey wool suit and ribbon-bowed navy blouse. As businesslike as the simple bob cut of sleek black hair.

The hand was tiny, white and cool in his own; he could feel her delicate bones in his palm, reminding him of an injured sparrow he had once held as a boy.

'Take a seat, m'dear,' he invited and instantly regretted his choice of words. Because, although she graciously accepted his offer, he did not miss the flicker of irritation in the beautiful dark eyes behind the unflattering round student's glasses.

No more sexist endearments, he told himself, and seriously considered whether to address her formally as Ms Kelly. But the problem was resolved with the arrival of Ian Findlay and Peter Rawlings – the senator decided on Christian name terms for all.

After serving coffee, he said: 'A short while ago I received an initial reaction from you two gentlemen regarding my proposal for Voting Registration as a way out of the Northern Ireland impasse . . .'

'It'll just prolong the agony,' Findlay interrupted defiantly.

Powers raised his hand. 'Please, Ian. Let us hear Fern's view.'

To the American's surprise she smiled at the volatile Orangeman as she placed a slim lady's briefcase demurely on her knees. 'It may surprise you to know, Senator, that I agree with Ian and Peter.' She flipped open the lid of her case and extracted her notes. 'To recap, you suggest that voters in the Six Counties register either as Irish or British citizens and thereby decide to vote for Dáil or Westminster MPs. A sort of make-your-mind-up time. To my mind, any Catholic registering as Irish will be effectively disenfranchised unless they uproot and move to Eire.'

'Irish voters would retain all their existing rights,' Powers countered, 'including local council elections, arguably the most important issues to affect the individual . . .'

'But excluding such *minor* matters as welfare and taxation,' Fern Kelly retorted. 'In effect, Catholics in Ulster could happily vote for tax cuts – or increases – in another country. One in which they have never lived. And most of us, myself included, already travel on an Irish passport.'

'That wouldn't have to change.'

She shook her head. 'Then the whole concept is another well-meaning fudge.'

'And a dangerous one,' Findlay interjected.

'I agree. It is divisive. Far from the intention of creating a bond of Irish unity and giving Ulster Catholics legal status, it is a recipe for civil war. Not exactly what we need at the moment.'

Abe Powers was stunned. How could this bright young middle-class Catholic girl be so dismissive of his carefully crafted idea? A former political student at Queen's, a skilful journalist and rising star in the SDLP – how could she reject this monumental leap in forward thinking, this radical suggestion already accepted in embryo form by London and Dublin as a way forward?

Stubbornly he said: 'We achieved an accord – I admit, a fragile one – between Israel and the PLO. If that can be done between sworn enemies, then surely we can make some concessions . . .?'

'Britain is not an occupying power, Senator,' Findlay snapped. 'And there is no comparison. If British policy was in any way parallel to the Israelis', then all IRA suspects would have been imprisoned without trial or dumped on the mountains of Donegal. Houses of IRA sympathisers would have been blown up and Dublin bombed for giving refuge to its supporters.'

Peter Rawlings agreed. 'That's not to mention forming a security buffer zone for several miles into Eire.'

'Do I need to go on?' Findlay asked. 'Remember this, Israel has always had backing from the United States. But when confronting the IRA, Britain has always been opposed by you Americans. In fact, if it hadn't been for Washington's pressure after the First World War when the twenty-six counties seceded from Britain, there would probably be no Irish Republic today.'

Abe Powers was angry. 'Don't expect me to apologise for that, Ian!' He watched his carefully built house of cards flutter to the ground.

It was Fern Kelly's small voice which broke the bitter silence that followed. 'If you'll forgive me for saying, Senator, no amount of tinkering with fine words in agreements and treaties or fudging parts of the constitution will bring an end to the violence, because you are trying to reconcile the irreconcilable. Believe me, my party has been trying very hard to find some common ground with Sinn Fein. The simple truth is only the IRA can decide on peace and what they want no one in this room is in the position to deliver, any more than Dublin or London can. They want the border torn down and that's something the majority of Protestants won't tolerate – as well as thousands of Catholics who also have no wish to become part of Eire.'

'Maybe the IRA merely want historical justice,' Powers goaded.

Findlay's laugh was brittle. 'I've yet to hear any IRA or Sinn Fein argument that doesn't go back to 1921 or beyond. They're living in cloud-cuckoo-land. And, Senator, to quote your own guidelines for these talks, what was it . . .?'

Fern Kelly helped him. 'Put the past behind us, live with and recognise present practicalities and resolve our differences in the interests of our children's future.'

'Your sentiment is right there, Senator,' Rawlings agreed. 'We need something that will *unite* our people in the north, not divide us.'

'But *excluding* the IRA,' Powers echoed, as though the very words themselves were a betrayal of Irish history that he'd been taught at his grandmother's knee. 'I don't think it will work without them, whatever you say. Unfortunately that is the one basis on which Downing Street allowed these talks.'

Fern Kelly said quietly: 'I wonder if there isn't only one way to unite a divided country like Ulster.'

Powers looked at her, thinking of the old English joke about towing it into the Atlantic and sinking it. 'And that is?'

'It's something I've thought about a lot recently. Not an entirely new idea, but maybe the time has never been so right to give it a chance. A fresh start. Give a divided people an incentive to work together. An *independent* Northern Ireland under the protection of the United Kingdom.'

Rawlings raised an eyebrow. 'You mean like the Isle of Man?'

She nodded. 'An autonomous Crown possession, totally self-governing apart from defence against foreign aggression. Our own laws, taxes, offshore status to pull in big investment . . .'

Findlay was dubious. 'How does this square with your party's aim of constitutional ties with Dublin?'

'It doesn't, but we each have to give something to find a solution. *Your* people would have to accept some form of power-sharing.'

Suddenly Abe Powers experienced a surge of excitement. Had they stumbled on a real possibility here? 'Would the IRA go for that?'

'No,' Fern Kelly replied, 'but under your Secret Protocol the ringleaders will be interned for the first three years. With a new constitution up and running, they'd stand no chance of restarting the fight. Only people without hope resort to guns.'

Powers was still puzzled by one thing. 'But, Fern, you've always believed in a United Ireland – like my own ancestors.'

She smiled gently. 'Do you know, Senator, if Ulster was truly independent and free of any claim by Dublin, I think you would soon see the people of north and south more united in spirit than you would ever have believed possible.'

Two hours later Casey paid off her cab outside Boodles. She experienced a small thrill of trepidation about entering the hallowed portals of the venerable club. It wasn't long ago, Mercs had told her, that women had not been allowed to visit. Was she wearing too much make-up? Was the bright floral summer dress really appropriate, even with the borrowed black cardigan to tone down the overall effect? She really began to wish she'd gone home and changed into her business suit with the padded shoulders that Mercs said made her look like a fullback for the Chicago Bears.

If Harrison thought she was wrongly dressed, he gave no sign as he waited for her in the lofty marble-floored lobby. He was wearing a slightly unfashionable charcoal suit and, she noted, the same tie he'd worn at the funeral. Felix the cat and the orange hand of Ulster.

As he greeted her, she was aware of the intensity of the expression in his dark eyes.

'I can't wait to meet the mystery man,' she said.

If Harrison was harbouring any anger towards her, he hid it well. He was relaxed and smiling easily. 'No real mystery, Casey,' he assured as he led her towards a quiet corner table in the fusty, panelled dining room with its starched table linen and heavy silver.

There were two men at the table. Immediately she recognised one as he sprang attentively to his feet. Don Trenchard was as dapperly dressed as the first time she'd met him at Dukes Hotel, a fawn cotton suit and striped shirt, the regimental tie fastened at the collar with a plain gold pin.

'Don you met the other day,' Harrison said.

Trenchard had a tan and the mischievous grin of a boy that made him seem younger than Harrison. His handshake was enthusiastic and playful, his ready smile alluring. She caught a

196

whiff of cologne. 'A delight to meet you again, Miss Mullins. Let me introduce Sir George Pepperell.'

The old man rose unsteadily from his seat. His bald crown was surrounded by a halo of white and wispy hair. Small bristles had escaped the razor on his bloodhound jowls which carried the broken veins of someone who suffered from high blood pressure. But it was the thick and greying eyebrows that dominated his face and emphasised the watery eyes. They fixed on her with a stare of disturbingly candid interest.

'Miss Mullins,' he acknowledged, reaching across the table. His voice was deep and smooth, containing both graciousness and natural authority. 'It's a pleasure. I've heard so much about you.'

She laughed uneasily. 'None of it true, I expect.'

'Oh, I'm sure it is.' As he resumed his seat, she noticed that the voluminous trousers of his pinstripe suit were hiked almost to his chest by Paisley-pattern braces. A gravy-stained matching tie hung low and wide, reminding her of a baby's bib. 'You seem to have made quite a mark for yourself in recent days.'

'Not a black mark, I hope?'

He smiled slowly and broadly, his teeth slightly yellowed by cigar smoke. 'Is that a Texan accent I detect?'

She realised he had overlooked her question. 'I'm a California girl,' she said brightly. 'They grow us big there too.'

One of the shaggy eyebrows lifted slightly and she wondered if he was amused or offended by her impertinence. His gentle smile, however, remained. 'But you are married to an Englishman?'

Damn, that was awkward, hardly the way she wanted to start this conversation. 'Well, just. To be honest we're not too close nowadays. Mostly we speak to each other through our lawyers.'

'I'm so sorry to hear that.'

She decided she wanted to know exactly who she was lunching with. 'I'm sorry, Sir George - is that what I call an English knight?' He smiled meekly and nodded. 'But you rather have the advantage over me. I really don't know why I've been asked here.'

197

Trenchard was leaning sideways in his chair, his arm draped carelessly over its back. 'Sir George used to describe himself as "something in the ministry". Very enigmatic.'

Casey heard the alarm bells ringing. 'Any particular ministry?'

Sir George waved a wrinkled white hand, its back flecked with liver spots. 'Doesn't matter, dear lady. I'm long retired now. Besides which, we're not here to discuss me.'

'Then why *are* we here?' Her tone was a little sharper than she'd intended.

'Just for a chat. I like to get to know ladies and gentlemen of the press. I've read your work with great interest. Tell me, are you fully recovered from your traumatic experience at Seven Dials?'

'I guess so. But I'm still getting nightmares. I'll have to give up cheese at bedtime.'

'And your daughter? Candy, isn't it? What a delightful name. Is she showing any ill effects?'

'She's a bit withdrawn still.'

'And she wants to be a dancer?'

God, what doesn't this man know? she thought. 'Today yes. A year ago she wanted to be a doctor, then an interior designer. I should have stopped her then, I could do with some decorating advice on my new place . . .'

And they settled into light-hearted banter, questions and interest from Sir George and quick-fire answers from Casey, who was anxious to please and impress. She wasn't sure why, it just seemed to be the wisest thing to do. The old man became visibly more relaxed. He caught onto her jokes and began to laugh quite a lot. When he raised his hand, a waiter materialised instantly at his side, order book at the ready. Sir George's recommendation of the melon with Parma ham didn't invite detractors, though no one took up his suggestion of poached fish. The other choices were plain, traditional and well-cooked although with a certain lack of imagination.

Casey noticed that Harrison was saying nothing and Trenchard very little. Occasionally the two friends would exchange glances;

Trenchard would give a small grin, and then they would resume listening as Sir George continued his skilful and gentle interrogation.

The two bottles of Nuits-Saint-Georges were rich and plummy, leaving Casey feeling quite light-headed by the time they had finished the dessert.

Over coffee Sir George Pepperell said: 'Of course, with freedom of the press must go a sense of responsibility, wouldn't you agree?'

That seemed reasonable to Casey; with her head gently spinning, most things would have seemed reasonable. 'Yes, I think so. I like to think I feel a responsibility to my readers.'

'I had more in mind the government, any government of the day.'

She tried to concentrate on what he was saying. 'I'm not sure about that.'

Sir George paddled his spoon in his coffee cup. 'Let's take an imaginary situation where a journalist – as often happens – wants to investigate events in Northern Ireland. Say, the work of the intelligence services or, perhaps, that one-time alleged shoot-to-kill policy – the RUC and army accused by certain parties of trying to force terrorists into fatal ambush situations rather than detain them and convict on *prima facie* evidence. He finds himself probing delicate matters and would, of course, receive only the most superficial co-operation from our public affairs people in Army HQ, Belfast.' He looked at her directly, the humour having vanished from his eyes. 'Is it right then that he should talk to the only ones who will answer his questions? Inevitably these are people with an axe to grind or grudges to bear. Does he then cobble together a story with only half the facts available and present it as the truth? And thereby put at risk agents in place whose only task is to destroy terrorism?'

'You mean name names?'

'Not necessarily, no. But to reveal organisational structures, the way in which things work – all information that can serve the enemy.'

Casey puffed out her cheeks. 'Well, if a journalist doesn't get

199

co-operation from the authorities, then I suppose he doesn't have much choice, does he? I mean he does have a job to do.'

Sir George's eyebrows met in a forbidding line as he frowned. 'But that's not very responsible, is it?' He waved his hand towards Harrison and Trenchard. 'It could put chaps like these at risk. ATOs like Tom, for instance. Surely the journalist could just go on to another story, could he not? Something a little less controversial.'

For a brief second she relived Seven Dials, remembered the shock of the blast. She felt suddenly awkward and momentarily tongue-tied, but she had no doubt about her view on the matter. 'Sir George, a journalist has a job to do. I believe that freedom of the press is more important than – than almost anything. Governments might say something is secret just because they know it's wrong, immoral or downright illegal. It's amazing what some governments consider secret. Without the press as a check and a balance, governments can drift into fascism and dictatorship. I'm sure Hitler, Mussolini and Stalin had very strong views about responsible reporting, don't you? Soldiers on the ground can find themselves acting illegally and it's no defence to say that they are just obeying orders.'

A smile drifted briefly across Harrison's face as he listened to her spirited defence of the media.

But Sir George's face had reddened. Casey noticed and added quickly, almost apologetically, 'But this is all very hypothetical.'

'No, Miss Mullins, it happens all the time.' It was noticeable that he had dropped the use of her first name. 'Every day so-called investigative writers, authors and TV reporters probe and dig, probe and dig with scant regard to the damage they do. It also happened with your own report yesterday, did it not? You attended a press conference at which the elected people's government gave its considered and responsible view of the current terrorist situation – which you chose to ignore.'

Casey felt a sudden rush of anger and indignation. 'Because it was a pack of lies.'

Sir George ignored her statement. 'Instead you made up your

own version of events using privileged information gained under false pretences. Not even an unattributable briefing.'

'Are you telling me what I printed was untrue?'

His eyes were bleak and washed of colour. 'I am saying it was irresponsible and certainly not in the national interest. And, like the journalist in my hypothetical case, when you received no official confirmation of the sending of a parcel bomb to a certain American senator, you proceeded to write a version that read as though it actually had happened.'

Casey turned to Harrison. He gave the appearance of being unconcerned, as though none of it had anything to do with him. When their eyes met briefly she could read nothing into their expression. She turned back to Sir George. 'I happened to be there at the time. I know a parcel bomb was *thought* to have been sent. If I'd been given a straight answer to my question – like it was a false alarm – then it wouldn't even have been mentioned in the article.'

Again Sir George appeared not to have heard. 'And for the life of me I cannot see what possessed you to name Major Harrison here.'

Casey shook her head, exasperated. 'It's hardly a state secret. Any Belfast journalist or competent defence correspondent can find that out.'

Sir George removed his napkin from his waistband and dabbed the coffee stains from the corners of his mouth. 'You realise that it sets the major and his family up as targets for the IRA? They will have to go into hiding and probably move house.'

That was something she did feel bad about and threw a sympathetic glance in Harrison's direction as she said: 'I know, I think it's awful, but we didn't indicate Tom's address. I'm not responsible for the excesses of the tabloids.'

'Ah, that word again. Responsible. It strikes me, Miss Mullins, that you do not consider yourself responsible for *any* of this fiasco. I am sure your editor would not take quite such an ambivalent view if I mention the problems that your reporting has caused when we meet tonight.'

The words were like an electric shock. 'You know him?'

The gentle smile had returned to his lips; he knew he'd got through. 'I know everyone, Casey. Your editor and I frequently bump into each other on the London social circuit. He even mentioned you to me recently, said what promise you had. His only regret was that you hadn't taken up British citizenship. You see, he is aware that, as a divorcee here on an American passport, you are liable to deportation if you break the law. Unlikely, of course, but it's so easy in your type of work to step over that thin line between what is legal and what is not. And England does have so many little arcane laws dating back to Tudor times. Never been taken off the Statute Book. I'm sure we all break the letter of the law every day without even knowing.'

Casey felt her stomach contract, too shocked to speak. It could hardly have been a more blatant threat.

She became aware that Sir George was still talking. '. . . Now that we understand each other, I'm sure we can establish a good working relationship. But remember what I said about responsibility. If you feel the need to do any probing or what-have-you, give me a ring and I'll give you all the help you need, steer you in the right direction. Don here will give you my direct line.' He leaned back in his chair, satisfied that he'd done an excellent demolition job. 'Just to make the point – much to my own personal amazement – Tom here has agreed to give you a personal but nonattributable briefing on the current situation. Proper channels, young lady, that's the thing to remember.'

With that he rose a little unsteadily to his feet. As he did so a waiter appeared at his side as though by magic, the old man's black Melton coat and walking cane in his hands.

'It was a lovely lunch, Casey, and you've been charming company. I like a lively discussion.' His handshake was dry and cool. 'Don't forget, call me any time.'

She watched as, supported by the waiter, the old man walked shakily towards the door. Then she fell back into her seat, feeling shell-shocked and drained. 'Wow!' she breathed, 'I think I've just blown my damehood.'

'Nonsense,' Trenchard laughed, 'he liked you.'

'Then I'd hate to be someone he doesn't.'

She made her excuses then and left for the ladies' room.

'Worked a treat,' Trenchard said. 'Sir George is a master at this sort of thing.'

'Poor girl was terrified at the end,' Harrison observed. 'Did you see the look in her eyes?'

'You're going soft, old son. She'll be like melted butter now, so it's all down to you.' He passed Sir George Pepperell's card across the table. 'Give her that, I'll make myself scarce now. Tell me how it went when you get back to my flat tonight.'

Don Trenchard had just disappeared through the door when Casey returned, looking a little more composed.

'Just *what* is Sir George, Tom? I mean, does he really have that sort of clout?'

'According to Don he's connected with the Defence Advisory Committee. Strictly speaking, that's Ministry of Defence, but in fact it can be used to cover most things not deemed to be in the national interest. By all accounts he's not a man to cross.'

The waiter came with more coffee. 'So you *hadn't* really forgiven me for yesterday? Or for gatecrashing the funeral?'

He looked abashed. 'Look, I've just been following instructions. I didn't know it was going to be like this, I'm sorry. So let's put all that behind us and start with a clean slate.'

'What did you have in mind exactly?'

'Are you free for the rest of the afternoon?'

She hesitated. 'I can be, if I can make a couple of telephone calls.'

He grinned. 'So, in the words of a certain nameless tabloid, let me take you into the mysterious world of the tick tock man.'

A Defence Ministry car was waiting outside Boodles when they left. The chauffeur unhurriedly negotiated his way through the traffic to Oxford Street, then north up Gloucester Place before picking up the Marylebone Road and the M40 westwards out of London. The traffic was light as they sped along the motorway, finally turning off at Junction 6 and making their way across country towards Oxford.

The entrance to Vauxhall Barracks, headquarters of 11 EOD Regiment RLC, was through a pair of unmarked security gates. She was mildly surprised to find that they were checked in by an armed soldier in helmet and full combat gear. The signal board on the guardhouse explained why. State of Alert: Bikini Amber.

'You're very privileged, Casey. Few journalists are given permission to come here.'

A short drive through tree-studded lawns brought them to the car park and the boxy redbrick headquarters building. From then on, the afternoon floated by in a bewildering haze, her mind filled with facts and statistics that she attempted to scribble in her notebook, an entire Pandora's box revealed to her. There were reconstructions, photographs and diagrams of every type of home-made bomb ever used: car bombs, culvert bombs, milk-churn bombs, beer-keg bombs, coffee-jar grenades, incendiaries and letter bombs. Memo Park timers from parking meters, electronic circuits, antihandling devices, they were all there and Harrison patiently explained the uses of each and the individual problems they presented to the ATO whose job it was to defuse them.

One particular weapon fascinated her with its clever incorporation of everyday household objects. The PRIG, in army jargon, Projected Recoilless Improvised Grenade, was a type of shoulder-launched bazooka capable of knocking out a lightly armoured vehicle with a warhead that mostly comprised a dog-food can filled with explosive. A plastic lampholder acted as the arming switch, and resistance for the backblast in the launcher tube was provided by two packets of digestive biscuits wrapped in kitchen J-cloths.

But it was the heavyweights that truly amazed her. The spigot mortars and the 'barrack-busters'. They truly defied the misleading description of 'home-made'. Amateur only in their ingenious improvisation, these were the business, precision-built and lethal. And there were plenty of wall-mounted photographs to bear witness to their awesome power. Entire town centres destroyed in Ulster, gutted and flattened, and craters in roads so massive they looked as though they'd been created by small meteors.

Harrison said quietly: 'You must realise that this is why Sir George was so hard on you. His fear is that this scale of damage could start happening here on the mainland.'

Next she was shown the UK operations room with large-scale wall maps that showed the locations of the ten army disposal teams and their fourteen backup units which were on short-term standby.

'We cover the whole country except London,' he explained. 'Even then we're available if requested.'

Outside she was taken to a large garage where some of the teams' white Transits were housed. Welcoming the diversion of a pretty red-headed American visitor, nothing was too much trouble for the WO2 and his crew. The men happily demonstrated their skills with the robotic Wheelbarrow and other equipment.

'What's that?' she asked.

'A bombsuit, miss,' the WO2 replied. 'Like to try it on?'

She looked at Harrison, her eyes dancing with mischief. 'I can't, can I? I'm hardly dressed for it.'

'Go on, miss,' one of the corporals urged and earned a disapproving scowl from his commander.

'Turn around then, and no peeking!' she laughed.

And when they turned back the floral dress had been tucked up inside the legs of her knickers like a schoolgirl in a playground. 'I haven't done this since I was seven.'

There was no shortage of willing hands to strap her into the heavy suit, her long tanned limbs swallowed up by the enormous leggings and the armoured jacket, then finally sealed with the claustrophobic helmet.

She and Harrison were still laughing about it as the chauffeured car sped back towards London in the early evening.

'I can't tell you how much I appreciated that, Tom.'

'A pleasure, you made the men's day.'

'I wanna be a bomb man.'

'You can't.'

'Oh, all right then.' She glanced out the window at the lush Oxfordshire countryside passing in a blur. 'All this makes me feel awful. You know – what Sir George was saying about you having to move house. Is that really true?'

'Yes, but it was going to happen anyway.'

'Really?'

He nodded. 'My wife and I are separating.' The words were out almost before he realised. Since Pippa's father had told him about her affair, he'd had little time to consider his own reaction. He'd been too tired, too busy. But then perhaps he didn't really need to think about it. The writing had been large on the wall for a long time, he just hadn't wanted to see it. It wasn't Pippa's adultery; he'd been no saint himself. They had just grown apart, it was as simple as that.

His only real regret was the anguish that their separation might cause his son. But then Archie was a tough little character.

'I'm sorry, Tom,' Casey said.

'Thanks, but it just stopped working out, that's all.'

'It must be catching. And it's not much fun. I hate sitting in every evening eating TV suppers.'

'What about your daughter, Candy?'

'The same house but a different planet. You know, all Walkmans or pop videos.' She looked at him and smiled. 'You won't be going home, not with the press waiting for you?'

'They'll have given up, I expect. Gone on to someone else. Anyway, I've moved in with Don.'

'You like him?'

'We've known each other a long time. He's a good mate.'

'Good-looking.'

'An eye for the ladies.'

'I noticed.'

On impulse, he said: 'About that TV supper.'

'Yes?'

'How about giving it a miss tonight.'

'The thing is, Casey, although what you wrote about me being called in from Belfast wasn't *incorrect*, it was only half the story.'

They were seated in a quiet Italian restaurant off Haymarket. 'What do you mean?'

Harrison said: 'The statement issued at the conference was also correct in so far as it went. I've been given permission to give you the full story – but it must be unattributable. I'm getting far too much publicity for a humble bomb man.'

She was curious. 'Why now and why me?'

He toyed with his wine glass. 'Now, because this is a very serious bombing campaign which shows no signs of letting up and the public should know that the Provisionals aren't having it all their own way.' He held her gaze with steady brown eyes. 'And you, because I think you can be trusted.'

She wasn't sure she believed that. 'I thought I was in the doghouse, especially with you.'

'I overreacted after the funeral. I was still angry after Jock's death and I thought you were like the rest of the gutter press. On reflection, I realise why you didn't advertise what you did for a living. Besides, I've since read the articles you've written. They were very compassionate, very touching. And, according to Sir George, you've virtually become accepted as Fleet Street's expert on this new campaign.' He raised his hands, palms out. 'So we thought it wouldn't hurt for you to understand more about what we do – hence the visit to our HQ.'

'And now?'

From outside came the plaintive wail of a police-car siren carrying eerily on the night air.

'You should know that the terrorists haven't been quite as successful as people think. We're receiving some excellent pre-emptive intelligence at the moment. That gives us a good idea of when and how the bombers are going to strike, if not exactly where. That means that 11 EOD on the mainland, as well as the various police Explosives Sections, are ready and waiting on instant standby. So when PIRA gives its usual warning, lately down to thirty minutes, which is hopelessly inadequate for evacuating an area, the bomb-disposal teams are in there like a shot. Device defused, panic over.' He hesitated as though deciding how much more he should say. 'You remember the van bomb at the

Chiswick flyover and the three hoaxes the other day? Well those hoaxes were in fact the real thing.'

'Why wasn't that admitted at the press conference?'

'To keep the enemy guessing, unsettle them and get them wondering what game we're playing. As you know, the Security Service, or MI5, is in overall charge of anti-terrorist activity. They have their own agenda of psychological warfare.'

'Is that the sort of thing that Don Trenchard does?'

Harrison was astounded at her perception; she'd only met him twice. 'What makes you think that?'

'I could just imagine him, that's all. He's so smooth.'

'Well, what Don does for a living is a mystery to everyone, including himself half the time. Always has been. But the point is that the IRA has been adopting a new combination of tricky antihandling devices. Difficult for us, but not quite difficult enough. Because the truth is we're right on top of them.'

'Are you quite happy for me to publish that?' She shook her head in amazement. 'I mean after that lecture I got from Sir George this afternoon. Is it really something you'd want the bombers to know?'

'It doesn't matter. When an ATO or one of London's Expos is tasked to a device he can never be sure what he is going to find. And over the years, each one of us has come across every variation imaginable. You can never double-guess a bomber. You can never take anything for granted. All I'm telling you is, at this stage of this particular campaign, we've mastered AIDAN's antihandling techniques and we're getting them defused well within the warning times . . .' His voice trailed off.

'What is it?' she asked, turning round in her seat to see what he was looking at.

The waiter had been standing on the pavement by the open door, his outline intermittently edged in blue light from a police car in Haymarket. Now he had been joined by the restaurant owner and one of the chefs; they were talking to a passer-by.

'Something's going on,' Harrison observed. They had both become aware of the sinister background howl of sirens above the low rumble of the city's traffic.

The chef turned back towards his kitchen, dessert orders to attend to. His expression was glum as he wiped his hands on his apron.

Casey called him as he passed. 'Excuse me, do you know what's happening?'

He shook his head sadly. 'There is a bomb warning fifteen minutes ago. The Trocadero centre in Piccadilly.' The Italian looked gloomily around the empty bistro. 'Look, tonight only you and one other couple. Another bomb alert. I do not think you will be coming back tomorrow, eh? Even for my famous *castagnaccio*?'

They all heard it then. A distant low thud. There was no mistaking the sound. The chef raised his eyes to the heavens and crossed himself.

11

Memories of Seven Dials flashed through Casey's mind. When she spoke, a slight quake had entered her voice. 'Is that it, Tom, the Trocadero?'

He shook his head, eyes narrowing as he calmly appraised the direction and volume of the sound. 'No, too far away for that. A smallish device. Just a few pounds, I'd say.'

'You can tell?' This man really was amazing, she thought.

'I've heard enough of them in my time.'

Then there was another, similar sound. But, although much farther away this time, its deep bass resonance was profoundly more chilling and ominous.

Harrison called for the bill. 'Casey, I need to find out what's going on.'

As he spoke there were two more explosions, almost simultaneous. One was much closer, causing the windows of the bistro to shake and the coffee cups to rattle on their table.

'Jeez!' Casey gasped, instinctively reaching for his hand as though his mere presence could in some way protect her.

'It's okay,' he reassured and, as she released her grip, she realised that her nails had been digging deep into his flesh. 'Do you want to wait here until I get back?'

She managed to regain some composure and forced a smile. 'C'mon, Tom, what d'you take me for? Am I an intrepid reporter or what?' A nervous half-laugh followed. 'Besides, I'd feel safer with you.'

Harrison settled the bill and they stepped out into the street, walking the short distance to the junction with Haymarket. It was a bizarre and nightmarish scene. The wide roadway had been sealed off by police at the north end by Piccadilly, cutting off the one-way traffic flow and leaving the normally teaming thorough-fare uncannily empty of traffic. A cacophony of car horns filled the air like angry birdsong as the surrounding streets became clogged with anxious and bewildered motorists.

Beyond the taped cordon, Harrison could see that two Explosives Section Range-Rovers had established an ICP. Flickering neon advertisements continued mindlessly on, the dark buildings bathed in the revolving sweeps of purple light from the emergency vehicles.

As they approached the cordon Harrison flashed his security pass at the young constable. 'And the lady's with me. Who's in charge here?'

'The Senior Expo, sir. Over there.'

Al Pritchard was standing by the open door of the leading Range-Rover, talking into the radio mike. Perspiration glittered on his balding crown and his eyes were dark-rimmed with fatigue. He caught sight of Harrison and lifted a hand in weary acknowledgment.

He continued talking for a few more moments before signing off. 'You a bloody clairvoyant, Tom? You're right in the thick of it.'

'Just happened to be passing, Al. So what's going on?'

'You tell me. Les Appleyard's in the Trocadero – a half-hour warning. Then fifteen minutes in, a device went off without warning at Oxford Circus, apparently concealed in a lamppost. Just after that there were three others – again, all in lampposts. On Piccadilly near Hyde Park Corner, at Leicester Square, then Cambridge Circus. All small but they caused some injury and damage – and total chaos!'

Harrison knew exactly what he meant. In the very heart of London, it was an area surrounded by a maze of streets. Thousands of people would be running in all directions from the smaller devices only to come up against crowds of pedestrians being evacuated from the original threat at the Trocadero.

Casey listened, horrified. It sounded as though the whole of central London had been surrounded with explosive devices. 'It's just like Seven Dials, but on a massive scale,' she murmured aloud to herself.

Pritchard noticed her for the first time. 'Who's the lady, Tom?'

'Casey Mullins from the *Standard*,' Harrison replied, expecting to feel the full power of Pritchard's wrath.

Only when the man said in a reasonable tone, 'Sorry, Tom, no press tonight, please,' he remembered that Trenchard had told the Senior Expo that she was being cultivated for public relations purposes.

But Harrison had been struck by Casey's words. Just like Seven Dials. 'Al, have all the manhole covers around here been checked?'

Pritchard clearly took the question as a challenge to his competence. 'Of course. And wastebins, postboxes, the works. There's no way I'm going to allow the police to let us walk into another Seven Dials.' Haymarket, the only traffic-free route out of the area, was now filling with hundreds of walkers evacuated from all around the West End. 'Look, Tom, by all means stay with us. But first take the lady away, there's a good chap. You'll probably find traffic's still moving in The Mall. Put her in a taxi and send her home.'

At that point Les Appleyard appeared from the Trocadero centre, carrying his bomb helmet under one arm and trailing a disrupter from his other hand. He crossed the eerily deserted street and approached the cordon. 'You're going to love this, Al. The bomb was an elaborate phoney. Fully working TPU with a trembler, but the Semtex was dummy material.'

'Christ!' Pritchard spat. 'They're just playing silly buggers with us.'

Appleyard sniffed heavily and wiped the film of sweat from his forehead as he viewed the tide of anxious humanity filling the Haymarket. 'They're trying to terrorise the city, Al, it's as simple as that.'

'And they're bloody well succeeding,' Pritchard growled. Then he noticed Harrison again, which did nothing to improve his humour. 'Are you still here?'

Harrison raised a hand in mock surrender. 'Okay, Al, we're leaving.'

Casey clutched at his arm. 'I can't, Tom, not down there.'

'Haymarket, whyever not? That's the way everyone's going.'

'No, Tom,' she said adamantly. 'It's just like Seven Dials. The street Candy and I took was the only one left to take and that's where the car bomb was that killed Jock.' She was close to tears. 'I just can't go.'

Pritchard watched her outburst with a curious expression on his face, as though he'd just swallowed something unpleasant. He said: 'We're off to have a look at those other devices. When you're ready, Tom, phone the office to find out where we are.'

Harrison steered the reluctant Casey back through the cordon as the engines of the Range-Rovers were gunned into life. He began to realise the hidden emotional scars that Seven Dials had left in her mind and his heart went out to her.

'I'm sorry, I was being silly,' Casey said as they began to be jostled along by the fast-moving welter of evacuees. 'Guess we can't spend the whole night sitting on the pavement . . .'

But conversation had become impossible. A party of Japanese tourists had engulfed them, jabbering excitedly as they attempted to keep up with their guide. The group collided with a collection of French students carrying rucksacks, emerging from Panton Street. Refugees from a Leicester Square cinema première were caught up in the swelling crowd, men looking incongruously exotic in tuxedos and black ties, glamorous escorts clinging to their arms. Momentarily Harrison thought he recognised a film star, but then the famous face disappeared amid a bobbing sea of heads which had now filled the entire width of Haymarket.

Up ahead, the crush of humanity was parting like a river around a lone and stationary police car which pointed into the crowd, its blue lights pulsing energetically. The driver and his colleague were struggling to open the doors against the flow. A helmeted constable was shouting at them from the pavement beside a parked car.

The momentum of the tide was becoming stronger, the pressure pushing in from all sides, threatening to sweep Harrison and Casey from their feet. They moved all the faster to avoid being overtaken by the weight of people behind them. Harrison saw one of the Japanese women crushed against a traffic bollard in the middle of the street. There was nothing he could do for her as she disappeared beneath thousands of running feet.

Casey clutched his arm tighter, terrified that she'd be torn from him. She gasped for breath, aware that the oxygen was being squeezed from the night air, becoming hotter by the second. Claustrophobic and starting to panic. Feeling faint and certain she would have fallen had it not been for Harrison at her side.

She suddenly became aware of stifled screams as people sank and drowned in the relentless ebb, and twice she stumbled on something soft under foot. A child, a woman? It was impossible to tell as they were carried inexorably on.

'BOMB!' yelled the constable on the pavement.

The two policemen, who had now managed to extricate themselves from their patrol car, looked at each other and then at the surrounding crowd. The ashen faces of the officers said it all. There was no way they could halt the overwhelming scrum of people bearing down on them.

Harrison managed to fight his way sideways, dragging Casey with him, until he was able to reach the wing of the patrol car. He clung to it like a man escaping the force of wild rapids.

'Get away, sir!' shouted the nearest policeman.

'I'm with the Explosives Section,' Harrison yelled back. 'What's the problem?'

The policeman's jaw dropped with incredulity. 'You are, sir?'

'Yes, dammit, what's the problem?'

As relief replaced his astonishment, the officer said: 'My mate reckons he's found a bomb in this parked car. Looks to me like he could be right.'

Harrison worked his way between the two vehicles and peered into the window of the parked Renault. In the footwell, half hidden by the seat was a small plywood box. Thin twin-core cable could be glimpsed at the edge of the rear carpet, disappearing towards the boot.

He turned to the police driver. 'Have you got a toolbox in the car?'

'Er-yes, of course.'

'Let me have it. I suggest you call up reinforcements to get this

214

area cleared and get a Section team down here pronto.' The driver nodded, reaching for the boot and the toolbox.

While waiting for backup manpower, the three policemen faced an impossible task, but they wasted no time in doing their best. With the radio messages sent, the driver proceeded to inch the car forward into the crowd, the doors wide open with an officer on each side to form a slow-moving wedge. If they could reach the first intersection with Charles II Street, they would stand a chance of diverting the endless procession of evacuees to safety.

'PLEASE STAND STILL!' the driver begged over the loud-speaker. 'PLEASE STAND STILL AND LET US PASS!'

If they could halt the flow, then they stood a chance of reversing it. But, of course, it was hopeless because of the pressure of new arrivals pushing in from the very streets up which the police now wanted them to return. Still people were streaming past the car bomb.

Harrison turned to Casey. 'Get away from here as quickly as you can. Go home and I'll be in touch later.'

She shook her head. 'I want to help.'

His anger suddenly flared. 'For God's sake, Casey, this thing could blow up at any moment. There's nothing you can do. I'm sorry, I don't have time to argue!'

Then he forced himself to turn away, stooping to open the toolbox and examine its contents for anything of use. Mostly spanners of different sizes. Hopeless! He continued rummaging. A torch – handy. What else? Thank God for that, a pair of wire-snippers. And a roll of insulating tape. What he really needed was a specialist spring-loaded centrepunch for such a delicate operation. And what did he have available? A sodding great wheel brace!

He straightened his back and looked along Haymarket towards Piccadilly. The patrol car had reached the intersection and was having some success in diverting the tide of evacuees. Now he focused his attention on the Renault, blotting out his awareness of the steady trickle of pedestrians still passing just a few feet away.

Cars and derelicts, he thought suddenly. It was years now since he'd personally had to deal with either. And he had believed he would never have to again. Inside this vehicle, anything could be waiting for him. This was AIDAN. Nothing might be what it seemed. Or it could all be an elaborate hoax.

Casey's words seemed to be echoing around his skull. Just like Seven Dials. A car, just like this, had faced Jock Murray less than two weeks ago. Now it was his turn.

He shone the torch into the dim interior, playing the beam across the roof until he found the courtesy light. Yes, there it was. The opaque plastic cover and the bulb removed, a thin wire trailing down towards the TPU. Any attempt to open the doors and, instead of lighting the interior, the current would pass through to fire the main charge prematurely.

Silently he cursed Al Pritchard for not keeping a Wheelbarrow always to hand. How he wished to God he had his Belfast wizards Heathcote and Corporal Clarke with him now. They'd be in and out in two minutes flat, crack open the boot and in with the Candle cluster charge. All over and let's go home.

Sweat gathered around his collar. He moved the torch beam towards the dashboard, looking for what had killed Jock Murray. And there it was. An innocuous black plastic module, a flex trailing to the cigar lighter. The same setup that had killed Jock the moment his hand went in through the broken window.

Some thoughtful bastard had taped over the tell-tale red glow of the tiny LED bulb. Was that how Jock had come to miss it? The tape also obscured the maker's name which may have offered a clue as to what activated it.

If it was passive infrared, detecting body heat, he might get away with it. But if it was ultrasonic then he wasn't at all sure. The mere change of air pressure when opening the door would be sufficient to trigger it.

He drew back, stripped off his jacket, then edged around to the front of the car. Placing one foot on the fender, he gingerly levered himself up onto the bonnet, feeling the suspension sinking under his weight.

He stiffened, shutting his eyes for a second, but still seeing the image of the mercury tilt switch behind his closed lids.

The shock-absorbers had steadied now and he breathed again. Twisting into a sitting position, he ripped out a length of insulating tape, cut it with his pocket knife and stuck it across the windscreen. Two minutes later the glass was crisscrossed with the stuff. He had absolutely no way of knowing if the movement of a falling segment could trigger the alarm sensor, or how great a change in air pressure would do the same job. Trying to cover both possibilities, he spread his jacket over the windscreen before picking up the wheel brace.

Finally he looked back up the street, praying for a sign that Al Pritchard had returned. That the awful decision had been taken from him. All he could see was the police car, still at the junction with Charles II Street and now having staunched the flow of pedestrians. But he was aware that he must act quickly while the street was clear. At any moment more people could break through the cordon in panic and find themselves walking straight towards the car bomb.

Weighing the brace in his hand, he lifted it and struck once, hard, just above the dash, his eyes closing in reflex as he did so. Nothing happened, the screen chipped but intact. He tried again, applying more force. The glass gave with a mushy crackling sound, frosting instantly.

Slowly, very slowly, he pulled away his jacket from the whitened screen and began to breathe again. It had all held together. Inside, hopefully, the air pressure had remained constant.

He reached forward and, with extreme care, began picking away at the trillions of clustered white diamonds. Just a small hole, that was all he wanted. Above the dash, behind the alarm module. Small enough not to cause a dramatic shift in pressure, big enough to insert the nose of the wire-cutters.

Blood was beginning to trickle from his unprotected fingers and it was seeming to take for ever as, in his mind's eye, he could visualise the face of the Memo Park timer as it edged towards zero . . .

Then he was through, a tiny aperture cleared behind the alarm. But now he must be exceedingly careful. Normally cutting the power supply could be expected to activate the relay and cause

217

the current to flow through the alarm circuit. He squinted through the hole until he was able to identify the actual alarm leads. Inch by inch, he edged in the clippers until he found purchase on the flex. Snip, so simple. And nothing happened. Then he was safe to move onto the lead that fed to the power supply from the cigarette lighter.

Another snip. He'd done it, hardly believing his own good fortune. Luck was certainly a lady tonight. At least so far.

Quickly he swivelled round on his buttocks, lifted his feet and kicked in the windscreen, the glass caving into the interior in great flexible chunks. He followed through, squeezing in over the dash until his feet landed on the front passenger seat. Turning awkwardly, he bent down to the TPU. The small plywood box was half hidden and there was a strong natural impulse to pull it clearly into view. But it could be fitted with a tilt switch, a trembler or even a pressure plate for all he knew. Instead he climbed over into the rear section wriggling between the bulky headrests.

Landing upside down in an ungainly heap, he struggled to right himself, his heart freezing each time he felt the suspension dip.

It was hot work, the car seeming airless and his legs cramping up on him as he crouched on the floor in the narrow gap behind the front seats. At last he traced the flex from the TPU that led through to the explosives in the boot. One careful halfway cut, insulating the end; then a second finally to separate the bomb from its timing and power unit.

And it was done.

His shirt was now sodden with perspiration, his face dripping and his eyes stinging with salt. He reached, exhausted, for the courtesy light and stripped away the booby-trap flex before throwing open the rear door. Feeling near collapse he just lay in the confined space, gulping down great draughts of cool night air, his eyes closed in a very private moment of ecstatic relief.

'Well, if it isn't our intrepid tick tock man,' Appleyard said.

Harrison opened his eyes. His friend was standing, grinning, Al Pritchard behind him.

'And just what the hell are you doing?' the Senior Expo thundered.

218

'Lending a hand,' Harrison replied, struggling out from his squashed position. He could see now that more police reinforcements had arrived to control the crowds.

'And how would it have looked if you'd blown yourself up, Tom?' Pritchard's voice was quavering with suppressed anger. 'You're not on our payroll, you've got no equipment, you're just a bloody adviser.' He indicated the curious faces of a few passersby who were now coming past, just as Harrison had feared. 'How many of these people would you have killed if you'd set the damn thing off?'

Harrison brushed himself down and picked up his jacket from the bonnet, too tired to argue. 'I made the best decision I could at the time, Al. Sorry if that upsets your sensibilities.'

'I want you off the Section.'

It had been a long day and frankly he was past caring. 'Then put in an official request, Al, it's your prerogative. We'll only know whether or not my decision was right when you examine the TPU. I haven't touched it in case our friend AIDAN attached something nasty. And I'd use a barrow to open that boot if I were you.'

'Thank you for that treasured advice,' Pritchard replied stiffly.

As Harrison moved away, Les Appleyard climbed into the car for a better look at the TPU.

Casey appeared with one of the police officers from the patrol car; they were both laughing, the Haymarket now fully cordoned off, the street clear of civilians.

She rushed towards Tom and threw her arms around his neck. Her cheeks were warm and damp with tears of relief, but she was too overcome to find the words she wanted.

'One lady returned safe and sound, sir,' the policeman said. 'Tried to make her go, but she insisted on helping. Thought we ought to make her a special constable.' He plonked his hat on her head.

She laughed, finding her voice. 'That's Americans for you, policemen of the new world order.'

Harrison didn't want to spoil her moment of glory, but there was still a risk until the boot of the Renault had been opened and cleared. 'Time to go home, Sheriff Mullins, let's get you a cab.'

219

As they began to walk, Appleyard called from the Renault. 'Thought you'd like to know, Tom, there were three minutes left on the timer.'

Al Pritchard glowered.

They eventually found a street where traffic was moving and hailed a taxi.

She gave the driver her address in Fulham before explaining: 'It's my new bachelor-girl pad. It's not much, a small flat, but it's home. I'm on an end with only one attachment.' She paused, aware she'd put it badly. 'Does that make me sound disabled?'

He laughed, already surprised at how easy he found it to relax in her company. 'Not disabled, just plain uncomfortable. I think you just mean your flat's in a semi.'

'Well, if it sounds uncomfortable, that's because it is. We only moved in yesterday. Still living out of boxes which all ended up in the wrong rooms. It was all such a rush really. I didn't have to leave the old place so quickly, but after Seven Dials I just didn't want to have anything more to do with my ex. You see, Randall could have picked up Candy before all those bombs went off. But he was just too busy. Busy, busy, busy.' She placed her hand on his arm. 'Why don't you come in for coffee? I might even be able to find the biscuits. We can have a Welcome-To-My-New-Home party.'

Somehow he couldn't face the idea of returning to Don Trenchard's flat and being quizzed on how the day with Casey had gone. If he left it until later, his friend would be asleep. 'I'd like that. But I'm not sure you can have a party with coffee and biscuits. Sort of contradiction in terms.'

'Not even if I wear my feather boa?'

In the event Casey found a bottle of cooking sherry to follow the coffee and biscuits. There was no music because all the cassettes and CDs were in Candy's bedroom and Candy was asleep. So they sat talking on the sofa, surrounded by tea chests and suitcases spilling open with Casey's clothes after her hunt for something suitable to wear that morning.

Two hours slipped by before either of them noticed as they exchanged life histories and light-hearted banter. There was something about her that lifted his spirits, just as it had at their first meeting and on the drive back from the funeral. Something that drew out his own dry and sometimes black military humour. When had he last laughed like that with Pippa? Perhaps he never had.

No further mention of the bombing campaign was made, he noticed, and he wondered if she was deliberately keeping off the subject. Perhaps she recognised his need to unwind and forget the tensions of the job.

He found himself watching her closely, transfixed by the expressive blue-green eyes as she delivered her quick one-line jokes that tripped off her tongue without a moment's thought. She had a wide, happy mouth with cute rabbity teeth, as she herself described them, a slightly turned-up nose and elfin chin. He liked her freckles and the wavy pale copper hair which she brushed absently with her hands or twirled between her fingers as she talked. Apart from mascara, she didn't wear make-up. Her clothes were smart and looked good, but they were unfussy and she wore no jewellery.

Unlike Pippa, Casey Mullins appeared to have little obvious vanity. And he knew for certain his wife would never have risked her life helping the police just a few yards from an unexploded bomb. But then why was he comparing her with Pippa? What was the point? His marriage was over in all but name. But then, he wondered as they talked, perhaps that was the point. It was time to look to the future.

'Oh, my God, is that the time?' Casey stared at her watch in disbelief. 'Gone two o'clock and I'm on the early shift.'

Harrison stood up. 'I am sorry, it was thoughtless of me, I didn't realise it was that late. I haven't enjoyed myself so much in ages.'

She looked up at him curiously, an uncertain smile on her lips. 'Hell, you know, like they say, time flies when you're having fun.'

He picked up his jacket from the sofa. 'Thanks for the party.'

'You're very English, Tom.'

'I'm sorry?'

'Very polite, very English.' She unfolded her long legs from underneath her and climbed to her feet. 'I mean it's not every man who takes a girl out for a romantic candlelit supper and ends up dismantling a bomb in the middle of the West End. That's some special kind of man. A quiet hero. I feel safe with you. There's no way you're going to jump on a girl and ravish her.'

His laugh was slightly uneasy, wondering if he detected a note of disappointment in her voice. 'We bomb men like to play a waiting game,' he joked, adding mischievously. 'As you know, we call it soak time.'

Her eyes were twinkling. 'Very appropriate.'

He indicated the phone. 'May I call a taxi? I can wait for it outside.'

'Sure.' She was very close now, watching as he punched in the numbers. 'You don't have to go.'

His eyes met hers, wide and misty with expectancy, and he felt her hand on his wrist. Slowly he lowered the receiver, aware of the discordant female voice on the other end, and dropped it onto the cradle.

The smell of her filled his head and her face filled his vision until he could see every pore in her skin, every freckle, and the whiteness of her teeth as he lowered his mouth onto hers. Her tongue was still sweet from the sherry, her breathing warm against his cheek as her nostrils flared and her arms went round his neck.

The kiss was long, hard and passionate. So long that he began to think he was drowning, aware only that he didn't want the moment to end, never wanted to come back to the surface.

When at last she pulled away, gasping for air and laughing as they found themselves back together on the sofa, she said: 'I think perhaps I got you wrong, Tom Harrison.' The smile faded on her lips and she looked closely into his eyes as though trying to fathom something she didn't quite understand. 'I mean it, I'd like you to stay. And I don't mean on the sofa.'

Yet it was to begin on the sofa, because the flame was lit and was burning fiercely. He could not remember ever wanting a woman the way he wanted Casey now. A woman who could combine intelligence, wit and desire in such a heady cocktail. Who now closed her eyes, trembling slightly, absorbing every minute sensation as he undid each button down the front of her summer dress.

A small gasp escaped her lips as she became aware of the cooling air on her skin and then the warmth of his mouth as it trailed across her right breast into the scented valley. Her lips parted, her eyes still tight shut, imagining the deft strong hands as they found the front fastener of her brassière. Those hands that, just hours before, had dismantled a bomb on a London street. Now those hands were slowly, surely dismantling her. She wondered if she would explode and the very thought sent a warm, moist sensation fizzling and bubbling between her legs.

They made love on the floor with just a dustsheet and a cushion on the bare boards. Their intimacy came with unexpected ease, the very spontaneity of their actions intoxicating as they urged each other on in hoarse whispers between snatched gasps of breath. He was stirred by her candour, her determination to satisfy both their needs with inventive and lustful lovemaking that had her acting out the whore with unabashed relish, moaning with pleasure as he invaded her. She arched her back against the floor, the skin of her belly drum-tight and her ribs high as her arms reached above her head in abandon. Her hair splashed onto the cushion as her head twisted from side to side, her breasts trembled under the unrelenting rhythm. Then she was gasping, begging for release from the exquisite torture as she hovered on the brink.

Her mouth opened in a silent cry, her lips forming around the unspoken words. Fuck me, fuck me. Yes, yes.

Never had he found such a hushed plea so erotic, an aphrodisiac that so spurred him on. Plunging deeper and without let-up, on and on until he saw the perspiration start to glisten between her breasts, gathering droplets forming like a tiny dew pond, the dampness trickling down across her abdomen to where their bodies touched. The wet slap of flesh against flesh, animal and exciting. Then the small fist tightening in his groin, the involuntary contraction of his balls and the sudden blessed relief. His own gut-wrenching cry mingling with hers, Casey's knees coming up high around his sides, squeezing into his flanks as she was carried on the wave.

Her knees dropped, her legs open and languid, his head against her breasts, the tension ebbing away like a turning tide, her hand running gently over his hair.

She said softly, slowly: 'Thank you for dialling my number, Tom. I must go to sleep now because I think it's just possible I'm in love. And being in love makes me very tired.'

He moved to one side, feeling himself slide gently, reluctantly from her body. Her face immobile, tranquil as though already asleep except for the gentle smile of satisfaction on her lips. Looking down at her, he couldn't find the words he wanted. It was like no time he had ever had with Pippa, but it sounded like a betrayal to say so. And he was afraid that it would have sounded crass to mention it. Instead he said, quietly: 'Sweet dreams.'

It would have been a magical end to a trying day had Casey's telephone not begun to ring. She stirred and sat up, pulling a dustsheet around her shoulders as she reached to answer it.

'Hello, Casey Mullins.' Her eyes widened, taken aback as she listened before turning to him. 'It's your friend Don. He wants to speak to you.'

Harrison's own surprise had turned to irritation even before he took the receiver. 'Don? Why the hell are you phoning at this time – and where the hell did you get the number?'

Trenchard's voice was brisk. 'Don't ask, Tom. I just guessed you might still be with her. I heard what happened in the Haymarket . . .'

'That can wait till we meet,' Harrison snapped.

'Did you see the newsflash on the television?'

Casey's set sat in the corner, not yet plugged in since the move. 'No, I didn't.'

'Then you don't know?'

'What, for Christ's sake?' Irritation turning to anger.

'That car you cleared. It blew up at the police station compound. They reckon there was a separate bomb built into a false exhaust pipe. Two coppers died and seven were injured.'

Harrison stared at the blank wall. Cars and derelicts. The old nightmare was coming back to haunt him.

12

The Home Secretary wore the benign expression of the schoolroom swot. The goody-goody teacher's pet who made head prefect before going on to Oxford and being called to the Bar. No doubt he'd have made judge if naked ambition for power hadn't side-tracked him into politics. Despite the horn-rimmed spectacles, he retained a youthful face that belied his years. His carefully cultivated reputation was one of fairness and approachability.

Nevertheless, Harrison felt less than comfortable standing before the minister's vast desk in the elegant, old office of state with its smell of beeswax and leather. He might have been more at ease if Al Pritchard and Jim Maitland of the Anti-Terrorist Branch had not been standing at his side.

And it didn't help that he'd had an argumentative meeting with Pippa at her father's house the night before. It had ended with young Archie in tears. Harrison realised in retrospect that he shouldn't have gone. Suddenly he didn't feel he could trust his own judgment any more. At least professionally, he hoped he still knew what he was doing.

It was two days now since the bomb in Haymarket and twenty-four hours since Casey Mullins's latest article had appeared in the *Evening Standard* to reassure Londoners that the bomb-disposal experts were beating the terrorists. How many readers believed her didn't really matter as Don Trenchard had pointed out. What was important was that the AIDAN active service unit believed it, and on that question only time would tell.

'Please take a seat, gentlemen,' the Home Secretary invited. His tone was humble, almost apologetic. 'You will appreciate that this is a very trying period and I thank you all for finding the time to put together proposals when I have no doubt that you are at full stretch.' He looked directly at the Senior Explosives Officer. 'Mr Pritchard in particular I thank for allowing our colleague Major Harrison to examine the *modus operandi* of his Section. However much I assure you to the contrary, I expect such action will inevitably be seen as a lack of confidence by Her Majesty's Government. That, however, I promise you, is not the case. But events in the last few days vindicate our decision to bring in a little recent Northern Ireland experience to the capital. I'm sure you'd agree?'

Al Pritchard's face was grimly impassive. He could barely bring himself to nod his acknowledgment, let alone force out the required response between clenched teeth.

'Yes, Minister.'

'I'm glad you see it our way.' He leaned forward, elbows on the desk and his chin cupped in his hands. A deliberately informal gesture to put them at their ease. 'So, Major Harrison, if we were to give you carte blanche, so to speak, what steps would you take to protect this fair city?'

Harrison cleared his throat and glanced at the notes on his lap. 'First, Minister, what I have to say is in no way critical of the Section or the way that it's been run.' That wasn't strictly true, but he wasn't looking to make a lifelong enemy of Pritchard. 'Secondly, I am fully aware of the political importance of not having London appear to have become as fraught as Belfast or Londonderry. After all, that is the reason the Section has maintained a low profile, although that has necessarily meant increasing the risk factor to its personnel in some instances. This approach has worked well, mostly, until now. But it has resulted in underfunding, which is again understandable given the demands for resources in other areas of policing. It has also resulted in a decline in expertise on the technical front.'

He was aware of the rasp of indignation under Pritchard's breath.

The Home Secretary raised his famous quizzical eyebrow. 'That's very blunt of you, Major. How do you mean?'

'As I'm sure you know, sir, in Northern Ireland we use the robot

226

Wheelbarrow for most jobs. Three types actually. The standard Mark 13, a new small version called Buckeye for high-rises or confined spaces and the big Attack Barrow specifically designed to tackle car bombs. With sufficient warning, in the city centres we can usually deal with any device in between two and three minutes of arriving on scene. The method's efficient and it's saved a lot of lives and property.'

The minister turned to Pritchard. 'I understand you, too, have these robots?'

'Yes, sir, the standard versions and not the very latest mark. But we do have call on army backup from 621 Squadron at Northolt.'

Harrison said: 'The point is that Northolt is thirty minutes' travel time to central London. And the Section's robots are kept in reserve and are rarely taken on a task. That inevitably means that the Expos become rusty as operators and the machines themselves fall into disrepair. Again funding plays a part. In normal times, this might not present a serious problem, but these are not normal times. Particularly in view of the renewed use of car bombs here on the mainland. And I'm given to understand that a long terrorist campaign is anticipated.'

The Home Secretary nodded his agreement. 'So what would you recommend? That the Explosives Section deploys its robots more frequently?'

'No, sir, it's too late for that. It would take months of practice for the Expos to reach what I would consider acceptable levels of efficiency and we don't have the time. My recommendation is that we bring out three top teams from the Province with their equipment, including the big Attack Barrows. Under less pressing circumstances I'd suggest we reinforce from 11 EOD here on the mainland – they have operators with recent Ulster experience. But complete teams from 321 have a wealth of special kit and are bang up to date. These should be stationed with the Section for the duration of the emergency to operate alongside Mr Pritchard's officers. I've taken the liberty of checking with my Chief ATO, Colonel Lloyd-Williams, and he concurs with my assessment.'

'Wouldn't that leave the Province itself vulnerable?' the minister asked.

Harrison shook his head. 'For the moment, the AIDAN team doesn't appear capable or inclined to operate in two places at once, which suggests they are a fairly small, independent unit. So, while they are on the mainland, that should be our main concern. We can draw on our other UK teams as replacements and step up Special-to-Theatre training. Meanwhile London would have the cream of our operators to combat the worst of the threats.'

The Home Secretary sighed deeply. 'The army on the streets of London, Major, it won't look good on the television news. There'll be a loss of confidence abroad and it will hit the tourist trade.'

'With respect, sir, I understand tourism has already suffered badly, and a limited army presence can't be worse than terrorists exploding bombs successfully.'

'I'm not sure the Prime Minister and my colleagues will altogether agree with you. It'll refocus attention on the whole Northern Ireland problem at a time when we're anxious to keep it out of the limelight.'

'It's your decision, sir, but I think the bombings are already doing that.'

The minister gave one of his enigmatic little smiles before turning to Pritchard. 'And what is the Section's view?'

'Such a move plays into the terrorists' hands in my opinion. It isn't the first time the Provos have tried to get us to overreact. We're coping well enough.'

'But are we, Mr Pritchard? You forget I get full reports on these bombings and it seems that you've had a fair degree of luck with the flyover bombs and Major Harrison's timely intervention in the Haymarket two nights ago.'

Pritchard wrinkled his nose. 'It's still the *army* on the London streets, Minister.'

Harrison said: 'We can spray our trucks white and wear civilian clothes – it needn't be obvious to the casual observer.'

The Home Secretary nodded thoughtfully, obviously recognising the advantages of the suggestion, before he addressed

Maitland. 'Chief Superintendent, you've been listening patiently. Your Section has one view and Major Harrison another, what do you think?'

Maitland was ever the diplomat. He said: 'I think, Minister, that London remains in acute peril and as yet we are not close to detecting this particular active service unit. Until we are, it might be expedient to take up Major Harrison's proposals, at least for a trial period, then review it as necessary. It is no less an extraordinary measure than those my commander wishes to take.'

'And they are?'

'To recall half of all previously serving Branch officers from the regions and deploy a massive covert force on the streets of central London as we did in the seventies. That, combined with vehicle spot checks with armed backup on all major routes into the capital.'

The minister frowned. 'To be honest, I think that more likely to alarm the public than army bomb-disposal teams on the streets. And, anyway, wouldn't such checkpoints be more cosmetic than effective?'

Maitland disagreed. 'You might be surprised, Minister, to know how few main arterial routes there really are into London. These can be monitored with relatively little manpower and checkpoints can be very effective if not publicly announced. We can also target the types of vehicles the terrorists are likely to be using for the transport of materials or for use as mobile bombs. In particular unmarked vans or trucks and stolen vehicles in general. Also, it has to be remembered that the amounts of home-made explosive required to be effective are quite enormous and an overloaded suspension is a big giveaway. That means we are putting the terrorists under great pressure. It might sound like hunting for a needle in a haystack, but we know the IRA will be coming into London regularly and we only need one lucky break. And that doesn't even have to mean an immediate arrest – a well-placed roadblock can be sufficient to persuade the terrorists to abandon a vehicle bomb and that's enough. There's little chance they'd return to a vehicle because the explosive's effective shelf life is little more than two weeks in total.'

To the Home Secretary it all made a horribly necessary kind of sense. 'I'll be having a meeting with the Prime Minister and the inner Cabinet tonight. If I get a general sanction then it'll get passed down officially through COBRA.' He rose to his feet. 'Thank you so much, gentlemen, for sharing your thoughts.'

Brief handshakes followed as the Home Secretary led them to the door. 'Would you mind waiting one moment, Major?'

Harrison turned, catching the scowl on Pritchard's face. His eyes said it all. Traitor, I told you so.

The door closed leaving the SATO alone with the minister. 'First, Major, I should like to thank you for your brave and selfless act the other night.'

For one perverse moment before he realised what the Home Secretary meant, the vision of Casey Mullins naked on the dustsheet in her new flat flashed into his mind. Of course, Haymarket. 'It was just good fortune I was there.'

Again the familiar raised eyebrow. 'In your position, I think I'd have considered it most *unfortunate*. Sitting on top of a bomb wouldn't be my idea of fun.'

'It's my job, sir.'

The minister looked at him closely. 'What is it with you people? The adrenalin fix, the challenge?'

Harrison felt uncomfortable under such scrutiny; he'd asked himself those questions a million times and still did not know the answer. It was a job he both loved and hated. One thing was certain, the longer you were in it the more profound your fear became. Felix. The deft cat with nine lives, and as you approached the next surprise package you had to wonder just how many you'd already used up?

The Home Secretary appeared to recognise suddenly that it had been an impudent question to ask. A sympathetic smile jerked at one corner of his mouth. 'Thank you anyway, Major.' He hesitated for a moment, as though uncertain how to proceed. 'The other reason I wanted a word was this business about the article in the *Evening Standard*. Suggesting that the bombers are clever, but not clever enough. That you're on top of the situation – because, as I told Mr Pritchard, I know that is not the case. A bit provocative, don't you think? Might it not persuade the terrorists to try for even more treacherous devices?'

Harrison said: 'I think that was the idea.'

The minister looked puzzled. 'You *think*? It was you who briefed the journalist, I believe.'

'Yes, on orders issued through MI5 and, I assumed, COBRA itself.'

'I see.' The calm eyes blinked behind the spectacles. 'Well, in fact, COBRA isn't always briefed on the minutiae of the anti-terrorist tactics used by the security agencies. My concern is that the more advanced technology the bombers use, then the more difficult it will be to counter the threat.'

It was difficult ground for Harrison to defend; he wasn't at all sure that he supported MI5's ploy. 'I believe the idea is to make the bombers get too clever for their own good.'

That eyebrow again. 'Own goals, is that it?'

'That's what's hoped. The policy has been used with some success in the past and it might give the police the leads they need to round up the AIDAN gang.'

The Home Secretary understood. 'But a dangerous gamble, don't you think? Whether or not it pays off, the bombs could become even more dangerous than they already are, isn't that so?'

'It's certainly possible.'

'So that was one of the reasons behind your recommendation for army help from Belfast.'

There was no need for Harrison to answer; the Home Secretary fully understood the risk involved.

Pat McGirl left the basement flat safe house in Slough and walked the half-mile to the lock-up garage where the stolen duplicate Sierra was kept.

Satisfied that he hadn't been followed, he drove towards the rented house near the Henley-on-Thames farm. After a circuitous route, he pulled in at a roadside telephone kiosk and rang to warn of his arrival in an hour's time. Five minutes later he passed the house, driving slowly round the surrounding streets looking for

231

anything out of place. Only then did he park in a lay-by from where he could observe the driveway.

During the following forty minutes he could detect nothing that suggested the house was under surveillance. Starting the engine, he drove back down the high-hedged residential road and turned into the gravel forecourt. By the time he reached the integral garage, the up-and-over door was already rising, allowing him to drive straight in. As he emerged from the car, the door was already lowering again, shutting out the daylight.

Clodagh Dougan stood silhouetted in the doorway to the kitchen. He noted her long black hair and the slender outline of her body, accentuated by the black denims and black turtleneck sweater. Then he saw the gun.

'You can put that away, Clodie. Don't want you shooting yourself in the foot.'

Her voice was quiet and assured. 'Don't patronise me, McGirl.'

He ignored her, brushing his way past into the kitchen, grinning into her face as he went. 'Where's the old man?'

Clodagh flipped on the safety and tucked the automatic in the waistband of her trousers. 'My father's asleep. He's had an exhausting time.'

McGirl regarded her closely. She was a handsome woman, he thought, slim but firm-bodied, and assertive. There was a challenge in the tone of her voice. Demanding respect for Hughie Dougan and daring him not to give it. She gave no indication of the fear usually found in those who worked under him and which he came to expect. Perversely he found himself smiling at her stand of defiance against his authority.

'I'd like a wee word with your da.' He felt oddly obliged to add: 'It is rather important.'

She held his gaze for a long moment, her dark eyes seeming to burn into his. It was as though she wanted to be sure he knew the score, accepted that no one pushed her or her father around. He knew Donny Fitzpatrick had been impressed by her and now he knew why. This was the woman who had avenged the man who she believed had betrayed her father. The woman who had calmly sat on the back seat of a car in County Sligo and opened her legs to that man. Who had brought down the hammer on his head as he had been lapping between her thighs. McGirl felt a twitch of life in his loins.

Clodagh said: 'I'll make some tea and wake him. He'll be parched.'

I'll do what you ask, but on my terms; he understood what she was telling him. 'I wouldn't say no to a cup myself.'

She glanced at him as she picked up the kettle and for a second he thought her expression had softened. That there might have been a hint of a smile on those lips.

He glanced round the kitchen as she prepared the china pot, the cups and saucers. The cupboard over the worktop was open, filled with half-a-dozen packets of essential groceries, nothing more. A few vegetables in the rack and, he guessed, a few cuts of meat in the fridge. There was no air of permanence; it was the larder of someone on a week's self-catering holiday.

Then he noticed the wheelchair in the corner. That had been Hughie's idea. To be a blind cripple pushed around in a wheelchair by his devoted daughter. Deliberately to draw attention and sympathy from neighbours and local shopkeepers, knowing full well that the sight of invalids made people feel uncomfortable and unlikely to ask too many questions. And if they did, there was a simple explanation: she and her father had returned to their original homeland having once emigrated to America. The old man had an incurable wasting disease and wanted to be on his own turf when he died, as he knew he soon would. That was why they just rented a house. A year, that was the most the doctors gave him.

People were embarrassed to ask more, and no one ever spoke to people in wheelchairs; it was as though they didn't exist. And if any local buck fancied his chances with the daughter, he would know better than to waste his time because clearly the old man could never be left alone.

McGirl had to admit they made the most unlikely pair of terrorists. He said: 'Anything unusual this week?'

She knew what he meant. 'A double-glazing salesman on Monday. I got his name and later phoned his company. He checked out.' She stirred the pot. 'Then a window-cleaner touting for business. He left a card and just a number. An answering machine so I can't be sure, but he seemed like the real thing.'

McGirl sympathised. 'Doesn't do much for the blood pressure.'

'And the local Methodist minister. I hadn't anticipated that. He was a real pain, the creepy do-gooder. Wanted to make sure the Social Services were giving us proper help. Offered to sit with Da if I wanted to go out of an evening. But the way he looked at me, I think he had something else in mind.'

I bet, McGirl thought. 'What did you say?'

'The truth, that we were staunch Catholics.'

McGirl chuckled.

The door opened. It was Hugh Dougan, his hair awry and his collarless shirt open at the throat. 'I heard voices.'

'It's Pat,' Clodagh replied. 'And there's a brew on.'

Five minutes later they were seated round the table, drinking tea and eating sweet biscuits. McGirl asked how the bomb-production operation was going. Dougan answered that it was going grand, all the TPUs and other devices for the next phase of the campaign were almost complete and would be collected by the unit's other members the following night and delivered to the nearby farm. There, two new van bombs would be fitted using the massive quantities of fertiliser and icing sugar that had now been refined. Other free-standing devices would also be assembled.

'About the new phase,' McGirl said, coming to the main purpose of his visit. 'I've heard from the Chief of Staff. He wants us to consider a change of tactics.'

Dougan blinked slowly. 'But it's all been agreed, planned for . . .'

McGirl took the newspaper from his pocket and unfolded it, spreading the pages across the table. 'Have you read this?'

Dougan took his half-moon reading glasses from his pocket. 'What's this?'

'Last night's *Evening Standard*. Quoting that bastard SATO

they've brought over from Belfast. Reckons they've got us sorted. Says these new devices are tricky, but they've got the upper hand.'

Dougan wiped the sleep from his eyes. 'That's bollocks.'

McGirl pulled a tight smile. 'He quotes the flyover bombs. Says they diffused three of them.'

'You don't believe that?' Clodagh demanded. 'Before, they claimed three were hoaxes.'

'How do I know what to believe, sweetheart? All I know is that, except for some restrictions at Chiswick, the rush-hour traffic still pours over them each morning . . .'

Dougan shrugged and sipped at his tea. 'So, you can't win them all. There was nothing wrong with Seven Dials and you know the chaos we caused in the West End. And the secondary on the Haymarket car.'

'We can't be complacent, Hughie. They've got the SATO over here now, maybe he's starting to make a difference. That's what the Chief of Staff thinks.'

The bomb maker slowly replaced his cup on its saucer; Clodagh watching him closely, keeping silent. 'This,' he said, tapping a forefinger on the newspaper, 'is crap. They're winding us up, trying to reassure the public. The bomb-disposal teams have got a bit lucky, that's all.'

McGirl helped himself to another biscuit. 'Then perhaps it's time they got a bit unlucky.' His teeth snapped into the digestive.

Clodagh could see her father's eyes narrowing, recognised the pulsing vein of anger in his temple. Gently she placed her hand on his wrist. 'Da, I think perhaps Pat has a point. There's the propaganda element to all this. They've said publicly that they've got us beat. We have to prove them wrong.'

Dougan sat back in his chair and sniffed heavily, saying nothing.

'Can you do it?' McGirl pressed.

'Of course he can,' Clodagh replied testily.

The bomb maker pursed his lips. 'It'll need some thought. I'll need some time.'

'How long?'

'A week.'

McGirl looked at Clodagh Dougan and smiled; her lips twitched momentarily before she averted her eyes from his.

'You've got it.'

Don Trenchard pulled over to the side of the road that ran parallel to the stony beach. It was bleak and windswept, just the distant figure of a man throwing driftwood for his mongrel dog at the water's edge.

Dull scudding cloud merged with the grey racing current of the North Channel, the horizon indistinguishable between the two. Only the ghostly outline of the Belfast-to-Douglas ferry, floating somewhere between sky and sea, gave any perspective to the distance.

In the passenger seat John Nash looked away from the beach to the neat pebbledashed bungalows with their trimmed hedges and wind-stunted cypresses, eucalyptus and acers. The heartland of respectable Protestant Ulster. Cultureless seaside suburbia with its net curtains, a healthy fear of God and an Orange Lodge hall in a community that had scarcely been touched by over twenty years of violence.

Trenchard wound down his window, allowing the salty air to gust in. 'Christ, John, a man could die of boredom here.'

Nash smiled, turning up the narrow collar of his leather bomber jacket. 'I can think of worse ways to die.'

'But not in a worse place.'

The MI5 man looked at the car clock. 'Will he show?'

'He'll show. They'll be watching us now, checking that no one is following. Another ten minutes, I'd guess.'

In fact it was nearer fifteen. On the beach the man with the dog had walked away before the pale blue Datsun approached from the opposite direction. It parked facing them, leaving a gap of some twenty-five metres. Two men, two blank faces indiscernible behind the gleam of the windscreen glass.

Nash drew the 9mm Browning from beneath his seat, held it low between his legs, and began to check the magazine.

236

'You won't need that,' Trenchard said tetchily. 'I'll go and speak to them. You come when I call.'

He opened the door, climbed out and slammed it shut. It was bracing, hardly summer weather. The wind buffeted him, tousling the tight gold curls of his head, dragging at his trousers.

The driver of the Datsun ran down his window.

'Hello, Spike,' Trenchard said. The muscular young man, who wore a denim jacket over his T-shirt, merely nodded and leaned back so that the Englishman could see his passenger. 'Hello, Billy.'

William Frederick Baker was huge, with the body of a heavyweight wrestler who had gone to seed. The rosebud mouth was too pink and too feminine for the flat bruiser's face with its broken nose. 'It's been a long time, Mr Smith. I was starting to think you'd deserted us.'

Trenchard ignored the jibe, but knew what he meant. In recent years the relationship between the Protestant paramilitaries and the security agencies had cooled, the RUC making its presence felt in the hard-line Loyalist ghettos, old favours forgotten on orders from Whitehall. The Anglo-Irish Agreement had started the rot and it had been downhill ever since.

'Fancy a stroll, Billy? I've someone I'd like you to meet.'

Spike gave his master an inquiring look, but the big man just shook his head dismissively and began struggling to extract his bulk from the confines of the seat.

The generously cut material of his fawn suit flapped around him as he made his way to the pavement, the wind snatching away his breath. Trenchard beckoned to Nash, then stepping down onto the shingle began walking slowly along at Baker's side.

As the MI5 man caught up with them, Trenchard said: 'Billy, I'd like you to meet my boss, Mr Jones. Mr Jones, this is King Billy. Billy Baker.'

They stopped walking and the two strangers shook hands, each taking stock of the other. Baker's huge grip was strong and prolonged as the lashless powder-blue eyes seemed to bore into

Nash's with the disturbing power of a hypnotist. He said: 'Mr Smith and Mr Jones. Not a comic double act, I trust?'

A joke, but there was no humour in it. Just letting them know that he knew the names didn't mean a thing. And that he was in no mood to be messed about.

Nash said: 'We need your help, Mr Baker.'

King Billy began to walk on slowly, one ponderous step after another. 'Then things must be bad.'

'They are,' Trenchard confirmed.

'The bombings on the mainland, I suppose? It would take that to bring you people scurrying out of the woodwork.'

'That's a bit unfair,' Nash said.

Billy Baker's rosebud smile deepened. 'You think so? Was a time when Mr Smith here would phone me and say there's a dead Provo in a field shot by our boys. Be a good lad and claim responsibility, will you? There's a drink in it for your trouble.'

Nash glanced at Trenchard, his disapproval plain.

Trenchard said: 'Things have changed, Billy. More rules, more regulations.'

'Tell me about it,' King Billy returned icily. 'Now you treat us like we're fucken taigs, or worse. And what have we done to deserve it? We've been called more British than the British and this is our punishment. I think the British Government has forgotten the difference between right and wrong. I'm not in the business of doing favours any more. If you want favours, go visit the Mountview social club on Enfield and ask for Mad Dog. See if he's feeling any more obliging than me.'

'We have, and he isn't.'

Nash said: 'You haven't even asked what we want.'

Billy Baker shuffled to a halt and spared him a contemptuous glance. 'Everyone knows what you want. I know, Mad Dog knows, the fucken IRA knows – the whole of bloody Ulster knows. You want the AIDAN bombers.'

Nash saw no point in prolonging the conversation. 'That's right.'

'Then go to your mate Gerry Adams in Andersonstown and ask *him*. I'm sure he'll oblige.'

'Be reasonable,' Trenchard said.

King Billy pulled an innocent po-face. 'You mean dear old Gerry's not saying? My-my, well, you certainly find out who your real friends are when you're knee-deep in shite, don't you?'

'We *need* to know, Billy,' Nash pressed.

The big man stared out at the leaden murk of sky and sea. Suddenly the rush of the waves on the shingle sounded very loud. 'There'll be a price to pay.'

'Name it,' Nash said.

'Representation at the Abe Powers' talks.'

'Not possible, Billy. All paramilitaries are excluded.'

'And no internment for my people.'

'It's not in my power to offer,' Nash replied. 'That's between London and Dublin.'

'But you'll draw up the internment lists when the time comes? They'll only know who to go for when you tell them.'

Trenchard knew he had a point. 'Go on.'

'Take out Mad Dog and his gang. The whole lot. If you need it, I'll supply the membership list. A few names that'll surprise you.'

Nash sensed King Billy hadn't finished. 'And?'

'Am I currently in the frame for any misdemeanor?'

The MI5 man glanced at Trenchard who shook his head.

'Then I want a seat – or an appointee – at the Powers' talks.'

'You're a paramilitary leader,' Nash hissed.

The rosebud smile stretched like elastic into a long, thin grin. 'I deny that. I just run a drinking club – can't be held responsible for what the members do. Like the internment lists, politicians are obliged to believe what you tell them. If I can identify the AIDAN members, then I expect my name to be removed from any of your paramilitary membership lists.'

Trenchard sighed. 'It's not possible, Billy.'

Nash stepped up beside Billy Baker and stared out to sea at his side. 'A seat at the talks, it means that much to you?'

The big man turned, his short white hair tugged by the offshore breeze. 'It's my friggin' country too, Mr Jones.'

239

'Can you deliver?'

'Try me.'

'Deliver, Billy, and you get your seat.'

The deployment of three teams from 321 EOD Squadron, Northern Ireland, to London with backup from 11 EOD was sanctioned by the COBRA meeting the day following Harrison's meeting with the Home Secretary.

By the time the signal was received by Colonel 'Taff' Lloyd-Williams and forwarded by the secure Brinton fibre-optic telephone line to Girdwood Park Barracks in the Ardoyne, off the Crumlin Road, Captain Peter Heathcote had already been on stand-by for twenty-four hours in anticipation of the move.

Four gleaming new khaki Tactica trucks, built by Glover Webb of Southampton, waited outside the reinforced blockhouse which housed the ops room. Three Mk8 Wheelbarrow robots were carried, complete with the latest remote colour TV equipment and all the other bomb-disposing gadgetry that had been developed over the years. The fourth truck carried a powerful Attack Barrow version of the robot, dedicated to destroying vehicle bombs in short order and capable of being rigged with a PAW-PAW warhead for use against vans or a RAID – Rapid Access and Instant Destruction – designed to counter car bombs. An additional standard Bedford truck would transport the crews and their personal belongings, including civilian clothes, on the journey to London.

Corporal Clarke delivered the message to Heathcote. He was grinning widely, looking for all the world like a naughty, podgy schoolboy at the end of term. The capital beckoned. Booze, good food and beautiful women. 'CATO confirms, sir. London awaits the timely arrival of the 5th Cavalry.'

They left at last light to avoid attracting the attention of Provo eyes which were always watching. As the gates in the high-security fence swung open, the small convoy sped through into the wet night.

Heathcote peered out of the window from beside the driver in the lead Tactica. Across the street from Girdwood Park was one of the most incongruous sights in Belfast, one that never ceased to fascinate and amuse him. On a patch of derelict land stood a small lone, single-storey building, closely surrounded by razor-pointed security railings and with a huge satellite receiving dish dominating its flat roof. For all the world it looked like a nuclear command bunker, yet Heathcote knew it was just the local Catholic betting shop.

He wondered what would happen between now and his return from London. Somehow he doubted it would be quite the picnic Clarke and the others assumed it would be. He'd read the reports. London was in the grip of terror; it was a capital under siege. And if he and his Belfast cats were wanted there, then it was for good reason.

They boarded the Liverpool ferry for the night crossing and made Vauxhall Barracks near Oxford by noon the following day. That afternoon the Tacticas were sprayed white, allowing the paint to dry overnight. The next morning Metropolitan Police livery stripes were added by the mechanics before the convoy continued its journey to Lambeth Road in the heart of London.

Their welcome at the Section was muted. Al Pritchard treated the twelve new arrivals almost as though they didn't exist. Al though he went through the motions of welcoming them, he did so without warmth and even without one of his sardonic smiles. It was all done with the minimum of required etiquette, nothing more. In the corridors he would pass by the army personnel without acknowledgment, his eyes fixed on some point in the middle distance.

'I feel like the bleedin' Invisible Man,' Corporal Clarke complained.

The Sexpo quickly and irreverently became known as Sexpot, Pilchard and then, bitterly, Prickhead.

Perhaps following their chief's example, many of the other Expos treated the army personnel with stiff courtesy or indifference, despite the fact that all had at one time served with 321 EOD.

Noticeably different in attitude were Les Appleyard and Midge Midgely. Having worked most closely with Harrison since his arrival, they had volunteered to share their offices with the men from Belfast. That in itself created chaos because the newcomers not only worked but also lived and slept in the confined space, erecting collapsible camp beds in every available corner.

Harrison apologised to Heathcote for the cramped conditions. 'I'd have us billeted at one of the London barracks, Peter, but if I did that we'd never get tasked. Al would just go out on call and conveniently forget to give us the location. He calls the shots here, remember, and it's his decision whether or not to send us out. But if we're camped all over his headquarters, he can hardly ignore us. The only time he'll be able to let the office cleaners in is if he sends us out.'

Yet, despite everyone's growing fears that Al Pritchard would never let them see action, they were deployed just two days later.

A white van – the description and registration plates of which exactly matched a legitimately owned vehicle in Milton Keynes – was abandoned in Oxford Street, its hazard lights left pulsing as the driver mounted the pillion seat of a motorcycle which roared away north up Duke Street. Within minutes an AIDAN warning had been telephoned to the Samaritans. Eight hundred pounds of ammonium nitrate fertiliser and a mere thirty-minute timer.

To Harrison's surprise, Al Pritchard had thrown open the door to the overcrowded office. 'We're tasked to Oxford Street, Tom,' he announced. 'Time for your lads to show what they're made of.'

Was that a smile on his face? As always it was difficult to be certain, but there appeared to be a certain glint in his eye.

Peter Heathcote and Corporal Clarke scrambled for the Tactica which carried the Attack Barrow, hurtling out of the compound doors in the wake of the Section's Range-Rovers. With siren caterwauling from the escorting police car as it carved its way through the commuter traffic, the two men were rigging the PAWPAW warhead to the big barrow.

The work was completed just moments before the vehicle came to a halt in a side street opposite the massive D.H. Evans department store. Before them lay a stretch of eerily deserted street, the pedestrians having been hastily pushed back behind the cordons. Yet many shoppers and office workers were still being evacuated through back exits to the surrounding streets; others with no alternative means of escape were crouched in rear rooms away from windows. Both police and public had learned quickly over the past few weeks, government-issued safety advice on what to do in bomb emergencies having been widely published in the national press. Now everyone was beginning to understand the power of explosives and what they could do; a bomb was not something to gawp at from an upper floor unless you wanted to be blinded or maimed by flying shards of glass.

Harrison arrived with Al Pritchard. By the time they'd scrambled from the Range-Rovers, the aerial had already been slotted into its position atop the Tactica and the Attack Barrow was already rumbling down its ramp, operated with relish by Corporal Clarke and his hand-held remote-control box.

Parked beside the pavement a hundred metres ahead was the white van, paintwork gleaming like a showroom model, hazards blinking steadily.

'It's your decision, Al,' Harrison said.

The hoods came down over Pritchard's eyes, reminding Harrison of a predatory hawk as he surveyed the scene, weighed up the odds. What had the warning said? Eight hundred pounds of high explosive; it had been quite specific about that. And here was the bomb, parked in a canyon of tall, glass-fronted stores holding millions of pounds' worth of merchandise. Any injuries would be unpredictable, the cost would not. And they were within five minutes of the warning deadline. Way outside the safe limit.

Pritchard swallowed. 'Tell your team to go for it. And I just hope they're as good as you say they are.'

Harrison turned and nodded to Heathcote and Clarke who stood poised, the Attack Barrow whirring earnestly as though eager to be going. The captain responded with a thumbs-up sign and the robot jerked into action, moving into the centre of Oxford Street and executing a neat left-hand turn.

Pritchard and Harrison backed to the corner, shielded by the wall to watch the vehicle trundle on its way, alone in the vast concrete chasm of the shopping centre, stalking its mechanical prey. Meanwhile the hazards blinked on unerringly, the harmless-looking van suddenly taking on an air of clinical menace. It was a bizarre sight, a remote and deadly battle between two machines.

Behind them Heathcote and Clarke studied the television monitors as the van filled the screen. The two men exchanged whispered words, as they had done a hundred times before in Belfast, watching the robot close in for the kill.

Harrison willed them on, glanced at his watch. Fifteen seconds to go. If the given warning time was correct. If the timer was accurate. If, if, if . . .

Decisively, Clarke swung the Attack Barrow round on its rubber tracks to face the side of the van square-on. He released the drive buttons and the robot lurched forward, the distant clang quite audible as the huge circular cutting charge was extended on the telescopic arm, jamming hard against the van's steel flank.

On command from Heathcote, Clarke thumbed the plastic tit of the first firing circuit on the control box.

The cutting charge blew, tearing a ragged hole in the vehicle's side. Clarke released the drive buttons and the robot pushed forward, its telescopic arm punching in through the gap with a cluster of six-ounce Candle charges.

The corporal hit the second tit. Harrison held his breath.

The pavement shook from the throaty roar and rumble as the barrow delivered its lethal sting. The van skewed sideways, the low-pressure blast blowing the bomb's circuitry and burning out the explosive in a fierce tongue of flame that set the vehicle ablaze. Greasy black smoke spiralled skyward into the bright summer sky.

A few plate-glass windows nearby had shattered, but that was all. Heathcote looked at Harrison and grinned broadly. Even Pritchard almost smiled.

After the hidden device in the Haymarket bomb, no one was going near this baby. It was allowed to burn out fully before it was finally inspected and cleared away.

Perhaps, Harrison thought, the tide had begun to turn against AIDAN.

Declan O'Dowd was a freelance novelty salesman.

The job didn't pay well and his wife, whom he only saw at

weekends at their family home in Luton, was forever chasing up shopkeepers who hadn't settled their bills for three months or more. But O'Dowd was his own boss and his work could take him wherever he pleased; there wasn't a town or city that didn't have a shop with a dispenser for practical jokes. Rubber spiders, sponge sugar lumps, itching powder and plastic dog dos. That was his stock-in-trade. And ideal cover for one of the Provisionals' mainland flying-column experts in R and R. Research and recce.

He hadn't been surprised when the envelope arrived at his home. It contained a newspaper clipping. The meaning was self-explanatory. A possible future target and an address somewhere in Pimlico.

It took him just over an hour to locate from the blurred press picture of the front door. The estate agent's For Sale sign made things easier.

There were several tatty tourist hotels in the street and, unusually for the time of year, all had vacancies. He chose one with a room which looked onto the street, with a clear view of the house that was for sale.

A call to the estate agent established that the owners were looking for a quick sale. The property was currently unoccupied and viewing was strictly by arrangement only; the agent would be delighted to show him round.

O'Dowd went out in the middle of the day, taking his case of samples to many little back-street shops in the West End and the southern suburbs. But in the mornings and late afternoons he sat at the window of his room with a pair of binoculars.

For two days he saw no one leave or arrive at the house. The target, he feared, had flown for good.

Then on the third day, a Friday afternoon, a BMW pulled up outside. A small, pretty woman climbed out. Smartly dressed and very self-assured, he thought. She looked to be in a hurry.

This might be his only chance. He ran downstairs and collected his estate car which was parked on a nearby meter. By the time he'd driven back the two blocks to his hotel, the woman was leaving with two suitcases.

With a smirk of satisfaction on his face, O'Dowd settled down to follow her car. He always enjoyed that sort of challenge.

It was to be a long drive to Wokingham.

He parked across the road from the gates of Hurlingham Boarding School. A banner had been strung along the adjoining railings: SUMMER FÊTE AND SPORTS DAY. Twenty minutes later Pippa Harrison's car re-emerged, this time with a boy of about ten in the front passenger seat.

O'Dowd selected first, signalled and pulled out to follow the BMW back to London.

13

Patrick McGirl had charged one of the mainland support teams with finding suitable locations of the type specified by Hughie Dougan. He had been quite precise. Three empty or derelict shops with easy access in different parts of the city, but away from the centre which would be swarming with alert cops. No evidence of dossers, junkies or glue-sniffers.

Several suitable sites had been found, stealthily broken into and Polaroid photographs taken. They settled on one corner shop in a Victorian estate due for demolition off the East India Dock Road near the Isle of Dogs. Another in Deptford and one more in the back streets of Lambeth.

On the day in question, McGirl received the first evidence that the effect of the campaign was starting to bite. Just a small picture caption story in the *Daily Mail*. It showed a deserted stretch of Oxford Street outside the D.H. Evans store. In the background was an Attack Barrow and a Tactica truck, painted white. The fact wasn't mentioned, but McGirl knew that both types of equipment had only ever been deployed in Northern Ireland.

The Renault van was a duplicate of one owned by a genuine firm of shopfitters in Shooters Hill; the bombers' vehicle had been hot-wired and stolen to order by the support team, then scrupulously valeted and stored in a lock-up garage. That afternoon it had been collected by one of the AIDAN team and driven to the farm at Henley-on-Thames. In the secure barn, false number plates were fitted as well as cheap vinyl livery graphics. At ten o'clock in the evening McGirl drove to the rented house, parking in the integral garage for ten minutes before leaving again. Only this time Hughie Dougan and his daughter were crouched on the floor under a blanket in the rear.

247

On his arrival at the fortified farm, he found the AIDAN team ready and waiting. This night two of the four would be accompanying Dougan and Clodagh on their mission. Moira Lock, the farmer's daughter from Fermanagh, and Leo Muldoon from Derry's Bogside district; neither had a record.

'Meet AIDAN,' McGirl said to them. 'You just need to know him as Hughie – and this is Clodagh.'

Leo was lanky, long thin wrists showing at the cuffs of his leather jacket, his ungainly movements creating the false impression that he wasn't fully in control of his limbs. His skin-tight jeans just served to emphasise his height as he lurched towards Dougan and extended his bony hand. 'You'll be doing a fine job, Hughie. It's an honour to meet you.' Beneath the wind-blown mop of black hair his face was pimply and adolescent, his long teeth seeming too big for the cheerful mouth.

Dougan's cheeks coloured with pride. McGirl had never been more than dour and matter-of-fact; even FitzPatrick had seemed aloof and sceptical about his capabilities.

Yet here was a front-line soldier, a young buck with nerves of steel and matchless courage who had been risking his neck almost nightly, running the gauntlet of the police on the streets of besieged London to place *his* bombs. Leo Muldoon's words and his smile appeared genuine, the look of awe and respect in his eyes was unmistakable.

Hughie Dougan was back. Living the dream of eighteen lost years. To where he had never truly been before. At the top of his deadly profession, respected for what he always knew he was. The best. They'd written songs about him once, but they were forgotten now. When this was over, perhaps they'd be heard again, resounding in the bars and clubs of west Belfast.

Meanwhile Clodagh regarded Moira Lock with mild interest. She was considerably shorter and of a lighter build than Dougan's daughter and several years younger. A lack of confidence showed in the way she carried herself with shoulders slightly hunched and in her nervous half-smile. Watching but not speaking.

The three bombs were identical: five-gallon oil drums, the bases of which had been cut away in order to fit the thirty pounds of

ANS explosive and a TPU before being fixed back on with Isopon plastic filler to make completely sealed units. Only a dowel pin was accessible by unscrewing the small top cap together with an LED light. While this remained unlit he was safe to pull the pin which would irreversibly trigger the switch to start the timer. That itself could be overridden at any moment by one of the three antihandling devices which came into immediate effect: a passive short-wave radio signal detector which would cut into a priority ten-minute fuse; an X-ray-sensitive switch used in the manufacture of hospital body scanners and a sensitive vibration trembler adapted from a cheap Taiwanese luggage alarm.

Dougan's combination was designed to thwart the use of a mechanical Wheelbarrow or a hands-on approach by the bomb-disposal experts. But for the last of the bombs that would be found that night, he planned an additional refinement. One he hadn't used for ten long years. The pressure mat. Ironical that. It had been the forensic evidence from that defused pressure-mat booby trap in Ballymurphy that had led to his second conviction. This time it would catch one of the so-called bomb-disposal *experts*, he was sure of that. Leastways the bastards would have to eat their words, would look like fools in the national press after that stupid, boastful article . . .

Now the Renault van was carefully loaded with the drums, each freshly sprayed in gleaming black paint, giving no hint as to the deadly tricks that lurked within them.

Toolboxes, timber and assorted light fittings were also stowed, together with a hastily contrived signboard that read: *Stebbings – Emergency Repairs and Overnite Shopfitting* and a genuine telephone number.

McGirl handed out blue overalls, the backs of which had been stencilled early that day by an innocent company of screen-printers in Kingston-on-Thames.

'Too bloody short,' Muldoon complained.

McGirl grinned malevolently. 'Don't worry, you're not goin' to a fucken fashion show.'

It broke the tension and the team members laughed nervously.

Muldoon swung up into the driver's seat, Hughie Dougan next

to him. Behind them the girls were climbing into a red Escort saloon, another duplicate of a genuine car. Automatic pistols were carried beneath the front seats.

'Ready?' McGirl asked.

The van driver took a deep breath and forced a smile. 'Can't wait.'

McGirl nodded to the farm manager who stood by the barn doors. The interior was plunged into darkness and the vehicle lights came on, engine noise and exhaust starting to fill the cavernous outbuilding. The doors swung wide, and the Renault's headlamps carved a swathe across the muddy yard, picking up the glistening veil of drizzle.

And they were off, out into the night, on the road towards London.

They made fast time down the M40 and Western Avenue, the traffic fairly light at this time of night. Muldoon regularly checked his speed, keeping to sixty, not wanting to attract attention by travelling too slow or too fast. He also kept watch in his rearview mirror for the lights of the following Escort which would provide the necessary armed backup and their means of escape if anything went wrong. In the meantime he noticed three police patrol cars passing at different times in the opposite direction; it struck him as more than might normally be expected.

But if he were perturbed in any way, Muldoon gave no outward sign. He chatted and joked, Dougan assumed, to cover his nerves. 'Must be some time since you've been on a job, Hughie?'

'Yes.' He didn't want to say no. That he'd always been the bomb maker, never the bomber. Didn't want to admit that his guts were churning like so much cold porridge. That he was scared, not of confrontation with the police or even death itself. It was the thought of another long stretch in prison that he couldn't face; wouldn't face.

'Sure you're all right if you brazen it out. Smile and be chirpy with the Brits. It works as well here as it does across the water. Cheerful, polite and no smart backchat.' He removed one hand from the wheel and tapped the side of his nose with his forefinger.

250

'But then they don't know what's going on upstairs. Like the song says, you can't go to jail for what you're thinking. That way we get the last laugh. Sure we're okay.'

Ten minutes later they were approaching the A40(M) flyover into Marylebone and his bravado evaporated. The nearside lane had been coned off. He glimpsed the POLICE SLOW sign and saw the patrol car with its blue flashing light and an officer with a yellow fluorescent jacket and storm torch waving traffic into the makeshift lay-by. A vehicle safety check.

Muldoon hit the brakes, checked that the Escort was close behind. They slowed to a crawl, both men feeling the increasing thud of their heartbeats, their mouths going dry. A Mercedes in front, a white Fiesta van in front of that, told to pull in. The Mercedes waved on. Now them, the officer flashing his torch in their cab, then along the side.

Then a wave of the torch, move on.

Dougan felt the relief squeeze out of him as Muldoon crept past, his eyes flicking sideways at the line of trucks and vans that had pulled over.

Muldoon chuckled suddenly, the release of tension having an effect like laughing gas. 'Did you see that, Hughie?'

'What, the vehicles?'

'Did you not notice anything?'

He shook his head.

'Unmarked, all of them. Safety check, my arse. No cars, you notice. They're only pulling in unmarked vehicles, don't you know. Sure the bastards never learn.'

Stebbings Shopfitters, Dougan thought. It had been their salvation.

There was no further problem as they continued on, following the A40(M) as it metamorphosed into the Marylebone Road, then Pentonville and City as it took them across the north of London towards Shoreditch. The square mile of the City of London itself had been sealed off since the Bishopsgate bomb and security had been tightened even further in recent weeks, so now they gave the area a wide berth. Muldoon confidently took to the back streets, working towards their first target, the disused corner

251

shop at the end of a row of dilapidated Victorian terrace houses off the East India Dock Road.

Muldoon jerked on the handbrake.

Dougan peered out at the faded fasciaboard above the shop. Patel & Son Grocers. Splattered with paint, daubed with fascist British National Party slogans and showing unmistakable signs of firebomb damage.

'Remember,' Leo Muldoon said, 'if we're challenged it's all front and bravado. No one will be expecting any trouble in this area . . .'

'I know that,' Dougan snapped, 'it was my idea!' Then he quickly apologised. The truth was, he felt terrified.

Muldoon took it well, smiling as though he understood, before checking his watch. One o'clock. Time for all the drunks to have wandered home from the pubs, to have had their fish-and-chip suppers. The street rain-slicked and empty except for a mongrel dog rummaging in the dustbins. Just two window lights visible. Pensioners with insomnia, Dougan guessed, or out-of-work adolescents playing rock videos into the early hours.

Muldoon checked through his side window. The Escort was parked just round the corner, its lights doused.

'Let's go,' he said hoarsely.

They climbed out and crossed the pavement to the door. As they did so Muldoon stepped unexpectedly in a dog turd and cursed silently.

'C'mon,' Dougan urged.

They used their bodies to shield the crowbar from view as Muldoon jammed the metal tip in the rotten wood by the lock, wrenching it open.

Somewhere a woman shouted, screamed. A man laughed, sounding drunk. An empty lager can clattered in the gutter, rolling in the light breeze. The expectant silence settled again.

They returned to the van, Muldoon taking out the sign and placing it beneath the boarded-up window. It was an elaborate precaution, seeming unnecessary – unless something really did go wrong. Then the two of them lowered the first drum onto the two-wheeled porter's trolley and rolled it into the shop.

Depositing the load in the storeroom behind the smashed glass of the counter, Muldoon held a torch while Dougan unscrewed the top cap and inserted his forefinger in the loop attached to the dowel pin.

He looked across at Muldoon, seeing the sweat on his skin and the fear in his eyes. 'When I pull this, Leo, the whole thing becomes live. The trembler's on a hair-trigger – it needs only the slightest vibration. So don't fall over anything on your way out.'

Suddenly Muldoon looked more gawky and awkward than ever. There was no humour in the grinning boyish face. 'Sure I'll be like a shadow, Hughie.'

They checked their watches. One fifteen exactly. The timer set to run for two hours twenty-five minutes.

Dougan nodded, eased out the dowel pin and delicately rescrewed the cap. Carefully Muldoon shone his torch beam so that they could both retrace their footsteps to the shop.

'Don't slam the door,' Dougan reminded.

His hand trembling slightly, Muldoon eased it closed. Suddenly both men realised that they'd hardly breathed for the last two minutes.

Then they were gone, driving away into the night, the girls still following closely in the Escort. The preplanned route took them back to the East India Dock Road, past the Isle of Dogs where they turned off for the Blackwall Tunnel which would take them under the Thames to Greenwich.

Clearing the far side of the river, Muldoon left the motorway at Shooters Hill Road, turning west to run parallel with the Thames and past the Marquis of Granby pub before driving into the Deptford back streets.

They drew up outside a parade of shops in a council estate, the Escort pulling in some fifty metres behind. This time the target was a shop that had obviously served as an outlet for Oxfam; now it was empty, its windows lime-washed white. Dougan and Muldoon followed an identical procedure to the first, returning to the Renault at precisely two o'clock.

Half-a-mile down the road they stopped beside a row of three telephone kiosks and Muldoon climbed out. As the support team's reconnaissance report had forecast, only the Phonecard machine had not been vandalised. He dialled the X number and waited. After four rings it was answered.

McGirl identified himself. 'Michael Collins.'

'Griffith here,' Muldoon replied. The names of two of the old IRA's founders in 1920. 'Two down and one to go. On schedule.'

When Muldoon hung up, McGirl replaced his own receiver at the call box in Watford, north London. He had memorised the number he was about to dial.

A disinterested male voice answered. 'Associated Newspapers.'

McGirl said: 'Casey Mullins – *Standard*.'

'I'll try it,' the operator said. He sounded doubtful.

It rang several times. Then: 'News desk.' Male.

'I want to speak to Casey Mullins,' McGirl repeated.

'Sorry, mate, this is news. Casey's on features. Won't be in till ten – or seven if she's on zombie shift.'

Shit, shit, shit! McGirl cursed silently. He'd thought because the first editions hit the streets by eleven, they'd all work through the night. He should have checked with the support team, they'd have known. So stupid, to have assumed . . . Too late now.

'Hello, are you still there?'

McGirl said: 'It's urgent. Have you got her home number?'

The man's tone changed; maybe, McGirl thought, he'd picked up the trace of Irish in his accent, putting the deputy night editor on his guard. 'Sorry, old son, we don't give out home numbers of staff.'

'I said this is urgent, a matter of life and death.'

There was a sigh that could have been irritation. 'If it's *really* that serious, I could try her number and get her to call you back. But it *is* after two.'

McGirl thought fast. He'd be taking a risk, a terrible risk. But then no one yet knew who he was or why he was phoning. He forced the anger from his voice, adopting a lighter tone and fighting to hide his accent. 'I would be most grateful.' He gave the number.

'A call box?'

'Afraid so.' Then added quickly: 'My car's broken down in the middle of nowhere. I'll wait, but please make it quick.'

'Of course. Who shall I say is calling?'

McGirl smiled to himself. 'Just say a friend of Tom Harrison.'

It took the deputy night editor five minutes to find Casey's new number, the sudden strident ring of the bedside telephone jolting her awake.

Groggily she reached for the handset, mumbling her new number and getting it wrong, brushing the hair from her eyes as she listened, scarcely comprehending, to the voice at the other end.

'God, Mac, I thought it was World War Three,' she mumbled, fishing for the pen and pad she'd knocked from the table. 'Call what number?' She jotted it down. 'Who'd you say it was?'

Casey frowned as she listened to the answer, now sitting up clutching the duvet to her naked chest. 'That's all right, Mac, you didn't interrupt anything. I was only in bed with Richard Gere when you woke me.' Slowly, thoughtfully, she hung up.

'Who was it? What's wrong?'

She turned to Harrison; he was leaning on one elbow, watching her closely. 'It was Mac on the news desk. A friend of yours rang. Wants me to call him back at a public call box. Says it's very urgent. Didn't give a name.'

Don Trenchard. That was Harrison's immediate thought. Only Trenchard was cavalier enough to phone at such an hour, only Trenchard knew where he could be found. 'The bastard. I'll call him in the morning.'

Casey was perplexed. 'Not you, Tom. This caller wants *me* to call, not you. Just said he was a friend.'

'Only Don knows I might be here.'

'Don doesn't have an Irish accent.' She had begun dialling.

'What?'

She covered the mouthpiece. 'Mac said he thought the caller was Irish.'

Suddenly Harrison was wide awake, uncertainty creeping like the fingers of a cold hand behind his neck.

The number stopped ringing as someone picked up the phone. 'Hello?' she said.

'Casey Mullins?' a voice asked. 'Listen and listen good, there'll be no second chance. This is AIDAN. A bomb is due to go off in approximately fifty minutes in Poplar, East London.' He gave the address, crisply and precisely, not hurrying. 'And a friendly warning – don't approach the device. Pass that on to your Tick Tock Man.' He slammed down the telephone.

Casey's mouth dropped open and closed again, speechless, staring at the receiver in her hand as though it were contaminated. Her eyes moved across to Harrison, trying to find the words.

He reached over, snatching it from her. There was nothing but the dead tone.

She cleared her throat, 'He's gone.'

'Who?' Harrison demanded.

Her mouth was dry, arid as a desert. 'It was a bomb threat. Somewhere in Poplar.'

Harrison shook his head, trying to clear his mind. 'This has to be someone's idea of a joke.'

'I don't think so, Tom.' He could see now that her face was pale with shock, the fear in her eyes all too real. 'It was the AIDAN codeword.'

That was it. No one but no one would make a joke about that, not even Trenchard. He took the note pad from her. 'I'll call the Section on my mobile. You ring AT Branch and give them that call-box number.'

'What's their direct line?'

'I don't know.'

Shit, she'd have to go through 999.

Harrison took the mobile from his jacket hanging on the chair and punched a single number. He recognised Midge Midgely's noncommittal voice.

'Listen, Midge, it's Tom here. AIDAN's just been on the blower. There's a warning for Poplar.'

The Yorkshireman seemed to be waking from a dream. 'Tom? You pulling my plonker? AIDAN phoned *you*?'

'It came through Casey on the *Standard*,' he explained vaguely. 'We're down to about forty-five minutes.'

Midgely realised it was no wheeze – until Harrison read over the address. 'Patel & Son, Tom? What the hell *is* this? A grocer's shop in Poplar.'

Harrison felt the ice running through his veins. 'I'll tell you exactly what it is, Midge, it's a come-on. Just make sure my boys get tasked in on the job.'

'I see.' He sounded dubious. 'I'll check it out with Al.'

'No time,' Harrison objected.

Midge sounded like he could be chuckling. 'No trouble, he's kipping in the duty office.'

Of course. Divorced, Pritchard had no home to go to. No doubt he couldn't sleep either.

Harrison said: 'Okay, Midge, I'm going straight there. You can get me on the mobile.'

As he replaced the telephone in his jacket pocket, he turned to find that Casey had finished her call and was already out of bed, tugging up tracksuit trousers over her naked body.

'Don't even think it, Tom,' she warned. 'That call was to my paper, so it's my story. We can travel together or else I race you across London.'

His scowl melted into a reluctant half-smile. 'And I can guess who'd get there first.'

By the time they'd reached Casey's parked Mini Cooper, the Section's Range-Rovers were screaming out of Lambeth Road, the lumbering Tactica in hot pursuit.

Muldoon swung out of Coldharbour Lane and into Brixton Hill.

'Time?' he asked.

'Two forty-five,' Dougan replied smugly. The precise time McGirl was due to ring the Samaritans with the Deptford bomb warning. He could imagine the growing pandemonium in the Met's Explosive Section. He was actually beginning to enjoy this.

'Sod it!' Muldoon hissed.

'What is it?'

The other man didn't answer. He didn't have to; Dougan could

257

see it himself up ahead in the dazzling reflection of shop window lights on the wet street, bouncing off the gleaming bodywork of parked cars. Amongst all this he'd missed the flashing blue light and the policeman in the yellow dayglo waistcoat waving them down.

'What are you going to do?' Dougan breathed, the knot of terror tightening like a balled fist in his abdomen.

'Hope the girls don't panic,' Muldoon replied tersely, beginning to wind down the window. 'Let me do the talking . . .'

The officer wore sergeant's stripes; he was middle-aged, his face pinched against the drizzle. 'Out late, sir?'

'Out early,' Muldoon countered cheerfully. Dougan noticed there was no trace of an Irish accent, the 't' dropped to sound like a Londoner. 'Brick through a shop window and the place vandalised.' He jerked his thumb over his shoulder, as if in explanation. The policeman shone his torch on the van's flank. 'Oh, I see, emergency shopfitters, eh? Bloody vandals around here – our loss, your gain.'

Muldoon chuckled; he seemed genuinely relaxed. 'What's going on, then?'

'Just routine. Out-of-date road fund licences and hooky goods, you know.'

I know, Muldoon thought, so what's that bastard doing in the flak jacket, hiding in the doorway shadows with a Heckler & Koch and a firearms-unit car parked farther up? The Escort had over-taken them, had pulled in just ahead of the police vehicle. If the shit hit the fan, Moira would know what to do. Take out the man in the doorway and splatter his backup as they sat in their car, tired and bored. They would run for the getaway car, Moira covering.

'Where are you headed, sir?'

'Not far. Off Streatham High Road.' Muldoon could see an-other officer now, looking directly at the Renault as he spoke into a radio mike, flex extending from the open window. Checking the registration number against the computer. No fears there. An identical blue Renault was owned by the genuine Stebbings company. Easy-peasy.

'Licence, sir?'

'Sure.'

No problem. Genuine licence that would check out. The Brits were so fucking trusting on their own turf.

'My son used to work for Stebbings.'

Sudden paralysis caught in Muldoon's spine, spreading up to his throat and jaw. He swallowed, hard. 'Pardon?'

'Has old Cyril retired yet?'

A shrug. 'No idea, I'm new.'

'I'd better look in the back.'

Shit! 'Sure.' Calm.

Opening his door, taking an age. Into the wet drizzle like the clammy hand of death. Slow-motion, all the time in the world, looking ahead at the Escort, knowing that Moira would be reaching for the gun. Bizarre and unreal, his heart pounding so hard and so deep it hurt his ears as the blood thudded through the veins in his temples.

The doors creaked open; the flashlight revealed the lengths of timber, the toolbox, the sign . . .

'What's in the drum?'

'Varnish.' Glib. So goddamn fucking cool.

The officer on the radio nodded at the sergeant.

'Thanks for your co-operation, sir. Watch your speed now, it's slippery tonight.'

YEEEAH!

Casey tore through the deserted London streets, slipping expertly through the gears in fluid heel-toe changes at the approach to each bend, bringing on the power at the apex, straightening out the Mini Cooper with a roar from the exhaust.

'Where the hell did you learn to drive like that?'

'My first husband drove dragsters as a hobby. He taught me to drive, then divorced me.' She grinned. 'He was lucky to get out of the marriage in one piece.'

'I can believe it.'

With Harrison navigating, they reached the corner shop in Poplar just five minutes after the Section convoy. Local police were clearing the area, attempting to hold back angry and anxious locals who were wandering around in nightdresses and pyjamas and pushing up against the cordon tapes.

Harrison pushed through the crowd, flashed his pass at the bewildered young constable.

Al Pritchard was standing by one of the Range-Rovers and saw him coming. He didn't mince his words. 'You know what this is, Tom? This is PIRA cocking a snook at your bloody bravado that we've got 'em licked.'

Harrison smiled gently. 'Then we're agreed on something, Al. Poplar means nothing to them. It's a blatant come-on.'

'And phoned in person to your journalist lady friend.' He almost spat the words, ignoring Casey's presence. 'Well, that's it and we've barely ten minutes.'

'Is the area cleared?'

Pritchard's eyes, red-rimmed, were like chips of frost. 'Is it fuck?'

'What's been found?'

'They sent in a local constable. Thank Christ the lad had some imagination – read your friend's articles, I imagine, found a bloody great oil drum. Front door'd been jemmied. He went in . . .'

'Jesus,' Harrison breathed. 'If AIDAN says don't go close, he means it.'

The local police inspector was standing listening to their conversation. Despite the pompous tilt of his jaw and the steely glint in his eyes, Harrison recognised instantly that he was a man out of his depth. 'Look, you people, I've still got officers clearing the area. There's an old people's home not a hundred metres away, over there, so what are you recommending?'

Pritchard said: 'Nothing's guaranteed, sir, but we've a squad from Northern Ireland here, the best. We're pushing the end of the time limit anyway. If they go in with a controlled explosion . . .' He glanced at Harrison.

The SATO nodded. They had nothing to lose, they were between a rock and a hard place and they knew it. A few minutes either way would make no difference.

'Go ahead,' the police chief decided.

Pritchard turned to Harrison, the invisible smile unmistakable. 'Over to you, Tom.'

Harrison called across to Captain Heathcote who stood beside the Wheelbarrow, Corporal Clarke next to him, big, eager and with his large red face perspiring brightly. 'Go!'

'WAIT!' Pritchard shouted suddenly.

All heads turned.

'Can you run her on cable?' the Sexpo asked.

Heathcote nodded. 'Sir?'

Pritchard was clearly tired, leaning against the side of the Rover, thinking back. 'This is AIDAN.'

Harrison nodded, indicating to his captain to rerig the robot. 'So?'

'Before your time, Tom. I'm reminded of the late lamented Hughie Dougan, back in – when? – the early seventies. He fixed some crude device from a radio-controlled model aircraft . . . The bomb was triggered by radio waves.'

'We've no ECM here . . .' Harrison began.

Pritchard regarded him closely, for once almost as a friend. 'Indulge an old man's whim, Tom.'

'It's being done, Al.'

Clarke had worked at lightning speed and already the robot was making its way down the street.

Harrison and Pritchard joined Heathcote at the back of the Tactica as he watched the monitor. The view from the Wheelbarrow's front camera swung round to show the corner shop, the picture jerking as the tracks negotiated the kerbstone, the telescopic arm probing at the front door. It swung open at a touch.

'How close did the constable go?' Harrison asked the local police chief.

'Just peered into the back room, thank God, then beat a hasty retreat.'

'Did he actually step into the room?'

'He says not, but then he was a bit unnerved afterwards.'

The barrow's spotlight played over the debris within the shop

261

until Clarke located the back door. Again the picture began to shake as the corporal tentatively edged the robot forward, its steel arm punching open the door.

They all glimpsed it: the squat, shiny black drum.

Then the picture trembled as the door crashed back against the wall and the screen went blank.

The sound was simultaneous, a low deep-gutted roar that shook the damp night air. They felt it through the soles of their shoes and the trembling of their hearts, vibrating like trampolines on stretched tendons. Falling glass made small sharp detonations as it shattered, followed by the heavier sound of roof slates crashing to the pavement.

'Jesus Christ,' Pritchard said and began running forward, Harrison and Heathcote hard on his heels.

Turning the corner, they came skidding to a halt, the scene before them reminiscent of the wartime German blitz. The shop doors and windows had been blown across the street and one wall had collapsed. Fire now engulfed the entire corner, flames leaping from the banisters and doorframes and rubbish that had accumulated on the derelict shop floor. A geyser of water fountained from a fractured main causing the fire to crackle and fizz, sending eerie elongated shadows dancing down the walls of the narrow street, flickering light glittering on the carpet of broken glass.

Only the base of the Wheelbarrow remained recognisable. The top hamper of the robot had been ejected skyward from the shop and had ploughed through the roof of a house opposite. Later it was found in the kitchen, having collapsed two ceilings during its fall from orbit.

'What do you think it was?' Heathcote asked.

Harrison's eyes narrowed as the flames devoured fresh material and increased in intensity. 'My guess is some type of trembler, but . . .'

Pritchard completed the sentence. 'I doubt we'll ever know. The bastards.'

The police chief had joined them, the fires from the street reflected in his eyes, his face devoid of colour. 'Why? Why here, for God's sake?'

'Who knows,' Pritchard murmured.

The policeman forced his attention away from the mesmeric scene. 'There were still some old people in that home. Only a few minor cuts, but some are badly traumatised. Can I continue to evacuate?'

Pritchard said: 'There could be a secondary. This bomber's known for it.'

'So what do I do?'

'It's your decision, but they're probably safer where they are. I'd get your men to search the entire block and surrounding streets first, if I were you.'

They turned at the sound of Les Appleyard running towards them. 'Al, it's Midge on the radio. Looks like there's another one.'

'I just knew it. Where?'

'Over the river. Deptford. Shall I task another of Tom's teams?'

Pritchard turned to Harrison. 'I hope you're satisfied, Tom? AIDAN's now having great fun deliberately wasting our barrows on low-grade targets.'

Harrison could find no reply. Pritchard knew he was waging a propaganda war, but how could he tell the man the full extent of the plan, a dangerous gamble of which he disapproved but had been obliged to participate in.

'The Provos could be drawing us out of the city,' Heathcote observed. 'Poplar, then Deptford. We'll have nothing left if they've got a spectacular planned for Westminster or the West End.'

Harrison and Pritchard looked at each other for a long and acrimonious moment; neither could deny the captain from Belfast might very well be right.

The Sexpo made his decision. 'Tell Midge we're on our way. Keep Tom's teams in reserve.'

Harrison touched Pritchard's arm. 'I don't think that's a good idea, Al. We've still got our two Mk8s immediately to hand as well as your two.'

The other man turned, the anger clear in his face. 'But for how long? You saw what just happened. We'll handle Deptford my way.'

Harrison caught Les Appleyard's eye, saw him give a shrug of resignation.

It was the last one.

Muldoon pulled in at the kerbside, his nerves still frayed after their close encounter at the police checkpoint.

Instinctively he didn't like the location. It was too bright with street lights, too overlooked. But it was also too late to do anything about it.

Same procedure, the girls parked behind in the red Escort while he and Dougan planted the sign by the window, forced the door of the one-time fashion shop and wheeled the final bomb inside. Barely seven minutes in total.

'I'll finish off,' Dougan said.

Muldoon nodded. This one was going to be different. A totally separate three-pound Semtex secondary charge wrapped in three-inch galvanised nails held in place with strips of plastic parcel tape. Detonated by a pressure mat hidden somewhere under the flooring. If that was triggered it would no doubt also set off the oil-drum bomb. Blow up half the fucking street, Muldoon thought.

He left Dougan to it, pleased to be away. His nerves had suffered enough for one night. Twice now he had backed away from one of Hughie's boxes of black tricks. Holding his breath, feeling the sweat coursing down his back, the damp seeping into his underpants. Terrified to breathe, terrified that he'd bang into something in the dark, create some inadvertent vibration that would be enough to set the bugger off. Or some local resident's radio alarm would go off for the early shift and trigger the passive signal detector. Only the X-ray-sensitive switch held no fears. As for the rest of Hughie Dougan's gadgets, hell, he wouldn't want to be the poor bastard who had to defuse them.

He lit a cigarette, looked up and down the wet, deserted street, at the bright shop windows and the pools of light. Nothing and no one.

Clodagh beckoned from the driver's window of the Escort. He sauntered back towards her.

The two women climbed out of the car, anxious to stretch their legs. Dougan's daughter said: 'It's just been on the radio news –'

'Christ, radio!'

The woman laughed. 'Wrong type of signal, Leo, don't worry. Worry if you see some kid with a radio-controlled toy car.'

Muldoon felt foolish. 'Sorry, what news?'

'The Poplar bomb went off. No details yet.'

The Irishman grinned 'That'll make the bastards eat their words.' He offered Moira Lock a cigarette.

As she looked up from the flame of his lighter, the expression froze on her face. She could see the distant white police car crawling beside the pavement, a routine night patrol checking the shops in the arcade.

'Peelers,' she breathed.

Muldoon glanced up. One beat officer out of the vehicle and going to a doorway. A dosser? A suspected break-in? Christ! 'Moira, go get Hughie, quick.' He turned to Clodagh. 'Back in the car and get it started.'

As Moira disappeared inside the shop, Muldoon scrambled into the Renault.

'Hughie! Quick!'

Dougan turned at the sound of the girl's voice, the dowel peg he had pulled still in his hand. Suddenly he realised where she was in the darkness. 'Don't move!' he yelled, flashing his torch.

'What?'

The last thing he saw in the circle of light was the expression of puzzlement on the pretty pale face as her foot stepped onto the loose lino.

A huge bursting bubble of lacerating glass and brickwork exploded across the street in front of Clodagh's eyes. She just saw the Renault van lifted bodily into the air, like some levitational conjuring trick and hurled across the street into the shop window opposite before the shock wave caught her own car. Her view through the windscreen was a swirling panorama of the devastation as the vehicle spun like a fairground dodgem, slewing across the road until it faced the opposite direction.

Miraculously the windscreen had not shattered. She stared

blindly ahead, hands grasping the steering wheel, her dark world closing in, the words screaming in her skull. Da is dead! Da is dead!

Rubble was bouncing on the car roof as it landed, glass crashing all around. She glanced back, saw Muldoon lurching from the van that had been concertinaed sideways by the force. Blood poured from his head as he stumbled blindly across the pavement. Beyond him the two beat officers had recovered from their shock and were running towards the scene. Lights were coming on in the bedrooms overlooking the street, heads appearing at shattered windows, people in their nightwear emerging, bewildered and bloodied, into the debris-strewn road.

Clodagh jammed the gear lever into reverse and stamped on the accelerator. The engine howled and tyres squealed, glass crunching noisily as she pulled alongside Muldoon.

He fumbled for the handle of the passenger door, yanked it open and fell inside.

She changed into first, her foot hard down, and the car screeched into the night.

'I don't like it,' Harrison said.

'You don't have to.'

Pritchard's mind was clearly made up. He walked away towards the Section's Range-Rover where Les Appleyard was waiting. After witnessing the Poplar incident the Expo was taking no chances and was kitted out in a full bombsuit and Nomex hood beneath his helmet.

Harrison crossed the street to the Mini Cooper where Casey Mullins was using his mobile, telling Hal Hoskins where to come to take the photographs.

She glanced up as he approached and he thought how efficient and professional she looked, yet how vulnerable. The drizzle had darkened her copper hair and flattened it against the sides of her head, the ends dripping onto the traditional reporter's trench coat and running down to the jogging pants and white trainers. No make-up – there'd been no time – and that made her look wide-eyed and almost childlike.

'What's happening, Tom?'

'Les is going in.'

'Al won't use another Wheelbarrow?' Her eyes were bright, but clouded with concern.

'I can't budge him. I can understand his point even if I don't agree with it. This bomb looks identical, which could mean the same highly sensitive trembler. Les can make a more stealthy approach than the robot. And there'll be no radio contact, just in case.'

'What will Les do? Use a disrupter?'

He smiled, amused at how easily she'd absorbed the language and the techniques. 'No, it's a sealed steel drum. He'll use a Flatsword – you know, the type I told you I used at the Europa recently. But Al wants a picture first.'

'Picture?'

'An X-ray, so we can get some idea what we're up against. With our experience we can recognise most electronic gizmos, circuitry and so on.'

'I see.' She brushed a strand of wet hair from her eyes. 'And the evacuation?' She meant the adjoining council estate.

'There never is enough time. But I don't think AIDAN's intention here is to kill innocent civilians.'

'Then what is the point, Tom? I don't understand.'

'It's to kill an Expo or an ATO. To prove I was wrong about what I said.'

She stared hard, trying to see behind those impassive dark eyes. 'In my last article, you mean?'

Harrison didn't answer, couldn't. How could he tell her she was an unwitting party to all this? Just another victim, just another small contributor to the jigsaw.

'God, Tom, that's terrible.'

Les Appleyard was on the move now, his helmet in place, waddling round the corner, carrying the blue plastic Inspector camera, and out of sight.

A portable camcorder and tripod had been erected at the roads crossroads which relayed Appleyard's rapid progress to a monitor in Pritchard's Range-Rover and Harrison moved across with Casey to watch.

Pritchard's driver called from the front seat of the Rover. 'Message from the Ops Room room, sir. It's Midgely.'

The Sexpo turned away from the screen as Appleyard was seen entering the one-time Oxfam shop. 'Yes?'

'Says to tell you there's been an explosion in Lambeth. He's tasking in an Expo team. Reports from two local coppers saw people acting suspiciously just before and after.'

Pritchard's impatience was on a hair-trigger. 'Meaning?'

The driver's smile positively beamed. 'Looks like an own goal, sir. Possible two of the buggers have blown themselves up.'

Harrison was only half listening, his attention riveted to the monitor and the street scene, deserted and brightly lit like a clapboard film set. He'd seen Appleyard go in, was visualising every movement of the stealthy approach he would be making, anticipating each of Les's thoughts, living each tentative footstep himself. Could imagine his friend stooping gently, carefully going onto one knee. Eyes transfixed by the solid black drum. Hating the thing like it was the very essence of evil. A living entity with a clockwork heartbeat and a black soul. Les watching for the slightest movement, careful not to make a loose floorboard tremble. Carefully placing the two taped-together Polaroid cassettes behind the device. Resting the X-ray camera on his knee, adjusting the focus.

Own goal! At last the driver's words permeated Harrison's brain. Registered. Sweet Jesus God! An own goal for AIDAN.

Totally alone in the empty Oxfam shop in the deserted street, Les Appleyard pressed the button of his camera.

Inside the oil drum, the X-ray-sensitive microswitch clicked position and completed the circuit.

Leo Muldoon had made a remarkable recovery from the shock of being blasted across the street. 'Slow down, Clodie, for God's sake. We'll be okay if you keep your nerve.'

She took a deep breath, lifted her right foot and tried to calm herself. Staring ahead as the wipers dragged aside the rain, she was scarcely aware which road she was on, blinded by the tears that welled in her eyes and ran freely down her cheeks. Occasional oncoming headlights rose out of the night dazzling and refracting brightly on the lacquered tarmac before screaming past in the opposite direction.

'I'm sorry, Leo.' Her voice was weak, fractured.

He looked at her, felt for her sorrow. He wanted to comfort her, this woman who had impressed him with her strength and dedication. But he couldn't find the words. 'Hold the faith, Clodie. I'm sure that's what your da would have wanted.'

His words finally registered and she took her eyes from the road for a moment. He saw her smile; it was the first time that night. A gentle smile of appreciation for his words; somehow he didn't think she ever smiled a lot. 'How are the cuts?'

He'd soaked three handkerchiefs with the blood but at last he seemed to have staunched the flow. 'Sure I'll be fine.'

They had passed through Kingston-on-Thames, crossed the bridge and skirted Hampton Court Palace, now taking the Lower Sunbury Road towards Shepperton.

Muldoon consulted the map as they passed the water towers and reservoirs. 'Slow here, take the next right.'

She checked behind as she turned without signalling. There was nothing else on the road.

Ahead the grey Nissan Sunny was where the other team members had left it, parked by the kerb, the key in the exhaust pipe. Clodagh pulled in behind it and switched off the engine. As they stepped out, the night was damp and chill, the only light from the moon which appeared fleetingly from behind the scudding rain cloud. Without exchanging a word, they stripped off their overalls and, taking new trainers from a plastic bag in the Escort's boot, changed their shoes. Everything worn on the bombing raid was then locked in before Muldoon swiftly unscrewed the registration plate and replaced the original number of the stolen vehicle.

He tried to sound cheerful. 'All done.'

She reached back inside and set the incendiary device timer for thirty minutes, then shut and locked the door.

They drove the Nissan Sunny straight on, rejoined the Staines road and continued for a mile before filtering onto the M3. At

Junction 2 they took the M25 orbital northwards, then turned onto the M4 just after Heathrow Airport and headed west.

Back in Sunbury, on the quiet reservoir road, the Ford Escort exploded and burst into flames.

14

Within twenty minutes of the Deptford explosion, Les Appleyard was admitted to St Thomas's Hospital in Lambeth where he underwent emergency surgery to remove his right leg. One testicle had been destroyed in the explosion and careful needlework was required to save the second; his remaining leg was horrendously pulped, but the surgeon believed there was a chance that it could be saved.

His buttocks too had been badly lacerated, but the bombsuit had taken much of the force, reducing the injuries to his pelvis and trunk. Both hands were burned, but not severely and the damage to his face looked worse than it was. Miraculously his eyes had escaped injury, but both eardrums were badly ruptured.

The following day, heavily sedated, he was transferred by ambulance to the Cambridge Military Hospital in Aldershot close to the family home in Guildford. Through the dreamlike veil of anaesthesia he was only vaguely aware of his arrival at the bleak brick Victorian building. The houseman's welcoming words of encouragement were lost on him, but he felt the reassuring squeeze of his arm before he began the rattling trolley ride down the corridor. Counting the endless lights passing high above his head, wondering about the strange smell of disinfectant and cooking cabbages from the adjoining kitchens. He was too weak, too disorientated to realise that his leg had gone, the wound left open, the flaps of skin from the lost limb preserved to cover the raw stump.

Ward Six and the face of an angel, the prettiest porcelain face he had ever seen, framed against the wide triangular cap veil. The loveliest and most compassionate eyes. He did not register the grey shirtwaister and red epaulettes of the Queen Alexandra's.

271

He told her how pretty she was, too, and wondered why she did not seem to hear.

But as Sister Di McGuire, a Dublin girl, looked down at her patient, all she saw were the cuts and the swellings, the glazed half-closed eyes and the almost imperceptible movement of the parched lips. She and the nurses knew who he was, what he did and what he had done. Tender, eager hands transferred him to the bed, their bodies strengthened by their anger and their pity, then watched while the registrar, an army major, made his examination and ordered the epidural. The sister nodded, turning quickly so that the surgeon would not see her tears as she thought of the terrible, awful waste of it all.

At lunch time Appleyard's wife Doreen visited. She sat beside him, ashen-faced with shock and her eyes red from hours of remorseless weeping, and watched. Because of his injuries she could not even hold his hand; she had to be content with a desperate attempt at thought transference, willing him to open his eyes, willing him to recognise her. Even for one flickering second, for one half-smile. What she would have given for that. But he didn't stir. Appleyard just drifted on through his sedated sea of dreams and the agony for Doreen was made worse because all she could see in her mind was her husband playing football with their two sons in the back garden earlier that summer. So fit and strong; always so strong. So unlike herself. She had always relied on his mental and physical strength, fed off it, she recognised that now. And here he was, more helpless than a baby.

'There's a possibility we can save his other leg,' the consultant surgeon explained. Lieutenant Colonel Wallace was in his fifties, stout and florid-faced, that curious blend of military man and physician, combining compassion with a no-nonsense acceptance of the facts. 'We'll operate this afternoon.'

It was a long moment before she could find her voice. 'Can you tell me – what you think, what are the chances?'

His smile gave her strength, despite his reply. 'Not good, I'm afraid. But your husband is a brave man and a fighter.'

'He'd hate to be in a wheelchair.'

Wallace nodded. 'But he'll be very pleased to be alive. Very pleased to see you and your children again.'

Those words were the comfort and hope she needed. And she took his advice to go home and to take strength from the support of family and friends who had gathered round. Yet all the time she had one eye on the clock, knowing that this was a critical period as Colonel Wallace attempted to screw an outer aluminium fixator into the bone of her husband's remaining shattered leg.

After a sleepless night and endless cups of coffee, it was finally dawn and she waited with trepidation for the telephone call inviting her to visit.

At last it came. The operation had been initially successful although its viability was still in question. At least Appleyard was conscious and asking for her. Much encouraged, she took a taxi to the hospital, not trusting herself to drive.

Wallace had been right, her husband was clearly overjoyed to be alive. When she arrived, Sister McGuire was holding a cup of tea for him which he drank through a straw. He was pale and weak and spoke in a hoarse whisper, hardly able to hear yet making feeble jokes about nothing in particular. They talked about her and the children and the kindness of in-laws whom normally they barely tolerated – his condition wasn't mentioned.

Fifteen minutes later Doreen thought it best to leave and allow him to rest, promising to return that evening.

As she stepped into the corridor she saw Tom Harrison and a woman she did not know; they were talking to Colonel Wallace.

Harrison recognised her. 'Doreen, sweetheart – I'm so sorry.'

There was no warmth in her eyes. 'What are you doing here?'

'I wanted to see Les. It's the first chance I've had to get away from London. How is he?'

'How do you think he is?' The anger, the accusation were unmistakable.

Harrison felt uncomfortable, unsure why she was so hostile. He put it down to shock. 'If there's anything I can do?'

'I think you've done enough, don't you? That nonsense in the newspapers, just goading those Irish bastards to try something.

Les thought it was a mistake. Well, he was right, wasn't he? But it wasn't you who paid the price – it was my Les.' She appeared to notice Casey for the first time, but her attention remained focused on Harrison. 'I heard that you and Pippa have split up.'

It could have been a sympathetic acknowledgment of the situation by a friend of both parties, yet Doreen's tone was again one of accusation.

As she glanced sideways at Casey, the meaning was clear. If this woman, this stranger, was the reason, then Pippa had done the right thing.

There was an awkward silence between Harrison and Casey as Doreen left and Colonel Wallace went to see if Appleyard was strong enough for more visitors.

'That was awful,' Casey said at last. 'I thought you were great friends with Les and Doreen.'

He swallowed hard. 'We were, once.'

She could see that he was hurt. 'Then why did she react like that? You didn't plant the bomb. It was hardly your fault.'

'Maybe, maybe not. One thing I've learned over the years – you see it all the time with victims and their relatives. They can't hate faceless killers. How do you hate someone you don't know, let alone understand?' It was as though he were trying to answer a private question of his own. 'Perhaps I'm just an easier target for her.'

Wallace emerged from the doors of Ward Six, the sister by his side.

'He'd like to see you, Major Harrison.'

'Five minutes only, mind,' Sister McGuire added.

Appleyard was propped up in bed at a slightly elevated angle, wired to the paraphernalia of the patient-controlled drip-feed of morphine, bottles and monitors. He looked exhausted and deathly pale, but he managed a smile.

'How are you, you old reprobate?' Harrison said.

His friend strained to hear the words. 'I've lost a bit of weight since we last met, Tom. Most effective diet I've ever tried.' The weak laugh didn't quite ring true. 'Anyway, it wasn't you I wanted to see – Sister said you'd brought the lovely Casey with you.'

274

She laughed lightly and leaned across to kiss him on the cheek. 'It's good to see you cheerful, Les.'

'That's made me feel better. Almost got the old third leg going then. I could even start to like Americans.' His effort at humour broke down into a racking cough. When it finally subsided, he said: 'Tom, I've asked but no one here seems to know, and Doreen wouldn't say, what happened in the end that night I copped it?'

Harrison said: 'You don't want to go into all that.'

'I'll be the judge of that.' He sounded a little breathless.

'There was a third bomb, similar to – to the one you tackled.'

'Yes?' His voice was slightly slurred.

'It went off while the terrorists were planting it. Killed two of them.'

Appleyard's eyelids fluttered. 'Sweet Jesus, an own goal . . .' He said the words slowly, almost as though he was savouring the taste of them. 'So this – my accident – wasn't completely pointless.'

God, Harrison thought, even Les blames me for this. Not like Doreen, not up front and full of anger, but underneath it all he holds me responsible.

'Tom, there's something wrong,' Casey said.

Appleyard was mumbling. 'Where's the bloody barrow? What's Al playing at? It's going . . . to be a fucking . . .' He was breathing hard now, his skin becoming grey and waxy with perspiration '. . . fucking great bang.'

Harrison was on his feet, moving towards the staff room. Sister McGuire met him halfway. 'What's the matter?'

'Les has had a relapse or something.' They were striding together, shoes clattering on the polished floor. 'He suddenly became disorientated, sweating. . .'

They stopped at the bedside. Sister McGuire took one look and said: 'Blast-lung. NURSE!'

It was a common occurrence, Colonel Wallace explained afterwards. 'Suddenly the oxygen and blood levels drop, often after twenty-four hours or so. His X-ray will show up cloudy.'

'Is it serious?' Casey asked.

'It's serious, but not usually life-threatening.' Wallace poured them tea in the staff room. 'I spent a year at the Royal Victoria in Belfast. There were a lot of bomb victims but we only lost one through blast-lung. Two or three days on a ventilator and he'll be as right as ninepence.'

'And his legs?' Harrison asked.

Wallace sipped at his tea. 'It might not seem like it to you – or to his wife – but he's been lucky. We've managed to save a hand's breadth of bone beneath the knee. That's enough to fit a prosthesis. Even if we have to take off the other leg – the one we're trying to save – there's a good chance that too can be fitted out artificially.'

'You mean he could walk again?' Casey asked.

'We'll make damn sure he gives it his best shot. Little Sister McGuire is quite the most awsome bully I've ever met. With her help we'll have him walking within the next ten days or so.'

Casey was astounded. 'That's incredible.'

'It's the best way,' Wallace replied evenly. 'Before muscle waste sets in and before the patient has too much time to feel sorry for himself.'

Harrison felt better for hearing the surgeon's bullish attitude. 'Les seems remarkably cheerful and confident.'

Wallace raised one eyebrow. 'Don't let that fool you, Major. Trauma amputees have no time for mental preparation, to think of the life that lies ahead of them. Les Appleyard is a tough nut, thinks and acts like a soldier. The more cheerful and jokey he is now, the deeper will be his depression when it finally sinks in. No more football, running or so many other things he probably liked to do. Post-traumatic stress disorder. He must grieve for himself sooner or later. It's a necessary part of the healing process. Mind as well as body.'

Casey said: 'How many bomb victims have you known, Colonel?'

He drained his tea. 'Not many here at the Cambridge. But dozens over the years, especially in Ulster. Of course, you read about them at the time or see the television coverage and you think, my God, how awful. Then you never hear of them again.

You're a journalist, Miss Mullins, you know what it's like. Another day, another story. But not for those people. For them time stopped on that day the second that the bomb went off. Sometimes I think the dead are the lucky ones. When we medics use the term "seriously injured", it isn't a glib choice of words, it means exactly that. Few people know what a bomb can do. How it tears a limb off a torso like a child's toy. Or what happens with shrapnel or flying glass. I've seen people's faces quite literally sliced in half, cheeks removed down to the gums and teeth, a woman's breast removed with the precision of a surgeon's knife . . .'

Casey winced. 'Please.'

It was raining outside and the tall windows were beginning to fog with condensation, the suffocating warmth of the hospital almost overwhelming. 'All those victims are still out there somewhere. A teenage boy blinded, tapping with his stick. The once pretty girl with a disfigured face and no legs, wondering how her husband can still bear to make love to her. They're all there still, struggling to get through what's left of their lives. Forgotten by a world which cannot bear to witness their torment.'

It was still in the quiet of the staff room, stuffy and claustrophobic. He was talking about Gwen and the years of plastic surgery and skin grafting that lay ahead. Casey shifted uneasily, thinking of the Seven Dials bomb that had so nearly caught her and Candy. They had almost become the people Wallace was talking about. Hoarsely she said: 'I think we really must leave.'

'Of course.' Wallace snapped out of his deep thought, and walked with them down the lofty corridor to the entrance. 'I made a point of boning up on Irish history when I was in Belfast. Read a lot, wanted to understand something of what it was all about, what the Provos were fighting about. And, you know, I could see their historical grievances and what they claim is the justification of their cause.' He stopped by the doors to shake hands. 'Then I asked myself, does it really justify the killing, the maiming and the wanton destruction?'

Harrison said: 'If I hadn't reached the same conclusion, I'm not sure I could do my job.'

They walked back to Casey's Mini Cooper without speaking. She was experiencing a wretched sense of hopelessness and sorrow and thought Harrison was feeling something similar. He rarely appeared angry but now, as she saw the grim set of his jaw, she sensed that he was raging inside.

As they climbed into the car he said: 'I need a drink.'

She started the engine. 'That makes two of us.'

He stared out of the rain-streaked windows, not seeing the pedestrians scurrying with their umbrellas tilted against the rain. 'You know, it's only just come home to me. Seeing Les like that, seeing what's happened to him, what they've done to him. Knowing that no one can turn back the clock.'

'You've known him for a long time.'

'As long as I'd known Jock. We were inseparable once. In Ulster the IRA managed to pick off some ATOs – often deliberately, like that business the other night. But never the three of us. We led a charmed life. Until now. Jock dead and Les crippled. There's only me left.'

'What d'you mean?'

But he didn't know what he meant. Anger was blinding him, the rage of it burning in his head. Seeing Les like that, seeing Doreen cut him dead in the hospital corridor, while somewhere, probably only miles from London, the bombers called AIDAN were sniggering at their victory, laughing at the press coverage of Appleyard being blown up and a Wheelbarrow destroyed. Licking their wounds at two of their own being blown up, but knowing there would be plenty of volunteers to replace them. Unemployed youngsters fed on the cruelty of Irish history, casting the blame for what they did on everyone but themselves. 'Look what they've made us do. Look at us, do we not bleed, do we not weep?' The battle that didn't end in 1921 with partition and the Irish Free State, and never would until the Brits were out and the border torn down. The subject of a thousand rebel songs, then as now.

The own goal was what Trenchard said John Nash of MI5 wanted. Harrison had wanted it too and that was what they'd got. But it was a hollow victory. And, as Doreen had rightly pointed out, it had been he who had called the tune but Les who paid the price. And for what? The snub to PIRA had been overshadowed by their own loss, the political point hardly scored, and the public hardly reassured. And the Provos had two more martyrs to add to the glorious memory of Bobby Sands and his fellow hunger strikers and the others who had gone before and since.

Casey pulled in at a drab roadside pub. Lunch time had passed; the place empty and dusty, with crisp crumbs on the worn carpet and the ashtrays overflowing. The barman absently served a pint of bitter and a half of lager, his attention on the horse race being shown on the television behind the bar.

'I've been thinking,' Casey said as they sat down on the torn windowseat, 'if I hadn't run that article, maybe Les wouldn't be like he is today.'

'Don't blame yourself.' His response was automatic. 'As you said yourself, I didn't plant the bomb. And neither did you.'

She stared down at the fizzing liquid in her glass. 'How can anyone do a thing like that?'

'You wouldn't understand.'

'I'd like to. I'd like to know who could do such evil. To know what drives them.'

'Don't waste your time.'

She picked up the glass, sampled the contents and found she suddenly had no taste for it. 'You're still blaming yourself, though, Tom, aren't you?'

He took the small briar from his pocket, stuffed the bowl with tobacco. 'Perhaps.'

'But you didn't run the story, Tom, I did. It was my decision.'

He turned to face her, his brown eyes intense and fathomless, moist with unshed tears. 'You were set up, Casey. Don Trenchard and I set you up on orders from MI5. You were on a roll with the bombing stories. They saw you were hungry for success. They even pulled in Sir George to give you a fright, to prime you up to co-operate.'

Casey didn't understand. 'I had no problem running the story. It was just your view of the situation and the public had a right to know.'

'It went a little deeper than that. Having examined the devices

279

AIDAN was using, it was decided that if they got any more complicated, there was a good chance that the terrorists would score an own goal.'

She was stunned, speechless for several long seconds. Slowly she said: 'Am I following this correctly? You deliberately manipulated me so that those two bombers died?'

He nodded, clearly unhappy with his confession. 'We couldn't be certain it would work, but we knew the bomb maker was technically untidy. Despite the cleverness of the antihandling ideas, the workmanship was a bit shoddy, poor soldering and bad connections. We knew that the more complicated they made them, the greater the chance they'd finally set off a device by accident. As it was, that wasn't exactly how it happened. It appears someone set off a separate booby trap. But nevertheless it was undoubtedly a direct or indirect result of that article.'

She stared at him. 'I don't believe I'm hearing this, Tom.'

He shrugged. 'There is a precedent, according to Nash. A similar ploy was used in Northern Ireland during the early seventies – press reports that led the terrorists to overcomplicate their bombs with the same result.'

'That same ploy resulted in Les getting blown up, is that right?' she demanded.

'It's possible, but we might never know for sure. It was either an X-ray-sensitive switch or Les just ran out of time. It all depends what fragments the forensic boys can piece together.' He stared down at his own beer, also untouched. 'I guess it doesn't help to say I'm sorry. That I wish I hadn't gone along with it.'

'It doesn't help Les.' Cold. 'God, I'd heard you Brits could be devious . . .'

'Sometimes you have to be when you're dealing with devious bastards like AIDAN.'

'And me, Tom? Was screwing me all part of your *devious* ploy? To prime me up, as you called it? Was that MI5's idea or yours?'

Anger flashed in his eyes. 'C'mon, Casey, it wasn't like that and you know it. I wouldn't be telling you this now if I didn't care about you.'

Her eyes narrowed. 'You bastard, Tom. You don't care about

me. You just care about your own guilty conscience. You've put blood on my hands – not just the blood of those terrorists but also Les's blood. I don't think I can forgive you for that.'

Don Trenchard left early in the morning to check over the security arrangements. He drove down the M3 motorway until, just past Basingstoke, he veered off on the fast A303 dual carriageway before picking up the old Roman road, the A343, which plunged through the rolling hills of Salisbury Plain to the ancient cathedral city itself.

Trafalgar House was on the southern outskirts. In its own parkland, the magnificent stately home stood on high ground overlooking the finger streams of the Avon where they formed part of the picturesque and famous water meadows.

The location had been chosen for a number of reasons. The building was empty and up for sale, plans to develop it into an hotel and conference centre having failed to materialise. Therefore the owner was more than pleased to agree a short-term lease to the government's Property Services Agency. Their experts swept in with lorry loads of furniture, antiques, oil paintings and *objets d'art* to fill the public rooms and bedrooms, as well as conference tables and chairs, while British Telecom installed the necessary secure communications equipment.

Another attraction of Trafalgar House as venue for the Abe Powers talks was its isolation. To the west it was flanked by the Avon, the few footbridges that spanned it being easy to seal off. Running parallel to the river in the east was a single winding country lane which served only to provide access to the estate itself and a few isolated farms. Closing the road would cause inconvenience only to a few locals who used it as a shortcut between the villages of Downton and Alderbury on the edge of the city.

And so the barriers had gone up, blocked by heavy-duty earth-moving equipment and manned by half-a-dozen burly public-works labourers. Local farmers and their workers were issued with special passes and were mildly surprised that Polaroid photographs were taken of them and heat-sealed into the small plastic ID cards. New EC rules, they were told, and everyone knew that Brussels bureaucracy knew no bounds. For effect, one or two sections of the lane were actually excavated, forming security pinch-points surrounded by discreetly armed labourers and more heavy plant. Only the local poachers were aware of the increased number of game wardens prowling the estate with walkie-talkies and shotguns. No one was aware of the covert observation posts in the surrounding fields manned by members of the SAS in plain clothes.

Trenchard came down the A338, turned off by The Bull at Downton, crossed the river and almost missed the northward turning. When he'd cleared the houses he came across the second Road Closed sign. The grim-faced workman in orange overalls checked his ID and waved to the driver of the mechanical digger to reverse up and let him pass.

Idyllic countryside, Trenchard thought, as he drove along the lane, taking the switchbacks carefully until he reached the second checkpoint and continued climbing towards the gatehouse at Standlynch where he swung into the estate.

The SAS major in charge of security met him at the steps to the house. He was wearing a tweed jacket and twill trousers.

'Any problems, Larry?'

The soldier shook his head. 'Sweet as a nut, Don. And I'll tell you something, I've served my time in Ulster over the past fifteen years and I've never known anything like it. The delegates in there are falling over themselves to accommodate each other. This idea of an independent Northern Ireland has really caught their imagination.'

Trenchard raised an eyebrow. 'Really?'

The other man laughed. 'There was a real sticking point this morning when the principle of some kind of equal power-sharing in the new Stormont parliament came up. The air was electric, I can tell you. Well, the Catholic SDLP guy stood up and suggested his formula for the number of seats. Then Ian Paisley took to his feet with his idea – which offered *more*! He got a standing ovation.'

'That's crazy.'

'Maybe not. With Dublin and London out of the picture, all parties are shifting position, having to change their manifestoes.

Basically the SDLP is swinging to the left and the Unionists to the right. As Paisley told me privately, it felt like the burden of being British had been lifted from his shoulders. He feels nothing but bitterness at what he sees as Britain's gradual betrayal over the years.'

'There's just one problem,' Trenchard said.

'What's that?'

'The Provos aren't part of this and they can't be wished away. They're the ones who say whether or not the war is over.'

The soldier smiled. 'Tough shit. I've never seen such optimism – those bastards are well out of it.'

Trenchard said: 'Unfortunately or otherwise, Larry, Ulster is *not* like the Isle of Man. It remains rather attached to Ireland, whether anyone likes it or not.'

He turned then and entered the building, leaving the SAS major to ponder his words. Again he showed his pass to the armed policeman on the oak doors that led to the main debating chamber. There was a large circular table at which the delegates sat: he recognised the party advisers who had been responsible for kick-starting the agreement: Fern Kelly, Peter Rawlings, Ian Findlay and the others. They were now joined by the more familiar faces of Ulster MPs and their counterparts from Westminster and Dublin.

Only Abe Powers was standing, dominating the proceedings with his impressive bulk, stripped to workmanlike shirtsleeves and braces, a floral tie loose at his throat and a lock of silvered hair curling over his forehead.

'Before we break for lunch and you return again to your individual working parties,' he announced, 'I thought you'd like to know the progress we've achieved in the past two days.

'Firstly, we now have constitutional experts here from both the United Nations and the European Community to discuss the legal implications of independence for Ulster and in exactly which form this might best be achieved. That independence has already been guaranteed by both Ireland and Britain, and both have offered a defence treaty in terms of protection against external threat.

'A date of six months hence from the final document signing

has been agreed for independence, prior to which certain security measures – agreed elsewhere – will be put into effect . . .'

Trenchard, watching from the door, understood exactly to what the American referred. The secret protocol. For the first time ever, there would be selective internment of known terrorists on both sides of the border. They would be held for three years by which time, it was believed, their support would have withered and died. A prosperous new country with everything to look forward to would have no time for the men of violence. So ran the theory.

'A newly structured police force will be in train,' Powers continued, 'with the aim of creating a fully representative Catholic–Protestant law-enforcement agency within five years.

'There is to be a new Right to March Act enshrining the right of the people to hold both an Orange Day and a St Patrick's Day march – but only on specified days and in an agreed public place. Mini practice parades, which create most resentment, will not be allowed and traditional rituals that cause sectarian offence, such as effigy burning, will be actively discouraged by political leaders. A new Independent Ulster Day, a public holiday, will be fixed at a date somewhere between the 17th March and the 12th July and will be supported by public funds.

'Discussions are in progress with the Roman Catholic Church with a view to further integrating the education system and adopting a less didactic religious bias which will be acceptable to both sides of the sectarian divide.'

Don't hold your breath, Trenchard thought to himself, and backed towards the doors.

'Two non-political forums are to be set up between Dublin and Belfast, one on Tourism and Culture and another on Trade and Economic Co-operation . . .'

He closed the doors behind him, Abe Powers' litany of agreement gently muffled as he waited until the delegates broke up for a finger buffet and glasses of inferior wine.

A world of their own, he thought. There they all were, carried along on a wave of blind enthusiasm and hope for a new beginning, while the people who really counted were out there somewhere planning their next strike.

284

While AIDAN was determined to bomb its way to the conference table – or destroy the talks completely – Abe Powers' dreams and those of the politicians would remain just that. Dreams.

Over lunch he made a point of talking briefly to Senator Powers and the other leading politicians present. Satisfied that there were no complaints on any aspect of security, he returned to his car and began the drive back to London.

He arrived in the capital just after rush hour, the worst of the commuter traffic travelling in the opposite direction.

When he arrived at the mortuary, only the duty officer was present to answer his questions about the victims of the apparent own goal in Lambeth.

'It's early days, Mr Trenchard. Humpty Dumpty had nothing on these jokers. Both were partially vaporised and we've a lot of bone fragments to piece together.'

'But you have some initial findings?'

The man gave a dry smile. 'I can tell you one was female, about five-four in height and light build. The other was male, possibly five-nine with some curvature to the spine which suggests he was in his late fifties or early sixties. Beyond that, it's pure speculation.'

'So no positive identification?'

'Well, normally the IRA get around to telling the world who their intrepid and heroic bombers were. Otherwise, it'll be a question of matching dental records – once we can reassemble all the bits. Not too difficult if the people concerned have served time.'

'How long is that likely to take?'

'Guessing, four to six weeks. Maybe less, maybe more.'

'And nothing else to go on?'

'A few personal effects.' He produced two polythene bags from a row of locked steel drawers. 'One pearl stud earring and an eternity ring from the woman. And this from the man's hand.'

Trenchard held the little bag up to the overhead light. A plain gold wedding band. And a Celtic Birds ring.

Eddie Mercs looked up from Casey's VDU. 'Is this true?'

'Verbatim.'

285

'I mean it's not a case of you not letting the facts get in the way of a good story?'

'I don't write fairy tales, Eddie.'

'You know it's dynamite, don't you? I just hope you're not doing this because you've fallen out of bed with lover boy?'

She smiled ever so sweetly. 'I'm not that sort of girl.'

'And it wasn't unattributable?'

'For Christ's sake, Eddie, no. He just told me. Period.'

Mercs grunted. 'Well, it's certainly got to be a breach of confidence.'

'That's my problem. The thing is, do you think they'll run with it?'

'Probably – provided the editor doesn't mind kissing his knighthood goodbye. Besides, the whole thing's going to break in the next few days.'

'What whole thing?'

'The link between the AIDAN campaign and those secret talks. You remember, Senator Abe Powers? There's been a leak from his home town, probably from one of his political staff there. It could be Powers' opening gambit to run for Vice President. A small item in the local newspaper hinting at an imminent breakthrough on the Irish question. It's been on the wires and I'm not going to be the only one who's picked up on it. I've been onto the Northern Ireland Office and they're still denying everything – but, unofficially, my contact says there *could* be an announcement next week.'

'So, what are you going to do?'

'Me, I'm packing my shillelagh and my mouth organ and heading acrus the wutah,' he replied, trailing into a dreadful Irish accent.

'To Belfast?'

'Belfast, Derry, Dublin – whatever it takes. Gerard Keefe owes me and it's time to call in the debt.'

'Let me come with you.'

Mercs was taken aback. 'You? Why on earth would you want to go there? There's no story in it for you.'

She slid her arm around his shoulder. 'I'm curious, that's all,

Eddie. There's been so much talk about Northern Ireland lately and I know nothing about the place.'

He grunted, aware that his resistance was token. 'You don't want to know either.'

'But I *do*, Eddie. I'll be no trouble, promise. I'm due some leave – is it a deal?'

Casey had no doubt that it would be and, despite his apparent reluctance, neither did Mercs. Indeed he'd be lying to himself if he said the prospect of her company didn't delight him. A willowy American redhead on his arm – it could do his credibility no harm at all. Privately he recognised that the prospect of luring her into his bed was remote, but he didn't dwell on the down side; with some things it was better to live in eternal hope.

The article revealing a Security Service plot to manipulate the press into persuading the IRA bombers to complicate their bombs sufficiently to blow themselves up was raised at the morning news conference. It was referred to the lawyers who were afraid that as only the *Standard* had carried the story the newspaper might find itself open to a suit for contributory damages from Les Appleyard and his wife.

When the story finally appeared in the midday Late Prices edition, all direct reference to Major Tom Harrison as the source was removed, as were all references to the fact that Appleyard might have been injured as a direct or indirect result of MI5's wheeze and the *Standard*'s own article. To avoid anyone else making the obvious connection after her previous articles, Casey Mullins's by-line was removed and replaced by an anonymous 'Staff Reporters' credit before it made the front-page headlines.

It fooled nobody.

Tom Harrison caught the full broadside of Al Pritchard's fury the moment he stepped into the Section's office after lunch.

'Of all the bloody irresponsible things to say!' the Sexpo fumed. 'Apart from anything else, how the hell are Les and Doreen going to feel with all this stuff over the papers?'

Al Pritchard wasn't the only one. John Nash was waiting by his side, his face tight with scarcely suppressed anger. However, he was a little more diplomatic. 'We need to talk, Major.' The use of his rank sounded ominous. 'I believe your office is free.'

Harrison led the way. As soon as the door closed behind them, Nash said tersely: 'I hope you've got a bloody good explanation.' He slapped down the latest edition of the *Standard*.

The SATO picked it up, dry-mouthed, and scanned down the column.

'Well?' Nash asked impatiently.

Harrison looked up. 'Well, what? It's true, isn't it?'

'That's hardly the bloody point, Tom! You had no business telling the Mullins woman that.'

'You were the one who wanted to win over the press. To take her into my confidence.'

Veins swelled in Nash's temples. 'Don't get funny with me. Haven't you ever heard of the Official Secrets Act, or did they just neglect to ask you to sign it when you joined the army?'

'I don't remember you saying anything about Official Secrets when you coerced me into this, John. And I don't remember you specifically telling me what *not* to mention.'

Nash scowled and thrust his hands deep into his trouser pockets. 'And, Tom, when I suggested you got into bed with her, I didn't mean literally, so stop playing silly buggers. The last thing I expected was this sort of pillow talk.'

'I can do without your cheap comments.'

A slow, bitter smile crossed Nash's face. 'Well, if my comments are cheap, Tom, yours are going to turn out to be bloody expensive. The brown stuff has already hit the fan – it's not only over my office but all over the Yard and the MOD – the Northern Ireland Office and Downing Street, too, are only a matter of time. You're going to regret this bitterly.'

Harrison turned slowly, his words precise and well chosen. 'The only thing I regret, Nash, is that I allowed Don to talk me into this in the first place. If I'd trusted my instincts, Les might still have his legs.'

'Is this what it's all about?'

'I saw Les yesterday. Not a pretty sight.'

For a moment Nash was unsure, his footing lost. 'C'mon, Tom, for God's sake, you're a soldier and this is war.'

Harrison's eyes fixed on his. 'Don't talk to me about soldiering and war. All you know is cloak-and-dagger stuff.'

'So you're blaming me for Les's accident?'

A hesitation. 'No, ultimately I blame PIRA. But you and I played our parts, didn't we? All too damn well.'

Nash looked momentarily chastened. He was beginning to perspire and fiddled nervously with the knot of his tie, letting air get to his collar. At length he said: 'Well, Tom, if it's any consolation, I don't think you'll be playing a part for much longer. The Anti-Terrorist Branch is acceding to Pritchard's renewed request that you be taken off the Section.'

'Maybe I *need* a touch of clean Belfast air. At least there I've got some idea who the enemy is.'

He knew he'd gone too far then when he saw the expression in Nash's eyes. 'You won't be returning to Belfast. I've already spoken to CATO. The colonel isn't too pleased with you. You've got leave due – you're to take it while it's decided what to do with you. Frankly, Major Harrison, I think your career has come to a premature end.'

Harrison leaned across the desk, his fists planted firmly on the leather top, his jaw jutting defiance. 'And frankly, my dear, after all this I don't think I give a damn.'

But he did. He knew the moment Nash stalked to the door and slammed it closed making the glass rattle. Even through his anger with the terrorists, with Nash and with himself, he knew he cared. His job wasn't just a job, it was a vocation. It hadn't started like that, but that was what it had become. It had been the same with all of them. Jock Murray, Les Appleyard and Tom Harrison, the three musketeers. And now there was only him left. If he were to be kicked out of the Service now, then the terrorists had won.

He needed to know exactly where he stood. Picking up the telephone, he dialled direct through to CATO in Lisburn. 'It's Tom here, Colonel.'

'Ah, you didn't waste much time, old son.'

Harrison closed his eyes in relief. The lilting sing-song accent

289

was as friendly as ever. An ally if ever one was needed. 'Sorry, I seem to have blown things this end. I was a bit cut up after seeing Les Appleyard yesterday and spoke out of turn to a journalist friend. It was a stupid thing to have done.'

There was a brief, considered silence. 'I thought there had to be a reason for it, Tom. That's somewhat reassuring. But bad news travels fast. The front page of the *Standard* has been faxed. I would be surprised if the Sinn Fein office hasn't even been sent one. However, I'm afraid your reasons won't cut much ice with the powers that be. They'd want your head on a pole if it wasn't that they'd prefer to hush the whole thing up as soon as possible. Afraid it might be seen as the government trying to influence these nonexistent talks that aren't going on.' On an open line, this was telling anyone who wanted to listen what he really thought of the Establishment's treatment of his Senior ATO.

Harrison said: 'Am I reading the tea leaves right, sir? My career's finished?'

There was a slight pause. 'You've powerful friends at court, Tom. Me for one and Don Trenchard for another are planning to have a word in the GOC's ear. Your future is safe. But the Northern Ireland Office won't want you back here, Tom. After that revelation, they say you're a liability, a natural target for the little people. And they could well be right. I'm sorry, you'll be sorely missed.'

Harrison knew exactly what the colonel meant. His job was safe, but his career was finished. The sentence was implicit: no return to Ulster meant he could never become CATO. Exiled for ever in the purgatory of some arms dump in one of Britain's shrinking overseas outposts making inventories of war stock and blowing up unstable old ammunition.

There could hardly even be a lucrative future as a civilian in the Section. Not now.

And his private life was similarly bleak. Not only had his marriage finally broken down, but he'd also managed to destroy the first real love to enter his life in years. Allowed himself to put duty before honour. Unlucky was starting to look like bloody carelessness.

As he replaced the receiver, with Colonel Lloyd-Williams confirming he would be relieved in London the next day by a major who was flying in from Germany, Harrison almost felt sorry for himself. Only the thought of Les Appleyard's plight kept him from self-pity and reminded him to make a call to the Cambridge.

His friend was still on a ventilator, Wallace told him, but his condition was stable.

He hung up and looked around the empty office. Two weeks' enforced leave lay before him. He was tempted to pack a tent and a backpack and take to the hills. Maybe South Wales or the Yorkshire Dales. Pippa might be persuaded to agree to Archie going with him. That would be good; oddly enough, since his split with Pippa, he and his son had been getting on especially well together. Harrison had managed to snatch the odd afternoon off to take Archie fishing, to the cinema or, if time was tight, just for a McDonald's. Thankfully Pippa had always been at work when he called. Yes, he decided, a camping trip would be fun.

And Casey?

Just the thought brought a smile to his face. He remembered her interest when he told her he liked to hike in remote places. 'I'd like that,' she'd said. 'I used to be a Girl Scout. And I like to think I can still switch from satin to denim. Next time you go just give me time to pack my rucksack and rollers.'

The telephone trilled on his desk, jolting him from his memories, and he snatched it up irritably.

'Tom?'

Was this mental telepathy? 'Casey.'

Her words came out in a gush: 'Tom, I'm so sorry. I've been a right cow. I was so angry with you I didn't realise what I was doing – God, I suppose you have seen it?'

'The front page. Yes.'

'They won't know it came from you.'

'They know.'

'I'll deny it. Protection of a journalist's sources and all that.'

Despite himself, he found that he was smiling. It must just have been the pleasure of hearing her voice again. 'Don't bother, Casey, it's all over. They know.'

'Will it affect your career?'

'What career? I've been suspended.'

There was a low whistle of surprise at the other end. 'God, Tom, I really didn't mean that to happen. When I got home at lunch time I told Candy what I'd done. She thought I was mad. She reminded me of that time in the Haymarket when you defused that bomb. She made me realise, Tom . . . You're the best thing that's ever happened to me.'

Momentarily he could hardly speak, an abrupt emotional charge swelling in his larynx. Hearing her voice was like a balm, his future – or lack of it – suddenly seeming of total insignificance.

'Tom? Are you there?'

'Let's meet tonight.'

'Oh, Tom, I'd love to.'

'But?'

'I'm taking a late shuttle to Belfast.' She added, lying, 'On assignment.'

She didn't add that it was her intention to find out the identity of the AIDAN bombers who were terrorising London.

15

The ten-wheeled, seven-ton dumper truck seemed to fill even the huge secure barn. Its gargantuan steel-ribbed cargo body obscured the overhead fluorescent tubes and cast giant shadows onto the concrete floor. The air of unreality was heightened by the drumming of soft summer rain on the corrugated-tin roof; the four of them and the monster bomb, hidden in the velvet darkness of the warm night, cocooned in light from prying eyes. At the country pub only two hundred metres down the road, the couples and their children out for an evening meal and the locals at the bar had no idea that three thousand pounds of fertiliser mix was being primed.

Leo Muldoon and Liam Doran from Tyrone had been loading the sacks. Now they sat, tired and sweating on empty oil drums drinking lemonade from cans.

McGirl stood back, a dog-end smouldering between his fingers, watching as Clodagh Dougan worked on the wiring connections between the tractor unit and the dumper trailer. His eyes narrowed, fixed on her denim-clad rump as she backed out of the confined space. Her sweater had ridden slightly and he glimpsed the smooth arch of her spine.

She was some woman, he decided, so unlike any other he had ever known. Not just her physical strength – he had immediately been aware of her firm, athletic build – but it was her inner strength seemingly fuelled by some personal hatred that intrigued and excited him. So unlike his common-law wife with whom he lived in Donegal, a waifish, pale-faced girl with the dark eyes of a frightened rabbit. Finola had perpetrated acts of terrorism, too, but almost reluctantly and certainly fearfully.

Not so Clodagh Dougan. She was a woman driven, possessed.

Even after the shock of her father's death, when she arrived back at the farmhouse with Muldoon, her tears had already dried and he had not seen them again since. It was as though the tragedy had spurred her on and she had urged him to drop the plans that Hugh had laid for a campaign of smaller explosions and go for a big one. Urged him? The thought brought an invisible smile to McGirl's lips. Urged was hardly the word. Clodagh Dougan had demanded. To hear her speak to him, you would have hardly thought he was Pat McGirl, seasoned commander of the Northern Brigade.

He had been irked by her manner but also beguiled by the passion of her plea and that strange expression in her eyes. Within hours he was in contact with Donny Fitzpatrick, supporting her request to go for an altogether more significant target. A day later, after an extraordinary meeting of the inner caucus of the Army Council, they had received the coded signal to go ahead.

And this was it. Three thousand pounds of it. Almost one and a half tons.

No, McGirl decided, Clodagh Dougan was an enigma. And by Christ he wanted her . . . He thought again of the folded newspaper in his pocket and wondered how she would react. The prospect intrigued him. He would have to choose his moment.

She dropped down from the tractor unit, landing solidly on her feet and brushed down her rumpled sweater. Almost immediately she saw the curl of smoke and the cigarette butt burning between his fingers. He saw the look of disbelief flash in her eyes as she walked straight across to where he stood.

Her voice was low and angry. 'Christ, what is this with you, McGirl? Some sort of macho thing? Put it out.'

He reacted with deliberate languor, taunting her, before dropping the stub to the concrete and crushing it underfoot. 'What's the matter, Clodie, nerves playing you up?'

She looked closely into his eyes. 'I can do without the schoolboy bravado. Save it for when you want to show off to your mates back home.'

He raised his hands in surrender, his patronising grin deepening into a mocking smile.

Clodagh ignored him and turned away, calling out to Muldoon and Liam Doran: 'It's all set, so don't touch anything. We leave in one hour. Nine o'clock.'

The men nodded grimly and watched as she left the barn for the car.

'Some woman,' Doran murmured.

Muldoon grinned cheerfully. 'You'd better believe it, Liam. That one has icewater running in her veins, so she does.'

'Still, wouldn't mind giving it one,' Doran admitted ruefully.

'You?' McGirl said. 'She'd eat you for breakfast and I doubt she'd bother to spit out the bones. Now get your mind back on the job. Check over the bikes.'

'We've checked them.'

'Then check them again.' McGirl turned and followed Clodagh into the churned mud of the yard, shutting the big doors on the awesome juggernaut bomb.

She was waiting impatiently at the wheel as he climbed into the passenger seat. Without a word she let out the clutch and began the brief journey back to the rented house. An antagonistic silence hung between them.

When they arrived, she went upstairs to her room and left McGirl alone to make himself a pot of tea and watch the television. There was an old comedy he'd seen a dozen times before; a banal game show. He wasn't in the mood and turned it off. From the stairs he heard the clank of metal and soft grunts of exertion coming from Clodagh's room.

On impulse he poured a cup for her and took it up.

Her door was ajar. He could see her standing before a full-length mirror, staring at her own image in denim jeans and an unfussy black brassière, legs planted firmly apart as she jerked on the dumbbells, each in turn, her biceps swelling hard to meet the challenge.

So that was why she looked so good. He'd assumed the demand for a set of weights at the house had been for Hughie Dougan to continue the fitness régime he'd followed in the Kesh. He'd been wrong. Judging by the sinuous muscles in her back and shoulders, he guessed she weighed maybe two stone more than she looked.

295

'Had your eyeful, McGirl?' She'd seen him in the mirror.

He nudged the door open with his knee. 'Couldn't knock, hands full. Thought you'd like some tea.'

Her expression softened momentarily; she made no attempt to cover herself, he noticed, and he tried to avoid looking at her breasts.

'Thanks.' She took one of the cups.

'Couldn't help noticing . . .' he ventured warily '. . . you look good. 'Keep yourself in shape.'

'I try.'

'Look good enough to be in that stupid TV show. You know, *Gladiators*. I like strong-looking women.'

She regarded him coolly over the lip of the cup as she drank. 'Is that your clumsy attempt at a pass?'

He felt his anger flare. Why was she always trying to belittle him? And why, although he hid it well, did he always feel like an awkward, tongue-tied adolescent in her presence?

'It was meant to be a compliment.'

'Don't bother.'

McGirl put down his tea on the dressing table. 'What is it with you? Is it just me, or do you hate all men?'

Her eyes hardened. 'Something like that.'

He was frustrated, hunting for the right words. 'I – I mean, you're an attractive woman, you must be nearly thirty . . . But no husband, no boyfriend . . .'

'Know all about me, do you?'

'The security section checks everyone. There's no man in your life, never has been.'

Was that a pitying smile on her face? 'It's what all men think, isn't it? Spinsters and widow women. Christ, she must be frustrated, begging for it. Either that or she must be a dyke.'

McGirl's cheeks coloured; somehow *that* prospect hadn't crossed his mind at all.

'Well, I'll tell you, Pat –' The artificial intimacy of using his first name had the opposite effect, distancing the two of them. '– if I'm lonely and frustrated, I do exactly what you do. I jack off, all right?'

She might just as well have smacked him full-square in the face. He blustered: 'No, Clodie, I didn't mean that, I wouldn't . . .'

'Well, now you know.' Her patronising tone now had an edge of anger. 'And for your information, I *did* have a boyfriend once.'

But he was hardly listening. 'God, Clodie, is it such a sin for a man to fancy you?'

His words jolted her. Maybe it was because she had allowed no man to get close to her, that she hadn't heard such words for so long. For a second she felt wrong-footed, embarrassed at the way she'd treated him. 'I'm sorry. You hit a raw spot, that's all. I didn't mean to give you a hard time.'

He smiled uneasily, fished in his pocket for his cigarettes. Women usually fell at his feet; he wasn't used to this. He tried to regain control of the situation. 'Want to tell me about it?'

'Not really.'

He laid his neck on the block. 'I'd like to know.' And waited for her to cut it off.

To his surprise she didn't. Instead she sat on the edge of the bed, nursing the hot cup in her hands. It was the first time he'd seen her look remotely vulnerable. She didn't look at him but at her own reflection in the mirror when she spoke, her voice low and distant. 'There was a serious love in my life once, around ten – nearly eleven years ago. I was studying at the Poly and I didn't have much time for boys. My father had been away in the Kesh since I was ten and all I thought of was working with him when he came out. Together we'd be the deadliest bombing team ever – to pay the Brit bastards for what they'd done to Ireland. What they'd done to Da, taken him away from me. We'd always been so close until the soldiers came and the troubles began again. It had started as a silly dream, but by the time Da was due out after nine years, that dream had become reality. I had exercise books full of ideas and designs for TPUs and booby traps hidden in my locker – you wouldn't believe it. And all my girlfriends could do at the time was drool over film stars and pop singers.'

But seeing her, listening to her talk, McGirl could believe it. Could visualise the life of the strange introverted daughter of a bomber, desperate to avenge the years of happiness they'd stolen from her and her father. He didn't interrupt, just sipped at his tea in silence.

'I'd told Da about it, but of course he never realised how serious I was. Parents don't, I suppose. Then, maybe a year before he was due out, I met this guy in the canteen at the Poly. Chris Walsh, he said his name was. He seemed a lot older than me at the time. Twenty-five, he said, but I'm sure it was more. A mature student, wanted to be an architect. His parents had emigrated to England from Armagh when he was young and he'd been brought up in London. He had hardly a trace of an Ulster accent. He'd been well-educated and got A-Levels, but hadn't been interested in university then, or so he said. He'd joined the British Army as an officer cadet, but then became disillusioned and left and spent years bumming around the world, working his passage or staying with families of rich friends. He moved in those sorts of circles. Then he began to realise he wasn't getting anywhere or going anywhere. He decided then to go back to university and get a degree; it was easier for a mature student to get a place in Belfast.

'He was very charming, very worldly-wise. Quite persistent in getting to know me, wouldn't take no for an answer. I guess I was pretty flattered by his attentions really. He was far older than most boys I knew; we could talk about anything. We ended up living together in his digs for three months. For the first time ever I felt I could trust someone enough to tell him about my secret plans – I'd only ever told Da. Chris laughed at me, told me I was crazy – we ended up talking about Irish history and arguing endlessly about the rights and wrongs of what the English had done. At one point he almost had me convinced I was wrong. For the first time thoughts of wedding bells and prams came to the fore. Then Da was released from the Kesh; he and Chris actually met once, seemed to get on all right. Then Da did his runner across the border.

'He managed to keep in touch with me, but I never told anyone, not even Chris. But then we found out later that Jimmy Coyle knew what Da was planning to do and blabbed to the RUC when they took him in for routine questioning.'

There was no emotion in her voice as she mentioned the man

she had killed as he attempted to make love to her. Fitzpatrick had related the story to McGirl. It had all the makings of Provo folklore, had earned her the nickname of 'Praying Mantis' behind her back. But more in awe than with any lack of respect for her action.

'At the time I didn't see the connection, but soon after Chris started asking questions about my father. Where was he, what was he doing? I remember, I was actually touched by his interest, his concern.' She shook her head at the memory. 'So bloody stupid! But then I suppose I was still very young. Just nineteen.'

It was intensely quiet in the bedroom, the lapse in Clodagh's story forming an awkward silence. McGirl's voice was hoarse. 'So you told him?'

She inhaled slowly, deeply, and shut her eyes. 'I told him. I thought not much at the time, but obviously it was enough. My father was caught at the border a few days later. And after a week or so, Chris just upped and disappeared. I came back to his digs one night to find him and all his things gone. Only later, much later, I realised he must have been a British spy. Trying to infiltrate any up-and-coming Provies on the campus. He appeared to have fingered two other male students, too, but they were already connected with the movement.'

'What happened to you?' McGirl asked.

One corner of her lips curled in a sardonic half-smile. 'Nothing. For a while RUC and army patrols made a nuisance at our home with their census checks and once I was taken in for interrogation. But they had nothing on me; I hadn't done anything. They had Da back behind bars and that was enough. They probably didn't put too much credence in Chris Walsh's reports.'

'And Walsh, what happened to him?'

'I've no idea.'

'And he's the reason *you* hate the Brits so much?'

'How many reasons do I need?'

Was this the moment, he wondered? He reached into his jacket pocket and withdrew the folded newspaper. 'Here's another one.'

'What?'

'Read it. Today's *Evening Standard*.'

299

Slowly she spread the tabloid across her lap, taking in the headlines, her head bowed slightly to read the text. She said nothing as she scanned down the column, her mouth moving in a silent curse. A small vein throbbed at her temple.

McGirl said: 'They set us up, Clodie. It's all there.'

She looked across at him and he could see the shock and anger in her eyes.

'They as good as executed your da. But it could just as easily have been you.'

Her voice was barely more than a whisper. 'And I fell for it.'

'We all fell for it. The English up to their old tricks again. They're the most devious bastards on God's earth, so they are.' He played his ace. 'But this time we know the individual responsible.'

'Who?'

'You can read it between the lines. It's the current SATO in the Six Counties. The man they brought over to London when they started running scared. Major Tom Harrison.'

'I remember the name, he was the one who gave the interview.'

He nodded. 'The man who set us up. And there's another reason for you to remember that name. Something you probably don't know. It was discovered by the security section when they reopened your father's file when you approached us through Killy Tierney. The man whose evidence actually got the conviction was the ATO who defused a booby-trapped device your da set. The man wasn't identified at the trial, but we placed the name. At the time he was just Captain Tom Harrison.'

Her eyes widened, not quite sure that she believed what she was hearing. 'The same man?'

He nodded. 'Small world.'

'Why are you telling me this?' she asked, but was sure she knew the answer. It was clear in his eyes which occasionally lingered on her body when he thought she wasn't looking. Irritated with herself, she stood suddenly and, picking up her sweater from the bed, slipped it over her head.

McGirl was saying: 'It occurred to me we could do something about it.'

'Like what? We'd never be able to get anywhere near him.'

Slowly, tantalisingly, he said: 'Would you be interested if I said I think I know a way?'

She had picked up the automatic pistol from the bedside table and was checking the magazine. One eyebrow arched as she looked directly at him. 'Interested in what exactly?'

'Interested in doing something about it,' he said.

Interested in letting me get inside your knickers, he thought. Then realised suddenly that she knew he was deliberately trying to get close to her, draw her into a conspiracy. He could see the knowing, disdainful look in her eyes.

She said: 'You know damn well I'm interested if I can get even with the bastard. What do you know about him?'

'Enough. And he'd be a legitimate target.'

She slipped the pistol into her waistband, pulled a short leather jacket over her shoulders. 'Let's talk about it tomorrow. Right now we've got work to do.'

He nodded his agreement, quietly satisfied at his progress.

'Just one thing, McGirl. You're married, right?'

'Not exactly.'

'With a child?'

He didn't answer; there was no need. She'd made her point.

The matter wasn't raised again before they drove back to the barn. Muldoon and Doran were waiting, the two motorcycles checked and loaded aboard the red Transit, the sides liveried with cheap plastic signs for a genuine motorcycle retailer in London. They all pored over the map for one last time, confirming the routes and synchronising watches.

Clodagh and McGirl opened the barn doors then and watched the van go. The next thirty minutes dragged by, then they climbed up into the high cab of the dumper truck. As the enormous engine thundered into life, the entire building trembled.

This would be a night London would never forget.

They took the seven thirty British Midland flight to Belfast.

Casey fretted over the wisdom of leaving Candy to look after herself in the house, even though a girlfriend was staying with her, and wished she'd been able to see Harrison before she left. At least he'd shown no sign of bitterness when they had spoken on the telephone and she loved him for that. The short flight was halfway over before it began to dawn on her exactly what she was trying to do; then the apprehension began to set in.

Eddie Mercs offered no comfort. A bad flyer at the best of times, he'd forgotten that it was a No Smoking flight and had become increasingly irritable, attempting to calm his nerves by emptying a row of miniature plastic whisky bottles.

'Not my fault I was a breast-fed baby,' he complained bitterly when Casey chided him about his alcoholic intake. 'They should make allowances for those of us who need oral satisfaction.'

The vision of a fully grown Mercs suckling blissfully at his mother's bosom brought only a momentary light relief from her fears of what lay ahead. That dread word. Ulster. That dark and evil place she knew only through television news and press reports. An endless round of bombs and shootings. She was entering an urban war zone for which she was totally unprepared. But it was also Tom Harrison's world and that, somehow, gave her a small measure of confidence.

They touched down at Aldergrove in failing daylight beneath a cloudy, rain-filled sky.

She had been expecting the terminal to resemble an armed camp, like some tinpot banana republic, and it was with a sense of relief that she saw only one armed policeman talking nonchalantly to some plain-clothes security personnel. No one stopped them, asked them who they were or where they were going.

The car-hire company had sent a small courtesy bus to take them to their vehicle and after a few minutes' form-filling they were on their way south towards Belfast.

There was one permanent vehicle checkpoint on the airport road, manned by the RUC. The policeman was polite, asked to see Mercs's driver's licence, then waved them on.

They continued on through the monotonous flat countryside, the rain becoming gradually more persistent. Within half-an-hour Mercs was negotiating the city-centre streets, taking the bridge across the River Lagan, which divided west from east Belfast, and was heading up Newtownards Road. It was a grey sprawling area of shabby high-street shops with side roads of Victorian terraced houses interspersed with some modern estates.

One brightly and crudely painted gable end, which looked onto the main street, left them in no doubt whose territory they were in. This was Protestant heartland.

'Not much chance of wandering into the wrong patch in this city,' Mercs muttered, 'unless you're a blind man.'

The Park Avenue Hotel on Holywood Road was large, bland and reasonably modern. The reception staff were friendly and asked conversationally whether they were visiting on business or pleasure. When Mercs replied: 'A bit of both,' they didn't inquire further.

Time was pressing. It was nine forty-five already, so after checking into their respective rooms, Mercs called for a taxi to take them back into the city centre.

This time an army checkpoint of khaki-coloured Land-Rovers had materialised on the bridge and Casey felt a sudden sense of unease at the sight of the young men in full combat webbing and helmets. They looked menacing with their SA 80 Bullpups and serious faces.

A brief inquiry at the cabby's window, a check on his licence and a quick glance at the passengers in the back. That was all and they were on their way.

'Don't you get sick of all these checks?' Casey ventured to ask the driver.

He chuckled and his accent was so harsh and heavy that she had difficulty in understanding his reply. 'Sure you get used to it. But sometimes 'tis a real pain, so it is. Though I think if we ever get real peace here, we might even miss it.'

She wasn't sure she'd heard right. 'You actually enjoy all the trouble?'

'No, love, not at all. But we're so used to it, we would miss it, kind of. Otherwise Ulster would be a very dull place. The violence gives it an edge, a buzz. But then you're American, yes? Sure you'd have to live here to understand.'

She glanced sideways at Mercs; he said nothing, just raised his eyes to the heavens.

They had arranged to meet Gerard Keefe at the Front Page public house in Donegall Street. It was Friday night and a favourite haunt of the city's journalists for celebrating the end of the working week. The taxi dropped them off outside the dark forbidding frontage with its blinking neon sign. Creaking stairs led the way to the upstairs bars. The noise of excited, gabbling voices and too-loud laughter hit them, the room thick with tobacco smoke and the yeasty smell of stout. It was packed, the rough pine bar and floor almost obliterated by the press of bodies, faces smiling and glowing with alcohol, unwinding fast after a frantic day. Above their heads the giant fan struggled to clear the air.

Mercs led the way, weaving through the bodies, treading on feet and mumbling his apologies, peering at groups of men and women as he attempted to find Keefe. Casey trailed behind, finding herself watching individuals, looking at their unconcerned and happy faces. And thinking, this is Belfast. This is the dark soul of Ireland.

Keefe was talking to a rapt audience – two long-haired and pretty girls who looked to be scarcely out of their teens. As he spoke earnestly across the table, decorating his words with a flourish of hand gestures, they appeared to hang on his every sentence.

He caught sight of Mercs edging towards him. 'Eddie!'

Casually dressed in a dark jacket and black open-necked shirt, his face was pale with dark worried eyes that were set closely together beneath wild eyebrows. The confusion of unruly hair made him look younger than his forty years.

'Thought you weren't going to make it,' he said, rising to shake Mercs's hand and quickly noticing Casey. 'Didn't know you were going to bring your girlfriend . . .'

'Unfortunately, Gerry, we only work together.'

'You're still a lucky man. I'm charmed, eh . . .?'

'Casey. Casey Mullins.'

He nodded towards the girls, indicating it was time for them to go; reluctantly they took the hint and he beckoned to the barmaid to take an order for drinks. Gerard Keefe was something of a minor, self-promoting celebrity, Casey decided, as he fixed her with a winning smile and an uncomfortably penetrating stare. 'So what d'you think of Belfast, Casey?'

'I haven't seen much of it. Except for the odd Land-Rover and foot patrol I've seen, it seems just like England. I'm not sure I was expecting that.'

'You'd notice the difference if you crossed into Eire. That's *real* Ireland, beginning with the state of their roads and their signs, of course. Yield instead of Give Way. It's all somehow less ordered, more relaxed.'

Thinking aloud she said: 'And there were no checks at the airport. I think that surprised me.'

Gerard Keefe gave the drinks order to the barmaid before answering, leaning forward conspiratorially. 'What you must never forget, Casey, is that over here nothing is what it seems. Remember that. You'll get no trouble from the security people unless they're interested in you and mostly they've their work cut out with known terrorists. There's no hassle for businessmen –' he indulged in a broad grin '– or journalists. But if they *are* interested in you, they'll know your every movement. Each time you stop at a roadblock your car registration number is checked against the computer. There are informers everywhere. For the army, the Provies and the Proddies. Unemployment's high, so there're a lot of bods about with bugger all else to do. When people innocently ask you which school you went to or where you live, what they really want to know is are you a Catholic or a Prod? Can I talk to you, can you be trusted? The young woman pushing a pram might have an Armalite in there with her wee child. The door-to-door salesman might be checking on Catholic families, finding a target for a sectarian killing. Last year near the border a farmer ploughed up an entire field. An alert army patrol leader, a country boy himself, thought it was an odd time of year to do it. When they checked it, it was an elaborate ruse to disguise the laying of a half-mile command cable for a bomb under the road.'

The drinks arrived; Keefe made no attempt to produce his wallet until Mercs paid and brushed aside the Irishman's belated offer to pay.

'There's always people listening,' Keefe continued. 'This place is a favourite haunt for the press. The *Irish News* office is just across the street. That's the Catholic daily. You often get their journos in here, and you'll find their perception of events quite different from those on the *Telegraph* around the corner.'

'And who do you write for?'

'Anyone who'll pay me. I just alter the slant.'

Mercs said: 'And just what slant would you put on Abe Powers' secret talks, Gerry?'

The journalist's eyes hardened. 'I'm still waiting for that earlier cheque you promised.'

Mercs was unfazed. 'Bloody accounts department.' He patted the front of his jacket. 'Never mind, I've a bundle of readies for the right answers.'

'I'm not sure I can give them.'

'Try, Gerry, there's a good chap.'

Keefe glanced around him to check no one was within earshot. 'First thing to realise, Eddie, is that this is like nothing I've ever known before. The Six Counties and the Free State have always been a hotbed of rumour and gossip. We all know no Irishman can keep a secret. Well, this time they have. You've got to ask yourself how they've achieved it?'

'How?' Mercs pressed.

'There's a strong rumour of a secret protocol. It was signed by Dublin and London in the early stages and formed the stick of Abe Powers' carrot-and-stick policy. Regardless of the shape of any final agreement, Dublin has promised to hold a referendum recommending the dropping from its constitution of Article Two, which lays claim to Ulster.'

Mercs shook his head. 'Why the hell should Dublin do that? They could have done that at any time in the past twenty years.'

'Because in return London promises to back Eire within the European Community on its claims to Regional and Social Funds and its interests under the Common Agricultural Policy. What you've got to remember is that Eire is ninety-eight per cent in debt. It's poor, inflation is rampant and its economy is in deep mire. Britain's robust support in Brussels means that Dublin

306

won't have to put up taxes and will have huge amounts to invest in infrastructure. Incumbent governments in Ireland are always losing elections over the economy and rising taxes. For once, they're virtually guaranteed to win.

'Dublin wants that agreement like crazy, especially as it means they'll never have financial responsibility for Ulster dumped on them. The Protestant parties here are also desperate to win the goodies in the protocol. For a start it virtually guarantees they'll *never* be part of the Republic and secondly it totally pulls the rug out from under the Provies.

'But the trick is that the protocol isn't ratified until the whole package is agreed. That has ensured that no one rocks the boat because no one wants to lose what is so clearly within their grasp. It has also guaranteed everyone keeps their mouths shut until the final deal is struck for fear of blowing the whole thing.'

Mercs frowned. 'Do you have any idea what form any final deal might take?'

'If I did, Eddie, I'd be a rich man. But I can tell you something, I've got a feeling in my water about this one. Nobody's giving details, but I've never known such optimism from both the Unionist and Catholic camps. They really seem to think an end's in sight. Abe Powers seems to have satisfied three sides of the square.'

'But is three sides enough, Gerry? From what you say, the Provos are the only ones to get nothing out of the deal.'

'And that's the reason for the AIDAN bombing campaign,' Casey added pointedly.

Keefe looked startled and dropped his voice another octave. 'A word of warning, Casey, don't go bandying around codewords. If they get generally known, all sorts of people can have motives to cause chaos and blame others. But yes, it explains the ferocity of the latest campaign in London. The Provies want the talks abandoned or a seat at the table – and they will stop at nothing. All I know is, I'm bloody glad the bombing has shifted to England. It was getting too hot for comfort over here, I can tell you.'

'These bombers, Gerry, are they just one gang or what?' she asked.

Keefe's eyes had become fixed on a lone drinker at the bar. A heftily built young man in jeans and a leather blouson was watching their table with studied nonchalance as he took sips from a straight glass of Guinness.

The journalist said: 'Look, this isn't the place to talk about such things. I've got to get home now, but I can give you a lift. We can talk on the way.'

Casey was slightly taken aback by the sudden change of tack, but remembered Mercs's warning that the mercurial Keefe rarely held a conversation without moving location half-a-dozen times.

They trooped out into the dark wet street and followed Keefe to the nearby car park. He checked carefully beneath his vehicle before he let them in, Mercs taking the front passenger seat.

'Look, Eddie, I've prepared a list of people you might like to speak to. Mostly they're on the political fringes. They might not know much about the talks, but at least they're willing to speak – for a price. Those who *do* know, aren't saying.'

'You're a gem,' Mercs said, accepting the sheets torn from a note pad and handing over a wad of sterling notes in return.

'Those people are expecting to hear from you.'

'And the bombers?' Casey asked.

Mercs became irritable. 'Let's drop that one, eh?'

'No, it's all right,' Keefe said. Casey wondered if he was afraid of having his reputation as the Ulster guru undermined. 'Look, I've got access to the very top of all the paramilitaries. They all trust or distrust me equally, depending on which way you look at it. But no one on the Republican side is going to give anything away about the AIDAN active service unit. Not a hint, not a whisper. I can pick up the phone and speak to Gerry Adams of Sinn Fein and sometimes even Martin McGuinness will talk to me. But they've become figureheads in the Republican movement, too well-known. This business runs deeper. The people you'd want are operational; those at the top wouldn't even know the details, wouldn't want to.'

'So how could I find out the identity of the AIDAN bombers?'

'Casey!' Mercs said, his face reddening with embarrassment. 'You just *don't* ask questions like that.'

308

'I just have.' She smiled one of her sweetest smiles. 'I'm an American.'

Keefe chuckled. 'Eddie's right. You're likely to be one dead American if you're not careful.'

'I'm serious, Eddie. Those people have killed an innocent child my daughter's age and maimed her mother who is a friend of mine. And they killed one bomb-disposal man and injured another I'd got to know. I'd like to be able to name them in print.'

'Still want your Pulitzer,' Mercs muttered despairingly.

Keefe smiled patiently. 'Look, Casey, sometimes a whisper goes out that so and so was responsible for some killing, or is on the gallop in England. Someone blabbing in Dublin or speculating in the Kesh. Nothing is ever confirmed, and even that happens rarely now. Security is much tighter. Other sources can be Army Headquarters in Lisburn or the RUC at Knock, but they need a reason for telling you and you never know what it is. Let's say at best their information is likely to be unreliable.'

'And there's no one else?' It sounded like a dead end.

'Well, if there's something you want to know about the Provies that they or the authorities can't or won't tell you, the best people to ask are their sworn enemies. One of the illegal Protestant gangs, the UFF, the UVF or the Red Hand Commandos.'

'Could I speak to them?'

'They might not want to speak to you. If anything they distrust journos more than the Provies. Feel the media's never given them a fair show. You should be warned, they're a dangerous bunch. If the Provies don't like what you print, they're likely to shrug it off, try to win you over another day. If you upset the Prods, they might just shoot you.'

Casey felt the clammy fingers of apprehension crawl up her spine. 'I'd still like to give it a try. Do you know someone?'

Keefe stared at the windscreen for a moment. 'There is a face. At least he *might* let you pose the question, even if he won't give you an answer.'

'Who's he with?'

'That would be telling.' Keefe took the mobile telephone from his pocket and punched in a number. After a long wait he said:

'Billy? – Gerard here. How's it going? Good. Listen, I've a couple of friends with me. Journos over from London. One's a very pretty American lass with gorgeous legs. Digging the dirt on the other side. I was wondering if you'd be willing . . .?'

Mercs leaned over towards the back seat. 'This is *not* a good idea. Let's drop it, eh?'

'No, Eddie.' She touched his arm. 'But I don't expect you to come along if you don't want to.'

'God knows what trouble you'll get into if I don't.' He shook his head unhappily. 'And who was it promised she'd be no trouble? I should have guessed.'

Keefe said: 'That's settled.' He put away his mobile. 'You've got an audience with King Billy. It was the gorgeous legs that sold him.'

Casey laughed. 'Wasn't that just the slightest bit sexist. When he finds out the truth, maybe it'll be you who gets shot.'

Keefe turned back, making an obvious point of looking at her knees. 'Oh, I don't think King Billy will be disappointed, Casey, I really don't.'

The heart of big Billy Baker's kingdom was a nameless drinking club in the Ardoyne, not far from the Peace Line. It was just a short drive in Keefe's ageing Toyota saloon. A dark street, the bulbs in the lampposts shattered so that no light was cast on the black-painted frontage. No one, Keefe pointed out, wanted to illuminate targets entering or leaving the premises.

Hardly had he applied the handbrake than the steel-reinforced door with its fisheye spyhole swung open. There was no light from the hallway and through the condensation of the car window, Casey was aware only of vague, fast-moving shapes as they were surrounded. All four doors were opened almost simultaneously, causing her to gasp with apprehension.

There was a slight quaver in Keefe's voice. 'Hello, Spike.'

'Mr Keefe.' The accent hard, the tone neutral. 'I've told you before not to park outside.'

'Not parking, Spike, just dropping off. Two visitors for King Billy. He's expecting them.'

Casey was aware of the tension ebbing as she struggled to

extract her long legs from the car and stand on the pavement. There were four of them. Sharp-featured young men, each one powerfully built and with his hair close-cropped.

Spike was the most muscular, pectorals and beergut straining against the rain-damp T-shirt. He also sported the shortest hair, razored to a dark bloom on his bullet head. His small fierce blue eyes looked her up and down, then switched warily to Eddie Mercs as the reporter stumbled awkwardly from the front passenger seat.

'Follow me,' Spike ordered.

She had expected Keefe to stay, not drive off into the night. Looking across the pavement, she could see that Mercs, too, shared her fear. Another of the young men placed his hand on her elbow, ushering her forward, following Spike's swaggering gait as he melted into the darkness of the hallway. She heard the front door crash shut, the heavy-duty bolts sliding home.

Abruptly the blackout curtain was jerked aside and the light hurt her eyes. As her vision adjusted to the brightness, she became aware of the thumping beat from a jukebox.

The faces of the people seated at the small round tables turned in unison. Laughter and conversation died away. There were strangers in their midst.

Mostly young men, Casey noticed, just a few old-timers in flat caps propping up the bar. A Union flag was draped above the optics and a mural of a mounted William of Orange, bearing the legend No Surrender, covered the entire far wall. It was a spartan and unwelcoming place, with bare floorboards and smelling of ale and stale cigarette smoke.

She felt quite relieved to see that two teenage girls had been dancing around their handbags in front of the jukebox. A semblance of normality. The murmur of conversation began again.

Her relief, however, was short-lived as Spike passed behind the bar and through another steel-plated door. Was this King Billy's fortress keep, she wondered, the bar acting as his moat if assassins breached the outer defences?

The stairs creaked underfoot as they climbed; a single bulb without a shade threw ragged shadows on the peeling wallpaper.

One door was open on the landing and they entered a small windowless room. It was empty except for a wooden table, a chair and a tattered doctor's screen. Her fear returned, her stomach beginning to churn.

Spike jerked the screen open, dividing the room in two. 'I'm going to have to ask you to strip off and be searched before we go in.' He spoke without emotion, as though it were the most natural thing in the world. 'Take one side each.'

Casey's fear turned to sheer terror, but she did her best to hide it. 'Can't you just frisk us?' she asked in a shaky voice.

'We're not looking for weapons.'

'And if I refuse, does it mean I can't see Mr Baker?'

'Yes, lady, you can see him. But you're journalists, right? So if you want him to talk about what we expect you want to talk about, you're searched first.' He waited for her to make her decision, adding: 'If we'd more warning we'd have got a woman in to do this. Don't worry, you're safe enough.' It was the nearest he came to apologising.

She glanced at Mercs. He'd made no attempt to undress and looked very uncomfortable.

Somehow, she wasn't sure why, she trusted the man called Spike. In a very small voice she said: 'All right.'

The young man indicated the table. 'Take your things off and put them on there.'

Christ, this was terrifying! This was the sort of place you heard about in Ulster. A quiet backroom, the kangaroo court, tortured for information with a black hood over your head, then knee-capped or murdered with a bullet in the back of the skull.

Her fingers were trembling so much she could scarcely undo the buttons of her blouse. Spike was already going through her handbag carefully, one of his companions checking Eddie Mercs's jacket and wallet. At least they did not appear to be watching her.

Standing in her brassière and American pantyhose, with tights and lacy black briefs combined, she clutched her hands to her chest and darted quickly forward, dumping her skirt, blouse and jacket on the desk.

Spike glanced up. 'Everything please.'

He looked down again at what he was doing.

Taking a deep breath, she stripped naked, standing and feeling foolish with one hand at her crotch and the other inadequately attempting to hide her breasts.

Spike had finished checking the seams of her underwear and suddenly looked straight at her. She expected there to be a lascivious smirk on his face, a leer. But the face was almost frighteningly impassive. 'Hands down and turn, slowly.'

Her eyes shut and she obeyed, experiencing the worst sense of fear and humiliation she had ever known.

Then it was over.

As disinterested as before, Spike moved her clothes back across the table top. 'Get dressed.'

Dammit, she thought, he's talking like a bloody doctor. It was unnerving. She dressed more quickly than she had ever done in her life, getting in a muddle in her desperation to pull on her pantyhose, snagging the nylon until it laddered the full length of one leg. Hot and uncomfortable, she finally felt a semblance of dignity return.

Mercs appeared from behind the screen, tucking his shirt into his waistband, and Spike was knocking on the door at the far side of the room. A gruff voice barked in response and the young minder turned the handle. 'Your guests are here, Billy.'

They were shown in.

King Billy held court behind a huge battered desk in a dark room illuminated only by a green-shaded editor's lamp. It lit up his huge frame, giving the impression that he was the only person there. Like a buddha, she thought, floating in the darkness. Only later, as her eyes adjusted, did she notice other things. There were two acolytes standing in the shadows behind him, hard-faced men in leather jackets. Over their heads on the wall were the colours of the local Linfield Football Club. In a far corner of the room she noticed an array of banners, all neatly furled in a rack, and a monstrously large Lambeg drum.

'Miss Mullins, Mr Mercs.' The big man struggled to his feet, his belly straining against the desk edge as he reached across to

313

shake their hands. His face was broad and blunt, the flattish nose curiously kinked where it had once been broken; his white hair was cropped and neat, his eyes the palest powder blue that Casey had ever seen. 'Sit, sit, please.'

As he resumed his own seat, she saw he was wearing a loudly patterned kipper tie and a shirt with short sleeves from which his massive pink arms protruded like legs of ham.

Casey smiled uneasily. 'I'm not sure whether to call you Your Highness or what?'

His laugh was like a volcano threatening eruption, a low rumbling roar from deep within the mountain of flesh, bubbling up to a wheezy chuckle in his throat. The sound was curious coming from such a pretty rosebud mouth. 'Very good, Miss Mullins. But no, no, King Billy is just a nickname. The boys like to have their fun. Billy like William of Orange, see? Appropriate that, bit of a joke. Just call me Billy.' He leaned back, grinning, the mirth subsiding. Then he appeared to notice her obvious nervousness. 'Oh, sorry about that outside. It's become routine nowadays, but we're not used to ladies visiting. I trust the boys conducted themselves properly?'

'Exemplarily,' she said, wondering if he noticed her sarcasm. 'But I don't understand the reason.'

For a moment he looked embarrassed. 'A few years ago that wouldn't have been necessary, but we can no longer trust the British. Nowadays they're always trying to get evidence against us Loyalist groups. There was one case, a woman – she was undercover for Special Branch – came to a meeting, the UVF I think, and recorded everything. Later they learned she'd had a highly sensitive microphone concealed – er,' now his face was the colour of rare steak, '– between her legs, shall we say? Sorry. It was connected to an aerial wire fitted in her bra with a small battery. The conversation was recorded by an unmarked radio van parked outside. Five good men were convicted.'

'I see.' It was just bizarre enough to be true. 'But you know we're friends of Gerard Keefe?'

Another throaty chuckle. 'So is half of Belfast. And if you were a spy, Miss Mullins, you would hardly tell him, would you?' He placed his hands in front of him, stretched out the plump fingers. 'Now what is it you'd like to know?'

Suddenly it seemed a fatuous question to ask. Nevertheless that was her reason for being here. Taking a deep breath, she said: 'Eddie here and I work for the *Evening Standard*. As you're no doubt aware there has been a terrible bombing campaign run by the IRA in London. I'd like to know the identity of those bombers.'

His eyes were focused on her, unblinking. 'Would you now?'

In the silence that followed, under King Billy's skin-stripping stare, she felt foolish. Wished she'd kept her mouth shut. Then, suddenly, she thought of little Shirley and Gwen. Of Jock's funeral and Les Appleyard lying in the Cambridge. She said with a defiance that surprised herself: 'I should like to name the bombers in the press.'

The silence continued for a few more moments as the big man weighed something in his mind. Slowly he said: 'It's strange how Ulster can be bombed and blasted for over twenty years and no one on the mainland hardly notices. Then a few bangs in the precious capital and everyone sits up. Do you know why the taigs are bombing London?'

For the first time Eddie Mercs spoke. 'It's these talks Abe Powers has been having.'

King Billy nodded. 'All the taigs ever want to do is destroy, Eddie, do you know that? Destroy the Ulster people, destroy democracy, destroy the Dublin Government if they could – and destroy the Abe Powers' talks. Or, I don't doubt, get a place at the table and hijack any agreement.'

'I'm sure they won't succeed,' Casey said. 'The British Government won't give into terrorism.'

Cold humour glittered in King Billy's eyes. 'Is that what you think? Believe all that rhetoric, do you? Then what followed hard on the heels of the Brighton bombing at the Grand Hotel that damn near killed Prime Minister Thatcher? I'll tell you, the Anglo-Irish Agreement, giving one sovereign state a say in the running of *another* country. It's a world precedent. So the Provos saw the door ajar – just one more push. The Number Ten mortar attack, the City bombs. Then we get Downing Street cosying up to Sinn Fein, pushing us inexorably towards Dublin. Each time the resolve of the government weakens. No, my friends, the Provisional IRA will destroy the talks and the hope for peace, or they will have their say. There are some pressures that no government can resist, no matter what they say. That is what terrorism is all about. And meanwhile we are left excluded. Our fate in the hands of others.'

'We?' Casey asked.

'Let us say those of us of a more determined persuasion.'

'You've got Protestant politicians.' Mercs's gruff voice intervened. 'I can't see them giving up without a fight.'

King Billy gave a derisory snort. 'Abe Powers is in the chair. A known diehard Republican sympathiser. He'll drive a tough bargain and our politicians will have to compromise.'

Mercs said: 'How can they be said to have compromised if they've won. If Dublin renounces its claim on Northern Ireland, then the Orange Ulstermen have nothing to fear.'

'That's a worthless piece of paper!' King Billy almost spat with venom. 'The *intent* remains and always will. News from the talks is scarce, but I understand it's all in the small print. Ulster will be left a political mish-mash, a vacuum, a nothing place, ripe for the Provisional IRA's final takeover. *Realpolitik* is what counts, not articles written into constitutions.'

Casey frowned. 'Do I gather you hate these talks almost as much as the IRA?'

King Billy glanced to one side to where Spike stood, his arms folded across his broad chest. The young man gave a respectfully knowing smirk. 'You could say that. But, unlike the taigs, we are not working to destroy them. Our intention is to help, to take some pressure off the British Government.'

'How?'

'Like you, however difficult it will be – and it will – we intend to find the bombers.'

Mercs was puzzled. 'What real good would it do you if the bombing stopped? What would you realistically stand to gain?'

King Billy hesitated in his reply, stared at his huge hands

clumped on the desk, sniffed heavily, then looked directly at Mercs. 'A place at the conference table. It's what we deserve. Forget the politicians, we are the real voice of the Ulster people.'

Mercs grunted. 'I think at least forty-three per cent of the population might disagree with you.'

Casey winced. She knew full well that Mercs considered King Billy and his ilk to be nothing more than racist thugs, no better and no worse than the Provisionals. This was not the place to make those views plain. Not in some dark, back-street building, alone and defenceless in the lion's den.

But, to her surprise, King Billy just leaned back and smiled benignly as though he had heard such sentiments expressed a million times before. 'Mr Mercs, do you know *why* we're here?'

'What you mean?'

'Or you, dear American lady, whose compatriots seem to believe that the British are an army of occupation? Do you know why *we* – the Scottish Irish, as the Irish Irish would call us – are here in Ulster?'

Casey looked vague.

'No doubt you've heard the disparaging jokes about history in Ireland being as close as yesterday? Two points you must never forget. The first settlers in Ireland in the Stone Age – caveman days – were the Cruthin, Nordic peoples in search of warmer climes. The taigs – the Celts who claim Ireland as their own – didn't arrive until the Iron Age. Came from central Europe. That's a gap of five thousand years. We, the Protestant Scots originally came from Northern Ireland anyway and returned to resettle a mere two thousand years later in Tudor times – a blink in history by comparison. Henry the Eighth had a row with Rome over his bigamous habits, you'll recall, and introduced the Reformation. In Ireland, steeped in Catholicism through historical chance, this was resisted and proved to be a thorn in his side.'

Casey blinked as she listened to this most weird of history lessons coming from Big King Billy. Her knowledge of the period was scant, learned mostly from Hollywood movies. Nevertheless she was intrigued.

'Then under Henry's daughter, Elizabeth the First, the

Catholic chieftains in Ulster tried to forge an alliance with England's oldest and bitterest enemy, Catholic Spain! The Spanish even sent a small armada, thank God defeated by the English.

'Is it any surprise the English began their so-called "plantation programme"? Land in the north was confiscated from the taigs and tens of thousands of Scots and English were encouraged to settle. And we've been here longer than the Virginian settlers have been in America – since 1607. They've got their bit and we've got ours. The trouble is, they want it all.'

Mercs said darkly: 'Maybe London thinks there'd be less hassle if they had it.'

King Billy didn't answer immediately. He reached forward and tilted his green-shaded lamp to shine on the wall above his head. There was a water-stained sepia print: rows of young men, all in khaki and most with drooping moustaches, standing woodenly as they stared at the camera. 'One of those is my grandda. Richie Baker of the 36th (Ulster) Division. Won the MC. Died, alongside two thousand fellow Ulstermen who *volunteered* to fight for the Crown, on the first of July 1916. The Battle of the Somme. That is our blood bond with Britain.' He paused to let his audience understand the significance of his words. 'And what were the IRA doing at this time? The Easter Rising against British rule in Dublin, that's what! With arms supplied by the Kaiser – although these were thankfully intercepted.

'Is it any surprise that when the Free State was formed in 1921, the sacrifice of my father and the others was rewarded with the right to remain British?'

'But the Irish never accepted that,' Mercs pointed out.

'Sinn Fein and the other diehards never have. I told you, they want it *all*. And if proof were needed of the taigs' continued treachery, when the Second World War came and Britain was fighting for its life, for the survival of free Europe, Ireland declared itself neutral. Bloody neutral! And here in Ulster the IRA were showing torches from the rooftops to guide the *Luftwaffe* bombers onto Belfast!' He shook his head as though he couldn't believe his own story.

Casey tried to lighten the atmosphere; it was so heavy with

hatred, it was almost tangible. 'But surely there have been times of peace? Can't you see a way of living together without violence?'

'There's never been peace, Miss Mullins. The IRA's presence has always been there like a guttering candle that won't go out. But you're right, there was a time at the start of these troubles in the early seventies. I admit we'd been a bit hard on the taigs – keeping them out of local politics and the best jobs – and I think we felt some guilt. The Civil Rights movement pricked more than a few consciences until it was hijacked by the IRA.'

'Was your conscience pricked, Billy?' Mercs asked innocently.

The big man laughed, a patronising laugh that he reserved for those who didn't understand. 'Not all Proddies were rich, middle-class and privileged, Eddie. I lived in what you would call a slum with no inside privy. Left school at fifteen to work as a stager at Harland and Wolff until my back gave up. My simple life evolved around supporting the Blues at football and playing the drum for the local Orange flute band. The taig kids used to walk past our house on their way to their good schools in their neat fancy uniforms. They moaned about living in the Divis Flats, yet my ma would have given her right arm to live in one of those modern flats. No, Eddie, the taigs didn't look so hard done by to me.' His smile melted away as if it had never been. Now the grim authoritarian face of the feudal chieftain had returned. 'They've done their best to destroy our cities and now they're out to destroy yours. We're on the same side, Eddie, fighting the common enemy.'

Casey leaned forward earnestly. 'So will you, can you, help us?'

'Where are you staying?'

'The Park Avenue.'

'And I'll want your home addresses in England.'

She felt her fear return in a rush. 'Why?'

'To check you out.'

Mercs thought, Jolly King Billy wants insurance. Cross him and one day you'll answer the door to a gunman's bullet. Reluctantly he put pen to paper and watched as Casey did the same.

'No promises,' King Billy said grimly, then his face lightened a little. 'And No Surrender.'

At that moment there came the sound of footsteps from outside the room and a hurried knocking at the door. One of Spike's fellow henchmen pushed his way in. 'Sorry to interrupt, Billy. Thought you'd want to know. I've just heard it on the radio. Something big is going down in London!'

Casey froze.

16

The monstrous dumper truck thundered up the A102 motorway towards the Blackwall Tunnel, its huge steel sides rattling with the speed. Its headlamps were like eyes burning fiercely into the wet night and the jetting sprays in its wake became glittering silver wings.

Its target was in sight. And closing.

High in the cab McGirl adjusted the driving mirror. Just treble-checking. The two motorcycles were still keeping position some hundred metres behind. Muldoon and Doran ready, the empty van already placed and waiting in West Ham across the river.

'Half-a-mile,' Clodagh Dougan confirmed.

They both wore balaclavas, rolled up to look like woollen hats.

McGirl nodded his acknowledgment, taking one hand from the wheel and fumbling in his shirt pocket for his cigarettes. He tipped the packet, pulling out one of its contents with his teeth, then hunted for his lighter.

Clodagh noticed. Nerves, she thought. This front-line Provie hero is human after all. 'No, Pat, not now.'

He glanced sideways, saw the dash lights throwing the taut pale skin of her face into highlight and shadow, and grinned. 'No, of course not.' And just clamped the cigarette in his mouth, unlit. A comfort to his jangling nerves.

'Something coming up,' he said, eyes back on the mirror. There had been little traffic at this late-night hour, but now a car was gaining rapidly in the fast lane. Doing a ton or more, he gauged, already passing the two motorcycles.

Motorway Ends.

The sign flashed by as the road began to narrow, their

northbound carriageway separating from the southbound as they hurtled towards the Blackwall Tunnel entrance.

Target close and closing. Huge circular gantries looming.

More height warnings for the old tunnel. Thirteen foot four inches. McGirl content, the tyre pressures reduced to clear them by a whisker.

Defeated by the spray from the dumper, the overtaking car had slowed to fall in behind the lumbering ten-wheeler. McGirl squinted in the mirror; it was white, flashy, judging from the grille, a Mercedes.

'Oh, Sweet Mother of Jesus,' he breathed. He could see the pulsing blue light catching up fast. Some zealous cop wanting to catch the Merc. An excuse to go back to the station, out of the rain and a cup of tea. 'Shit!'

Clodagh turned in her seat. 'What is it?'

They were plunging down towards the tunnel now, the cutting lit in a blaze of yellow sodium light, height-alarm gongs hanging overhead and the bright mouth opening to swallow them.

KEEP IN LANE – KEEP IN LANE demanded the signs.

'Police car,' McGirl snapped. 'About three vehicles back.'

'After us?'

And they were in, the pressure blast hitting them, shaking the windows, the stark strip lights enveloping them, the noise of the dumper reverberating around the tunnel as it closed in over their heads.

'No!' McGirl had to shout above the deafening din. 'After a speeding car behind us!'

The illuminated tarmac ribbon opened up ahead of them, the first red tail-lights visible fifty metres ahead.

McGirl grinned harshly, the cigarette shredding between his teeth. He spat it out. 'Time for an executive decision.'

'This is my da's dream, Pat. My dream.'

He spared her a fleeting glance, then averted his eyes back to the mirror. 'Then we go!'

Balaclavas down.

Shifting his foot, he stabbed the brake pedal. Then again, and again. Then he hit the airhorns. A double blast like a soul from hell, the aching sound of a dying whale, trembled along the tunnel. In his mirror he saw the Mercedes backing off as the dumper's red lights continued blinking. McGirl stamped on the brakes again, this time long and hard, heard the hiss of compressed air as they began to bind.

Now, now, the silent voice yelled in his head.

He spun the wheel, felt the monster begin to slew, aware of the plaintive shriek of burning rubber. Saw the signal flasher of the Merc. Could imagine the face of the impatient driver as he pulled out to overtake.

'Stupid bastard!' McGirl screamed.

The dumper's wheels locked, seven tons of truck and three thousand pounds of explosive on the slide. Its front nose struck the tinplate crash-rail, friction sparks trailing like a shooting star, the cargo body rocking as it swerved to block both lanes.

As it came to an ear-grinding halt, the nose embedded in the buckled rail and began to tear at the tunnel lining. Simultaneously they felt the earth-shaking thud of the Mercedes as it crumpled into the dumper's side.

Christ, McGirl thought.

'Get going!' Clodagh shouted. Already she was adjusting the final settings to the complex TPU that would protect and then ultimately fire the mammoth bomb.

McGirl took the automatic from beneath his seat, switched on the vehicle's hazard flashers and kicked open the door. Looking back along the flank of the dumper, he could see only half of the Mercedes. Its bonnet had disappeared under the truck's chassis and the roof had caved in beneath the steel-ribbed underbelly. Steam and scalding water billowed and the saloon's hooter had become jammed on at full pitch, its piercing wail filling his head, blotting out his thinking process.

He jumped the few feet to the oil-sodden tarmac. A black slick like treacle was advancing from the wreckage where he could see the crushed driver, the man's blood-splattered face mouthing silently for help.

He ignored it, and glanced across the tunnel to check his handiwork. Excellent! The dumper's rear end was just feet from the far wall. No room for a car to pass, but enough for a motorcycle. The following cars had come to an untidy halt, each driver having to swerve to avoid the vehicle in front. McGirl shielded his eyes against the dazzling array of light, one throbbing blue police car strobe amid the white brilliance of headlamps. The two motorcycles had slowed with the rest of the traffic, waiting for everything to stop. Now Muldoon and Doran revved their machines, bucking as they raced to join the dumper and leaving skid marks scorched into the road surface as they braked.

Muldoon jerked to a standstill beside McGirl and handed over a spare helmet. While he put it on, dazed drivers were emerging from their cars, doors opening. Then the two police officers pushed through, hastily pulling on their peak caps, ready to take charge, beginning to run.

McGirl raised his automatic. 'GET BACK! THIS IS A BOMB!'

The policemen took a second to comprehend, to register the gun and the meaning of the words, McGirl's harsh Ulster accent. They skidded to a halt in mid-run, one sliding on the spilt oil and stumbling. The other was younger, looked no more than an adolescent. He reached out his hand, palm up.

'Don't be silly, sir. Hand over the gun.'

Christ, thought McGirl, what the fuck do they teach them at Hendon? 'IT GOES OFF IN ONE HOUR!'

The officer didn't flinch, didn't appear to hear. Took a step forward, then another. His hand still held out. 'Let's be having it, sir.'

Are you fucking deaf?! 'THIS IS AN IRA AIDAN BOMB, GODDIT?! AIDAN! YOU'VE GOT AN HOUR TO CLEAR THE TUNNEL! AND DON'T APPROACH IT OR IT'LL BLOW!'

'Andy!' called the policeman on the ground. 'Keep back, it's the bloody IRA!'

Another step forward. McGirl's eyes seemed to zoom in like a camera on the thin young face, the clear eyes, the pimples on his chin.

The single shot took him out. Ear-shattering in the enclosed

324

space, the 9mm round acted like a rug pulled from beneath the officer's feet, flinging him backwards onto his companion.

Clodagh shoved the gun into her pocket, pulled on her helmet, and threw herself astride Doran's pillion. 'LET'S GO.'

The gleaming tail pipes exploded in a cloud of choking exhaust and the first motorcycle was on the move, slowing for a wobbly passage between the dumper's rear end and the tunnel wall. Then it was away, the noise of its violent acceleration vibrating back and forth beneath the Thames, McGirl and Muldoon adding to the nerve-shattering clamour as they followed close behind.

On the ground Police Constable Pete Williams hugged PC Andy Collins in his arms, seeing the gaping chest wound and feeling the life leaking out of the young body.

With his free hand he pressed the send button on the radio clipped to his lapel, gave his call sign. He heard a response, the voice like it was coming from Mars, the signal breaking up.

Underground, he thought, and tried again. Nothing but hiss and static.

Underground. His eyes travelled to the massive dumper jammed across the tunnel, then up to the arched roof.

A massive bomb, how big? The blast directed straight up out of the steel sides of the cargo hold. And above, how many million gallons of river water pressing in on them? Immense, unimaginable pressure. God knew how many cars were now bumper-to-bumper in the jam. Young Andy dying in his arms.

And his sodding, fucking, bloody bastard radio didn't work.

The shutter of the camera blinked silently again as they left.

From the pavement opposite it was impossible to see the image-intensifying telephoto lens, hidden as it was in the shadow of the missing roof slate.

The technician from 14 Intelligence Company was satisfied. He slid the slate back into place, hunkered down in the confines of the roof space, and pulled off his earphones.

Beside him the SAS minder, wearing a civilian green anorak and with a stubby Heckler & Koch sub-machine-gun resting across his knees, nodded sagely. 'Interesting?'

'Could be, Ran.' The technician switched off the tape machine, made himself comfortable and began scribbling in his note pad.

Ran Reid watched him without comment. The technician was an insular bastard, he thought. Kept things to himself. Operational silence was second nature to them both. Especially in OPs. But, after all, this was a permanent covert OP in a safe house. An occasional exchange of words wouldn't go amiss.

The previous owners had been driven out nine months earlier when the place was firebombed. It was an anonymous attack and no one knew who was responsible, although Ran Reid could guess. There had not been much damage but it was enough to persuade the Protestant couple that it was time to move for the sake of their child. The husband worked for a construction company contracted to the RUC and he knew for that reason he was considered fair game by the Provisional IRA.

The property had come on the market at a snip, the new owner a single woman in her thirties who said she worked as a secretary in the Northern Ireland Office. In fact she was RUC Special Branch.

It was an ideal situation because every day she could take the tapes and rolls of film into work without the need to make surreptitious journeys.

That wasn't to say that Ran Reid or the technician, or the other teams on rota, could ever afford to drop their guard. Because if King Billy ever discovered the bug transmitter that fed perpetually off the electrical circuit in his drinking club, or the OP in the rooftop opposite, they knew he would not hesitate to act. The betting was it would be an incendiary device that would roast them alive. No one doubted that in truth King Billy's loyalty as a Loyalist was nowadays mostly to himself. It was anyone's guess if the Quick Reaction Force from the local army base would arrive in time to rescue them.

The technician passed the note to Ran Reid. 'Can you encrypt and send, please. Priority.'

It took just a few minutes for the words to be electronically coded and then fired into the airwaves in a burst transmission lasting a fraction of a second. The signal was so fast that it would defy any of the scanners known to be used by paramilitaries on both sides.

The duty officer in the high-security operations room of the Intelligence and Security Group Detachment at Lisburn received the signal and decoded it minutes later. Known colloquially as 'Int and Sy', or more menacingly as simply 'The Group', it was, depending on one's viewpoint, the most revered, despised, feared and notorious of the several covert intelligence units operating in Northern Ireland. In order to preserve its shadowy anonymity, its official title and that of its component parts had been changed from time to time over the years to mislead the enemy as to its true function. The Group comprised 14 Intelligence and Security Company, drawing on suitable officers and NCOs from all branches of the army and Royal Marines for undercover surveillance work, the Field Intelligence Unit – manned by the Army Intelligence Corps to run agents in the field, who were frequently 'turned' terrorists – and a small contingent of SAS troopers for hard backup.

Lieutenant Bryant read the signal for a second time before calling Don Trenchard on his bleeper. The liaison officer had been enjoying a round of cards and sharing jokes with colleagues over a late coffee in the mess bar. He always found it easy to relax in the place with its plush burgundy carpet, matching drapes and heavy mahogany panelling: it simply reminded him of home on the Bedfordshire estate that had been in his family for generations.

Feeling tired and more than ready for sleep, he overcame his initial irritation and walked briskly back up to the ops room, leaving his winning hand unplayed.

'Thought you'd want to see this. From the OP opposite Billy Baker's club. That's the gist of the meet. Full transcript and photographs will be in by 0830 tomorrow.'

Trenchard studied the signal, lowered himself into a chair. 'Eddie Mercs and Casey Mullins,' he murmured.

'Says she wants to name the bombers.'

'Don't we all.'

'What's King Billy up to, Don?'

327

'Judging by the lecture on the Protestant case, he's out to win friends and influence people.'

Bryant shook his head. 'I don't mean that. The way he's left it. It's almost as though he thinks he can help them. As if he knows something.'

'More likely bravado and pride. Doesn't want to admit he knows bugger all.'

'But if he does?'

'He knows we've got first call.'

'So what do we do?'

Casey Mullins, Trenchard mused. Friend, now lover, of Tom Harrison, Ulster's Senior ATO and up to his neck in AIDAN's London bombing campaign. Made the story her own, latest darling of what was Fleet Street, hungry for success and on the scent.

'She's at the Park Avenue. Get someone down there to keep a watch. Check with the airport car-hire companies and get a registration number if there is one. Then feed everything into Crucible. Our access only. I want to know everywhere she goes and everyone she sees.'

'It's as good as done.'

It was half past midnight when the first signal came through to the Section admin office.

Midgely had just glanced at his watch. 'I know a place where we can get a late-night curry and a lager, if you fancy it? Celebrate your departure in style.'

Harrison put a brave face on it. 'Sounds good, and it's the best offer I'm likely to get. But promise me, no crying in your beer.'

The Yorkshireman almost smiled. 'I don't know how I'm going to live without you.'

'You'll get over it in time. Al will look after you.'

Midgely chuckled and glanced over his shoulder to be sure Pritchard wasn't around. The Senior Expo had come in with the twelve to eight a.m. shift, overlapping with their own by one hour. The terrorists' favourite time to strike.

Not that they were expecting anything. Since AIDAN's own

goal in Lambeth, there had been a sudden lull in activities. Clearly the incident had set the Provos back, maybe even resulted in a premature end to the whole campaign.

Perhaps his successor, arriving from Germany the next morning, would have nothing more exciting to do than supervise the 321 squad's return to Belfast. Either way, it was no longer any of Harrison's concern.

He put down the copy of the *Royal Logistics Corps Gazette* he was reading as he heard the duty officer take the radio call. 'Central Ten Five Five receiving . . . Yes . . . Where? . . . Location Westminster Bridge, status not confirmed . . .' The man swivelled in his seat, still listening intently to the voice in his headset and gave a thumbs-up. 'Wilco, sir. We're on our way. Please clear the area and check and secure an ICP on the north bank.'

Midgely was on his feet. 'I'll call Al.'

The desk phone rang and Harrison reached for the receiver. 'I'll take it.'

As the Yorkshireman disappeared into the corridor, the voice of the Anti-Terrorist Branch detective was almost shrieking on Harrison's line. 'Call from the Samaritans. Car bomb threat for vicinity of Westminster Bridge. Forty-five minutes warning received 0028 hours.'

'Anything else?' Harrison demanded.

'That's it.'

'No codeword?'

'No.'

Shit! A hoax or what? 'Definitely not AIDAN?'

'Negative.'

He hung up and the duty officer called across from the radio console. 'Is that our confirmation?'

'Yes, but no codeword.'

'It looks like a car pulled up on the pavement, dead centre of the bridge. Hazard flashers on, bonnet up, and the driver walked away. Sound familiar?'

Harrison paled. 'The flyover bombs.'

Another signal was coming up on the console and the duty officer turned away.

Al Pritchard strode into the room, Midgely at his heels.

'Suspect car bomb on Westminster Bridge now confirmed,' Harrison reported and gave the details.

Midgely grimaced thoughtfully. 'No codeword, so it could be a copycat.'

Pritchard's eyelids half lowered. 'Or a rerun of the flyover bombs.'

'And no codeword – to deliberately slow our response?' Harrison suggested.

The Sexpo nodded. 'Midge, put out an all-units to have all bridges in central London checked and watched. If it is them, let's get ahead of the game.'

But it was already too late for that. The duty officer had finished with the latest caller. 'Vauxhall Bridge now, Al, the same setup. And this console's lighting up like Blackpool seafront. I need backup, fast.'

Midge yelled down the corridor for the new shift members to man the switchboard and Harrison's phone rang again. It was via another branch of the Samaritans. Vauxhall Bridge confirmed. No codeword.

'You want my lads tasked, Al?'

Pritchard had accepted the inevitable. The prospect of car bombs, even if they weren't AIDAN's, left him with no real choice. 'Your lads, Tom, but not you. You've barely fifteen minutes left to run, so let's call it a day, eh?'

Bastard! 'Sure, Al, if that's the way you want it. You're the boss.'

The acid smile. 'I always have been.'

Within five minutes four Range-Rovers and four Expos with their backup were on the road together with three British Army Tacticas, which included the big Attack Barrow. They were racing after a rapidly mounting number of suspect river bridge car bombs, Waterloo and Battersea Bridges now added to the list.

Only Harrison and Midgely were left. The Yorkshireman telephoned the remaining Expos on leave and told them to report in – like yesterday! He also requested the army unit at Northolt be put on immediate standby.

Earlier Harrison had found himself thinking about Casey and whether they might be able to steal a few days away together. Maybe a quiet country hotel somewhere. Now all such fantasies were pushed rudely to the back of his mind. 'Something else is brewing,' he observed, lighting up his small briar pipe. It always helped his concentration.

'How d'you mean?'

'These bridge bombs aren't hoaxes, Midge. No hoaxer abandons four cars – even someone else's – simultaneously on one night. To my mind, no such idiot would find three friends daft enough to go along with it. That means it's PIRA – but no codeword.'

'So?'

'They're going for a spectacular. I don't know where or how, but that's what they're setting up. I can feel it. Maybe these bridge bombs are quite basic, put in place by a regular mainland active service unit, or even their regular logistics people. They've spread our resources and now they'll go for the big one. *Then* we'll get our codeword.'

Midgely looked chastened, shivering suddenly in an imagined draught. 'Al was right, Tom, you've just a few minutes left to run. Why don't you go home? Close the door on all this. It's not your worry any more.' He smiled and placed his porky hand on his friend's arm. 'Sorry about that curry.'

The duty officer was busy again; both men turned as he completed his conversation. 'Got something here, Midge,' he called. 'A fucking great dumper truck in the middle of the Blackwall Tunnel. And it's AIDAN.'

'Oh, sweet Jesus,' Midgely murmured, stepping forward to snatch the task-sheet. He stared at it, hardly believing. 'A truck blocking the northbound tunnel. Car crashed into the side of it with a couple and a baby trapped. One policeman shot dead . . . What the fuck, this is some kind of sick joke!' He shook his head. 'Forty-five minutes to go, verbal to surviving police officer who confirms AIDAN codeword and a specific warning not to approach the vehicle.'

Harrison stared at the large-scale wall map of the London

streets. 'No one else is going to be free for half-an-hour at best, Midge. When will the first relief get here?'

'He's driving in from Carshalton.'

Too long, Harrison decided. 'Then it's you or me. I'll toss you for it.'

Midge said: 'Someone's got to stay here, Tom, and you don't qualify. Take the last Rover and get down there, I'll join you as soon as the first relief arrives. With a police escort hopefully he'll make it in another ten.'

Harrison was already on his way to the door. 'I'll need a complete sitrep on my way, Midge. Update me on the radio.'

Outside the tarmac of the compound glistened with the rain that had been falling all evening without let-up. He splashed through the puddles as he ran to where the Range-Rover stood, white and shiny under the bright lights of the open garage. As he swung up into the driver's seat, the allocated police escort vehicle was already moving into position, its blue strobe gyrating around the compound.

In minutes they were racing east along the northern embankment before sweeping up through the backstreets to avoid the building congestion of traffic at Waterloo and then Blackfriars Bridge where the Section's Expos were at work. It was a diversion that cost them many precious minutes.

By the time they were approaching St Paul's Cathedral, Midgely was on the radio with his updated sitrep. 'We've got a problem, Tom. Police on the scene say some sort of anti-approach device has been rigged to each side of the dumper. Looks like those automatic porch lights, similar to the one they used at the West Drayton flyover bomb.'

That's all I bloody need, Harrison thought angrily. 'Go on.'

'As you know, the tunnel runs south to north. The south side is chocka with cars, but at least it's now been cleared of people, apart from those poor sods trapped in the Mercedes. Of course, no one's been able to get near them. The ICP has been set up in the empty north sector – fire brigade, police and paramedics in attendance. Again, they haven't approached within a hundred and fifty metres.'

'How much longer on the clock?'

'If you want to believe them – and it's been confirmed this time in calls to Reuters and AP and traced to Dublin – you've got thirty-four minutes precisely.'

'Cheers.' He set his watch.

Now they were overtaking a long line of jammed traffic, Harrison following the police escort on the wrong side of East India Dock Road. The road-blocking cordon was opened to admit the two-car convoy before it turned onto the A102 tunnel approach road which was totally and eerily devoid of traffic.

The tunnel mouth beckoned, emergency vehicles queued in one lane, ready for the all-clear and the call to action.

It was strange to be suddenly enveloped in the soulless man-made artery beneath the Thames, with its stark and clinical overhead lighting and soot-encrusted walls discoloured by the exhaust from the thousands of vehicles that passed through each day. At any moment Harrison half expected to be confronted by the headlights of cars bearing down in the opposite direction.

How small and confined the two-lane carriageway suddenly seemed, its historical origins now blatantly clear. Built in 1897, Harrison knew, for the horse and cart. The second tunnel had been added in 1967 to carry southbound traffic and was over two feet higher. It didn't sound much, but it made a big difference.

The patrol car was slowing, pulling over behind three ambulances and two fire tenders. Harrison continued to crawl forward, finally braking beside the lead vehicle.

And there it was. Over a hundred metres distant, slewed at an angle like a steel blast door blocking the tunnel completely, the upper edge of the dumper's cargo body seeming to touch the roof.

The senior police chief was at his window. 'God, am I pleased to see you. How d'you want to play this?'

It was no time for niceties. 'First of all, you'll have to back these vehicles right out of the tunnel.'

'We wanted to be able to move in the moment you're finished.'

'I understand. But if that bastard goes up you'll be blown out the tunnel like a cannon. Better to drive out in one piece and wait there. Now tell me, is this the closest anyone's got?'

'On this side, yes. But on the other side one of our officers was within forty feet.' In the tunnel the man's voice had an echoing ring to it.

'How long ago?'

'Just after the incident.'

That didn't mean a thing. There must have been a time delay before the anti-approach devices were armed in order to allow the terrorists to make good their own escape. 'Infrared?'

The police chief nodded. 'Almost certainly passive infrared linked to the registration of movement.'

'Usual range about ten metres?'

'Yes, but these ones are sited high up on each side of the cargo body, so there's probably a longer throw than in the usual domestic situation. I wouldn't take any risks under twenty metres.' The man looked painfully worried. 'I've got a firearms unit on standby. I wondered if you wanted to shoot out the sensors?'

Harrison shook his head. 'Too risky. It might do the job but it's just as likely to trigger it.' He turned round. 'Fetch me the senior paramedic, will you?'

The officer beckoned a man in green overalls. He must have been in his fifties: white hair, a lined face and steady dark eyes.

'Do you have space blankets on board?' Harrison asked. 'You know, the foil types used for hypothermia?'

'Sure.'

'Get me two. Some scissors and some cord.'

'What are you going to do?' the policeman asked as the paramedic returned to his ambulance.

'Infrared reacts to body heat. Foil has a reflective quality. That's the theory anyway.'

'Does it work?'

'We experimented in Belfast at a friend's flat with an interior security sensor. Used a whole roll of Bacofoil.'

'Did it work?' the officer repeated.

'Almost. Nearly crossed the room before it registered. We'd run out of foil for one arm.'

'Jesus.'

The paramedic returned. 'Tie one round my waist,' Harrison ordered. 'Like an apron.'

For someone of his age, the man worked with remarkable deftness; after years of witnessing motorway horrors and countless dangerous situations, he was totally unflappable. Once fitted and adjusted over the trousers of his flameproof overalls, the hem of the blanket rested just half-an-inch above the tarmac.

'I'll need a ladder to get me up to the sensor,' Harrison said, then fitted his bomb helmet before the second blanket was placed over his head, covering the armoured flak vest like a poncho. He stood, sweating in the darkness, until the paramedic had cut an eye-slit away in front of his visor.

Christ, he thought, I must look ridiculous. A lampshade made of silver foil.

His watch told him that there were just twenty minutes to go. There was no time for second thoughts. For a moment he watched the first of the emergency vehicles begin the long reverse back out of the tunnel. Then, picking up the Pigstick disrupter on its anglepoise mounting, and the lightweight aluminium ladder from the fire brigade, he began walking towards the dumper.

All he could hear was his own laboured breathing and the gentle rustle of the space blankets. He was alone now, totally. The tunnel began to take on a character of its own, seeming to adopt a new shape, shrinking in on both sides, the roof lowering as he walked. The white centre line on the tarmac and the crash barriers on each side emphasised the perspective like the work of a surrealist artist. All lines narrowing, leading to infinity. Infinity ending at the huge slab side of the dumper.

God, he felt lonely.

There was no one else in the world. It was like walking through a bad dream. His heart thudding, sweat running down his temples, along his jawline and starting to drip from his chin. His visor starting to fog despite the internal helmet fan. Bloody things never did work like they were supposed to.

He drew to a halt. That was it. Twenty metres, give or take. He could see the small white plastic sensor now, just below the upper

335

rim of the cargo body. Tilted slightly down. Like a watchful eye. AIDAN's eye. Ready, alert, all-seeing. Itching to react. Daring him to make a mistake. Willing him to.

No going back now.

Instinctively he drew his hands up under the blanket poncho. Unable to be sure, he prayed neither showed beneath the foil. If they did, AIDAN's eye would see them. Just a glimpse of warm flesh would be enough for the passive infrared sensor.

Cars and derelicts. The old dreads. Only this time it wasn't a car, it was something a thousand times worse.

He took a tentative step forward. His heart was going like a hammer drill. Another step, then one more.

Keep going, you fucking coward. There's a baby in a Merc on the other side. The father with a steering wheel in his chest and the mother with her legs crushed . . . How would you feel if that was your child trapped in there? And what would Archie himself think if he saw you hesitating now? Wouldn't be so proud of his father then, would he?

He forced himself on, each foot seemingly weighted with lead. Refusing to obey the commands of his brain, his body reluctant to be dragged, inwardly screaming, towards its inevitable fate. His eyes transfixed on the small plastic lens, waiting for the little red pilot light to blink on. *Aha! Caught you!*

Shit! Stop thinking, just keep going. Not too fast, don't create an airflow to lift the protective flap of the blanket. Not too slow or the clock will beat you.

Christ, Casey, I love you. Where the fuck are you now, and what the hell are you doing in Ulster? I should be in bed with you now, not walking under the Thames like a grand master of the Ku Klux Klan in silver paper!

He heard it then. Above the drumbeat thud of his own heart, above his rasping lungs and the sound of the blood rushing in his ears. The high-pitched cry of a baby. High-pitched, then subsiding into the painful gurgle of distress, regaining its strength in order to scream again.

He shuffled on, looked up.

God, the dumper was big. It towered above him, a rusting flank

336

of steel with ribs and rivets. Filling his vision until that was all there was in the world.

Would this be the last thing he ever saw?

He stopped, bending tentatively at the knees, lowering the Pigstick to the tarmac, careful for his hand not to show. It dropped the last inch, toppled over, the metallic clang echoing along the lonely tunnel. His eyes shut, then opened. No time to pray.

Inch by inch he swung his left hand up, shifting the six-foot ladder from the horizontal to the vertical. Gently he allowed the ends to touch the dumper's side. Daren't look at his watch, daren't reveal his wrists.

Up, up, you bastard, don't tell me you've suddenly developed vertigo?

One foot, first rung. Next foot, up, up. Nearly there.

Above his head the cyclops eye watched. Impassive. Now he could even see the indented lincs on the plastic lens, the attaching bracket and the screw heads, the thin twist of flex disappearing over the rim.

Perhaps the bloody dumper was empty? Nothing in it. Just another of AIDAN's practical jokes. That's what his instructor had told him once. That was the real essence of the booby trap. Forget your technical theories, when it came down to it a booby trap was just a practical joke by someone with a truly black sense of humour. You had to laugh really . . .

Last rung. Precarious and vulnerable, having to risk showing his hands now, hopefully under the sensor's line-of-sight, palms on the rough cold steel for support. His wristwatch showing.

Twelve minutes to go. God, where had the time gone?

He reached beneath the poncho, pulled out the wire-cutters from his trouser pocket then stretched up. Too short, damn it! The tip of the jaws just an inch below the flex. He bunched the muscles in his calves and pushed his soles against the ladder rung.

It moved, jerked suddenly, the legs sliding on the oil-smeared tarmac. His hand shot out, palm jammed against the steel rib to halt the movement.

Calm, calm, he told himself. A long, slow deep breath. Another stretch. More careful this time, measured, reaching out with

337

gentle pressure. Watching the jaws edge towards the exposed flex. Sweat running into his eyes. Through a painful and salty blur he saw the tip touch the flex.

He opened his palm, allowing the spring-loaded action to separate the jaws, felt them grip the flex. Then he shut his eyes and he closed his fist around the handles. A tiny harsh snap, feeling it through his fingers rather than hearing it.

Again he breathed, squeezed the sweat from his eyes, blinked, and looked.

The cut flex hung free. Sweet Jesus Christ, he'd done it!

'*Tom, how's it going?*'

The sudden sound of the metallic voice coming from his transceiver took him by surprise, almost toppling him from the ladder.

'Midge? Where are you?'

'*At the tunnel entrance. What's happening?*'

'I've just reached the truck and taken out the first infrared sensor.'

'*Thank God for that. What do you want me to do?*'

'The Pigstick's firing cables go back to my Rover two hundred metres back. I need a long extension to clear the tunnel.'

'*Wilco, Tom, we're on our way.*'

Ten minutes to run and no time to lose. Harrison jumped back down to the tarmac, scooped up his ladder and the Pigstick and rounded the small gap between the dumper's end and the tunnel wall.

Now he saw the Mercedes for the first time. It was hideously crushed, half buried beneath the dumper's chassis. The roof came down to meet the dash and in the apex of crushed metal he could just see the drained face of the woman. Young, maybe pretty, but splashed with blood. The skin around her closed eyes was grey from the mascara that had run with her tears of pain.

Unconscious, he thought, and thank God for that at least. Oblivious to the pain now.

He moved cautiously around the rear of the car, until he was in view of the second sensor on the dumper's other side. Peering into the distorted car window as he passed, he saw the baby's carrycot.

It was upturned in the rear seat well. A tiny white hand protruded, pink fingers wriggling from a white woollen sleeve. Alive.

He moved on, repeating the procedure against the second sensor, easier and quicker this time as his confidence increased.

Climbing back down, he stripped off his blanket poncho and apron, and removed the helmet. Cool air, tainted with the distinct smell of oil, rushed at him, drying the sweat from his skin. Roughly he ran his hands through his sodden hair, scratching his scalp in an effort to clear his mind.

First things first. Could he locate the timer and power unit? Was it accessible for a quick knockout with the Pigstick?

Quickly he moved the ladder along to the tractor unit. His mind was already filled with the next prospect: entering the cab. Sod, the door firmly shut. AIDAN would surely have thought of something here. What was it this time? The courtesy light or another car alarm like the one that had caught Jock? A trembler or a tilt as well? Almost certainly.

To climb up the foot and handholds to the cab would rock the springs and that was something he couldn't risk. So he replaced his helmet and used the ladder again, inching his way up until he could peer in through the driver's door.

The dash, the seats – Nothing obvious. His eyes drifted to the squab seat at the back, trying to penetrate the shadows. Somewhere, he knew, must be the TPU. But where?

He almost missed it. Naturally he'd been looking at the cab floor, expecting to find the unit beneath the seats or in the footwells. On the point of giving up in exasperation, his eyes lifted. And there it was.

His stomach turned to liquid. The neat little plywood box was swinging gently like a flypaper, suspended by a length of tightly coiled spring from the cab roof. All that kept it from rotating were the wires feeding from the back, disappearing down behind the squab seats.

The TPU resembled a PIRA Mk 16, as the ATOs had dubbed it. Two empty dowel holes to release two mechanical timers hidden inside: one to the main charge in the dumper's cargo body, the second a time-delay to activate the antihandling devices.

And there was one of them staring him in the face. He blanched. The tiny globule of mercury was sealed in its transparent plastic capsule, its pivot mounting adjusted so that the slightest motion of the cab would tip the mercurial blob to the other end where it would link the two terminal ends and complete the circuit.

No deal! He'd have to try another way.

Climbing back down the ladder, he moved to the gap between the tractor unit and the trailer. He scrambled up quickly, knowing exactly what he was looking for. Amid the connecting cables for brakes and the vehicles' electrical system, ran a length of black garden hosepipe. It was the link between the TPU in the cab with the perforated firing tube in the rear body which would detonate the inevitable sacks of fertiliser mix.

Fishing in his pocket again, he drew out his favourite craft knife and extended the blade. This was no time for hesitation. Like a surgeon in a life-threatening emergency, this was the time to kill or cure. In went the razor point, carving into the plastic, moving around the tube until he was able to tear off a ring of the stuff and reveal . . .

Two lengths of smooth white cable. Det cord? Please, God, let it be! If it was Cordtex he could just cut straight through it. Separate the brain from the monstrous body at a single stroke.

But the light was poor and he couldn't be certain. The trouble was the stuff looked almost identical to coaxial cable. And if he cut through that with a steel blade, he was dead meat. Involuntarily he glanced up at the tunnel roof, just feet above his head, and wondered what would happen if the dumper blew.

Feverishly he went to work, scraping with the blade at the first length of cable. Chips of plastic sleeve flaked away and then – careful now – the white fibre inner. A further, really cautious cut . . . and the compressed white PETN powder of the explosive inner core spilled out.

He grinned smugly. Det cord. Carrying the detonating wave at a rate of six thousand metres a second. With a confident flourish he produced his cutters and snapped it through.

His hand moved to the second cable. Backup, he decided, a

340

failsafe in case the first malfunctioned. Typical AIDAN thoroughness. He opened the jaws.

No shortcuts! A voice rang in his ears. His old instructor, long ago retired. His own voice, too, when he'd given lectures.

He dropped the cutters and picked up his craft knife. More steady whittling, flecks of white plastic scattering onto his knees until . . .

Oh, shit! Light gleamed on the inner wire core. It was coax. And he was a millimetre from death.

Instinctively his sphincter tightened as his bowels turned instantly to liquid jelly. In time, but only just.

The second cable was backup all right, but electrical not explosive det cord. A deliberate ploy to defeat the bomb-disposal officer in just this situation?

No matter. There was nothing for it. Like it or not, he would have to tackle the TPU in the cab.

Five minutes to run.

At that point he heard Midgely's Rover arrive, parking next to his and linking up the extended firing cable he'd been unreeling behind his vehicle.

Harrison turned back to the cab. The temptation to risk opening the door was colossal, but he forced himself to resist. AIDAN was hardly likely to miss a simple trick like that.

He went back up the ladder, feeling the cab suspension start to give. Hardly anything, but it was just enough to set the TPU dancing gently on its spring. Another hurried rummage in his pocket, greasy fingers finding the spring-loaded centrepunch.

He pushed the instrument against the toughened side window, heard the crack and saw the glass frost over instantly. Without hesitation, he began tearing aside the coagulated crystals from the frame with his bare hands. Then he was in, struggling to lift one leg through the jagged aperture, then the next until he was kneeling on the driver's seat, facing the back with the steering wheel digging uncomfortably into his backside. He cursed himself now for not using the passenger window, which would have allowed him more space. But time, running out by the second, was now the sole dictator of unfolding events.

Midgely appeared on the ladder now and, without wasting words, handed in the disrupter and its awkward anglepoise stand. 'Three minutes,' he warned gruffly.

Harrison nodded. 'Get back to the firing point, Midge. I want to Pigstick this the moment I'm clear.'

To wish good luck was to invite disaster. 'Go for it, my son.'

'Bugger off.'

The florid face disappeared from the window and Harrison concentrated on opening up the concertina joints. But it was difficult in the confined space, the helmet restricting his vision. And while searching for a clear gap behind the seat for the stand legs, the metal slipped through his greasy fingers. The stand banged against the cab side and, as he jerked the end clear, the clamp holding the Pigstick hit the TPU. He could not believe it! It swung gently left and right, a deadly pendulum, just ten inches from his face. He stared at it, his eyes glued to the little bead of glistening mercury. God, he could swear it was deliberately taunting him.

Ignore it, you fool! Get on.

Slowly the TPU lost its momentum, finally coming to a precarious standstill. As he heard the sound of Midge heading back out of the tunnel at top speed, he positioned the stand so that the Pigstick was just inches from its target.

That'll have to do. No more time to wait.

The disrupter would smash the unit, hopefully just microseconds before the detonator in the explosive could heat up. It was that close.

He twisted around on the seat and edged his backside out through the window, feeling the material of his overalls tear on the jagged edge. One leg extracted beneath him, knee jammed, then pulled painfully free. Then the second. Feeling like a contortionist as he half climbed, half fell down the ladder, landing on his back, but managing to break his ungainly fall with his forearm.

The watch face glared back at him. One minute fifty-five seconds.

He scrambled to his feet, the stinking coils of exhaust from Midge's Rover rasping in his throat. Starting to run now, he passed the end of the Mercedes. Then stopped. The sound was small, like no more than a whimper.

One minute forty-five.

Was there time? He looked up at the massive dumper. Christ! What would Archie think if he didn't at least try?

The rear window was shattered, the roof crushed down until there was an impossibly narrow gap between it and the top of the door. Twelve inches, ten? He launched himself at the aperture, scrabbling in until he found the metal closing like a vice around his hipbone, holding him fast. He stretched out his free hand, a mere inch from the baby's tiny hand. Their flesh touched for an instant, the skin cold. He grunted, pushed a little harder, his hand still slippery with oil and his own blood.

He had the little forearm, felt it wriggle, his grip better now on the woollen sleeve. His fingers tightened around the arm where it joined the shoulder. The baby emptied its lungs, screamed like a demented soul.

Pushing his knees against the buckled outer door, he levered out the rest of his body, feeling the teeth of glass raking along his back, then scraping over the top of his helmet.

He managed to get his second hand to the child, supporting its urine-stained rump, and crushed it protectively to his chest as he found his feet.

Then he was running. Running as he had never run in his life before. Through the gap between the dumper and the tunnel wall. Eternity stretching ahead of him, the endless ribbon of tarmac and the trail of firing cables.

Pounding, pounding, pounding. Blood pumping at his temples, his lungs stretched to bursting with the effort. On, on, on. Would there be enough time to reach his Range-Rover, still fifty metres off?

He tilted his wrist on the hand that cradled the baby's head. Oh, shit! The watch alarm began its rapid bleeping.

His feet skidded as he changed direction, stumbling, nearly falling, limping to the edge of the tunnel. He looked around. No hiding place.

He laid the infant on the tarmac and stretched himself out over the helpless bundle. Then fumbled for the send button of the transceiver on his lapel. 'Midge – FIRE!'

The harsh crack of the disrupter reverberated along the tunnel walls.

It was followed immediately by the explosion. The entire tunnel quaked, lit for one split second in an awesome blinding pulse of white light before the ear-splitting sound and the maelstrom of displaced air overtook him. And the lights went out.

Oh, Jesus fucking Christ! He'd got it wrong!

He heard the debris falling all around him in the darkness. Shards of hot metal lanced into his back as he pressed down on the baby, feeling it struggle against his belly. Waited for the tumultuous impact of the water as the tunnel caved in under the almighty onslaught of the Thames above.

Forgive me, Archie, Pippa. Casey, I love you. I'm sorry, so sorry . . .

He lifted his head. His deafness was stunning. The tunnel lights flickered on. Emergency generator, he thought.

Twisted round. There was the dumper, unmoved. Only its cab was all but demolished, the passenger door blown to smithereens and the seats ablaze.

He closed his eyes. He'd done it. After all, he had bloody well done it. The baby began to bawl.

Fifteen minutes later, after he and Midge made the final inspection, they took a calculated risk in allowing volunteer fire crew and paramedics in to cut the Mercedes' occupants free. The driver was dead, but the baby's mother was given a better than even chance of survival, although it was doubted she would ever walk again.

Midge pulled the melted wire from the passenger seat of the dumper cab. 'Not much left of the pressure mat. Separate eight-ounce charge of Semtex, I reckon.'

Harrison felt sick. How close had he come to kneeling on the passenger seat, rather than the driver's? If he'd had more time to think and plan, that's exactly what he would have done.

344

'I guess the Pigstick set it off. Smashed the TPU then rico-cheted around the cab, hit the seat . . . who knows?'

Another Range-Rover pulled up and Al Pritchard climbed out. His face was impassive. 'Had to go out on a high note, didn't you, Tom?'

Harrison glared. He didn't need this.

The Senior Expo smiled. 'Thanks, Tom. I owe you. Now that *was* more exciting than an episode of *Coronation Street*.'

Harrison shook the offered hand.

After the experience with the Haymarket car and its hidden exhaust-pipe bomb, the dumper was towed to an open field in Leyton where it was left isolated and guarded overnight. At six in the morning it exploded. A separate extended timer and detonator had been secreted within the main explosive charge itself.

No one was hurt.

But of the four car bombs on the main river bridges of London, two exploded before they could be defused, resulting in the need for extensive engineering repairs and massive disruption of traffic for several months.

17

Senator Abe Powers heard the news bulletin on the radio at two in the morning. He had just retired to his suite in Trafalgar House, having spent a long evening socialising with the delegates followed by two exhaustive hours going over revisions of the day's minutes and agreements with the secretarial staff. They would be working through the night to produce the documents for the next day.

As he poured a bourbon nightcap and switched on the radio, he had felt quietly satisfied with the progress. There was a good chance there'd be signatures on the dotted line tomorrow or the day after. No, that was too optimistic. Time for a little more brinkmanship from one side or the other. Threatening a walkout, demanding a small gain here or there. But he was ready for that. Tomorrow, the end of next week, what did it matter?

What mattered was peace in Northern Ireland. More importantly a peace that he, Abe Powers, had achieved. Virtually single-handed. No one in the outside world knew it yet, but when they did he would be heralded as the greatest American statesman since Kissinger. He would be the toast in every Irish bar from the East Coast to California. His name would be on the lips of every New York cop, every Boston taxi driver. The entire Irish political lobby and the forty million who claimed Irish ancestry would be in his pocket. If he played his cards right – and he intended to – then it was almost a foregone conclusion that he would be Vice President in the next Democrat administration. And after that . . .

'*A massive IRA bomb has been defused by experts in the Blackwall Tunnel in east London. If it had exploded and the tunnel had collapsed, the costs of reconstruction and resultant chaos to the city's transport system would have run into countless billions of pounds . . .'*

He listened intently to the full details. Imagined the magnitude of the immediate damage and years of inconvenience and financial loss that would follow had the Provisional IRA been successful – as clearly they so nearly had been. Could visualise the effect on New York had a similar device been exploded in one of the tunnels there.

And what next time? More bridges? Another tunnel bomb, maybe in another British city? On the tube line? Next time there might not even be a warning; he could understand that, what with the run of bad luck the freedom fighters had been having.

'Freedom fighters?' He'd thought in those terms quite unconsciously, he realised suddenly, but then he always had. Today's freedom fighters were tomorrow's politicians. How true that had proved in recent years.

How long, he wondered, would the British Cabinet stubbornly stick to their precondition of these talks? Insisting that the very people at the centre of the Irish problem in recent years be excluded from a voice in their own destiny. Unless they first renounced violence? And he knew they couldn't do that, as did the British Government. Because violence was the only way the terrorists would ever win the concessions they wanted.

He'd always thought it wrong to exclude the Provisional IRA, but had managed to assuage his conscience with the usual pragmatism of the seasoned politician. Press ahead anyway and hopefully the freedom fighters would be satisfied with the result. But could they ever be satisfied with something in which they had played no part? Now that agreement was so, so close, it seemed foolish to deny them still.

And how many innocent civilians in London and elsewhere would have to die, how many millions of dollars of damage squandered until the Brits relented? Next time PIRA might get lucky. Real lucky. Next time, next time . . . Maybe that would be tomorrow.

And the blood and the ultimate injustice would be on his hands. Because he alone – Abe Powers, future Vice President of the United States – was the only man in the world with the political power to change the rules.

It was now two thirty. Nine thirty in the evening in Washington. Early enough. He made his decision and reached for the telephone with its special scrambler unit.

Seconds later he was through to the White House, the President interrupted at the banquet he was attending.

They spoke together for an hour, the President relaxed and in no mood to rush back, happy to enjoy a cigar in the privacy of his office. Aides were hurriedly summoned in from State, sat around drinking coffee, answering the President's occasional questions and giving their advice.

Abe Powers III was a powerful and eloquent persuader and he knew how to add just the right historical slant that appealed to a romantic sense of justice against colonial repression. It could have been his own grandmother talking. When he hung up the telephone, his recommended plan of action had been sanctioned by the most powerful leader in the world.

Yet the senator could not sleep. To any fly on the wall he would have appeared a strangely vulnerable sight. The huge frame in striped pyjamas padding the suite, his mind and thoughts in turmoil. Waiting for the first dawn light to shed its quicksilver gleam across the running water meadows of the Avon.

Time then to raise his aide from his bed. To execute the plans, to have a person-to-person telephone conversation with the just-awakened Prime Minister in his Downing Street flat.

The ripple effect was like no pebble in a pond. It was as though he had thrown in a brick. Suddenly with no appetite for breakfast, the Prime Minister had called back to Trafalgar House to speak to the Northern Ireland minister who was clearly stunned by the development. The Royal Air Force helicopter was already on its way to ferry him to London as the PM's principal private secretary telephoned the homes of the Foreign Secretary, the Home Secretary, the Minister of Defence, the Attorney General and other key figures.

The extraordinary meeting of the inner Cabinet was arranged for ten o'clock.

It was a fierce and acrimonious debate. That morning they had been due to go public on the existence of the Trafalgar House talks. This was because, the night before, the editors of Britain's national press had met in a private function room above the Wig and Pen Club, symbolically at the heart of old Fleet Street. There they discussed the D-Notice restrictions on reporting the talks and the growing haemorrhage of news leaking from across the Atlantic. Already it had been picked up by *Le Figaro* in France and *Die Welt* in Germany. For once united, the most powerful editors in the land served notice on the government that they were going to publish. Damned or not.

The dilemma for Downing Street was simple. Senator Abe Powers III, with the backing of the President of the United States, had decided in view of the ongoing terrorist campaign in London that the Provisional IRA should be given a voice in the closing stages of the Trafalgar House talks. Aware that the British Government would be adamantly opposed to this, Powers warned that he would go public on the whole matter that was otherwise so nearly 'in the bag'. That would clearly embarrass Britain as, seen in an international perspective, it would be regarded as the party responsible for the breakdown of the peace negotiations. Furthermore Washington threatened to raise the Irish question forcibly at the United Nations, urging for positive action to be taken on the world stage.

Government ministers huddled and argued for over an hour before a counterproposal was struck, aimed at damage limitation. Whilst the attendance of any member of the Provisional IRA remained firmly unacceptable until the movement categorically renounced violence, an independent spokesperson of extreme Republican persuasion would be acceptable as a face-saving compromise.

This, the wily Secretary for Northern Ireland pointed out in a phone call to Abe Powers at Trafalgar House, might also save him the almost certain embarrassment of Ulster Unionist politicians walking out on this point of principle.

Further, the inclusion of this independent voice could be dressed up at the imminent press conference as success for the genuine bipartisan nature of the talks, rather than as a climb-down in the face of terrorism.

By midday Abe Powers III had agreed.

One hour later Donny Fitzpatrick received a telephone call at his home in Scotstown from Sinn Fein headquarters in Dublin, informing him of the decision.

The name?

The Most Reverend Bishop Joseph McLaverty. The eighty-five-year-old rogue clergyman, long retired from active participation in the affairs of the Roman Catholic Church in Ireland, whose outspoken views on the justice of the Irish Republican cause was almost evangelical in its fervour and heartfelt intensity.

Fitzpatrick replaced the receiver and turned round. His wife, sensing something, stood expectantly at the door.

In a rare show of emotion, the Chief of Staff of the Provisional IRA let out a whoop of triumph and punched the air with his right fist.

'We've done it! We've got our man at the table!'.

At the time Donny Fitzpatrick received his telephone call, Tom Harrison was in a taxi heading for Heathrow Airport.

The day had begun with the bedside telephone at Trenchard's flat shaking him from a deep and exhausted sleep. In his dream he had been back aboard the dumper truck, confronted by a snake-like clump of wires the thickness of a human wrist. Only one wire out of, perhaps, a hundred would be right. As he snipped with the cutters the bell started ringing.

He was still drenched in the cold nightmare sweat as he reached for the receiver.

'Tom!' It was Casey. 'Thank God you're all right.'

'I'm half asleep, that's all.'

'I heard about the Blackwall Tunnel bomb last night. I was terrified you might be involved . . . I tried calling, but there was no reply.'

350

'I got in late.'

'And were you there?'

He smiled, touched by her concern. 'You know me, can't resist a challenge.'

'God, it must have been awful.'

'I can think of better ways to spend an evening.' He didn't want to dwell on the subject. 'How's your trip going with Eddie?'

'Interesting. You know, it's an experience. Lots of contacts . . .' Somehow he thought she sounded evasive. And was there just a note of apprehension in her voice?

He said: 'Don't let the place scare you. Its reputation's worse than its bite. Individually they're a nice and friendly lot. The Proddies *and* the Catholics. Just don't go nosing into any dark corners, if you know what I mean.'

'Don't worry, Tom. Eddie knows his way around,' she said quickly. Perhaps a little too quickly, he thought.

They hung up and Harrison looked round Trenchard's spartan guest room. Late summer sunshine streaked through the window onto his two small suitcases. All he had in the world now. Suddenly, inexplicably, he felt as though a great burden had been lifted from him. Like this room, his life had become unexpectedly uncluttered, free of responsibility and commitment. The accumulated emotional baggage of life left behind. Pippa would be keen for a divorce and he had found Casey. His job at the forefront of bomb disposal was over and, much as he regretted it, the idea of no more life-threatening danger had its own attractions. Particularly after the previous night in the tunnel. Perhaps it really was time to step down. Let younger men take over.

By the time he'd shaved, showered and dressed he had made his decision. He telephoned Pippa's father and asked to speak to his son.

Archie was excited. 'Dad, that bomb in the Blackwall Tunnel – did you sort it out?'

'I did my bit.'

Archie was well aware of his father's self-effacing euphemisms.

351

'Great! What happened? The boys at school will want to know all the details.'

'When we meet. Listen, how d'you fancy a few days' hiking and camping?'

'Terrific! It's so boring here with Mum at work and it's *days* before I can go back to school.'

'Then I'll clear it with your mother and pick you up at lunch time tomorrow.'

And I'll pay a visit to Les Appleyard this afternoon, he thought as he hung up.

The telephone rang again as he was making coffee. It was Trenchard.

'Hallo, Don, what gives?'

'Your lady friend, Casey Mullins.'

Harrison frowned. 'What about her?'

'She's over here in the Province.'

'I know.'

'And d'you know what she's doing?'

'Vaguely, Don, she and Eddie Mercs are doing some research on the Abe Powers talks.'

'It goes a little deeper than that.'

'How d'you mean?'

'She's trying to track down the AIDAN bombers. And she's getting mixed up with a bad lot.'

Although he heard the words, he could scarcely believe his own ears. 'D'you mean Sinn Fein or PIRA?'

'Not over the phone,' Trenchard came back sharply. 'I'm not at liberty to say anyway. This is strictly on the old pals' act, Tom. She's in danger of getting mixed up in stuff she doesn't understand. If I were you, I'd have a word in her shell-like.'

If anyone knew what was going on in Ulster's murky world, Trenchard did. No doubt this conversation was strictly off the record. 'I will, Don, and thanks for the tip-off.'

'What tip-off? This phone call never happened. But anything for a buddy.'

As soon as Trenchard hung up, Harrison dialled Casey's hotel.

Apparently she and Mercs had already left, leaving a message for any callers that they were unlikely to be back all day.

He made a snap decision, packed an overnight bag and left the apartment, hailing a taxi to take him to Heathrow.

He'd decided on an Aer Lingus shuttle to Dublin. If he passed through Aldergrove, his presence would undoubtedly be noticed. Questions would be asked. High-ranking officers were expected to be met by armed drivers. Anyway, where was he going and what was he doing?

The flight was quick and chaotic as the attendants attempted to distribute snacks and liberal amounts of alcohol before landing. He hired a small Ford Fiesta at the airport and immediately struck north, heading up the N1 towards the main border crossing with Ulster forty miles on. As he anticipated, there was no problem at the checkpoint. Because the car carried southern plates, he was questioned briefly by the soldier who examined his driver's licence.

'English, sir?'

'Yes, over on business.'

'And may I ask what that is?'

He thought of the only business he knew anything about outside his own; Pippa's. 'Public relations. I'm seeing clients. Setting up a new product launch.'

The trooper tried to look as though he understood. 'Very well. Carry on, sir.'

Harrison glanced at his watch. It was seven thirty and Belfast was still the best part of an hour away.

As he drove towards Newry, Casey Mullins was luxuriating in the bath at her hotel, legs outstretched beneath the foam and a vodka and orange in her hand. It had been a long hard day, she and Mercs cramming in as many interviews as they could manage with those on the fringes of the leading political parties. There was a lot of talk, but precious little solid information was gleaned. As Gerard Keefe had predicted, only those who knew little were willing to talk; those who were on the inside track weren't saying.

Then at three in the afternoon the news broke. It was

announced simultaneously in London and at Stormont. The Trafalgar House talks *were* in progress – official. If the communiqué was to be believed, agreement was close and in view of this the famous Irish clergyman, Bishop Joseph McLaverty, renowned for his outspoken support of the Republican cause for over fifty years, had been invited to contribute in the closing final stages of the debate.

The rest of the afternoon disintegrated into chaos, Casey and Mercs having to race back to their hotel to file supporting stories for the late editions and follow-up, in-depth features for the next morning. Eddie Mercs had been in his element, talking excitedly down the telephone to the copy-takers with cigarette clamped, unlit between his teeth. Casey, however, had found the whole experience overwhelming.

When he set out that evening to unearth more background, she declined to join him.

Now she cursed as the telephone rang. The office or maybe Tom? Hurriedly wrapping a towel around her, she dripped a trail of water across the tiles and into the bedroom.

'Casey Mullins.'

'Miss Mullins,' the voice low and harshly accented, 'can you be ready to take a wee trip?'

She suddenly recognised the speaker and experienced a crawling sensation down her spine. 'Is that Spike?'

'No names please.'

'Of course, I'm sorry.' She glanced around the room, wondering what to say, what to do. 'Look, Eddie's out and I don't know what time he'll be back. Probably late.'

There was a hesitation. 'No matter, you can come alone. Billy didn't take too kindly to your friend anyway, didn't like his attitude.'

She recalled her ordeal the previous night, remembering how she stood naked, hands down, for Spike's disinterested inspection. 'Listen, I'll come, but not if I have to go through that business again. Know what I mean?'

'Sure, lady, that's no problem.'

'I need to get ready.'

'Half-an-hour enough?'

'Yes.'

'Then take a taxi to the Washington pub on Howard Street next to City Hall. Sit at the bar and order a drink. Try and keep one seat free next to you. You'll be contacted.'

'Where . . .?' she began but the cut-off tone was already drilling in her ear.

Next she tried telephoning two places where she thought Mercs might be; he wasn't. Resigning herself to going alone, she put on a plain black jersey dress and low-heeled pumps, then telephoned reception for a taxi. On the way out she left a note of where she was going with the duty manager.

As the taxi pulled out of the grounds into Holywood Road, she was unaware of the unmarked or 'Q' car leaving the parking lot, the driver talking into his concealed throat-mike.

The Washington was large, open-plan and busy, although it was too early to be crowded. She found two empty stools at the large semicircular bar and sat on one, placing her shoulder bag on the second. Wanting to keep a clear head, she ordered a sparkling mineral water and began studying her surroundings. Most of the customers were working men, although she spotted a few office girls talking to their male colleagues. Some were watching the television placed over the front door, others grouped conspiratorially in the dark wooden alcoves. No one paid her any obvious attention, yet she guessed someone was watching her closely, making sure she hadn't been followed. It was an unnerving feeling.

While she waited anxiously, Tom Harrison was pulling up outside the Park Avenue Hotel.

'I'm afraid you just missed her, sir. She left about twenty minutes ago.'

Another woman was just going off duty and overheard. 'Miss Mullins left a message. In her cubby hole.'

She looked at the name on the paper. 'It's for Mr Mercs, another guest.'

Harrison wasn't about to be deterred. Bad lot, Trenchard had said, and now the phrase was ringing in his ears. 'Mr Mercs didn't go with her?'

355

'No, sir.'

'May I see the message? It's extremely important I find her.'

'I really can't do that, sir.'

'I *am* her husband.' His smile was the most charming he could muster given his rising anxiety.

'Oh, I see.' And as she hesitated he quickly eased the note from her grasp.

'Thanks so much.'

He read quickly: *Eddie – I've had a call from King Billy's man, Spike. Wants me to meet at the Washington in Howard Street about 8.45. Please, please try and make it. I'll stall for time if I can. Your intrepid reporter assistant. Casey.*

Christ, Harrison thought, King Billy! Surely she hadn't got involved with him? Harrison had never met the man, or even seen his photograph, but the name had cropped up from time to time at high-level intelligence briefings in Lisburn. He couldn't recall which of the Protestant terror groups he was involved with, but that hardly mattered. Billy Baker was regarded as little more than a gangster and a thug by the security forces and was known to have been behind a number of sectarian 'doorstepping' campaigns, murdering Catholics who unthinkingly answered their doorbells after dark.

He looked at his watch. It was eight forty now. He'd never make it. Turning on his heel, he raced back to his hired car.

Yet it was ten minutes later before the stranger approached Casey in the Washington. She was beginning to think the meeting had been abandoned when he spoke and startled her, causing her to spill her drink.

'Is this seat taken?' He was in his twenties and wearing a denim jacket. His hair was short and his chin unshaven.

She moved her bag and shook her head nervously.

He sat, placed his cigarettes and plastic lighter on the bar, then beckoned for a half of Guinness. As he waited to be served, he moved his cigarette pack and lit one of its contents. It took a moment before she noticed the little square of paper. Just three lines were written in poorly constructed capitals.

356

WHEN I LEAVE,
FOLLOW IN A FEW MINUTES.
TURN RIGHT OUTSIDE.

The cigarette pack covered the note again and the man exhaled into the barman's scowling face as the Guinness was served.

Five long hard swallows was all it took and the glass was empty. The man levered himself from the stool and sauntered back out towards the street.

Her heart pounding, Casey drained her drink and glanced at her watch. Almost nine.

Dammit, Eddie, where are you?

She waited two more minutes, then reluctantly collected her bag and followed the stranger's footsteps. Outside, the pavement was almost deserted; there was no sign of the young man. She began walking towards the next junction with Queen Street.

He was waiting round the corner, a car at the kerb with its engine running. First peering back along Howard Street to the Washington, to be sure no one had followed her, he said: 'Get in the back.'

Now I *am* committed, she thought. No going back.

The exhaust burbled softly and the car sped away into the night.

As it did so, the hired Fiesta pulled up outside the Washington and Harrison crossed the pavement quickly. He pushed open the doors into the noisy chatter and smoke, edging his way through the crowd, looking around anxiously for some sign of her.

'You're too late, old lad.'

He turned, taken aback. 'Don.'

'I thought you were going to talk to her, Tom.'

'That's why I'm here. She's been out all day – I couldn't reach her by phone.'

'That's a pity. She's just left with one of King Billy's lads.'

Harrison noticed for the first time that Trenchard wasn't dressed in his usual flamboyant style. Just dark jeans and jacket and a black polo neck. 'And you just let her go?'

357

'Let's talk outside.'

Trenchard led the way. Once beyond the door, Harrison rounded on him. 'What were you thinking of, Don? Why didn't you stop her?'

'Because the soppy tart has just wandered into a security operation.' His boyish grin was meant to reassure. 'I didn't know she was going to come here. I've had her under surveillance, but I didn't know what she was doing until five minutes ago when she got into one of King Billy's cars – which just happens to be one of the vehicles in the operation that's going down.'

Christ! 'What sort of operation?'

'Don't know, Tom. It's all whispers over here, as I'm sure you're aware.'

'Is she in danger?'

Trenchard shrugged. 'There's always a risk, but my boys are fully briefed about her. The last thing anyone wants is a dead journalist on our hands, least of all an American one.' He lit a cigarette. 'Look, let's get back to my car. We'll monitor everything from there.'

'I could bloody kill you, Don.'

Again the boyish grin. 'Don't worry. Casey will be all right.'

Even as he spoke, the saloon carrying Casey was stopping outside a neat Edwardian house off the Donegall Road in the south of the city. When she and the stranger crossed the pavement to the front door, they broke the magnetic field of the sensor secreted in the headlamp of the empty car which had been parked outside the neighbouring house that morning. The miniature ultralow-level light camera automatically clicked twice, adding two more identifiable profiles to the roll of film that had been recording the day's visitors to the house.

The front door was opened by Spike. He glanced quickly up and down the road before closing it behind them. Without a word he led the way down a dark passage to the dining room where the heavy curtains had been drawn. A 'Jesus Saves Sinners' embroidery hung over the empty open fireplace. She noticed he made no attempt to conceal the heavy automatic pistol stuffed into the waistband of his trousers.

'This is my aunt's house,' he said suddenly. 'The ol' biddy's in the front parlour watching telly and sucking sherbet lemons. Doesn't know what year it is, let alone what day.'

'She doesn't mind you using her house?'

Spike gave a mean chuckle. 'I doubt she even realises.' He pointed to a pair of black tracksuit trousers, a man's navy sweater, and a dark jacket on the table. 'I want you to change into those. And can you pin your hair up?'

She was bewildered. 'Yes.'

'Don't want anyone to be able to identify you.'

He left her then to strip and change into the unfamiliar clothes. The trousers were elasticated and fitted well enough; the sweater and jacket were enormous and smelled of stale smoke and beer. She had just pinned back her hair when the door opened again.

Spike handed her the chequered cloth cap. 'It's time to go.'

To her surprise he led the way through the kitchen to the back door. As they walked briskly down the rear garden path, she glimpsed the unkempt shrubs on either side, the long grass going to seed. A gate in the back fence opened onto a narrow alleyway. Another car waited with several men inside. There was no courtesy light inside and it was impossible for her to recognise the faces of the men she was squashed between in the back seat. They were young, though, she was sure of that, the testosterone musk and the smell of lager quite unmistakable.

'Where are we going?' she asked as they drove off.

'You'll see,' Spike replied. 'Let's just say we're doing a wee favour for Her Majesty.'

'Favour?'

'Oh, it's a favour, so it is. No doubt about it. King Billy always liked to oblige the Crown. All different now, of course. It all went sour after the Anglo-Irish Agreement in '85, and Dublin's boot boys – sorry, I'll be referring to the RUC – started treating us no different than the murderin' Provos. Area saturation, special support units and informers. And we've heard the politicians from Westminster sniggering at us behind our backs. Loud and crass, that's what they think we are. Our Unionist politicians are snubbed now by the Northern Ireland Officer here – the English arse-lickers from Whitehall prefer to consult with ministers from Dublin rather than the elected representatives of the people. They don't like us because we stand four-square and say exactly what we mean. Unemployment, housing, education, the money is all spent on the sayso of the Republic now and it's all directed at the Catholic community. You're a journalist, you can ask questions. You'll see if I'm not right.'

'You sound angry.'

As soon as she said it, she thought how she was stupidly stating the obvious, but Spike didn't seem to mind. He just gave a harsh, humourless laugh. 'Oh, I'm angry, all right. We're all angry. We've become strangers in our own land.'

'Beleaguered.'

'That's a good word, lady. Yes, that's what we are. But make no mistake, we'll not be giving in. Recruits are flooding to the Protestant paramilitaries and we've arms coming in from South Africa and eastern Europe. Some of our people are learning from the Provos. We're making bombs too now, and we'll be taking them to Dublin.'

The mention of bombs made her blanch and she thought of Harrison, wished he was with her now.

'And Westminster still doesn't see the writing on the wall,' Spike was saying. 'But when they hear King Billy's Lambeg drum again, they'll know we're on the march. The Balkans – Bosnia and that lot – you'll have seen nothing yet.'

God, she thought, he means every word.

'We're nearly there,' the driver announced suddenly.

She peered out of the window, but all she could see was the dim outline of hedgerows and flat farmland beneath the fleeting nightclouds. All she knew was that they'd started travelling west and she'd seen a signpost for Ballymacrevan some way back. Otherwise they could have been anywhere.

Their car slowed and turned off the road without signalling; the suspension bucked and jarred, the headlamps showing the overgrown brambles on each side of the narrow farm track. Ahead another car appeared, tucked into a field gate lay-by with its lights off. Their car pulled alongside and stopped.

'Wait here,' Spike ordered and climbed out. Now she could see that he was talking to another man who was dressed in black and carried a walkie-talkie radio.

After a few moments Spike returned. 'Our taig friend has just left. He lives and spends most of his time in the west Belfast heartland. Rarely makes excursions, so it's been difficult for us to get to him. But his aunt lives on this farm and she's been poorly. A priest is calling every day, so she's not expected to last.' He added matter-of-factly: 'Her misfortune is our good luck. We've a man up watching the house.'

'Here it comes,' the driver said.

She turned and saw it then, the tell-tale beams bouncing over the hedgetop, obscured by a bend in the track. Then it turned into the straight, the brilliance of the car lights suddenly blinding. It kept on coming, the driver unaware of what was waiting.

'NOW!' Spike shouted.

Their driver accelerated hard, turning the wheel so that the saloon slewed across the track. Brakes screeched, loose shale ringing against metal as the oncoming driver attempted to stop, the car sliding to a halt just inches from the blocking vehicle.

She glimpsed two white shocked faces in the windscreen. One male and one female, she thought. Saw their panic as the engine revved and screeched and the gears crunched as the startled driver attempted to engage reverse. But he had left it too late. Dark figures had appeared, wrenching open the doors and waving guns.

The woman screamed, hysterical, flailing her arms against the man at her door.

'Shit, there's a wee child in the back!' the man called.

Then Spike was out and on his feet. 'Bring the man. One of you stay with the mother and the child for half-an-hour until we're clear.'

Already the victim had been dragged away, a black plastic bin liner pulled over his head and his hands secured behind his back with freezer ties. Before Casey had a chance to protest at the man's treatment, he had been bundled into the other car and it had begun to move.

361

Spike returned and slammed the door. 'Let's go.'

'Who is he?'

'Fucken IRA.' She noticed his voice had lost its calm, excited by the action. 'Sorry, I'm forgetting my manners.'

'You're sure he's IRA?'

Spike allowed his ghostly smile to make an appearance. 'D'you believe all that crap in the press? That our gunmen go out to kill innocent Catholics?'

'I don't know.'

'Well, sure they're all innocent. Then a couple o'years later, when the dust settles, you find their names at Milltown Cemetery on the Provos' roll of honour.'

'And that poor man?'

'That poor man is a Sinn Fein councillor in Andersonstown. He's also a member of the Provos' security section. Vetting new members and old-timers coming out of the Maze. If anyone knows who your bomber is, he does.'

'How do you know?'

'We've got our sources.'

'And what's his name?'

'Killy Tierney.'

It was half-an-hour before they pulled off the road and drove up an incline of cracked and weed-infested concrete. The two cars stopped outside a boarded-up, single-storey building that had once been a transport café.

Muffled cries of protest were uttered as Tierney was dragged towards the door, his voice silenced by a hard fist aimed at his kidneys.

'I want no part of this,' Casey protested as Spike ushered her in.

'Shut up and just listen!'

Once inside, the door was closed and the area lit by a paraffin lamp. It was a frightening and macabre sight, the men in black standing around the lone seated figure with his head bowed. On the floor broken glass and dog faeces, on the walls an ice-cream poster with a smiling maiden on an exotic desert island. No one moved.

362

What were they waiting for?

Then the back door creaked open and the big man stepped in, his loafers crunching on the glass. Immediately she recognised the massive form in the outsize grey suit and mustard-coloured polo that caught in the folds of flesh around his neck. The huge padded shoulders made King Billy's head with its thatch of pure white hair seem ridiculously small.

Spike stepped forward and unceremoniously stripped the bin liner from Tierney's head. A narrow pale face and wide frightened eyes stared at his tormentors in the shadows. His wire-framed spectacles fell to the floor, to be crunched slowly and deliberately underfoot by a smiling gunman.

'What do you want?' The words were croaked, scarcely audible.

'We ask the questions.' It was King Billy. 'And you have a simple choice. To answer them the easy way or the hard way.'

Tierney glared at the blur of faces. 'I'll say nothing!' he said defiantly.

King Billy chose not to hear. 'Your name is Kilian Tierney. Aged forty-three. Married with one child. You have served time at Her Majesty's pleasure for riotous behaviour and again later for firearms charges . . .?' He allowed the words to hang in the air and cocked his head to one side. 'I hear nothing.'

'Because I'm saying nothing!' Tierney spat.

There was an uneasy shuffling movement amongst the onlookers.

'There is no right to silence here,' King Billy said with slow menace.

'Please!' Casey cried.

Spike grabbed her arm, his fingers like steel claws in her bicep. 'Shut it,' he hissed.

'You are a councillor for Sinn Fein,' the Orangeman continued, 'and you are also a member of a proscribed organisation, namely the Provisional IRA.'

Silence.

'Please confirm.' For the first time he glanced in Casey's direction. 'We must be sure we have the right man.'

Tierney's mouth was clamped shut, his eyes so wide they looked in danger of falling from their sockets.

She wasn't prepared for what happened next, hadn't seen the man step out of the shadows. From the corner of her eye she saw it fall, wincing involuntarily as the sledgehammer head slammed into Tierney's bent right knee. His entire body jerked as though struck by a bolt of lightning. His cry, wrenched from deep within him and forced out through the constriction of his throat like an explosion, rang around the derelict building in a prolonged and ragged echo.

He tried to nurse the shattered joint as the blood bubbled up through the material of his trousers, but his hands were still tied behind him, so he was reduced to squirming on his seat in his agony and frustration, half falling in the process.

Rough hands straightened him. Then they all noticed the putrid stench. 'Oh, fuck, he's shit himself.'

Casey had turned her head away, still held fast by Spike's iron grip. Now she heard King Billy's voice again. 'You've a nice wife and a nice wee lad, Killy. Don't make yourself a total cripple for them. Just tell us what we want to know and we will leave you in peace. We'll even telephone an ambulance. You'll be in the Victoria before you know it.'

Tierney was sobbing, his head hung low, his knee a bloody pulp.

'Now, please confirm your identity.'

His head nodded, the hair dishevelled. Tears dripped onto his trousers, onto the floor.

'That's better. Now, let's not hang about. You know the identity of the AIDAN active service unit, right?'

A shake of the head, a sobbing sniff of self-pity.

'I just give the word, Killy, and it'll be your second knee. Then your right hand.' He paused to let the words sink in. 'Our sources tell us that you know. And we are all aware that it is a very great secret. So think hard, think of your wife and wee boy, and of that comfortable hospital bed waiting for you at the Victoria.'

The following silence was probably only seconds, but to Casey

364

the time yawned into an endless abyss. She found herself staring at the spreading pool of blood around his brightly polished shoe and the mesmeric drip of brown liquid that had flooded over the seat.

Tell them, she prayed silently, for God's sake tell them what they want to know!

Tierney said hoarsely, wincing through his pain: 'Have you got a cigarette?'

King Billy looked up at Spike, nodded. A pack was produced, one of the contents placed between the parched, bloodless lips and a match struck. The man inhaled deeply, lay back in the chair. Spike removed the cigarette from his mouth.

'Dougan,' Tierney murmured, smoke drifting up over his face. 'Hughie Dougan is the bomb maker.'

King Billy looked at Spike, Spike looked at King Billy. 'YOU LYING FUCKEN BASTARD! DOUGAN IS FUCKEN WELL DEAD.' Spike was yelling in Tierney's face, his mouth just inches from the other's eyes.

Tierney looked up pleadingly, his cheeks sodden with tears. 'Sweet Mother of Jesus, believe me. Hughie Dougan *isn't* dead. It was a setup down in Sligo, a fake. Hughie Dougan makes the bombs and he's been planning the campaign. Him and his daughter Clodagh.'

Spike stepped back. 'You'd be having us look for a ghost, Killy?'

'That's the whole point.' Exasperated. 'No one looks for a dead man, that was the idea.'

King Billy didn't look convinced. 'Who else is on the unit?'

'Pat McGirl.'

That figured. McGirl was one of PIRA's seasoned front-liners, but with no recent convictions. 'And?'

'The others are from the south. No records. A girl called Moira Lock and two others, Leo Muldoon and Liam Doran. Another man called Houlihan.'

They were names that meant nothing to King Billy or his men. 'You had an own goal,' Spike said, 'Who was killed?'

Tierney shook his head. 'I don't know, I just do the vetting.

They're running this from the top and no one's saying anything. Presumably it was Lock and Muldoon or Doran who got blown away, but I'm just guessing.'

'And where are they operating from?'

'God, you don't think they tell me that? You'd have to ask the man himself, Donny Fitzpatrick.'

King Billy looked once again at Casey. 'D'you hear that? We know who the bastards are at the top. And the Brits know too. But nothing ever happens. How d'you think that makes us feel?'

Spike prodded Tierney in the chest. 'And what makes you think I believe you know nothing?'

Tierney met his gaze, his eyes glazed in pain and defiance. 'Because you've broken my fucken knee and you're about to break the other, you bastards!'

Spike stepped away and looked at King Billy for approval. The big man nodded.

Two men stepped forward, one grasping Tierney's shoulders from behind, the other replacing the bin liner over his head. The struggle was token, the outcome a certainty.

King Billy was saying: 'Killy Tierney, you have been tried and found guilty of being a member of an illegal organisation, of aiding and abetting murder here and on the mainland, and of treason against your country. You are hereby sentenced to death, and may God have mercy on your soul.' He drew himself to his full height. 'God save the Queen.'

Casey jumped at the sharp report of the pistol that had been held to the back of Tierney's head. Only when he pitched forward did she see the weapon and the serpent's coil of gunsmoke. No one moved to stop the body as it fell, blood bubbling from the torn black plastic bag over the debris on the floor.

Now she stared at the corpse in total disbelief.

'Phone for an ambulance once we're away from here,' King Billy said. 'We'll issue a statement tomorrow.'

It was Spike who heard it first. The pulsing thud of the helicopter; it had come in upwind giving no warning of its arrival. Abruptly the entire building began to tremble in its downdraught, the Nitesun lamp dazzling as Spike rushed to the door and threw it open.

'THIS IS THE POLICE! YOU ARE SURROUNDED!' The bullhorn echoed like the voice of God.

Others joined Spike at the door. 'Christ!'

One man raised his gun.

'No!' Spike warned.

But it was too late. The marksman's round caught the man in the chest, propelling him back into the café as though pulled by elastic.

Casey shrieked in terror.

'THROW YOUR WEAPONS DOWN! COME OUT WITH YOUR HANDS ABOVE YOUR HEAD!'

Spike turned back to King Billy. 'The bloody twisters.'

The big man nodded grimly. 'What do you expect? Now, you'd better go. They're not known for their patience.'

The young man gave a half-smile. 'No surrender, eh?'

'No surrender.'

Spike dropped his weapon, raised his hands and walked slowly out onto the floodlit concrete of the old car park. He had barely glimpsed the lowering Puma helicopter, the groups of flak-jacketed RUC officers and their vehicles, before he was rushed by the soldiers on either side of the door. Expertly he was tripped and spreadeagled, face down on the ground, hands checking for hidden weapons.

The rest were similarly treated until King Billy himself emerged. Perhaps because he was such a large man, or perhaps because they knew exactly who he was, the SAS soldiers did not subject him to the same rough treatment. More circumspectly, they ran their hands over the mountain of flesh where he stood, virtually ignoring them, watching instead the approaching group of men in civilian clothes.

One of them broke into a run. 'CASEY!'

'Tom!' Trenchard warned, his words wasted.

Casey Mullins appeared timidly at the door, her slim body swamped in the male clothes, but the cap removed and copper hair hanging so that no one would shoot her by mistake.

'God, Tom!' Her face broke into a smile of relief. 'What are you doing here?'

He crushed her in his arms. 'Thank Christ you're safe.'

King Billy looked at her accusingly. 'You?'

Over Harrison's shoulder she shook her head.

Trenchard arrived with a senior Special Branch detective. 'Hello, Billy, been up to your old tricks again?'

The Orangeman's stare was glacial, his bulk unmoved. 'Whose tricks, Mr Smith? Mine or yours? Where is Mr Jones?'

'Mr Jones' was the name John Nash had used, Trenchard remembered. 'He's in London.'

'Then get him here.'

Trenchard watched as the Special Branch detective stepped tentatively into the café. 'If we find what I think we're going to find, you're not going to be giving orders to anyone for the next twenty years.'

'We've got the information you wanted. The identity of the AIDAN bombers. Hughie Dougan was behind it all.'

A sneer crossed Trenchard's face. 'Dougan's dead, Billy. Don't you read the papers?'

'His death was faked, Dougan has been behind it all the time.'

'You can do better than that, Billy. I was there. I saw his body, saw his Celtic birds ring.'

King Billy looked puzzled. 'I don't know about that. But what I tell you is the truth, may God help me. It's what Killy Tierney told me before he died.'

'One of your kangaroo courts, was it? I wouldn't put much store by that.'

Casey pulled away from Harrison. 'It's true, Don, I heard the poor man say it before they killed him. He didn't sound like he was making it up.'

Trenchard turned towards her angrily. 'Shut up, woman, or you'll find yourself arrested for conspiracy to murder.' He looked at Harrison. 'Get her away from here, Tom. We've never seen her tonight.'

'What's going on, Don?' his friend demanded.

Trenchard snapped: 'Don't meddle in things you don't understand. Now go.'

The Special Branch detective stepped back out of the café, his face pale. 'Two corpses,' he announced. 'One of Billy's men and a bound man with a bag over his head. Bit of a mess.'

'Killy Tierney,' Trenchard said.

Turning to King Billy, the detective said: 'William Frederick Baker, I am arresting you for the murder of Kilian Tierney –'

The Orangeman turned to Trenchard, his big face impassive. 'I had a deal with you and Mr Jones. A favour for a favour.'

Don Trenchard looked towards the café. 'I don't recall any deals, Billy. Sorry.'

18

'I read somewhere that violence turns women on,' Casey said.

Harrison leaned on his elbow and looked down at her naked body stretched out languorously on the hotel bed beside him.

'Did it affect you?'

She wrinkled her face in distaste, the memory of Killy Tierney's torture and execution was still vivid in her mind. 'It's a horrible thought, but I think it must have in a sort of way, don't you?'

'Something certainly did. I thought it was me.' He traced his finger over her nipple and watched with fascination as it puckered and hardened in response.

'Oh, it is you, Tom, believe me.' She sounded breathless. 'I suppose it's men of violence, rather than the violence itself. I mean, boxers for instance. Big ugly brutes most of them, but there's never any shortage of pretty girls hanging around.'

His hand followed down across the flat plain of her belly, lingering in the gingery wisps between her legs. 'You don't think of me as a man of violence?'

She was beginning to stir again now, pressing up hard against his fingers, her face flushed and her words coming out in short gasps. 'But – you deal in violence – in a way you deal with the most violent – thing imaginable . . .' And she was away, her hands sliding over his shoulders, fingertips kneading the clenched muscles of his broad back, her knees opening to draw him in.

Somehow it was different. Now it was the lovemaking of two people who were certain of each other and committed. There was no shame between them, no obvious secrets. Only once Harrison

370

thought fleetingly of Pippa, how it had never been like this with her. How, if it had, things might have turned out differently.

He had fallen asleep after that second bout of coupling, so long and unhurried. It was about three in the morning when he awoke again, instantly aware that Casey was missing from the bed. She was in her dressing gown, standing at the window and staring out into the night.

'What's the matter?' he called.

She turned, the light from the car-park floodlights creating a halo behind her hair. 'I didn't mean to wake you, I couldn't sleep. Things just keep on going round and round in my head.'

He rubbed his eyes with his hands, swung his legs off the bed. 'Hardly surprising. It was a pretty gruesome experience.'

'I know. But it isn't that. It's the confession that poor man made and the way Don dismissed it.'

Harrison shrugged. 'I can see why, I'd dismiss it too. People just don't go around faking their own deaths.'

'Some do – to disappear or to get insurance payouts.'

'True, but they don't usually supply a corpse.'

She nodded her agreement, but clearly wasn't convinced. 'But it could be done, Tom, couldn't it? It isn't impossible?'

He thought for a moment. There was no denying that it wasn't *impossible*. And hadn't he been struck all along by a similarity in the workmanship of the AIDAN devices with those of Hughie Dougan so many years before? He began to understand Casey's concern that Trenchard had dismissed the allegation out of hand. He said: 'Did you know it was my evidence that convicted Dougan the last time?'

Her eyes widened. 'Really? Jeez, that's uncanny.' She looked at him long and hard, turning something over in her mind. 'Tom, I've been thinking. Perhaps I should pay a visit south of the border.'

'Where?'

'Sligo. That's where Dougan was supposed to have died.'

'Don't get involved, Casey. This is the IRA you're talking about.'

She smiled at his concern. 'Oh, don't worry, I'll be discreet. I'd ask Eddie to come, but he'll be tied up with interviews.'

Hughie Dougan, Harrison was thinking, the trickiest bomb maker he'd ever known. The man who had tried to catch him out all those years before. Thirteen thousand pounds, that had been the price on Harrison's head. Thirteen thousand pounds for a dead ATO. Was it just remotely possible that Tierney's tortured confession was true?

He made his decision. 'I'll come with you.'

'What?'

'To Sligo, I'll come with you. I'm on leave, there's nothing to stop me.'

'Isn't it against some army rules or something?'

'Probably, but only if I get found out.'

'Oh, Tom, that's wonderful. We can go tomorrow, first thing.'

'Then you'd better get some sleep.'

She giggled, reaching across the gap between them and running her hands tantalisingly over his thighs towards his groin. 'Oh, I can't sleep now. I'm too excited. I want to make love again.'

He laughed. 'I don't think I've got the energy. Three times in one night – I'm not as young as I was.'

'You're the bomb man, Tom, and I feel like I'm about to blow up.' She looked closely into his eyes, feeling his body harden in her hands. 'Defuse me. A controlled explosion would be nice.'

'It was the X-ray-sensitive switch that finally did it,' Detective Superintendent Jim Maitland explained at the briefing of Anti-Terrorist Branch officers.

Detective Sergeant Myers, who'd been assigned to the laborious chore of tracing down the source of component parts used in the AIDAN bombs, said: 'Before they used that, the other leads were too vague. Hundreds of firms in dozens of countries make different microswitches, tilt switches and timers for use in everything from pinball tables to video recorders. Most companies willingly co-operate here, but abroad our requests for information are mostly ignored. We scoured the lists of Maplin's and Radio Spares, the main mail-order suppliers of electronic parts, but no real pattern emerged. Just a lot of fruitless legwork in prospect.'

'Until they used the X-ray switch,' Maitland intervened. 'These gizmos measure levels of radiation which cause the component to change its electrical characteristics – in layman's language, it's a current change that's sufficient to trigger an audio or video signal, or in AIDAN's case, a bomb.'

'Who uses these things?' someone asked.

'Variants are used in body-scanners or for checking safety levels on VDU screens in offices. And Harwell sells detection guns to local councils for checking natural radon levels. You know, like in Cornwall and north-east Scotland.'

'The point is,' said Myers, slightly irked that the big chief should be stealing his moment of glory, 'that it's a very specialised area with only a few manufacturers and very limited uses. When we ran their customer lists through the computer and matched them with those of Maplin's and Radio Spares – bingo! We'd isolated Solent Electronics Manufacturing. An address in the run-down Chapel area of Southampton . . .'

'Our target for this morning,' Maitland announced with triumph.

Local Special Branch officers had been keeping the ground-floor office and storeroom under discreet surveillance overnight. On orders from London, no inquiries were made either directly or through neighbours or the landlord for fear of tipping off the terrorists.

Maitland's team arrived before dawn with full armed backup from a specialist firearms unit. They were in position by first light and waited anxiously for the city to come alive.

At five past nine, a stocky man in jeans and T-shirt, with an aggressive-looking face and close-cropped hair, arrived to open up.

'ALL UNITS GO!' Maitland ordered into his radio mike.

Bystanders screamed in surprise as cars and unmarked vans opened up to disgorge armed men in flak jackets and SWAT-style baseball caps.

The man with his key in the door was frozen to the spot, paralysed with fear, as the policemen swooped.

Only afterwards, seeing the sign outside the rented office for Videomail Enterprises, did Maitland acknowledge that the bird had long flown. The previous renter of the premises – a Henry Roke of Solent Electronics Manufacturing – had left two months earlier. Not surprisingly, he'd left no forwarding address and no one was able to give a useful description of him.

But there was an upside. The office was filled with banks of wired video recorders and the owner of Videomail was arrested for trading in pirated tapes and pornography.

That, however, was of little consolation to Jim Maitland. Inquiries continued.

Casey looked drawn and tired as she packed, but was determinedly cheerful.

Harrison closed his suitcase. 'You look like a woman who's spent the whole night making love.'

A pink tongue poked in his direction. 'Rubbish, I'm always a happy waker-upper. I just don't get smart until about nine thirteen, that's all. Then you have to catch me before nine forty-seven or it's all over.'

Harrison telephoned Archie to postpone their camping trip. His son was clearly disappointed, the situation made worse when Pippa came on the line and threatened to deny him access to his son if he couldn't keep his promises. It was a ridiculous and acrimonious conversation that left Harrison feeling depressed, not least because there would now be little time left to make it up to Archie before his imminent return to school.

The call over, Harrison joined Casey and Eddie Mercs downstairs for breakfast. A decidedly unhappy waker-upper that morning, the reporter was nursing a ferocious hangover. 'I'd forgotten what stamina it takes to have a quiet night out over here,' he complained.

On Harrison's advice, Casey had made no mention of the previous night's events, merely saying that King Billy's contact failed to show up, but that Harrison had. 'And you don't mind if I take off for a day or two?'

'I'll be heartbroken.' He grinned at Harrison over his cornflakes. 'Just have to accept that the best man won.'

'Idiot,' Casey said. 'I *mean* can you manage without me?'

'You're on holiday,' Mercs reminded. 'I'll cope.'

'Did you learn anything last night?'

Mercs shrugged. 'Not much. Except one thing. That Irish bishop – what's his name, McLaverty – who's attending the Trafalgar House talks as an independent and token Republican.'

Harrison had heard news of the official admission about the talks on his car radio the previous afternoon. 'Yes?'

'My sources reckon he's in bed with the IRA. Knows all the top men personally, even if he's not a paid-up member.'

Harrison stared at him, his blood running cold. Jock Murray dead, Les Appleyard a cripple and the Provisional IRA at the conference table. He felt suddenly sick.

Mercs said, unaware of Harrison's involvement: 'They reckon it was the Blackwall Tunnel bomb that did it.'

Harrison said little more until he and Casey were on the road, cruising westward down the motorway towards the border crossing at Aughnacloy.

'I'm sorry, Tom.'

His anger showed in his clenched fists on the wheel. 'It makes it all such a bloody waste. For a second in that tunnel I thought I'd never see you again and Archie would be left without a father. I really believed that. It seems I hardly need have bothered.'

'No, Tom. That mother and her baby. They're only alive because of you. They wouldn't agree.'

He pounded the wheel. 'Christ, I hate politicians!'

It was lunch time when they turned into the narrow village street. The place had a forlorn air about it, just a couple of shabbily dressed locals and a stray dog on the pavement beside the peeling shop fronts.

They found the church on the outskirts, an ancient stone building, its walls and square tower mantled in Virginia creeper. The elderly priest stood by an elaborate and luridly painted carving of the Crucifixion, talking to two women.

Harrison parked and they walked back along the road bordered by a low stone wall.

The priest broke off his conversation as Casey approached him. 'Hi, Father, I wonder if you could help me?'

His whiskery face brightened. 'Of course, if I can. An American, yes?'

'Sure.'

'May I welcome you to Ireland.' The women made no attempt to leave, watching darkly, their distrust of strangers plain.

'Thank you. I'm Casey Mullins and this is my English friend, Tom.'

The priest nodded his acknowledgment, but his eyes only left Casey for a moment. 'Casey Mullins. That's a very Irish name.'

'On my father's side. But the reason I'm here is to look for the grave of a distant relative.'

'And who might that be?'

'His name was Hugh Dougan. I believe he might be buried here?'

Wispy eyebrows raised above his pebble-lensed spectacles. 'Indeed he is. He died just last year. Such a tragic case. All that time in prison, fighting for his beliefs and then to perish in a car accident.' He interlaced his fingers in front of his smock. 'But then the Lord indeed moves in mysterious ways. Perhaps his death was meant to give strength to someone else. It works like that sometimes, you know. For instance, a widow may find her own inner resolve when she loses her husband. Although not in Mr Dougan's case, of course. I do believe his wife had predeceased him by some years. Anyway, let me show you the grave.'

The women watched as the priest led the way through the unkempt churchyard, brambles and nettles growing unchecked beneath gnarled crabapple trees.

'I was a little surprised,' he was saying, 'that the family didn't want his remains taken north. It wouldn't have cost that much and I am sure the movement would have paid.'

Casey feigned ignorance. 'The movement?'

'The Irish Republican Army.' He used the old term. 'Mr Dougan was a member in the proud old tradition.'

'Perhaps his family preferred him to be buried here.'

'Evidently, Miss Mullins. But the movement usually likes to honour its Belfast dead in Milltown Cemetery at the martyrs' plot for the fallen.

'How exactly did he die?'

'A car crash – terrible business. There was talk that it was deliberate, but I doubt that. It happened on a notorious bend. And there was little doubt he'd had a drink.'

They rounded an overgrown shrub. 'Ah, yes, here it is.'

It was a simple slab of black marble, the inscription carved in gold lettering.

'Flowers,' Harrison observed.

'His daughter.'

Harrison frowned, trying to remember what he'd read on Dougan's computer file. 'I thought she was working in Canada.'

The priest looked at him. 'Perhaps one is. There are two daughters. It is the youngest who comes, who came just a few days ago. Caitlin, that's her name. Still lives in Belfast. My heart goes out to the dear child. It really broke her up when she identified the body. Not that there was much to identify. The car had exploded after the crash, you see. But there were his rings, they survived intact. Young Caitlin had a wee babe with her the other day. It doesn't take much to work out that she was carrying at the time of her father's death.' The thoughts of her suffering brought tears to the old man's eyes. 'I'm sorry. Tell me, is there anything else you'd like to know?'

Casey looked at Harrison; he shook his head. 'Father, you've been most kind.'

He left them at the crucifix by the gate where the two women had been waiting.

As they walked back to the car, Casey said: 'He nearly had me crying myself then. And I'm not sure I've learned anything at all.'

Harrison said: 'Perhaps we have. Firstly, cars *can* explode in crashes, but it's quite unusual – despite what you see in the movies.'

'Really?' Not quite believing.

'That Mercedes I told you about in the Blackwall Tunnel, for example. It didn't explode. I've spent many happy hours shooting at car petrol tanks, trying to make them blow. You need tracer rounds at the very least. The other thing is, as the priest pointed out, why wasn't the body taken back to Milltown?'

'Is that important?'

'It could be significant if we're to believe the story Tierney told before he died. A death south of the border makes checking forensic identification of the remains – dental records, fingerprints – very difficult. Neither the Garda nor the Catholic Church in Ireland are very co-operative with the RUC. But if Dougan, a recently released terrorist, had died like that in the north, Special Branch would have certainly made checks. As it is, exhuming the body from here now will prove virtually impossible.'

Casey opened the car door thoughtfully. 'I've just remembered, Tierney said that one of the daughters was involved, Clodagh.'

'The one who's supposed to be in Canada?' Harrison remarked as he climbed in.

'I wonder if it would be possible to find her sister, the one who brought the flowers?'

Harrison nodded. 'If the priest is right and she's still living in Belfast, then it shouldn't be a problem.'

He started the engine, swung the car round in a circle and headed back towards the border. When he had started out that morning, he'd been cynical of Casey's suspicions. But now, uncannily, everything was beginning to fit. His head began to spin with the implications. Just the possibility that he and the ATOs in Northern Ireland and the Section in London had been up against Hughie Dougan all the time . . . His old adversary, reaching out to get him from beyond the grave. At the very thought he felt his heart begin to pump and the adrenalin start to course.

Jock Murray, Les Appleyard . . . just one to go. Tom Harrison.

It was mid-afternoon when he dropped Casey back at her hotel then drove straight back down the M1 to Army Headquarters at Lisburn.

The office at 321 EOD Squadron was an unmarked Portakabin affair situated beside the main crescent-shaped brick building in the secure inner compound. He parked outside and then met the surprised stats sergeant on the steps.

'Hallo, sir, didn't expect you. Thought you was on R and R?'

Harrison smiled. 'Just picking up a few things, Sergeant. Is the colonel around?'

'He's at GOC's prayers, sir. Bit of a flap on with these talks going on at Trafalgar House. You know, anticipating trouble from one side or the other.'

Harrison was relieved that 'Taff' Lloyd-Williams was in conference, otherwise he'd have been obliged to explain his actions and he was certain his commanding officer would disapprove of his personal involvement. Had their situations been reversed, Harrison was sure he'd feel the same.

'Not to worry,' Harrison said, 'you're just the man I want.'

'Sir?'

'Can you run up a couple of names for me on Crucible?'

'No problem,' the sergeant replied, moving back towards the cramped Statistics Office where the computer terminal was housed.

He took his seat before the screen. 'What name is it?'

'Caitlin Dougan. Is there an entry?'

The sergeant punched up the file. 'Ah, daughter of the late Hughie, eh, sir? Snuffed it last year. She's now married to Peter Moore, a part-time RIR man.'

'Let me just take down that address.'

'Anyway she's clean. Just refers back to her old man's file.'

'Try Clodagh Dougan.'

'Right you are.' He waited for the file to swipe onto the screen. 'Just a sec . . . oh, that's odd.'

Harrison peered over his shoulder. 'Access Restricted.'

The sergeant chuckled. 'Looks like Clodagh Dougan's been a naughty girl. Refers to 14 Int only.'

Shit! The sneaky-beaky mob playing silly buggers again. 14 Int, Special Branch and MI5 each jealously guarding their own little pile of dirt.

'Want me to phone up for clearance, sir?'

Harrison shook his head. 'I'll leave it for now.'

He didn't want anyone to start asking questions and it was likely that the clearance level would have to be CATO himself or even

379

higher. It wouldn't do to alert those who would resent his interference.

' 'Ave a good leave, sir,' the sergeant called as Harrison returned to his car and set off back towards Belfast.

Warm and dusty sunlight was settling over the estate of small newly built houses in Ballynafeigh as he and Casey drove into Caitlin Dougan's road. Children played on many of the open-fronted lawns, watched by parents who were washing cars, planting immature trees or weeding flowerbeds.

'We can't just wander in and start asking questions,' Harrison had warned.

Casey had just laughed. 'Leave it to me. Everyone loves Americans and everyone has relatives in the States.'

As they pulled up outside the box-like semi with its white plastic cladding, he hoped she was right. Heads turned at the sight of the unfamiliar car and neighbours watched warily as the two walked up the path to the glass-fronted door. It took several seconds for the chimes to be heard above the background burble of a television and the crying of a baby. Then the thin shape of a young man emerged in the hall, blurred through the fluted glass.

The door opened a cautious three inches, restrained by a security chain. 'Yes?' The hair was dark and cropped, the eyes anxious.

'Mr Moore?' Casey inquired with a smile.

'Who's asking?'

Her laugh was uneasy. 'This is going to sound crazy, but I could be your wife's long lost stepcousin from California!'

A blank expression stared back at her. Then, hesitantly: 'What? Are you from the Jehovah's Witnesses or something?'

'No, I'm Casey, Casey Mullins. I'm American.'

'I gather that.' He sounded a little more relaxed.

'And if I tell you my stepfather's name was Dougan?'

The man nodded. 'That's my wife's maiden name.'

Casey smiled in triumph. 'Exactly! I'm over here on holiday – this is my English friend Tom – and I thought I'd try and discover my roots. You know, work out the family tree.' The man was still hesitating, clearly unsure. 'Look, I'm sorry if it's inconvenient just now, but I'm due to catch a flight home tomorrow. It's taken ages to track you down and it would be such a shame to go home without . . .'

'No, no,' he interrupted, unbolting the chain. 'Sorry to seem so cautious, but you can't be too careful, you know, the troubles – sure at least we can offer you some tea and cake.'

They were in. The front room was crammed with obviously second-hand furniture and a lobsterpot playpen taking up much of the space. There was a sickly sweet smell of milk and soiled nappies, Harrison noticed, as the man called up the stairs to his wife.

Caitlin came down a few minutes later, a timid wan-faced creature, small with painfully thin wrists and ankles. She patted nervously at her lank fair hair. With an uncertain smile she apologised for being dressed in the shellsuit with baby food stains, for the untidy state of the room and for the fact that she could only offer a jam roll with their tea.

Casey reassured her and launched into a major charm offensive which involved a convoluted family background in which she claimed that her fictitious stepfather's grandfather or great grand-father, she wasn't sure which – with the family name of Dougan – had emigrated to America.

Caitlin sat, clearly bemused and stiffly polite, balancing one of the unmatching china cups and saucers on her knee. 'I think some of the family did go to America, but I don't know who. I'd have to ask my Uncle Tommy. He knows all about our family history.'

Like Harrison, Peter Moore had said little, just leaning back on the sofa, watching and listening with intelligent interest. He said: 'There are a number of Dougans. How do you know Cait's is the right family?'

This was going to be the tricky part, Harrison realised.

Casey said: 'My stepfather has an aunt who seems to know about the family here.'

'Oh,' Caitlin said with renewed interest, 'what's her name?'

'Er, Hetty, I think, but I've never met her.' She added quickly:

'America's a big place, you know, and she lives over in Boston. That's like the other side of Europe to you.'

Caitlin shook her head. 'I don't recall anyone having mentioned her.'

But Casey was steaming on regardless: 'It appears she received a letter from someone over here saying how your poor father died last year. It must have been absolutely terrible for you.'

In an instant the atmosphere had changed. Harrison noticed Peter Moore's knuckles tighten and the warmth drain from his eyes.

Caitlin said: 'It's always a shock to lose a parent.'

'Were you close?'

'Not as close as we should have been.' There was an expression on her face that could have been guilt or resentment, it was hard to tell. 'I wonder who wrote the letter to America. Perhaps it was Uncle Tommy, but he's never mentioned it. And he doesn't write much now. Arthritis.'

'Is it right you have a sister?'

Caitlin's eyes brightened. 'Oh, yes, Clodagh. She's my big sister.'

'You sound fond of her.'

'Oh, yes. Ten years older than me, so she is. Much brighter, too. She went to university and now she's got a job in electronics. Always looked after me. Tried to protect me from things, you know, the troubles and that. For a while she belonged to the *Cumainn na n Ban* and didn't want me to get involved.'

'I'm sorry?'

'The women's branch of the Provies. Clodagh gave it up and steered me away. If she hadn't, I'd probably never have met Peter. Or else he wouldn't have wanted to know me.'

'Mine's a Protestant family,' her husband offered. 'Things are difficult enough as it is. All Cait and I want is to be left in peace and to have the best chance in life for the wee chap.'

'Where's Clodagh now, could I see her perhaps?'

Caitlin laughed lightly. 'Not really, she's in Canada.'

'Never!' Casey faked surprise. 'Perhaps I might get to meet her. Do you have an address?'

'Sure.' The girl stood and collected two postcards with forest

382

scenes from the Rocky Mountains. 'Suite 200, Stanley Tower, Marine Drive, Vancouver.'

'And a phone number?'

'She's not on the phone.'

'Never mind.' Casey glanced at her watch. 'Goodness, is that the time?'

Caitlin showed them to the door. 'It's been lovely to have met you.'

Peter Moore shook hands with Harrison. 'Sorry we didn't get a chance to talk, Tom.'

'Chattering women, eh?'

'Work here in Belfast, do you?'

'No, just over for a few days with Casey.'

They stepped outside, Caitlin and her husband waiting and waving as their unexpected visitors climbed into their car.

'That was a nice surprise,' Caitlin said.

Peter Moore was uncertain. 'I'd still like to know exactly how they got this address.'

Caitlin frowned. 'Didn't she say?'

'She said a hell of a lot, but not actually that.' He grimaced. 'And I wasn't too sure about your man.'

'Tom somebody.'

'I'm sure I've seen him before somewhere. Somehow he looks familiar.'

'The gentlemen are here, sir,' the sergeant announced.

Colonel Taff Lloyd-Williams rose from behind his desk and looked across the office at Harrison. 'I'm sticking my neck out for you, Tom. I just hope you're right. There are no prizes for standing on the feet of MI5 or Group.'

'I know that, sir, but this is also our domain. We've lost one ATO and two injured to AIDAN, plus Jock and Les in London. We need to know.'

John Nash entered first, his suit still crumpled after the early shuttle from London. Trenchard followed, as immaculately turned out as always, bespoke suit and cavalry tiepin; but his manner was less carefree than usual.

Nash stifled a yawn. 'Hello, Taff, hello, Tom. This had better be good, I can hardly justify the time away from London now that Trafalgar House has gone public.'

The colonel shook his hand. 'I wouldn't ask you to come, John, if I didn't think it was important.'

Trenchard found himself standing next to Harrison. 'What's going on, Tom?' he asked tersely. 'Why the hell has Nash been dragged over?'

'Just so the left knows what the right is doing, Don, that's all.'

'I'll let Tom here kick off,' the colonel said.

Harrison turned to Nash. 'Presumably you're aware that Billy Baker was arrested the night before last?' He was aware of Trenchard's eyes boring into him.

Nash nodded. 'Of course I am, Tom. For murdering a Sinn Fein councillor known as Killy Tierney.'

'Did you know Tierney was tortured before he died?'

An urbane eyebrow was raised. 'I haven't seen the report details, but I'm not surprised.'

Harrison took a deep breath. 'And did you know that he was specifically tortured to make him identify the AIDAN bombers?'

'For God's sake . . .' Trenchard began.

But Harrison continued regardless. 'And that Billy Baker claimed he was doing this at *your* request? That's yours and Don's here.'

It was Nash's turn to glare at Trenchard. 'Don, d'you mind telling me what the hell is going on?'

'I think Tom is getting out of his depth,' the intelligence officer replied snappily. 'These are highly classified intelligence matters, nothing to do with the practicalities of bomb disposal.'

The colonel intervened. 'Not quite true. To know the identity of a bomber is to know your enemy.'

Harrison snatched a dummy time-and-power unit from the cabinet and tossed it to Trenchard who caught it in midair. 'Imagine that's attached to a thousand pounds worth of explosive and you've got to destroy it. Who made it? Behan, MacEoin, the Midlander? The names probably mean little to you, but they can mean a lot to us. There's the world of difference between a bomb

384

made by Behan and *Hughie Dougan*! Ask Jock Murray's widow or Les Appleyard lying in hospital with his legs gone.'

'Steady, Tom,' Lloyd-Williams warned.

But Nash had caught the name. 'Hughie Dougan died last year.'

'Not according to Killy Tierney. While he was having his kneecap smashed, he was pleading to be believed. Dougan is still alive – his death was faked. And he's working with his daughter Clodagh. Tierney also named the other members of the AIDAN unit.'

'Tierney was talking crap to save his life,' Trenchard replied testily. 'I saw Dougan's body and can confirm that the daughters identified it.'

'*If* a car explodes, which is fairly unusual in itself,' Harrison replied, 'there's precious little left to identify. Just possibly that was the idea. Was it by accident or design that the crash occurred in Eire? And why didn't PIRA have the remains of a martyr and former hunger striker brought back to Milltown Cemetery?'

'You seem to know an awful lot about this, Tom,' Nash began to realise.

Harrison glanced at his colonel. 'I realise what I've done is out of order, but I was on leave and asked a few questions in the village where Dougan supposedly died.'

Nash chewed on his lower lip. 'And this business about Billy Baker and what Killy Tierney said? How d'you know about that?'

Harrison hesitated. He and Trenchard had been friends for a long time; mention of his own and Casey's involvement, which he understood had not been reported, could land the man in deep trouble.

'My fault,' Trenchard intervened. 'I told Tom about it in the mess, but then he is a senior officer and he's been very much involved . . . The difference is that Tom thinks that Killy Tierney might have been telling the truth. I don't.'

Harrison drew himself to his full height and addressed himself directly to Nash. 'There's one way to confirm this, John. I also visited Dougan's youngest daughter yesterday and obtained

Clodagh Dougan's supposed address in Vancouver. Maybe your people could check it out? If she's there, obviously I'm wrong.'

Nash was irritated, with Harrison for delving into matters that weren't his concern, and with Trenchard for sharing confidential information. 'Anything else?' he demanded sarcastically.

Harrison nodded. 'Clodagh is close to her sister. Yet she said she had no telephone number – she didn't even give one for her place of work.' He paused. 'I also learned that Clodagh is a highly paid electronics expert.'

It was the same full picture that had convinced CATO that there could be something in it.

Nash made his decision. 'I'll have the address checked out and we'll take it from there.'

'And you'll let us know?' Lloyd-Williams pressed.

'Of course. Now if you'll excuse us, I need to catch the next available shuttle.'

He motioned Trenchard to follow him and the two men walked out of the office to the waiting car.

Nash said: 'I don't believe you, Don. We set up a deal with King Billy and we weren't too particular how he chose to achieve his side of the bargain. Yet when he had that information, you chose to ignore it.'

'I haven't ignored it, John, it's in your report. I just chose not to act on it, because I think it's a load of bunkum. I still do. I thought we had enough on our plate without a wild-goose chase.'

'Well, you work for me now, not Group. If I didn't know you better, I'd say you were taking advantage of your old contacts with 14 Int. Well, I want you out of the Province and back in London. Do you know which man actually pulled the trigger to kill Tierney?'

'Yes.'

'It wasn't Baker himself?'

'No.'

'Thank God for small mercies. Then charge the murderer and get King Billy and the rest released on a technicality. I'll square it with Knock and the DCI.'

'So Billy will get his place at the talks?'

'It's not up to me, but I doubt it. He'll be happy enough to be released. I gather they've enough problems at Trafalgar House without King Billy throwing in his ten penn'orth.' Nash climbed into his car beside the driver and lowered the electric window. 'But before you do that, check the Vancouver address. Report to me with the result in London – in person.'

From the window of CATO's office, Harrison and Lloyd-Williams watched the car pull away.

'I just hope that's not my pension driving off, Tom.'

'So do I, sir. Let's just hope I'm right.'

Lloyd-Williams continued watching the disappearing car.

'Don't suppose you know much about Celtic legend, do you?'

'Not much call for it outside Wales and Eire.'

'I'm talking about AIDAN – derived from the name of the ancient Celtic god of sun and fire. I've been digging around in some old books. The English equivalent is Hugh.'

Harrison stared at him in disbelief. All the time Hughie Dougan had been enjoying a smug little joke with them.

'Pack your bags, Tom,' CATO said softly, 'and go back to the mainland. I don't want you setting foot in the Province again. That's official.'

19

'Sure 'tis a grand drop of malt, so it is.'

Abe Powers sat on the edge of his armchair, elbows resting on his knees and his big hands clasped together, and glanced sideways at the Secretary for Northern Ireland. Sir Ralph Maynard, a man almost as large as the American in physical stature, met the senator's eyes momentarily. A tic of a smile flickered across the Englishman's otherwise impassive face. Clearly they were both bemused, unsure what to make of the elderly and bewhiskered clergyman.

'Another glass?' Powers offered.

Bishop Joseph McLaverty was like a shrivelled little gnome, dwarfed by the huge armchair in which he sat. Clerical collar, tweed jacket with leather patches and pince-nez balanced on the tip of his nose. Hardly the strident-voiced ogre that both men had been expecting.

'Some temptations are more difficult than others for a man to resist,' he chortled. 'But at my age, there can be little harm in it.'

Powers reached for the bottle and topped up McLaverty's glass; Maynard declined a refill. 'Tell me, Bishop,' the senator asked. 'You've been here at Trafalgar House for three days and so far you've declined my offer to address the delegates. I'm curious to know why?'

The clergyman nursed the glass of malt lovingly between his rheumatic fingers. When he spoke his voice was quiet and slightly squeaky, the words selected with deliberation and delivered in a rambling, humorous tone. 'If I were to open my mouth and say just one sentence, all the Unionist politicians would stand up and walk out. And I really don't want to be seen as the man who destroyed the chance of peace.'

'I'm sure the Unionists would hear you out,' Powers said. 'We've developed a very co-operative atmosphere here.'

But even as he spoke the words, he knew they weren't strictly true. Divisions were becoming more apparent between the parties as they got down to the fine details of the proposals. He was beginning to get an uneasy feeling of impending doom. He wondered if the bishop's presence had had anything to do with it, had somehow changed the atmosphere?

McLaverty's watery eyes twinkled. 'Sure there's a lot of give and take and I'm most impressed. In fact I've spent my time just listening and inwardly digesting. Sitting in on all the little subcommittees and working parties, finding out what it's all about.'

'And what do you think?' Sir Ralph Maynard asked directly. He was finding the old man's shilly-shallying more than a little tiresome.

'Your proposal for an independent Northern Ireland?' He contemplated his glass. 'Novel, so it is. Novel, but not new.'

Powers picked up on the patronising tone. 'Not new, Bishop, but maybe the mood of the people is right for it now. Not back in the seventies or eighties, but today, when everything else has been tried, perhaps the time is right.'

'Perhaps, but will it stop the violence?'

Maynard's smile was as stiff as his starched white collar. 'I think you're more the one to answer that,' he said pointedly.

The bishop's eyes crinkled benignly. 'Ah, well, I've heard a lot of reference to this Secret Protocol. I've seen nothing in writing, but then if I had I suppose it wouldn't be secret. Anyway, everyone knows about it. A promise by Dublin to co-operate with the implementing of selective internment for suspected IRA members for three years?'

'It's been rumoured,' Sir Ralph confirmed.

'And Dublin removing Articles Two and Three from its constitution, which lay claim to the Six Counties?'

Abe Powers nodded.

'Then, if you will indulge an old man, allow me to remind you of something you may have overlooked. In 1921 the Irish

Government accepted the North's right to self-determination in return for dominion status. Self-determination for the North was again accepted by Dublin in 1925 in exchange for British economic aid. In 1985 they did the same thing in order to get the Anglo-Irish Conference. Now they are again saying that they are prepared to recognise Northern Ireland's right to self-determination – blithely ignoring the fact they have reneged on their promise three times before.'

Abe Powers frowned.

Bishop McLaverty took a sip of his whisky. 'Only an Irishman would sell the same horse to the same man four times. And only an Englishman would buy it!'

The American senator stared and swallowed hard.

'Oh, Dublin will accept British support in the EC for all the aid it can get. And it will go through the motions of trying to change its constitution. But that means a referendum and we all know the results of those depend on how you put the question. Not to mention where Dublin puts its propaganda effort. My humble prediction, gentlemen, is that it will never happen. Even if it does, the *intent* and *will* of all true Irishmen to be united as one will remain.'

'And joint internment?' Sir Ralph asked, guessing the reply he was going to get.

'Dublin might feel obliged to appear to go along with that, but they won't have their heart in it. And the Irish legal system can be fickle at the best of times. You've never yet had proper security co-operation with Eire and you never will. I'm afraid the men of violence may suffer a setback or two, but they'll still be there. Stronger than ever. And your embryo nation, like the offspring of the Devil himself, will be strangled at birth with its own umbilical cord!'

Small specks of spittle had gathered around the old man's mouth, and Abe Powers found himself staring at it with a kind of morbid fascination.

'You see,' McLaverty continued with a benign smile, 'what you have created here at Trafalgar House is a type of monstrous hybrid that denies its natural parentage. It is a denial of

390

everything Irishmen have fought for through the ages. To free itself from the shackles of British occupation. Is this really what the martyrs of Ireland – from the Easter Rising to Bobby Sands and the hunger strikers – all died for? A little offshore nonentity like the Isle of Man or the Caymans. Or those who have spent the best part of their adult life in the cages of the Kesh – ask them. You'll have your answer. No, dear friends, you will not get peace.'

'Does this mean a return to the bombing?' Sir Ralph asked, scarcely bothering to keep the contempt from his voice.

'Sure as a man of God, I'd know nothing about that. I have no influence in such matters.'

Abe Powers said: 'You appear set solidly against everything that has so far been agreed here at Trafalgar House, Bishop, yet you have made no alternative proposals of your own.'

A gentle smile. 'I have not been asked.'

'I'm asking you.'

'Well, the answer has been staring successive British governments in the face for years, certainly since the latest troubles started. But it will take a British Prime Minister who is a man of immense vision and exceptional courage.'

'Courage to do what?' Powers asked.

'To tear up his bogus alliance of convenience with the Orangemen of Ulster. To stand before the world stage at the United Nations and admit the historical wrongdoing that has been done to the freemen of Ireland by Britain. Not just to Catholics, but Protestants too. They have been shamelessly used to fuel your industrial revolution and to fight your wars. The courage to tear down the border and to invite UN troops to replace British soldiers on the streets while the new constitution and arrangements for All-Ireland elections are being made.'

'That's a non-starter and you know it,' Sir Ralph snapped, his patience finally breaking.

'Pray why?' McLaverty asked. 'It is the simplest, most honourable answer of all. Why is it, as that clergyman and writer Sydney Smith once said, that "the moment the very name of Ireland is mentioned, the English seem to bid adieu to common feeling, common prudence and common sense, and act with the barbarity of tyrants and the fatuity of idiots". '

'A lot has changed since the days of the Black and Tans,' Sir Ralph growled.

'Or the B-Specials?' the old man countered quickly.

Abe Powers waved his hand in an attempt to referee. 'But surely there'd be civil war – the Ulster Protestants would never stand for it.'

'That view has been grossly exaggerated,' the bishop replied reasonably. 'Ask any Orangeman why he doesn't want to be a part of Free Ireland and I guarantee he will cite contraception and the price of beer. He does not really know why, it's just what his father's told him and his father before him.' He paused for another sip of his whisky. 'Did you know that the first Irishman to lead the fight for freedom from Britain – the famous Wolfe Tone – was a Protestant? We have nothing against Protestants, there are thousands of them in Eire, living peacefully and prosperously with their neighbours. We, the Irish Irish, welcome the Protestant Irish with open arms. All this silly talk about Independent Ulster – well, it's much ado about nothing.' He looked directly at Powers. Sir Ralph had fallen into a hostile and truculent silence. 'Persuade the British, Senator – and you can, because they've tried everything else – and you'll go down as the greatest true Irishman in history. It could even mean the Nobel Prize, I wouldn't be surprised. And I think you'll find neither America nor the EC will stint in its generosity to a new United Ireland . . .'

The old man's words faded towards the end and his eyelids flickered momentarily.

'Are you all right?' Powers asked.

The eyes opened again. 'I'm not as young as I was and this *is* an excellent malt. It really is past my bedtime.'

Powers helped McLaverty to his feet, handed him his stick and showed him to the door.

'We warned you it was a bad idea,' Sir Ralph Maynard told the American as he left a few minutes later. 'We've heard it all before.'

Then perhaps you should have listened, the senator thought to himself.

He turned down the main light and stared out of the tall window. Under the full moon, the finger streams of the Avon were gleaming like quicksilver.

It had been uncanny, listening to the voice of the old clergyman. As though his own grandmother had been talking to him through a medium.

He felt tears in his eyes. Sadness? No, he knew what it was. Shame. Shame that he had betrayed his own people. His own grandmother. Shame that he had bowed to British pressure and taken the line of least resistance.

But now cracks were starting to appear in the plans for an Independent Ulster and he wasn't sure the consensus would hold together for much longer. And if it didn't, as McLaverty had pointed out, there was only one thing left to try.

Could the British be persuaded to do it? God knows they'd tried everything else recently and it had all come to nothing. Perhaps they were just weary enough to go that extra mile. To think the unthinkable.

If he applied American pressure now? The President had little love for the Brits and his wife, Powers knew, was sympathetic to Irish aspirations for unity.

He closed the curtains and made his way to the bedroom, his decision almost made.

That night he dreamed of his grandmother.

Three days later Donny Fitzpatrick's alarm went off at three in the morning.

He slipped out of bed, leaving his wife still asleep, then dressed in the dark, not bothering about a wash or shave. She barely stirred when he kissed her goodbye and went downstairs, feeling his way in the darkness.

Closing the back door behind him, he crossed the garden and scaled the rear fence. He walked the two blocks of the residential estate with his hands in his pockets and his shoulders hunched against the chill, the hood of his windcheater covering his head.

The car was waiting where expected with its lights off. He climbed into the back seat; without a word, the driver started the engine, switched on his headlamps and began the journey south.

There were to be two vehicle switches on the way to the pub on the outskirts of Dublin. Unlike the Garda in general, there were some elements of Irish Special Branch who were dedicated to eradicating the movement. Driven by frustration at the lack of political will by their masters, some had attempted to take the law into their own hands on occasion. Although Fitzpatrick knew the identity of most of them, he was nonetheless obliged to take elaborate precautions for his own safety. Then, of course, there was also the danger that the Brits would mount a deniable operation of their own against him . . .

The upstairs room had been booked the day before in the name of the All Ireland Philately Society. Fitzpatrick was the last to arrive, the door being opened by one of the Dubliners.

The man reholstered his pistol. 'It's promising news, Chief.'

'Good, I could do with some.'

He nodded to the motley gathering around the trestle table, which included the Quartermaster General, Maedoc Mallally and a retired priest known as Father McCabe.

The old man was anxious to tell the Provisionals' Chief of Staff what he had heard. 'The bishop sent a letter to me yesterday by safe hand. He reports that the talks are in increasing disarray. He has been talking to the representatives from the Dublin government and the SDLP people from the north, persuading them to strengthen their position and their demands in these Independent Ulster proposals. Now he believes that the Democratic Unionists are on the verge of walking out.'

Fitzpatrick smiled gently. 'So much for the demolition. What about the constructive side?'

'He's had several private sessions now with Abe Powers. He believes he's winning the senator round. In fact Bishop McLaverty says the American has made several calls to the White House to try and win support for the idea.'

Mallally, known as Q, was dismissive. 'We know the Brits will never wear it. Don't get your hopes up.'

'I'm not so sure,' Fitzpatrick said. 'We know the government is still smarting over American involvement in this process and they've been getting an increasingly negative press over it.'

'They'd regard the UN supervising a United Ireland as even more humiliating,' commented one of the Dubliners.

'Or maybe they're just weary enough to grab *any* solution that takes the problem out of their hands,' Fitzpatrick replied irritably. 'They'll have seen the latest opinion polls – that the majority of the British public just want their troops out of Ireland.'

'Perhaps they'll wait until Labour wins the next election,' Q suggested, 'and let them do the dirty work.'

'*If* they win,' Fitzpatrick replied. 'On the other hand, maybe the current government will see some mileage in solving the problem once and for all. Backtracking on ideals doesn't seem to worry politicians nowadays, and most of the English regard the Proddie bigots as no better than ourselves.'

'You could have phrased that better,' Q pointed out.

'We must keep up the pressure,' one Dubliner said.

'True,' agreed another. 'Let AIDAN off the leash again. Concentrate their minds.'

'We can't do that,' Q said. 'We can't be seen to be using violence now we're at the talks. That would be counterproductive. We need something a mite more subtle.'

It was then that Fitzpatrick remembered the signal from McGirl. The flying column had found a way of reaching Major Harrison and he wanted permission to follow it up. Clearly he had in mind assassination, but there was another way . . .

He could visualise the news arriving at Number Ten: Prime Minister, I regret to tell you that the IRA is holding a senior British Army officer hostage. In fact this officer has become something of a national hero in the press and on television . . . The Provisionals say they will keep his abduction under wraps and eventually release him if you accede to current American and growing UN demands for a United Ireland . . .

If not, they will reveal to the international media how a British hero was sacrificed to political intransigence in defiance of popular world opinion.

McGirl couldn't sleep.

He'd woken in the early hours after a nightmare, his body slick with cold sweat. A crazy dream. He was walking down a long dark forest track; ahead was a tunnel of light where he could see the distant shadow of a gallows. Behind him he could hear the muted thunder of horses' hooves and knew the riders were gaining on him. Yet he could not run . . .

For an hour he'd twisted and turned, but his mind just kept spinning. He knew what the problem was. Everything had been put on hold. There had been no activity now for several days, since the announcement that Bishop McLaverty was joining the talks.

And with nothing to do, his mind began to dwell on those nagging inner fears. What were the police doing, how close were they? He had no illusions that the full might of the British security apparatus was ranged against them. The police, Special Branch and MI5. Out there somewhere in the darkness, never sleeping, never resting. Insidious, creeping, edging ever closer to him.

The bombings had been a humiliation for the British Government, the newspapers and television headlines screaming capitulation to terrorism, and the politicians, he knew, would be baying for blood at any price. His blood, his and Clodagh Dougan's.

He left the bed, pulled on his jeans and stood by the window of the cottage. Outside, the road was deserted, dimly lit by a nearby street light. Beyond, the outline of the trees was growing more distinct against a lightening sky.

Dawn would not be long.

He lit a cigarette and looked back at the bed. Subconsciously Clodagh Dougan seemed to sense him watching, her naked body suddenly restless beneath the sheet, twitching and moving as she slept. It was like that between them now, and he would never have believed it.

The Blackwall Tunnel bomb had changed everything. Was it

the excitement, the adrenalin? The sense of power and achieve-
ment, the sharing of danger?

He didn't know, and it didn't matter.

What mattered was that when the team split up after the
attack, each member returning to a separate safe house, Clodagh
had asked him to go back with her. At first he had assumed it
was the loneliness she felt now without her father there. The
need for protection, a guardian who knew his place. But he soon
realised it was more than that. Suddenly there was some unspoken bond between them.

Without a word she had led him into the front room and
poured two drinks. Then, as he stood beside the cold stone
fireplace, she had knelt at his feet. It took him by surprise, feeling
her hands on his thighs, moving over his crotch. Then her fingers
plucking at his zipper, the abrupt indraught of cool air and the
delicate moisture of her mouth as she took his penis between her
teeth. Not once did she speak; not once did she allow her eyes
to meet his. She was alone down there, mistress in her own
world, oblivious of him.

He had been too shocked to speak, not wanting to break the
moment as he felt himself swelling to touch the back of her throat
resting on the warm bed of her tongue. Then she was on her feet,
gripping him there with her right hand, leading him to the sofa
like a dog on a lead. Her face was close now and he could see
that, for the first time since he had known her, she was smiling
as though she meant it. The light of mischief and provocation
dancing in her eyes.

Then he had ravished her. Hard and powerful, heedless of
her needs, aware only of his own. Driven by the overwhelming
desire to release the tension of the days and weeks of fear and
undercover living, to drown it all out in one glorious moment
of ecstasy. And to his surprise it was she who had climaxed
first, clawing her nails across his back so deeply that he felt
the wetness of the blood trickling from his skin. That had
stoked the final fire, and he drove into her, merciless until his
final rush.

As he fell beside her on the sofa, he anticipated her scorn and

397

sharp tongue. But he was wrong. Instead she just smiled, her mouth swollen and bruised, her eyes misty and unfocused.

Her voice was low when she spoke. 'If you're interested, that's my first time in ten years.'

He wanted to ask her why, but somehow didn't dare.

And she seemed grateful for that, clutching his arm and drawing close. Her head on his shoulder, the softness of her hair against his neck. As he glanced at her, he thought how like an adolescent she looked, a teenage girl who had just discovered her first love.

From that moment on it had been the same between them. The antagonism had evaporated, equals, as though both recognised that their fate was shared. For good or ill.

Still he wondered what had brought about the change in her. The next day, after they had made love again, she had whispered something that he thought might be a clue.

'I feel I've completed my father's life's work, Pat. Achieved what he always wanted to achieve. He gave eighteen years of his life in the fight for peace and freedom. Peace had to be achieved through violence, he knew that. Sometimes it's the only way.' She had kissed him then. 'There's only one thing left I have to do now.'

'What's that?'

'Not for my da, for me. To kill the man who lured him to his death. You said you knew a way.'

'I do.'

Remembering the conversation now, McGirl looked back out of the bedroom window and allowed himself to speculate. Peace. Down south of the ancient cathedral city of Salisbury. Trafalgar House. Was that really where it was all going to end? The struggle over after all these years? Perhaps even the tricolour flying over Stormont. It was hard to believe.   •

It occurred to him abruptly that his life would alter beyond recognition within months, maybe even weeks. There would be no place for him amongst the politicians. Street killers like Pat McGirl would just be an embarrassment, he was aware of that. After the accolades and platitudes for the foot soldiers of the Provisional IRA, he'd be cast aside. Forgotten, a social leper.

But he'd known no other life since his late teens, and he'd been unemployed then. Peace might yet prove a bitter victory for many. Suddenly he could see that there was no future, not for him.

Clodagh stirred again, this time propping herself on one elbow and shielding her eyes from the strengthening dawn light. 'What's the matter?'

'Couldn't sleep.'

'Why?'

'That signal to Donny Fitzpatrick, asking permission to go after Major Harrison.'

'Yes?'

'I've had the reply. We're cleared to go.'

The military attaché at the British High Commission in Vancouver received the coded signal from Vauxhall Cross, MI6's new headquarters in London, at eleven local time.

He telephoned his regular contact in the Canadian Security Intelligence Service and arranged to meet him at noon. The two of them took a taxi to the address the attaché had been given on Marine Drive in the south of the city. Stanley Tower was a twenty-storey office block and a fast elevator lifted them to Suite 200 on the nineteenth floor.

The legend stencilled on the glass swing doors read COMPLETE OFFICE SERVICES: EXECUTIVE SUITES, DOCUMENTATION FACILITIES, FAX, TELEPHONE RECEPTION, MAIL BOXES.

That's the answer, the attaché thought as they spoke to the primly dressed receptionist who interrupted her director's meeting.

'We have no client called Clodagh Dougan,' he said.

But his receptionist recognised the name. 'She's not a client, but we do receive mail for someone of that name.'

'Can you explain?'

'The arrangement was set up by an American lady.' The receptionist consulted her client book. 'Mrs Deborah Mayo from Connecticut. She called in personally and paid for one year's service up front. Cash, as I recall.'

'Can you remember what she looked like?'

'I do as it happens. Quite striking, in her late twenties or early thirties. Dark hair, black I think. Her accent was a little odd.'

Could be, the attaché thought. 'What arrangements does she have?'

'Well, it's on behalf of a friend of hers, this Clodagh Dougan. That's why it rang a bell, because it was rather unusual. Anything I receive addressed to Miss Dougan, I'm supposed to place in an envelope, readdress it to Mrs Mayo and post it on.'

'Where to?'

'Post office in England. To be collected.'

The attaché's mouth dropped open. Bullseye!

'But it's two-way,' the receptionist added. 'Sometimes Mrs Mayo sends me an envelope containing a sealed letter or post-card, whatever. I'm then expected to post those on from here to whatever address is written on them.'

'Thank you so much for your help.'

Don Trenchard accepted the signal from the cipher clerk and sat down slowly in his seat, spreading the paper out across the blotter on his desk and picking up his first coffee of the day.

So that's how she'd done it.

Clodagh Dougan was Mrs Deborah Mayo. Note the Irish name. American passport. Probably a genuine application but a substituted photograph. The wife of an Irish American supporter of the cause, cash for a favour one drunken night. It was likely the woman had never been abroad and didn't even know the application had been made.

This way Clodagh's sister Caitlin, relatives, friends and others who might expect to write to her in Canada could do so. And she could reply, each letter or postcard with a Vancouver post-mark. Perfect cover.

But now Trenchard had little time. Once he had passed the information on to Nash, events would take on a momentum all their own which would be impossible to stop.

The hands of the office clock showed eight o'clock. Just time to catch the City Prices edition. He made his excuses and left

Thames House, taking a taxi to Kensington High Street where he made the call from a public box.

'Mullins – features.' The familiar Californian twang.

'Hallo, Casey, it's Don here. Don Trenchard.'

'Oh.' Uncertain.

'Look, Casey, I feel I owe you an apology. That business over in Ulster.'

'Yes?'

'I'd like to make it up to you. Can we meet?'

'I'm tied up this lunch time,' she lied, not keen to see the man again.

'No, *now*. I've something important for you. I'm just across the street. There's a café.' He gave the name. 'Can you meet me there in five minutes?'

'I suppose so.' Hesitant.

'Great. And don't tell anyone you're coming to see me, there's a good girl.'

It was with considerable misgiving that she grabbed her bag and coat, left the office and took the lift and escalator to reception. Outside, the breeze along Kensington High Street had a cool autumnal edge to it, unwarmed by the sunshine. She found Trenchard seated at one of the pavement tables, his fedora and two coffees placed in front of him.

'What is this, Don?'

'I owe you. Nothing was published in the *Standard* about that King Billy fiasco. I appreciate that. Or the bombers that Tierney named.'

'Tom advised me not to. Besides, my paper could hardly accuse people on the uncorroborated word of a dead man.'

He gave one of his charmer's smiles, but it seemed to lack its usual confidence. 'Grateful anyway. I was rude, angry, at the time.'

'You had a right to be. I'd got in out of my depth.'

Trenchard waved a dismissive hand. 'Anyway, I've a little scoop for you. But it'll have to make the first edition or else all the other papers will be running with it.' He saw her glance at her watch. 'Is there time?'

'Just – if I'm quick.'

He slipped the photograph from beneath his fedora and pushed it across the table to her.

'Who's this?'

A plumpish smiling face stared up at her, a pretty teenager with a black fringe and beautiful sad eyes. The sweatshirt she wore was emblazoned University of Ulster.

'This is strictly unattributable, right?'

'Yes, I understand.'

'Come hell or high water? And that must include Tom.'

'Don!' Both exasperated and intrigued. 'I promise you my lips are sealed.'

'Everything Killy Tierney said was true.'

'And the photograph? Who is she?'

'That's the only picture in existence. She's with the AIDAN bombers. Here, now. Seven Dials, the flyovers, the Blackwall Tunnel . . .'

Casey's eyes widened.

'That is Clodagh Dougan.'

As Trenchard had anticipated, by the time he returned to Thames House representatives from the Anti-Terrorist Branch, the Home Office, Special Branch and the Director of Special Forces were already gathering for the emergency meeting that John Nash had called.

The Director General was in the chair, indicating the significance of the meeting, but Clarissa Royston-Jones left Nash to outline the latest developments.

'So there we have it,' he concluded, 'all this leads us to believe that the active service unit calling itself AIDAN is, in fact, headed up by Hughie Dougan. Patrick McGirl, PIRA's northern commander is involved, either in overall control or in a liaison capacity, I should think. Four other names have been mentioned: Moira Lock, Leo Muldoon, Liam Doran and a Londoner called Joe Houlihan. All with no previous and all except Houlihan coming from Ulster, but living in Ireland. Lock was almost certainly the female killed in the Deptford "own goal", along with one of the men, all of whom could be classed as ordinary IRA foot soldiers.

'The most interesting development of all is the involvement of Dougan's eldest daughter, Clodagh. She had no real form except a mild flirtation with the *Cumainn na n Ban* in her early teens. Went on to study microelectronics and until recently held a good technical post at a Belfast components firm. I hardly need to spell out the relevance of that. Just before the latest campaign began she took up a job in Canada. We have since learned that this was completely bogus and that she was using the name Deborah Mayo, backed up with an apparently legitimate passport. My supposition is that she's working with her father on the manufacturing side, probably updating him on technology, some of which he may only know in theory. The others, under McGirl, would do the planning and carry out the assignments.'

The Special Branch officer raised his hand. 'In the hour I had before this meeting I have been able to check with Immigration. I can confirm that an American subject by the name of Mrs Deborah Mayo entered this country by ferry from Norway on May 30. If she has left since, it wasn't on that passport.'

Clarissa Royston-Jones took over. 'I cannot overemphasise the importance of catching this team. The lull in their activities shouldn't make us complacent. As soon as the Trafalgar House talks don't go the way PIRA wants, we can expect AIDAN to be back with a vengeance.'

At that moment Jim Maitland of the Anti-Terrorist Branch entered the room. He waited patiently at the door, listening as the Director General continued: 'But now we have a strong lead. Not only the team's identity, but also a possible indication of the general area they may be working from. The *poste restante* post office that Clodagh Dougan has been using regularly is in the town of Marlow on the Thames. This district would make logistical sense as it is relatively close to the M4 and M40 motorways to London and just a little farther for the M3, all of which link in with the M25 orbital city motorway, giving them access to London from any direction they choose. Now perhaps, gentlemen, you'd care to update me on your anticipated response to this new information.' She wagged a warning finger. 'But whatever is planned, discretion is paramount. Nothing must alert these people that we are onto them.'

'I'm afraid it may be too late for that.'

It was Jim Maitland who spoke. All heads turned as he held up a copy of the *Evening Standard*. The headline leapt at them: BOMBER RETURNS FROM DEAD TO BLITZ LONDON. Beneath it was a picture of Clodagh Dougan.

'Christ!' Trenchard said.

Clarissa Royston-Jones shut her eyes. She really didn't want to believe this.

'Not much substance,' Maitland said, indicating the small column of copy set in largish type to fill the available space. 'But there's enough. Quotes reliable intelligence sources and names the suspected AIDAN team. All spot on.'

'Where on earth did they get that picture? I haven't even seen that one.'

'I think I can guess,' Trenchard interrupted. 'One of their reporters – the Mullins woman – has been over in the Province digging around. Our people were alerted and she was put under low-level surveillance. Visited King Billy's headquarters, then visited the village in Sligo where Dougan was supposedly buried. She also called on Clodagh's kid sister. My guess is that is where the photograph came from.'

'It's a bit academic now,' Nash said quickly before the conversation turned to how Casey Mullins had heard the names from Tom Harrison after Trenchard's indiscretion. The brown stuff was hitting the fan and it was all likely to end up in his lap.

'I agree,' the Director General said. 'It just means we'll all have to act that much faster.'

Trenchard relaxed back in his chair. 'Oh, for the freedom of the press,' he muttered beneath his breath.

By the time the meeting broke up an hour later, the hunt to find the AIDAN bombers was already in full cry.

Anti-Terrorist Branch detectives had earlier paid a discreet visit to Marlow post office where one letter awaited collection by Deborah Mayo. A plain-clothes officer was stationed behind the counter and a surveillance car placed nearby with a technical expert from SO7 on hand who would attempt to place a magnetic signal beacon on any vehicle used by Clodagh Dougan.

Inquiries were now concentrated between the M40 in the north and the M3 in the south, the area's eastern boundary formed by the M25 and, in the west, by a line drawn north and south of Reading. In time those boundaries would expand as necessary.

Although the process of examining all possible bomb factories had begun some weeks before, the effort increased a hundredfold with detectives from the AT Branch reserves drafted in from other areas. As large bombs had been used, then similarly large premises would have been required to conceal the carrying vehicles, in particular the Blackwall Tunnel dumper truck. However, the task remained enormous. There were literally thousands of possible warehouses and storage depots and hundreds of industrial estates in the region as well as out-of-the-way open sites like car breakers, farmyards and quarries.

Only photographs of three of the bombers were immediately available from security files: Hughie Dougan, Pat McGirl and a teenage Clodagh Dougan, taken when she'd been involved with the *Cumainn na n Ban*. In Ulster the RUC Special Branch was visiting the parents of Lock, Muldoon and Doran to try and obtain recent photographs from the family albums.

Police vehicle checks were set up on the approaches to all motorway junctions in the target area, each with firearms-trained officers in attendance. Every available unmarked car was deployed on the motorway system itself, on the lookout for recently stolen vehicles, unmarked vans and lorries and anything that might raise suspicions. Speeding motorists, the most unlikely suspects, would never know how lucky they had been that day.

Meanwhile the HOLMES computer was being reprogrammed to concentrate on the target area. Over the weeks, hundreds of wholesale and retail suppliers of ammonium nitrate-based fertilisers had been contacted nationwide and asked to draw up lists of customers, particularly new ones, who had ordered large quantities. These lists were gradually becoming available, but the results were patchy, depending on the quality and detail of the records kept.

Many customers could be deleted from the lists: local council parks and other government departments. Thousands of others comprised mostly garden centres, nurseries and farms, all of which would have to be checked.

On a parallel programme, catering suppliers had been asked to supply lists of anyone buying unusually large quantities of icing sugar which would have been mixed with the fertiliser to make the explosive mix. Unfortunately a high proportion were cash-and-carry customers.

By three in the afternoon five farms in the target area were showing up as having had large deliveries of fertiliser in recent months.

One in particular was of special interest. The farm had unusually occurred on the lists of three different suppliers and, illogically, all out of its immediate vicinity. Individually the deliveries weren't excessive; added together the amount was considerable.

'Get me Henley nick,' Maitland ordered.

The call to the chief inspector at Henley was patched through minutes later. 'Just caught me before I went home. What can I do for you?'

'High Farm, south of Henley. Anyone there know it? I need an idea of its acreage.'

'When do you want the information?'

'Yesterday.'

The chief inspector telephoned back in twenty minutes. 'High Farm is a smallholding. Hard to be exact, but between ten and eleven acres, I'd say.'

'Know anything about farming?'

'Some. Try me.'

'Might it use nine thousand pounds of fertiliser in a year?'

The voice chuckled. 'Only if they're growing exhibition specimens. No, I really don't think so.'

Maitland replaced the receiver, just as one of the HOLMES operators approached. 'Something of interest here, sir.

406

Remember the guy who ran the Southampton scam on electronic parts? Used the name of Roke. Well, here's a Henry Roke who ordered a big supply of icing sugar. He paid cash, but the wholesaler's kept a note of the delivery address.'

'What is it?'

'Top Flight Bakery, High Farm, Henley.'

Maitland snatched up his phone. 'Let's go. Ops room in five minutes!'

20

'The suitcases are in the car,' McGirl said. 'Leo and Liam are outside.'

Clodagh Dougan nodded her acknowledgment and glanced round the room, checking for the umpteenth time that nothing had been overlooked. If the Trafalgar House talks went their way, they would not return to the house and High Farm would be put back on the market; the movement might even make a small profit with land prices inching up again. But if Bishop McLaverty failed and PIRA's demands were not met, she and McGirl would be back.

Either way, no trace should be left in the meantime. The place had been scrubbed from top to bottom, all surfaces washed or polished to remove fingerprints. Apart from those retained in one of her suitcases, all the leftover circuit boards, components for making the TPUs, together with surplus supplies of Semtex, were buried in waterproofed toolboxes in the garden under a flagstone, where they would be retrieved at a later date by the mainland flying column.

She and McGirl had lit a bonfire in the overgrown vegetable patch and burned any rubbish that might have provided forensic clues, along with all of her father's clothes. That had been painful, yet, strangely, spiritually cleansing. She might never know the location of her father's grave, but at least the bonfire had been like a symbolic cremation. Better than nothing. At last she had been able to grieve, to allow the tears to flow as she clung to McGirl's arm. Although he said nothing, she sensed that he understood and she was grateful for that.

Now they would move on, to a new safe house provided by the flying column and their network of fixers, either willing or unwitting.

'Come on,' McGirl urged.

The telephone rang. Its strident tone abruptly shattered the quietness of the room. She stared down at the receiver.

Five rings, silence; then it rang again.

'Answer it, then,' McGirl said irritably.

'Hello.'

'Mrs Mayo?' It was the liaison officer of the flying column.

'Yes.'

'Have you seen this afternoon's *Standard*?'

'No.'

'Your picture and all the team names.'

'Christ!'

'Get out now. Make absolutely *certain* you're not being followed. And don't go near the farm.' He hung up.

She told McGirl what had been said.

'Don't panic,' he replied. 'If they were that close to us they wouldn't be putting our names and your picture in the press. They're after information from the public. If they've got names it'll be a leak from over the water. Some loose-mouthed bastard will be going for his tea.'

She knew the euphemism for execution. 'What do we do?'

'Continue as planned. Stay calm.'

'I want to call in at the post office in Marlow. See if there's mail from Caitlin.'

McGirl laughed harshly. 'I said stay calm, not calmly stick your head in a noose. Forget it.'

She followed him out, turning off the lights and locking the door behind her. There were two cars in the driveway, Muldoon and Doran were in the first. As McGirl opened the door of the second, they heard it. The screech of tyres from behind the boundary hedge, the high-revving engines, the white police car glimpsed speeding northwards past the gate. Then another and another. No sirens, no flashing lights. Heading towards High Farm.

Muldoon drove out onto the road first. And turned south.

'Hurlingham School,' McGirl said.

As always, the novelty salesman's intelligence was faultless.

Clodagh Dougan looked across the road from the passenger

409

window of the car. Twin spreadeagles of carved stone stood atop the gate posts, between which the gravel drive swept into the grounds of the Wokingham private school.

'Must cost a fortune to send a child here.'

'Harrison's on a major's salary and his wife's family's got money. All good chinless English stock.' He tossed his cigarette end out of the window. 'All set?'

She nodded grimly. 'How do I look?'

At the safe house, a rented basement flat in Slough, she had plucked her eyebrows and redrawn them in pencil. She had also dyed her hair mid-brown, which she now wore pinned up with a tortoiseshell clip. The mustard-coloured business suit, white blouse and sheer white tights completed the effect.

'Good enough,' McGirl said, engaging first gear, 'I'd trust you with my old granny.'

The car turned into the drive, crunching its way between the cropped lawns and herbaceous borders to the converted Tudor manor house, ivy crawling over the worn red bricks and timber beams. As they opened the car doors, they could hear the excited distant shouts of young male voices.

'Wednesday,' McGirl said flatly. 'Rugby.'

Someone had already appeared at the top of the steps, a boy of about eleven in grey flannels and a school blazer. Clodagh noted the floppy wing of hair over the open smiling face.

'Hello, can I help you?'

Clodagh whispered: 'Stay here,' to McGirl before turning to the boy. 'I've come to see the headmaster.'

'Oh, of course, is he expecting you?'

She smiled tightly. 'Can you just show me the way?'

He thought better than to argue. 'Yes, if you'd like to follow me.' The doors opened onto a chequered tile floor, the walls and stairway in dark timber and smelling of polish. 'Mr Hugget likes parents to make appointments.'

'I'm not a parent.'

'Oh.' Then a thought, cheeky. 'You're not a schools inspector?'

Clodagh smiled. 'No, I'm not a schools inspector.' She frowned suddenly. 'What's your name?'

'Jamie –' He corrected himself: 'Well, actually I prefer James.'

Worth checking, she thought. 'Well, James, do you happen to know a boy called Archie Harrison?'

' "Bomber" Harrison, oh, yes, he's a friend of mine. He's playing rugby at the moment.'

'You're not.' They were in a panelled corridor now.

'Sprained knee, rotten luck. Why, has Bomber done something wrong? You're not from the police?'

'Nothing so exciting, I'm afraid.'

He stopped outside the heavy polished door with the brass plaque and knocked.

'Come!'

James pushed it open. 'Please, sir, there's a lady here who'd like to see you.'

Rows of books lined the wall behind the leather-topped desk where the headmaster worked, his bald head looking up from an accounts book. 'Oh?'

Clodagh stepped forward. 'I'm so sorry to intrude, Mr Hugget.'

Pale grey eyes blinked in the narrow, waxy-white face, the thin lips curling into a somewhat insipid smile as he registered his glamorous and statuesque visitor. Self-consciously he removed the round wire spectacles and adjusted his master's cloak. 'Oh, dear, have I overlooked an appointment, Mrs –?'

'Mrs Scaife-Compton,' she said with a stiff smile. Go for a double-barrelled name, McGirl had advised; the English class system was such that no one ever questioned someone with a double-barrelled name. 'And I don't have an appointment. I'm from the MOD, Ministry of Defence.'

'Oh?'

'Welfare Department. I'm afraid it's about the father of one of your boys, Archie Harrison.'

Mr Hugget's face paled as the name registered and he anticipated what was to follow.

'Yes, I'm afraid he's been injured. Oh, not too badly I'm pleased to say.'

She heard the gasp of surprise from young James behind her, as the headmaster said: 'Was it a bomb?'

'No, some accident with routine ordnance handling.' She thought that sounded convincing. 'The thing is he's in hospital and is asking to see his son. It would be a great comfort to him.'

'Of course, of course.'

'I've been asked to take him along.'

Mr Hugget looked visibly shaken by the news. 'I'm just surprised his mother hasn't telephoned me.'

Clodagh concealed her smile of triumph. 'I'm afraid we couldn't contact her. They've separated, you know, and we didn't have an address or telephone number.'

The headmaster raised a forefinger. 'Ah, I can help you there! If only you'd phoned first.' He reached for his telephone. 'I'll call her now.'

Suddenly Clodagh panicked; she hadn't anticipated this. 'It's most important I take the boy . . .'

'Come, come,' Hugget chided as he dialled. 'Philippa Harrison must be told. And if the father isn't critical, then it's only right that his mother goes with Archie. I'm sure that's what she'll want. Bit too much for a young chap to take – even a Hurlingham boy.' He placed his hand over the mouthpiece. 'What hospital?'

She'd rehearsed that, read a newspaper story about the injured Expo called Appleyard. 'The Cambridge Military in Aldershot.'

'Good, that's not far, and it doesn't take Mrs Harrison long to drive here . . . Ah, Mrs Harrison! Hugget here from Hurlingham, I'm afraid I've some bad news . . .'

Clodagh was hardly listening. Damn it, damn it! What the hell was she doing? Just standing here taking this crap? There was McGirl sitting outside with a gun and she was letting the headmaster take control because – Christ, because he *was* the headmaster! She almost laughed through her frustration.

Then, as she listened to the man explain the situation to Philippa Harrison, she forced herself to keep calm and to think. She could hardly demand Archie be dragged off the rugby pitch at gunpoint with an entire school of onlookers. Someone would phone the police or raise the alarm. A time lapse after the abduction was essential in order to cover their tracks and get clear of the area. Besides which; it was imperative that the whole

412

business be kept low profile. Headlines about the Provies kidnapping schoolboys would not go down well with Fitzpatrick and the other IRA leaders just now.

And there could be another bonus. Philippa Harrison would be an additional hostage, another lever of pressure. She could also console and look after her son, saving them the trouble . . .

Hugget replaced his receiver. 'She's on her way.'

While she waited apprehensively, the headmaster went with James to the rugby field to break the news to the boy. It was half-an-hour before they returned, Archie having showered and changed into his uniform, his neatly parted hair still damp.

'This is Mrs – er?' the headmaster began.

'Scaife-Compton.'

The boy had been crying, the skin red round his eyes. He sniffed heavily as he extended his hand to her. 'I'm very pleased to meet you. How is my father?'

Christ, she thought. How bloody English, formal and stiff upper lip! They start them young, so they do. And the handshake, those little bones in her palm, so strong and manly.

Ridiculously she felt her heart go out to him. Recognised the pain in his eyes, the bravery of the man's words spoken with a boy's voice. Doing what was expected. She wondered if he in any way resembled his father. 'He's fine, Archie. Well, not fine exactly. A few burns and stuff, but he'll get better soon.'

The assertive clatter of high heels beyond the door heralded the arrival of Philippa Harrison. As she entered, Clodagh was surprised how petite she was, almost fragile. Yet the illusion was shattered by her confident stance and her articulate speech. 'Thank you so much for calling, Headmaster. I don't know why they couldn't find my number. Typical army incompetence, I suppose.' She turned to Archie; he was almost his mother's height. 'Don't worry, sweetheart. Daddy will be all right.' She hugged him briskly. 'Don't go letting him see you cry now.'

Clodagh was becoming impatient and increasingly agitated. 'We really ought to go now.'

Philippa appeared to notice her properly for the first time. 'You're the person from Army Welfare? Really, you ought to get

413

your act together. I'm still Tom's next of kin and you really should have my new address details.'

'I'm sorry.'

She sighed, resigned. 'Oh, well, I suppose you do have the *right* hospital? I phoned the Cambridge before I left and they knew nothing about Tom.'

Clodagh felt suddenly malicious. 'As you said, we *ought* to get our act together – anyway, I expect Major Harrison just arrived *before* his medical notes. Bureaucracy. That would explain it.'

'And exactly how is he?'

'Really not too bad, Mrs Harrison, I'll give you the details in my car on the way –'

'Oh, but mine . . .'

'*My* car,' Clodagh insisted. 'There are a lot of roadworks and a new traffic system – it's easy to get lost. We'll drop you back here.'

For a moment Philippa's wide and wary eyes stared directly into hers. Was she annoyed at Clodagh's insistent tone? Or was there just a hint of doubt? Then: 'Very well.'

Outside, McGirl stood with the front passenger door open and smiled as he helped Philippa inside. Clodagh joined Archie in the back. McGirl climbed in and pressed the central locking.

The vehicle jolted forward, heading up the drive.

'This is fairly old for a Ministry car,' Philippa observed sniffily.

'Defence cuts,' McGirl replied with a grin and swung into the road, heading north towards the M4.

'Is that an Irish accent?'

'Ah, to be sure,' he joked. 'We're both Irish.'

Archie looked up at Clodagh. 'You sound English.'

She laughed. 'When I make the effort.'

McGirl glanced at Philippa and saw the transformation on her face, the cloud of concern in her eyes, the tightening of her jawline as she looked at the passing roadsign.

'This isn't the Aldershot road. That's the other way.'

Clodagh reached into her bag on the floor and drew out the pistol. The muzzle was pressed against the back of Philippa's neck. 'One more word from either of you and you're dead. Now shut up!'

McGirl kept to the country lanes, threading his way on a route that ran westwards, parallel with the M4.

To begin with, Philippa had attempted to bluster defiantly until McGirl was obliged to take one hand from the wheel and slap her hard across the cheek. Only then did she seem to accept her fate, sitting in shocked silence with tears dripping down her cheeks, muttering words of comfort to her son.

Harrison has been married to this woman, Clodagh thought, as she studied the slender neck beneath the gun muzzle. She could see the tiny hairs, each pore. How close and familiar had Harrison been to *this* same skin, smelled *this* same expensive perfume? Run his hands through *this* hair before her eyes? Made love to *this* same trim body; laughed with *this* woman, got angry with her?

Somehow it made Clodagh feel almost as if she knew the man she'd never met. It was being so close to those who were part of his life, sharing their intimate secrets. Was she any nearer to knowing the man for this? Probably not. More likely she'd see the nature of Harrison in the boy. The white frightened creature sitting rigidly next to her with his hands on his knees. A tear-stained face, but not crying now. Eyes wide and alert and terrified and watching her every move. Being brave.

Yet somehow she rather liked the boy. Stupid really. This was Harrison's boy. He'd screwed *this* woman with her neck so thin she was sure she could snap it with her bare hands. He and she had produced *this* child. Archic was Philippa's and his flesh, part of him. And the funny thing was, she would have been proud to have a son like him herself.

Soon McGirl pulled over into a lay-by that was screened from the road by trees. Both mother and son were blindfolded before Philippa was ordered into the boot and Archie made to lie on the floor in the back before the journey resumed.

The old brewery building stood beside the Kennet river. A four-storey Edwardian structure, it had since been converted into a light-engineering factory until the company had apparently collapsed at the start of the last recession. A weather-tattered Land for Development sign stood beside the tall wiremesh gates, one of which was swung open by Muldoon as they approached. The car swept onto the weed-ridden concrete concourse and round to the rear of the building where the second car had been parked.

Philippa was shaking when she was released from the boot, unable to see the decrepit wall towering above her and the hundreds of broken windows like sightless eyes. She and her son were led through the back entrance and up several flights of steps to the top floor. There Muldoon and Doran had taken over the row of partitioned offices once used by the production manager and his staff.

The hostages were taken into one of them and ordered to sit with their backs to the old-fashioned radiator to which one arm was handcuffed. Their shoes were removed and then the blindfolds. Two camping mattresses had been unrolled over the broken glass and smashed floor tiles. A yellow plastic bucket stood between them. By awkwardly stretching out an arm and sliding the handcuff along the radiator pipe they could either sleep or use the bucket. But nothing more.

Philippa glowered up at them. 'What are you going to do with us?'

'Nothing,' Clodagh said. 'Provided your husband co-operates, you and the boy will go free. We'll take him in your place.'

'And if he doesn't?'

'He will.'

McGirl said: 'She should have his telephone number. Save us some calls.'

'Whose?' Philippa asked.

'Your husband's stupid,' McGirl snarled.

Philippa felt suddenly, deeply nauseated as the true nature of the situation sank in. The feeling of relief that at least Tom hadn't been hurt had long passed. Now she was being asked to betray him. Archie's father. Inexplicably a vision of their wedding day flashed through her mind. Not like a photograph, but like virtual reality. The feel of the white satin cool on her skin, the scent of the rose bouquet, the warmth of the sun, Tom's hand in hers. Warm, dry. A squeeze of reassurance to quell her nerves. She was being asked to weigh the value of her life and Archie's against Tom's. How could she make such a choice?

McGirl drew the heavy automatic and purposefully pumped a round into the chamber. He didn't need to point it at Archie's head.

Philippa was flustered, tried to think logically. 'I don't know where Tom is. He's on leave now, he could be anywhere.'

'Where does he live?'

'He's with that . . .' She nearly said tart. 'He's living with a journalist.'

'Have you got the number?'

'No,' she lied.

'What's her name?'

'Casey Mullins.'

'Her?' McGirl was incredulous; but when he thought about it, it made sense. She was obviously one of his press contacts. Now he knew it was more. Explained a lot of things. 'That was going to be our original route.' He put the gun away.

Clodagh left with him then, closing the door behind them. There was no key for the lock, but Doran had fitted two heavy-duty bolts. The remaining two offices were as empty and derelict as the makeshift cell, each with two more camping mattresses. A stock of provisions had been purchased – mostly boil-in-the-bag dishes, coffee and powdered milk – and a Trangia camping stove that ran on methylated spirit.

'We've got to decide,' McGirl said, glancing at his watch. They hadn't known how long the abduction might take; already it was forty-five minutes later than planned. 'It's three thirty. Do we go ahead now or wait until tomorrow?'

'Now.' Clodagh was decisive. 'The longer we wait, the sooner for someone to realise what's happened or for something to go wrong. Surprise and shock tactics.'

'If we can't reach him?'

'Then it'll have to be tomorrow, but we must go for it now if we can.' She looked at McGirl and waited for his agreement, wondered if he still thought of himself as running the show. 'First we'll tape-record the boy reading something from today's news-paper. Then you must get well away from here before you call. An hour's drive. Depending on where Harrison is, give him the minimum time to get here. He must have no time to think or to plan. No time to collude with the police or intelligence people. Pile on the pressure. Leave him in no doubt what will happen because, by Christ, it will if he doesn't show.'

'Did my grandmother teach me to suck eggs?' McGirl shook his head. 'Who found this place, Clodie, who showed you how it could be done?'

She placed her hand gently on his arm. 'I'm sorry, Pat, sure I just got carried away there for a minute.'

To his surprise she kissed him, albeit briefly on the cheek, in full view of Muldoon and Doran. They shuffled their stance uncomfortably.

She turned on them sharply. 'Right, while we do the tape-recording, you unload the explosives. This place is going to be turned into one gigantic bomb.'

'Where are they now?' Casey asked.

She had just returned from a late pub lunch at the Elephant and Castle in Holland Street. It was someone's birthday and a group of them had followed on to a wine bar to celebrate. Now she was feeling deliciously light-headed.

Eddie Mercs was just back from the Anti-Terrorist Branch's briefing. 'Where they always are, Paddington Green. One Irishman – no name released, but I got it on the nod that it's none of those you named. The other bloke was a local lad, maybe an unwitting accomplice.'

'And it was a farm?'

Mercs nodded. 'Near Henley. Bleedin' great barn full of ferti-liser explosive. Reckon if the place had gone up it would have been like a nuclear explosion. It would have levelled the pub just down the road.'

'God, how awful.'

A shrug. 'They don't care about things like that. Caches are always turning up in flats and garages in residential areas.'

The telephone rang on her work station.

'Mullins – features.'

'It's Bill here, friend of Tom's. I expect he's mentioned me.'

Casey laughed. 'Tom's got a *lot* of friends, Bill! But anyway, I'm sure he *has* mentioned you, I've just got cloth ears, that's all.'

'Look, sorry to trouble you, but I'm trying to reach him. It's quite important.'

'Oh, I see. Well, he's sorting out some paperwork at Vauxhall Barracks this afternoon.'

'Where's that?'

'Near Oxford.' She frowned. 'You're not with EOD then?' The drink had slowed her reactions, at first allowing her to miss the Ulster accent that slipped into his speech. Suddenly she experienced alarm bells ringing. 'Not Irish, Bill, are you?'

'Listen, cow, this is AIDAN!' The strident Ulster voice was unmistakable now, the strangulated vowels harsh with his anger. 'Don't say anything! Don't call anyone! We've got Harrison's son and his wife. Understand? You take one step out of line and they get blown away, got it?'

She'd already beckoned Mercs closer, now she pushed him away. He thought she was joking, pressed forward. She glared with enough ferocity to draw blood. 'Yes, I've got it.'

'Shut up and listen. Tell him his wife and son are sitting on three pounds of explosive. It goes off in exactly one hour and thirty minutes unless he hands himself over to us. In return they go free.' He was speaking faster, carried away on his own adrenalin rush. Mercs now sensed that something was wrong, saw it in the frozen rigidity of Casey's stance, her knuckles white on the receiver. He edged closer and she tilted the earpiece so that he could share the words. 'He drives *alone* to the village of Inkpen, that's to the west of Newbury. Check your watch. It's four forty-five now. We don't want to kill them because of a silly mistake like that, do we? He must be there by six fifteen. I'll want to check his progress, so he'll need a mobile phone. I've also got a tape of his son I'll play him.'

Casey thought quickly. 'I don't think he's got a mobile.'

'Then he'd better borrow one,' McGirl snapped. 'I'll phone you back for the number in half-an-hour.'

Christ, she thought, I can't be stuck here. 'Look, I've got a mobile, take the number. It'll be more secure than going through our switchboard.'

'Give!' he ordered, jotting it down as she told him. 'Remember, no police, no reporters, nothing *if* that wee boy and his mother are going to live out the next two hours.'

The telephone went dead in her hand, the tone drilling harshly into her ear, leaving her with an aching sense of uselessness.

'AIDAN?' Mercs asked. She nodded. 'And he's talking about Tom?'

'They've got Archie and his wife. They're offering a swap.' She felt the panic swelling in her chest. 'God, there's no time to do anything.'

Mercs stared at her, still not quite comprehending. 'I suppose that's the idea . . . I'll call the police.'

'No, Eddie!'

He started at the fierceness of her words. 'This is between me and Tom – I shouldn't have let you hear anything. Please, please don't say anything,' she pleaded.

Mercs raised his hands. 'Okay, okay.'

Already she was dialling Harrison's number. 'Tom must decide about the police.'

She caught him at Vauxhall Barracks just minutes before he was about to leave for the drive back to her flat. He was laughing, sharing a joke with the duty officer as he answered. Suddenly his world collapsed, her words sending his head swimming in shock and disbelief.

Then there was silence for a brief moment as he struggled to recover. 'I'll have to check with the school,' he said at last.

'Of course.' She hadn't thought of that. 'But I'm *sure* it was genuine, Tom. He actually said he had a tape of Archie's voice. No one would pull a practical joke like that.'

'Hold on,' he ordered and used another line. It took just four minutes to confirm the story without revealing his identity or alerting the headmaster to the nature of the problem. He prayed it was a cruel hoax, believed that somehow it just had to be. It wasn't. His voice was quaking with emotion as he came back to her. 'Look, there's a mobile I can use and I've got the car. I'm not sure where this Inkpen is, but presumably they've left sufficient time.'

'Tom, you can't go!' she protested.

'I've no choice.'

'You've no guarantee they'll let them go.'

'But I've got to try it, Casey. I've no other option.'

'You must tell the police. I can call . . .'

'NO!' There was a brief hesitation. 'Sorry. Christ, this is a nightmare. Look, they've allowed us no time. If we involve the police, it'll be the local plod, some inexperienced rural chief constable who sees this as his moment of glory, some gung-ho regional SWAT team.'

'Tom, think it out, for God's sake. If you don't call the police, nobody will know where you or Archie and Pippa *are*.'

Be rational, he told himself. 'Archie and Pippa are no use to them. It's me they want, Casey, I'm the senior British officer they'll want to swank about – to kill or to hold hostage, although God knows why?'

Suddenly she realised. 'The Trafalgar House talks, Tom. To use you as a bloody bargaining chip, that's why. It must be.'

'Then no police.' He was adamant. 'Let them dump Pippa and Archie somewhere, then we'll bring the police in.'

She had an idea, but time was running out. 'I must see you, Tom. I'm leaving now and I'll meet you somewhere on the road. Give me the number of your mobile.'

As soon as she'd taken it down, she hung up without giving him the chance to argue. She looked around frantically, surprised to find that Mercs had already located a road atlas and had spread it out on the empty work station next to hers. 'I've found Inkpen. I can see why they chose it. It's in the North Downs and bloody miles from anywhere. All farmland and country lanes.' He looked up. 'And he won't call the police?'

She shook her head. 'He says there's no time. It would just lead to a cock-up. I see his point.'

Mercs nodded his agreement. 'There'd be no time for them to set up covert surveillance. That's what's needed.'

God, she thought, was there no solution? She turned to him. 'We could do it.'

'Who?'

'You and me. Two cars and two mobiles.'

'Don't be stupid.'

'Why not, Eddie?'

'It's fucking dangerous for one thing.'

'If no one follows, no one will know where Tom is. Or his wife and son if those bastards decide not to release them. We've got to, Eddie, don't you see?'

He frowned and puckered his lips. 'It could be a good way to get Tom killed. If they know we are following . . . I know something about this sort of work. I did this report on undercover police units once. You use at least four vehicles. Form a box, they call it. One vehicle takes over from another, then if the quarry stops suddenly, you drive past and another takes up the tail.'

'That's not so difficult.'

'Motorcycles are good. Don't get stuck in traffic and can go anywhere.'

'Hal,' she said. 'Is Hal in? I thought I saw him a few minutes ago.'

Mercs stared at her. 'Casey, this is bloody lunacy.'

Harrison drove out of Vauxhall Barracks in a daze. Traffic registered, but it was in a kind of blur, his driving purely reflex and automatic, his mind trawling over the implications of what had happened. Trying desperately to inject some logic into what action he should take.

Time and again he went over what he had told Casey. That the release of Archie and Pippa was paramount, his own safety secondary. He'd used the same criteria for his decision to avoid police involvement at too short notice. Even he was panicking that he wouldn't make the rendezvous on time; he could imagine the chaos as the police tried to locate expert covert forces and deploy them to the scene against the clock. Yet despite that, Casey's warning echoed in his head: no one would know where he or his family were.

It was like evaluating a bomb threat, weighing the odds and probabilities, but never being absolutely certain . . .

At first he'd been hostile to Casey's suggestion that they meet somewhere on the road, but as he made good time down the A34, crossed under the M4 and proceeded through the town of New-bury, he began to welcome the thought of a few minutes with her. It might be the last they ever spent together.

She had kept in touch by mobile, her progress unbelievably quick. Thankfully the *Standard*'s offices in Kensington High Street were on the direct urban artery that fed into the M4 motorway. Even so she had some forty-seven miles to cover in order to reach Newbury. It would be touch and go whether or not she would make it.

He had just pulled into the village of Hamstead Marshall, a mere three miles from Inkpen, when she came through again.

'I've got us another fifteen minutes,' she said breathlessly. 'When he called through for your mobile number and your car registration, I said you'd been caught up in heavy traffic.'

'You took a risk.' He was angry that she'd done it, relieved that she had succeeded. 'Where are you now?'

'Getting lost in Newbury – no, it's okay. I need both hands in these country lanes now. I'll be with you in minutes.'

He put down the receiver and lay back in his seat, shutting his eyes. His heart was pounding. Keep calm, he told himself, keep calm.

The mobile bleeped. He opened his eyes and stared at it. There was little doubt who it would be. Suddenly that small comforting piece of plastic was transformed into something altogether evil and contaminated.

Slowly he reached out. 'Harrison.'

'Where are you?' The accent was harsh Ulster, full of scarcely suppressed venom.

'Newbury,' he lied. 'I'm stuck at traffic lights.'

'Don't fuck me around.'

'I'm not. I'll make it.'

'That's right. Listen.' There was a buzz and a whir, the tinny voice of a child, a boy. The reassuring tones of Pippa, her words calm but threatening to break up in hysteria.

'Turn it off,' Harrison snapped. 'I believe you. I'll be there.'

'Inkpen in twenty minutes or I phone the order.' The man had hung up.

Rage boiled over. He pounded his fist on the wheel, yelled at his own reflection in the mirror. 'BASTARD!!'

He threw open his door, stepped out into the lay-by, gulping down draughts of fresh air, his entire body trembling.

Casey rounded the bend then, the Mini Cooper in a four-wheel drift, tyres screeching and headlamps blazing even though it was still daylight. The vehicle slid behind his and her long legs appeared out of the door. Before he knew it, she was in his arms, her tears hot against his cheek. 'God, Tom, I'm so, so sorry. I can't believe this is happening.'

He eased her away. There was so little time. 'Listen, I'll tell them to contact you about the release of Pippa and Archie. That way you'll be the first to know.'

'When do you think they'll let them go?'

'It should be immediate, but I suppose I should allow twelve hours or so for unexpected eventualities.' He didn't really want to dwell on the negative aspect.

'And if I haven't heard then, do I call the police?'

He shook his head. 'Contact Don. He'll know the right buttons to push. If anyone comes busting in, I want it to be the SAS, not some local police firearms unit.'

She wondered again whether to tell him what she intended to do, but feared he would reject the idea. And she understood all too clearly why he might. But while she shared his desperate concern over Archie and Pippa, the safety of Harrison himself was even more important to her.

'I must go now.'

'Yes.' She kissed him hard on the lips. 'I love you.'

He pulled away then and walked back to his car. She watched him drive away, the memory of the exhausted and haunted expression in his eyes, she knew, would be etched in her mind for ever.

As his car disappeared from view, the first motorcycle came along the road from the other direction and swung in.

Hal Hoskins steadied himself and flipped up his visor. 'Hi, Case, am I in time?'

'Just,' she replied with relief, 'Tom's just gone.'

At that moment the second motorcycle appeared, ridden by a friend of Hal's, 'Bodger', who was another photographer.

'I'll work with you,' Hal told her, 'and Bodge will form a second team with Eddie.' He punched the single digit code into his mobile and almost immediately Mercs answered. 'Where are you, Eddie?'

'Just past a place called Crockham Heath. Can't be more than minutes away. Sorry I'm late – took a wrong turn.'

Hal looked at Casey and grinned. 'Let's go. Bodge will wait here for Eddie. We can move up to Inkpen, and then I'll follow your instructions.'

Instructions, that was a joke. 'I'm so grateful, Hal. But whatever you do, don't get too close. Those people will be armed.' She climbed back into her car. 'Keep behind me unless I lose Tom, then overtake. If Tom or whoever pulls over suddenly and I have to go past, you stop – well back – and get ready to take up the chase. If you lose both of us, stop immediately and get on the mobile.'

Hal appeared to be treating the whole thing as a game. 'Roger, Ten Four,' he said and gave her the thumbs-up sign.

She started the engine and turned the Mini Cooper onto the Inkpen road. Her hands were shaking. With full radio communications they might have been in with a chance. But reduced to using mobiles, which meant Hal and Bodger had to stop in order to speak or take a message, the omens were not good. Over the telephone on their separate drives down from London, she and Eddie had discussed the best method of operating. But she doubted now that it would be good enough. And if it wasn't, then Harrison could very well end up dead.

He arrived at Inkpen village with three minutes to spare. The AIDAN caller had not been specific about where he should stop, so he pulled over outside the first house of the village. It was a picture of rural tranquillity. Looking around he could see no sign of the terrorists' presence. A few parked cars, a woman pushing a pram, a couple of elderly men gossiping by a cottage gate. He looked in his rearview mirror, saw a car and wondered. But almost immediately it pulled in, much too far away for him to identify the make.

The mobile rang and he snatched it up. 'Harrison.'

'You're there?'

'Yes.' Irritable, angry and impatient.

'Leave the line open. I'll give you directions to Walbury Hill. Now start driving south through the village . . .'

He let out the clutch and pulled out. 'Keep going . . . take a left, then a right.' After a mile or so he was in open country, the road starting to climb, through a cutting towards the beauty spot and the viewpoint north over West Woodhay Down.

'Turn left,' ordered the voice and Harrison obeyed.

As he did so he spotted the Mazda saloon pull out from the cinder car park and fall in some fifty yards behind him. That was it, he decided. The instructions continued.

Minutes ticked by, the navigation tortuous as the terrorist slowly negotiated his way through myriad country lanes. It was only because the sun was mostly behind him that Harrison was able to establish that they were heading in an eastward direction. Place names vaguely registered. Woolton Hill. Penwood. Whitway.

They'd joined the A34, moving south, and now turned off left, moving east again towards Kingsclere.

'Slow down,' McGirl ordered, after they'd been travelling nearly forty-five minutes.

Crossroads ahead. Narrow farmtracks to either side.

'Keep going.'

The road dipping now.

'Pull over by the bridge.'

Harrison applied the brakes and steered into the grass verge, the Mazda pulling up close behind him.

Another car drove quickly past. Then nothing.

'Get out, face away from the car with your hands behind your back.'

He climbed stiffly to his feet, noticed that there was now no other traffic on the road, just undulating farmland all around. Turning towards the bridge parapet, he could see that the road carried over a steep-sided cutting, part of a disused railway line. It was dusk now and he could just determine the overgrown track of cinders, brambles and weeds that curved away to the north.

Then he felt the cold steel of the gun muzzle in the nape of his neck. 'Nice and easy, Harrison.'

A plastic loop was slipped over his wrists, the freezer tie rasping as it was locked tight. He was pushed sideways towards the broken wire fence at the edge of the bridge. He stumbled, slid on the muddy slope, his shoes slipping on the steep gradient of the cutting. He half stepped and half fell his way down, skidding on his bottom until he could regain purchase with his feet, the hand behind relentlessly pushing him on. By the time they reached the old railway track, his clothes were torn by brambles and caked in mud.

From somewhere in the twilight, perhaps from the bridge above, he heard the passing burble of a motorcycle exhaust.

'I've lost them,' Hal said.

'Where?' Casey demanded.

'On the bridge where they stopped. Both cars are abandoned. There's a disused railway line and I think they're walking along it.'

'Which way?'

'North.'

She cursed. The narrow farm road she was on, didn't even feature on her road map. 'Look, Hal, they're obviously not going to walk for long. See if you can pick up a road or something alongside the old railway track.' But she wasn't as optimistic as she sounded. 'Meanwhile, Eddie and I will position at the next two main villages and hope we can pick them up on their way through.'

Casey was plunged into the depths of despondency as she called up Mercs and ordered him to Ecchinswell while she drove on to Kingsclere. The terrorists' plan was clearly to switch vehicles and throw any would-be tail by using the railway line. So neither she nor Mercs would know what make of car they were looking for even if they saw it.

And, as it turned out, had it not been for their good fortune in having Hal Hoskins's motorcycle, that would indeed have been the end of the trail. But heading north along the narrowest of lanes towards Burgclere, which he reasoned could be running parallel with the railway, the photographer had passed a car parked on a short side road in the shadow of an industrial building. He glimpsed the dark shape of a man waiting beside it, looking anxious as he dragged on a cigarette.

Hoskins drove on for fifty metres, pulled over and, taking his mobile with him, retraced his tracks.

From a hidden viewpoint on the overgrown verge, he saw two figures approach the car: one man, looking dishevelled and exhausted, pushed along by the other.

The photographer pressed the dial code. 'Casey, I think I've got them.'

Doran opened the gate and Muldoon drove through.

Sitting blindfolded in the back seat, Harrison could see nothing.

'Out,' McGirl ordered as Muldoon opened the rear passenger door.

The air was chill for the time of year, an eddying breeze sending an empty can rattling across an open space. Harrison smelt the decay, the atmosphere of abandonment and desolation. Felt the weeds underfoot, growing between cracks in the concrete. A derelict factory, he thought, or possibly a warehouse. Nearby he detected the gurgling rush of water. Somewhere an owl hooted, adding to his sense of isolation.

He was frogmarched forward. Suddenly there was a distinct stench of damp bricks and rotting garbage.

His blindfold was pulled free and instantly torchlight dazzled him, as rough hands pushed him into the entrance of the building.

'Careful!' someone warned. 'She's got booby traps everywhere. Turn that torch off until we're round the bend.'

'What?' McGirl demanded.

'A photo-slave cell. Shine a light on that and we'll all go up.'

They stumbled forward in the gloom, Doran leading the way to the base of the stairwell. Then he turned on his torch and began climbing the first flight, glass crunching beneath their soles. Harrison could hear the distant drip of water, its melancholy plink magnified and echoing in the open body of the factory.

It was a wearying haul to the top floor. Eventually they followed the torchbeam across what was once a clerk's office. A broken desk remained, an upturned chair and posters and charts hanging in tatters on the wall. Three doors confronted them. Only one was open, illuminated by the flickering light of a hurricane lamp. The unmistakable shape of a woman stood silhouetted in the door-frame, legs apart and a gun in her hand.

'A present for you,' McGirl said, pushing Harrison forward.

He stumbled and the girl stepped back, the light of the lamp catching both their faces.

She regarded him for what seemed like several long moments, her eyebrows arched in an expression of curiosity. 'So you are Harrison,' she said at last, as though she could not quite believe it herself. Or was she just relishing the words, savouring her victory. 'Major – Tom – Harrison. The man whose evidence convicted my father . . .'

It had to be her, he thought. 'Clodagh Dougan?'

She didn't confirm it. 'According to the papers we've been playing quite the hero, haven't we? And then you deliberately set us up for an accident. I couldn't believe that at first when I read it.' She was close now, her eyes only inches from his own. They were dark and fathomless, burning with an intensity that was both beautiful and disturbing. He could see each pore of her skin, the whiteness of her teeth. Smell the shampoo she'd used on her hair. 'I wondered what sort of man could do that? What he would look like.'

He ignored her rambling. 'Archie – my son. And my wife. You agreed they were to be released as soon as I arrived. Well, I'm here. You can let them go now.'

'You're not giving orders here, *Major*,' McGirl sneered.

Clodagh appeared not to have heard either of them. 'You don't look much really,' she was saying. 'Quite ordinary really. Not the sort to deliberately lure an old man to his death. That was a pretty sick trick.'

Harrison glared back at her. 'What are you talking about?' He glanced around, searching for the face now so familiar from the file. 'Presumably your father's here?'

Her laugh was brittle. 'Hardly likely, Harrison. His remains were spread over half of Deptford.'

That shook him; everyone had assumed the unidentified terrorist had been one of PIRA's expendable footsoldiers. Nash's ploy had worked more effectively than any of them could have hoped, and they didn't even know. He said: 'That's an occupational hazard.'

'Funny man,' she sneered.

'I've faced the same occupational hazard every time I've had to tackle one of your father's bombs. He's killed several of my colleagues over the years. So don't expect my sympathy vote.'

She wore an expression of contempt. 'None of that would have been necessary if you bastard Brits had got out of Ireland.'

It was difficult to believe that this was the sister of Caitlin. The timid mouselike mother and housewife who wanted nothing more than to be left in peace, yet dreaded either Provo or Orange gunmen at her door because she'd married a Protestant.

Harrison said: 'I'm not political. My job is to save life and property and that's what I do.'

'Very noble, I'm sure.'

'Not really, I get paid for it,' he answered back sharply. 'Now, can I see my wife and son?'

For a moment she paused, unsure whether to give him another verbal lashing, then changed her mind. 'Take him in.'

McGirl shoved him unceremoniously sideways towards the second door, Clodagh following with the lamp. The door was unbolted and pushed open, a feeble light illuminating the bare room with its crumbling plaster and a heavy blanket covering the window.

Pippa was jolted awake by the sudden entry and looked up from the floor where she'd been dozing with her back to the radiator and Archie's head in her lap. Harrison had never seen her look so small and weak. A frightened animal, her hair dishevelled and falling over her face, her tights laddered and skirt torn.

She shielded her eyes against the influx of light. 'Tom?'

He went to her, knelt down, feeling anger and humiliation because he couldn't even hold and comfort her. 'Pippa – are you all right?'

Her free hand reached out, round his neck, and drew his face to hers. She didn't speak, couldn't. Her throat was choked with emotion, tears drenching her face.

'Dad, is it you?'

'Hello, son.' Tears were in his own eyes now, but the hot tears of anger that they could have done this. He forced out his words in an effort to comfort the boy. 'Been looking after Mummy?'

Archie nodded, sniffing hard, and stretched his unclasped arm round the necks of both his arents.

Clodagh remained at the door, McGirl by her side. 'Very touching,' he said.

Then Harrison turned towards them, climbed awkwardly to his feet, unbalanced by the bound hands behind his back. 'Where will you take them? I'd like them picked up as soon as possible.'

McGirl looked at Clodagh. 'I was thinking,' he said quietly, 'we've got no real need to release them now that we've got Harrison.'

'It's what we agreed, Pat.'

'That hardly matters, c'mon now. It's possible they know more than we think. They'll have a description of the inside of this place. It'll make it easier for the police to locate and then it'll have all been for nothing.'

Clodagh hesitated.

Harrison said: 'They're harmless, innocent. You can't keep a young boy and his mother like this. It's inhuman.'

'Shut up,' Clodagh snapped. 'You've still got your son. My father lost his children for nearly twenty years while he was inside. Do you think he *wanted* that?'

'He didn't have to do the things he did.'

Clodagh glared. 'Oh, yes, he did, Harrison. That's what you Brits have never understood. He *had* to do it, just like you'd fight anyone who invaded your country, occupied your towns and cities.'

431

'Don't waste your time on him,' McGirl said. 'Let's at least keep them for a few days. Maybe by then the Trafalgar House talks will have reached a conclusion.'

'You can't do that,' Harrison protested.

McGirl reached into the room for the handle of the door and, without a further word, slammed it shut.

The bolts went home.

21

When he went to bed in his room at Trafalgar House that night, Sir Ralph Maynard thought the day couldn't have been any worse. He was wrong.

As the Secretary for Northern Ireland shut his eyes and tried to sleep, the events of the day stubbornly refused to leave his mind.

It had begun with the Democratic Unionists walking out of the talks and holding an impromptu press conference with reporters who were camped out in the village of Downton at the edge of the sealed-off security area. The plans for an Independent Ulster were in tatters, they said, and blamed the collapse on a hardening of Catholic attitudes since Bishop McLaverty's arrival on the scene and rumours about Washington pushing for a United Ireland solution.

The disaster was all over the midday television news programmes.

In the afternoon had come the call from Number Ten. The US President had telephoned the Prime Minister suggesting that, in view of the breakdown of the talks, the possibility of a new All-Ireland initiative be explored. The American Ambassador to the United Nations had accordingly been ordered to raise the matter. It had been an embarrassing and acrimonious conversation.

Now, just as sleep began to creep up on him, Sir Ralph's aide knocked on the door. 'Sorry to trouble you, sir.'

Trenchard was by the man's side. 'We've received a call from Dublin, Sir Ralph. Codeword AIDAN.'

The minister's eyes were still bleary and unfocused. 'God, not more bombings.'

'No. They've kidnapped Major Tom Harrison and his family.'

'Harrison? Who the hell's Harrison?'

'The Senior ATO from Northern Ireland – or was. You know, the Blackwall Tunnel bomb?'

'Oh,' realisation dawning, 'him!'

'The IRA say he'll be released when we agree to the American plans for a United Ireland currently being brought before the UN. They say they'll keep the lid on it mediawise.'

Of course he immediately anticipated that he'd be required to drive straight to Downing Street and it was a fast journey in the chauffeured limousine on the deserted roads to London.

The Prime Minister was waiting in his study. Sir Ralph had never seen him look so angry and haunted; the pleasant, young-looking face had aged visibly since he'd last seen him.

Clarissa Royston-Jones, the Director General of MI5, was already sitting in one of the chairs. They discussed the latest developments earnestly for fifteen minutes, the Prime Minister concluding: 'It's imperative we find the remnants of the AIDAN unit and the location where they're holding this Harrison chappy and his family.'

'We'll leave no stone unturned,' Clarissa assured.

'The Home Secretary will authorise *any* additional resources you might require.'

It was *that* serious. 'Thank you, Prime Minister. No effort will be spared.'

He knew she meant it and had great faith in her tenacity, not least because he knew of her rôle in the Stalking Horse affair which had preceded the Gulf War. 'We're being boxed in. Heavy pressure from Washington and now this squalid little threat by the IRA. Something needs to be done.'

'Bishop McLaverty is the problem,' Sir Ralph said.

'But not the driving force,' the PM replied. 'That's the American, Senator Powers. Somehow we must seize back the initiative. Is there some way Powers can be dissuaded from pursuing this course?'

It was an open question. Clarissa was quick to read between the lines. Discredit the man, dig up something from his past, rattle a skeleton in his cupboard. Some sort of financial or sexual indiscretion. But, always trying to keep ahead of the game, she'd already looked. He was pure driven snow.

She chose her words carefully. 'What means should be used to dissuade him, Prime Minister?'

'I'm being pushed and I don't want to jump. All necessary means. Powerful diplomatic pressure.'

There it was, hidden in his reply for the benefit of any tape, known or unknown, that might be recording their every word.

All necessary means. Whatever you think fit, I don't want to know. Whatever it takes to make sure Senator Abe Powers III stops pushing the United Ireland proposal with Washington.

And, as she was driven away from Number Ten, Clarissa was in no doubt that such a directive, the first of its kind she had ever received, would be difficult to fulfil.

On returning to her house in Pimlico, which was only a few streets away from where Pippa Harrison had lived until recently, she telephoned John Nash and asked him to come over.

He arrived at first light, just minutes after the milkman had left one pint of skimmed.

'I want you to handle this personally, John,' she said.

Nash glanced at the bare table. 'No file?'

Her face was deadpan. 'No file.'

Hal Hoskins wriggled back through the long grass from the river's edge with his camera and telephoto lens until he was safely hidden behind the embankment. Only then did he stand up and, out of view from the old brewery on the far side of the water, walk back down the mud track to where the cars and motorcycles were parked.

'Nothing?' Casey asked.

He shook his head. 'They're still in there. On the top floor, I think. A face peered out earlier – seems they've put something up at the windows.'

Mercs looked at his watch. 'Ten minutes to noon. That's more than twelve hours.'

'Bastards,' she said.

Mercs was unmoved. 'What d'you expect? They're terrorists, not officers and gentlemen.'

'You've got to do it,' Hoskins said.

Casey was still unsure. 'I just hope it's the right decision. If the place is assaulted, they could all get killed.'

Mercs nodded grimly. 'But I'm afraid it's a risk we're going to have to take.'

Casey dug the mobile from her pocket and consulted her diary. Apart from Trenchard's flat number, which she knew, Harrison had given her several others where his friend might be reached.

He answered on her third try.

'Don, it's Casey.'

'Hallo, sweetheart, I thought you'd stopped speaking to me.'

'Don, this is serious. The IRA have got Tom.'

There was a tense pause. 'I know.'

'What?'

'There was a call to Trafalgar House last night. But how did you find out? Never mind, look, this has *got* to be kept under wraps. If you – if *anyone* – publishes anything, then it could be curtains for Tom and his family. They've told us the hiding place is packed with explosives. So you can imagine the danger they're in.'

'Don, listen . . .'

But he steamrollered on. 'We're desperately searching for clues to his whereabouts. Every copper in the south of England is on the lookout for him, COBRA's in session and the SAS are on standby . . .'

'Don, shut up!' she yelled into the mobile. 'I *know* where they are! In fact, I'm standing barely a couple of hundred yards from the place. I followed Tom to his rendezvous with them.'

An incredulous 'Christ Almighty' was his reaction. Then: 'Give me the details.' She told him the location, a deserted factory on the Kennet near Newbury. 'Stay put, Casey, the police will want a full debrief.'

She folded away her mobile.

Mercs looked cheerful. 'This is going to be the story of the decade and we're in on the ground floor. Hal, I suggest you and Bodger go and hide yourselves somewhere that'll give you the best angle. Otherwise the cops will kick us out as soon as they arrive.'

'Eddie,' Casey said reproachfully, 'how the hell can you think about that at a time like this?'

'Because, dear heart, I want to get back on the nationals.'

The first to arrive were CID detectives from Newbury, including one former Anti-Terrorist Branch Officer. Their approach was stealthy and on foot, rendezvousing with the reporters on the opposite side of the river to the old brewery. Casey and Mercs outlined everything they knew about the building and its grounds, the number of terrorists they had seen and their transport.

Ten minutes later an armed response vehicle arrived on the scene together with the uniformed chief inspector of Newbury who deployed them discreetly to cover the gates to the factory yard from the roadside ditch. The Territorial Support Group began sealing off the area. Cars were strategically positioned in case the terrorists succeeded in making a breakout without their hostages.

Casey and Mercs were led half a mile away on the far side of the bridge to a playing field which had been designated the emergency RV.

'Ours is just a holding operation until the big boys arrive,' the senior officer explained. 'It's not helped by the fact that the Paddies have such a commanding view. Anyone is going to be a sitting target who pops his head up.'

The next thirty minutes were the longest that Casey could remember. Absolutely nothing happened. The chief inspector kept glancing at his watch, the other detectives shuffled their feet impatiently. Mercs yawned. Birds sang in the trees. A train rattled by on the nearby track towards London.

Then suddenly everything seemed to be happening at once. First the Chief Constable arrived by helicopter. Then a police car, with flashing lights but no siren, appeared at the edge of the field leading a convoy onto the grass of the marshalling area. Next came the command and control vehicle known as Zulu.

Police began spilling out of patrol cars, unmarked Q cars and white Transits, in just minutes the field filled with reinforcements from the Anti-Terrorist Branch and marksmen in blue overalls from the SO19 'Blue Berets' unit who began unpacking their sniper rifles. Others were experts from TO7 Technical Support Branch and SO7, known as the 'Dirty Tricks Department'.

With the sudden influx of new arrivals on the village green, the place was fast taking on the atmosphere of an intensely earnest carnival. Then the second helicopter arrived in a special area that had now been cordoned off for the purpose.

As the passengers stepped down, Casey recognised Don Trenchard. Others, whom she didn't know, were John Nash from MI5, Jim Maitland of the Anti-Terrorist Branch, a Home Office adviser, a Special Forces brigadier and two police superintendents who had taken a special two-week course in hostage negotiation at Bramshill. They went immediately to Zulu Control for a meeting with the Chief Constable.

Shortly afterwards two more helicopters, both Pumas, arrived with a contingent from the Duty SAS Squadron at Hereford, the leader of whom also made straight for Zulu Control to thrash out an Immediate Action Plan in case of a need for an immediate response.

While they were in conference more vehicles arrived: three fire brigade tenders and six ambulances were followed by two white Tacticas which had recently been withdrawn from London to 11 EOD at Vauxhall Barracks.

Then, quite distinctly, a distant single shot was heard. Casey looked at Mercs, who shook his head and shrugged. Suddenly all sense of carnival died in an instant. A little later an ambulance drove off; there was no siren.

It was two-thirty in the afternoon when the meeting ended and Trenchard emerged, making his way across to where Casey and Mercs stood.

'I think congratulations are in order,' he said. 'I can't say what you did wasn't foolish and dangerous in the extreme. But as you got away with it, I can't say I'm not pleased you did.'

'What happens next?'

'Well, we've replaced the local firearms officers with SO19 marksmen, so now the place is fully surrounded. Unfortunately the terrorists spotted someone during the manoeuvre. A policeman was shot dead. Since then the terrorists have been on the blower to Trafalgar House making all sorts of threats.'

Casey paled. 'Oh, my God!'

He smiled reassuringly. 'No, don't worry. It was inevitable really. That old brewery is too well sited for a covert approach in daylight. And, anyway, threats are to be expected. The fact is the game is up for them and they know it. It's just a matter of time.'

'How long?'

'As far as they're concerned, until the talks are concluded in their favour. Abe Powers reckons that could be at any time.'

Mercs had been listening in his usual deceptively casual manner. 'So when do the Hereford hooligans go in?'

'Speculation of that sort isn't helpful. We'll want to try and get the hostages out first. Try and negotiate something. Besides, we're told the factory has been rigged with explosives and booby traps for a prolonged siege. Even the roof apparently, to stop anyone having any bright ideas about landing helicopters. And as this is the AIDAN team, I think we need to take the threat seriously. Can't really be too Rambo-ish about sending in the SAS.'

Trenchard left them then to join Nash and Maitland who waited by a Newbury Q car to take them nearer to the factory. He hadn't mentioned to Casey or Mercs that it was he who had the job of initial negotiation. Only his fellow professionals knew why and even they were unaware of his own, very personal reasons for volunteering.

The police negotiator had persuaded the terrorists that it would be best for them to communicate by a secure land-line telephone rather than mobiles, the transmissions of which could be intercepted by radio hams or the press. It was going to be Trenchard's job to take it in.

As they drove by the perimeter hedge, they passed Captain Heathcote, complete in khaki bombsuit, checking the roadside ditch for explosives, using a 'grudge' detector to locate any hidden command wires.

'I hope they're playing this straight,' Nash said.

Trenchard seemed unconcerned. 'At worst they get a fourth hostage. At best we get three out.'

The car stopped behind the screen of trees and they climbed out. Trenchard shouldered himself into the police flak jacket and picked up the telephone and bolt cutters. 'Good luck, Don.'

He stepped out in front of the gates, one SO19 marksman hidden to one side in the ditch. Trenchard raised both hands and waved them slowly so that the watching terrorists realised who he was and what he was doing. Then he proceeded to snap the padlock chain and pushed open one of the wiremesh gates.

Maitland and Nash moved up behind him as he began walking across the expanse of concrete yard towards the distant factory, telephone in hand and the cable trailing out behind him.

'Rather him than me,' Nash observed.

'And you say he volunteered?' Maitland asked. 'That'll be worth a gong. Even if it is posthumous.'

The ATO was now splashing about in the ditch beside them where the water passed under a culvert in front of the gates. He pushed up the visor of his helmet. 'Excuse me, gentlemen,' Heathcote said. 'But I wouldn't recommend stopping there. I think you'll find you're standing on what *could* be about thirty pounds of Semtex. In an oil can. No firing cable I can see, so it's probably radio-controlled.'

Maitland looked at Nash; Nash looked at Maitland. Both men looked down at their feet.

'Oh, shit!'

Heathcote chuckled, dropped his visor and scrambled out of the stream. His was a slow, waddling walk back in the wake of the car into which Nash, Maitland and the SO19 marksman had scrambled in undignified haste.

Trenchard approached the old brewery building in a kind of daze. His mind was racing back over the years. Like blurred photographs in the pages of a book being flicked through. Nothing definite, just glimpsed images that seared through the eye and etched themselves in the back of the brain. Barely remembered, but never forgotten. The old days. Indelible. The dirty rain of Belfast, the bombed-out ghettos on the Peace Line. The sanity-saving black humour in the squalid barracks, the smell of sweaty feet, polish and graphite oil, far worse than any back-to-back terrace. Ugly contorted faces screaming their stupidity and their bigotry. Old ladies smelling of lavender and offering cups of sweet milky tea. The strut and swagger of the flute bands. But most of all the unremitting boredom, the sheer tedium of routine patrols, day in day out, week in week out. Nothing ever happening. And then the sudden gut-wrenching fear. The explosions, the hysterical crowd, gunfire, the stink of CS and the crack and *thwack* of baton rounds. The absolute paralysing terror of it all.

And the teenage girl, sitting on the campus lawn and smiling bashfully at the camera, University of Ulster emblazoned on her sweatshirt.

Now he turned the corner of the building and saw the figure in the entrance portico. In the shadow, face hidden by a balaclava, the pistol held in a double-handed grip.

'Forward, slowly now,' McGirl said. 'Nice and steady.'

Trenchard edged forward, tugging the cable as it became snagged at the corner of the building.

'You can leave it here,' the gunman said.

'I've been authorised to talk to you.'

'Then you can use this telephone – from the *other* end of it.'

'No,' Trenchard insisted. 'Face to face. Inside.'

McGirl's laugh was harsh. 'So you can report on everything you see? I don't think so.'

'I don't intend leaving.'

'The Brits are giving us hostages now, are they?'

'You've got three innocent people in there. Let's talk about it.'

'Piss off!'

A second dark figure appeared at McGirl's side. Despite the balaclava, there was no mistaking the female shape. The voice confirmed it. 'What's going on?'

Keeping the gun levelled, McGirl glanced over his shoulder. 'This prick is offering himself in return for the other three. Some sort of fucking hero.'

'Hello, Clodagh.'

Her dark eyes bored out of the holes in the balaclava, seeing, but not believing. Unsure.

Trenchard said: 'It's been a long time.'

Still she stared. He watched her lips as slowly they mouthed the name. 'Chris?'

He nodded. 'Chris Walsh. It's been a long time. We need to talk.'

McGirl took a sideways step. 'You *know* him?'

She took a long, slow, deep breath. 'Oh, yes. I know Chris Walsh.'

'We need to talk,' Trenchard repeated.

Clodagh hesitated for a moment, then said decisively: 'Bring him in.'

In the darkness of the entrance, Trenchard was frisked, bound and had a strip of cloth tied around his eyes before being guided up the stairwell to the dilapidated office suite on the top floor. When the blindfold was removed he was standing in a darkened room with old blankets nailed to the windowframe. Boxes of provisions were scattered around, a stove, and two Armalite rifles rested against one wall.

'You're planning a long siege,' he observed.

'You'd better believe it,' McGirl said. 'Let the SAS come bustin' in here and they'll be in for a nice surprise. In fact I'm quite looking forward to them trying.'

'You could be bluffing.'

Clodagh stripped off her balaclava, shook her hair free. She said icily: 'It's no bluff. If anyone forces an entrance, they'll get blown to smithereens, but forgive me if we don't show you where everything is.'

'You can't possibly get away with this.'

'We'll see,' McGirl said. 'We've got hostages and they'll be the first to die if anyone rushes us.'

Trenchard indicated the covered window. 'There's a whole army of armed police and SAS out there. They'll just sit it out and wear you down.'

'We've just got to wait until the Trafalgar House talks are concluded,' Clodagh said. 'We'll be part of any final deal.'

'Not if you're holding hostages, you won't. The government won't allow a gun to be held to its head.'

442

McGirl sneered. 'And they won't let hostages get in the way of a peace settlement. They want it too badly.'

'Wrong,' Trenchard replied. 'But there is a way.'

'Is this a negotiation?' Clodagh asked sarcastically.

'If you like. You've got three innocent people in there. A woman and a child, and a man whose only job in the army is purely humanitarian, to save life and property. Release them and keep me. Then we'll allow you to sit this out until the talks are finished. And the government won't object if your release is part of the final deal.'

McGirl glanced sideways at Clodagh to gauge her reaction; he saw none. 'Harrison isn't so innocent,' he snarled. 'You must have read the press stories. Setting us up for an own goal. The one that killed Hughie Dougan.'

Trenchard shook his head. 'That wasn't Tom's idea. It came from MI5. Tom just carried out the orders, did what he was told.'

Clodagh's eyes narrowed. 'Harrison didn't know my father was the one killed at Deptford. You don't seem surprised.'

He hesitated before replying, wondered if this was the time to say it. 'I knew, Clodie, I saw his Celtic bird ring at the mortuary . . . and I knew the girl who was killed couldn't be you. Too short from what I was told but I didn't say anything.'

'Why not?'

Trenchard shook his head. 'I'll tell you, but not like this. Just you and me, in private.'

'I don't trust him,' McGirl said. 'Divide and rule. He'll just try and drive a wedge between us. And don't believe any of this crap about letting the hostages go and getting a deal. If we win through, it'll only be from a position of strength.'

Trenchard ignored him, looked directly at Clodagh. 'Five minutes, that's all I ask.'

The short silence was heavy, the atmosphere in the small room claustrophobic and charged with an electric tension. At last she said: 'You're the last person in the world I'd trust, Chris – God, I don't suppose that's your name for a minute . . . But I'll give you five minutes. For my reasons, not yours.'

'It's a mistake,' McGirl warned.

'Please, Pat, leave us. Shut the door. I'll be all right.'

The terrorist glared at Trenchard, shook his head in disapproval, and left the room.

Trenchard watched him go. 'Is there anything between you two?'

'Not really. What's it to you?'

He shook his head. 'You're not going to believe what I'm going to tell you.'

Her smile was bitter, resembling a snarl. 'That's true enough, so it is. I wouldn't believe you if you said the Pope was Catholic.' She waved the automatic in her hand. 'In fact I don't know why I don't shoot you now. No one has caused me the pain you did, Chr—'

'Don. Don Trenchard, that's my real name. Straight up, no lies. And what I was doing then, when I was on the campus, was just my job. In fact it was my first assignment. I was young, really keen.'

Her eyes blazed. 'Keen enough to shaft me – in every sense of the word!'

'What I hadn't bargained on was falling in love with you.'

Sitting there in the semilight, ten years on, in a besieged and derelict Edwardian brewery – talking to this man who now seemed a total stranger – she couldn't even find the words to express her anger, her confusion.

He smiled the smile she remembered. That slightly amused and patronising smile he used when she would earnestly explain her Republican beliefs over coffee in the university canteen. 'I told you you wouldn't believe me.'

'I don't.' Acid.

'Well, in fact, only I can know the truth about this. And I did. I did fall in love with you. I didn't mean to, didn't want to. But I did.' He held his bound hands in front of him, interlaced his fingers. Tried to remember how it had been. 'Remember those talks we had? In the canteen, in the park. In our digs. Over a bottle of Blackbush until two in the morning. Discussing politics and Irish history. You giving your views and me trying to talk you round. The arguments we had, the laughs.'

444

For a moment her face seemed to soften, the pupils dilating hazily. 'I remember.'

'I'll tell you something. Something strange. Something I didn't even realise myself at the time. In fact not until some five or so years later. By then I'd got sick of it all. The endless cycle of killing and violence. The dirty tricks on all sides – I knew all about them, because I was in it myself up to my neck.' He paused. 'I often thought about you, wondered. Remembered the things you'd said. Then suddenly, one day, I realised you had been right. No matter what the army and RUC did – from internment or the so-called shoot-to-kill policy – nothing would crush the IRA. It just kept coming back for more. For them it was just a continuation of their forefathers' fight against the Black and Tans before partition.'

A frown fractured the smooth skin of her forehead. 'You expect me to believe I converted you to the cause?'

'I've no reason to lie to you. It wasn't an immediate thing.'

'But you're obviously still with them. With British Intelligence or something. Still with dirty tricks.'

'Yes, but then it's my career. Too late to become an accountant or a solicitor now. But I do my bit to help if I can. Like when I recognised your father's Celtic ring at the mortuary, I realised he was dead. But if that had been known – that the old master bomber had returned from the dead only to be killed by his own bomb – it would have seemed like a victory to the British Government. They'd have been able to turn it into a far greater propaganda coup than they did. And I didn't want that.'

'No?'

'I was on the inside track, Clodie. I could see how scared they were of AIDAN, the pressure the campaign was creating, how close you were to succeeding . . . I knew how the talks were going, but without the IRA they were doomed to fail whatever was agreed. We'd seen it all before. And I didn't want that. While I couldn't condone the death and injuries your bombings caused, more than anything I wanted peace over the water. Just one more push and you could do it, I sensed that. And I was right. The

445

Blackwall Tunnel bomb was the turning point. That's why I said nothing.'

'And *did* nothing,' she said sarcastically.

'Not quite. The Prods had found out the truth about you and your father and I put my neck on the line in an attempt to suppress it.'

'Yes?' Not believing.

'They tortured and murdered Killy Tierney.'

The blood drained from her face. 'Holy Mother.'

'I'm sorry. I tried to stop it. I was too late. And when MI5 knew your identity, I leaked it to the press to give you warning.'

She was off guard now, her long black hair hanging limply over her face as she looked down at her hands, holding the gun between her knees. In a hoarse voice, she asked: 'And what about me?'

'I don't know.'

'You said you often thought about me, wondered what had happened to me?'

'Yes.'

'Yet you did nothing. You're in intelligence. Surely it would have been the easiest thing in the world to find out.'

His smile was crooked, unsure. 'I couldn't bring myself to. I actually took steps to avoid it. I knew I'd betrayed you. Betrayed your trust. And in that way I'd betrayed myself. I felt guilt – or maybe it was shame.' She was looking at him now, her eyes clear and candid. Somehow she seemed different from when he'd first walked into this awful place. Younger, almost vulnerable. As he remembered her, the earnest student. 'You could tell me now. What did happen to you?'

'I can't believe you don't know.'

'I only know what I see now. Someone hard and bitter.'

Her eyes narrowed, the vulnerability gone. 'And you know who made me like that?'

'Your father?'

She shook her head in exasperation. 'Sweet Mother of God, no. Da believed in what he did, that he was fighting for me, like I'm fighting for a future for Caitlin and her wee child. No, Don, it was you who made me like that. If ever I had cause to hate the Brits, it was you. You made me betray my own father without me even knowing it at the time. Sending him back to the Kesh for another nine years. How d'you think that made me feel?'

'If I could turn back the clock . . .'

'Oh, God, I wish. Because there was more to it than that – if you'd bothered to find out. If you really regretted what you did to me, at least you could run away. I couldn't.'

'What do you mean?'

'You left me with child.'

He stared, his mouth dropping open.

She laughed, the note brittle. 'Oh, you won't find that in your intelligence files. I was utterly ashamed, horrified. A Catholic girl made pregnant by a British spy. It would have been like giving birth to the Devil himself, to have had your child. But the abortion had to be secret and on the cheap, had to be on a student grant. So it was a back-street job.'

'I see.' Chastened.

'No, you don't. Because now I can't have children, you fucking bastard!' She stood up suddenly, her anger and grief returning. 'So I'm pleased with your conversion to the cause in your own sweet time. But it hasn't cost you anything, no pain and no suffering. Nothing!'

He looked up at her. 'That's what I'm trying to tell you, Clodie. I volunteered to walk in here. No one asked me to. It's time to pay the price.'

Her eyes were wide, the whites glistening with unshed tears.

'Christ!'

The door opened abruptly. 'Something wrong?' McGirl asked sharply.

Clodagh shook her head, unable to speak.

'Let them go, Clodie,' Trenchard urged. 'I'm of as much value to them as Tom Harrison, probably more so.'

'Don't listen,' McGirl said.

The woman sniffed, wiped the back of her hand across her eyes. 'You wouldn't understand, Pat. We'll keep him and release the others.'

'You don't believe that nonsense about a deal!'

She looked one more time at Trenchard. 'It doesn't much matter – but, anyway, I think perhaps I do.'

Making her decision, she pushed past McGirl and strode towards the adjoining door, sliding back the bolts. Three faces turned towards her, pale and drawn in the dim light.

'You okay, Tom?' Trenchard asked. 'Pippa and Archie?'

Harrison squinted into the light. 'What the hell are you doing here?'

'I'm your substitute.'

Clodagh bent to unlock his handcuffs. 'Be quiet, all of you.'

'Not the boy!' McGirl said.

Harrison began rubbing his chafed wrists as Pippa was released.

'This is madness!' McGirl shouted and stepped forward, jamming his pistol against Archie's temple. 'Leave him be, before I blow his sodding brains out.'

Harrison went to move towards the Irishman, then froze. The finger was taut on the trigger. So close, but there was nothing he could do.

'Listen, Pat –' Clodagh began.

'No, you listen! I don't know what this bastard said to you, but forget this business about deals. It doesn't work like that. The Brits, the Prods, the bloody Army Council, they'll all drop us in the shite if it suits them. And if there's an agreement, however much we've helped, we'll just be an embarrassment. Harrison and your man here, they both take the Queen's shilling. They're soldiers, expendable when it counts. But a wee boy. He's our real insurance. They won't sacrifice a wee boy to the IRA in a deal for peace – the tabloids would never let the politicians forget it. So if you want to live – and I do – then keep the boy, too.'

She hesitated, then slowly withdrew her hand and the key from Archie's handcuffs. In a quiet voice she said: 'The boy stays.'

'I'm sorry, Tom,' Nash said after Harrison's immediate debriefing. 'We had no idea it would work out that way.'

They were standing by Zulu Control on the village green. Harrison was choked with emotion. Anger, bitterness and a burning thirst for revenge. All played a part. But the most gut-wrenching feeling of all was that of absolute helplessness.

Jim Maitland said: 'Terrorists are an unpredictable lot, Tom. We thought it would be a good move. Although God knows what prompted Don to do his Sidney Carton bit. You know, it's a far, far better thing I do, and all that. At least we've got you and Pippa out. A small mercy, I suppose. Although I don't expect you to see it like that.'

Pippa out, Harrison thought. It may have been a consolation to him, but it was none to the woman herself. Like him, she'd rather have stayed in danger than abandon her son. If Archie died, she would die. Not immediately, but slowly over the years. Already something had died inside them both. And if the brief few hours of their reunion in the factory cell had brought them together again as a family, their forcible removal when Trenchard arrived had cruelly shattered all that.

Pippa had been hysterical, inconsolable, and had run to the arms of her father who had been brought to the scene. In some perverse way she blamed Archie's plight on Harrison and, of course, indirectly, he knew she was right.

He tried to clear his head, took a deep breath and looked around. Dusk was settling now. There were vehicles everywhere, uniformed police, marksmen and another group some distance away with two unmarked furniture vans who kept themselves to themselves. SAS reinforcements, he guessed.

Then he saw Casey, keeping back as she watched. Clearly unsure of herself, of him. Not wanting to intrude on his grief. Not knowing how he would react to her and what she had done.

Slowly he walked towards her. She was wearing her reporter's trench coat, eating a hamburger, cupping one hand to catch the crumbs.

Scared, he thought. Scared and not knowing what to do, like a girl. Her eyes were watchful, worried.

He stopped in front of her. 'Thanks, Casey. Thanks for what you did.'

Still she wasn't sure. 'Do you mean that, Tom?'

'I mean it.'

'I'm afraid it didn't help. I'm so sorry.'

'It was a brave and crazy thing to have done. But if you hadn't, all three of us would be in there and the police might never have found us. I took a gamble and lost.'

'As you said, you had to try.' Suddenly she realised how foolish she looked, a squashed hamburger in her hand, relish dripping through her fingers. 'I was hungry. I haven't eaten all day. Would you like some?'

Even now she could make him smile. He shook his head.

'What happens next, Tom?'

'We wait. It could take days. The negotiators will be asking to speak to Archie every day. Make sure he's still all right. Clodagh Dougan's agreed to that.'

'Is she running things?'

'Hard to say. She and McGirl between them.'

'What's she like?'

'Not like Caitlin. Clodagh's – I don't know – strange. Sort of hard and soft. Like there's some inner conflict. I'm sure she'd have released Archie. Something Don said perhaps, I don't know. McGirl stopped her.'

'Pippa's taken it badly.' As she spoke the words she realised it was a stupid thing to say; stating the obvious.

'She's under sedation. I'm afraid she blames me.'

Casey touched his arm. 'She shouldn't do that, Tom.'

'She has a point.'

There was a sudden commotion at the Zulu Control trailer. Voices were raised in vehement argument. Several officers stood around the entrance, looking in with curiosity. After a few moments Jim Maitland emerged, glanced around, spotted Harrison and strode towards him.

'Look here, Tom, we're beginning to get developments and I don't like the look of them. McGirl's starting to get very twitchy with the negotiators. To be truthful I think his real predicament is starting to sink in. He's beginning to dismiss the idea that their release will be part of a final deal at Trafalgar House.' Maitland grimaced. 'And I can hardly say I blame him there. The point is, he's demanding a helicopter flight now to take all of them to Eire with guarantee of no interference here and immunity from extradition by Dublin.'

'And?'

'He's threatening to shoot Trenchard if he doesn't get it.'

'What's the likelihood London and Dublin will agree?'

'Slim. But that's not the point. If anything happens to Don, we lose any chance of negotiating your son's release. He'll then be their *only* insurance and they'll keep him with them until the bitter end.'

Harrison experienced an awful churning sensation in his gut, the bile rising. The thought of his friend dying because of him, and his son still held captive was all too much. And just when he'd almost reconciled himself to the possibility that the siege could end peacefully. 'What are you proposing?'

'That we prepare for the worst. McGirl has given us an ultimatum to agree to his demands. Three hours. That'll take us to midnight. Our negotiators will try to dissuade him, play a stalling game . . .'

'But?'

'If Don is killed, I'm afraid COBRA will give the order for us to go in. Standard procedure once the shooting starts.'

'Christ.'

'The thing is, Tom, this is likely to get messy. You've been debriefed on what you saw of their explosive defences and they've left us in no doubt what to expect. The SAS have now updated their first Immediate Action Plan and are going to require backup from bomb disposal. Colonel Lloyd-Williams is flying here direct from Aldergrove by helicopter to take overall charge of the EOD operation. He's agreed, albeit reluctantly, to let you lead in the main assault to clear the way for an SAS follow-up and support from the 821 Squadron boys.'

'No!' Casey protested. 'You can't ask Tom to do that.'

Maitland looked grim. 'Please keep out of this, young lady. No one's forcing him, it has to be his own decision. But quite obviously Tom's the best qualified for this particular job. He's been inside the building and he's worked with the SAS.'

Harrison said: 'I wouldn't want to be anywhere else, Jim.'

Casey looked on in horror and disbelief. But she knew he would ignore her protest.

At that moment the Wessex appeared over the nearby village rooftops, fresh from the front line of Northern Ireland, in its battle livery of green, black and brown. Taff Lloyd-Williams had arrived.

Maitland said: 'The briefing starts in five minutes.'

McGirl's deadline of midnight came. And went.

London had agreed, the negotiators told him, had a helicopter on standby. But Dublin was dragging its feet. Unexpected that. The politicians there were wringing their hands with the moral dilemma.

Another half-an-hour, McGirl agreed.

He paced the outer floor beyond the offices like a caged tiger. Kicking at debris, winding himself up.

Clodagh leaned against the wall and watched him in silence, arms folded across her chest. Muldoon stood at one of the windows at the far end of the room, the sniper rifle with its nightsight poised, eyes relentlessly scanning the bald patch of concrete.

He looked back inside towards McGirl, the man's stalking figure lost in the elongated shadows where the moonlight glistened on the broken glass on the floor like crystals of blue ice. Liam Doran, covering the side of the building, was distracted too.

'Keep still, Patrick, for God's sake, can't you?' he said. 'You're making me nervous, so you are.'

McGirl scowled at him, walked menacingly towards him.

Doran turned his head away at the other man's approach, looked out towards the river. He'd always expected he'd die violently one day, had never guessed it might be quite like this. Not on the eve of peace. Ironic that. He said hoarsely: 'Why haven't the police lit up the place like a picture palace?'

'The Brits like operating in the dark. Like slugs and rats.' McGirl turned away sharply, walked purposefully towards Clodagh. 'They're playing silly sods with us, you know that?'

'I know that, Pat. What did you expect? It's negotiating procedure.'

She noticed he was agitated, perspiring. Not prepared to meet thy doom? She felt like asking but didn't.

He came to a decision. 'Then it's time to let the shites know we mean business. Call their bluff.'

'We can sit it out.'

He looked her hard in the face. 'Why? Don't believe our friend in there, do you? It'll all end the same way, sooner or later, if we don't keep the pressure up.'

'I call the tune, Pat. It's what was agreed.'

'No, Clodie, that was your father, not you. I'm giving the orders now.'

'Not the wee boy.'

'No, not the boy.' McGirl jeered. 'It's time for your man to pay the price.'

'Price,' she repeated, remembering Trenchard's words. 'Christ, were you listening at the door?'

He regarded her with contempt for a moment, not bothering to reply. Then he turned to the door of the improvised cell.

'Not in front of the boy, Pat!'

McGirl was inside. There was the sound of a punch being thrown and Archie screaming. Then Trenchard was being half pulled, half dragged out of the doorway, one knee scraping over the glass on the floor as he tried to gain his feet, still doubled over with the pain of McGirl's blow.

'For God's sake,' Trenchard cried, his voice strident with panic, 'don't be stupid. I'm worth nothing to you dead. Alive I'm your insurance!'

'You're right about one thing,' McGirl sneered, bringing his knee up into the face of the kneeling man, 'you're worth *nothing*. You said it.'

Tears began to fall down Trenchard's cheeks, his bound hands visibly trembling as he brought them up in a gesture of prayer and appealed to Clodagh. 'Tell him, Clodie! Tell him I'm worth more to you alive! Tell him!!'

McGirl stepped behind the bowed body with his automatic, saw the spreading puddle. 'Our hero's just pissed himself.'

Clodagh said: 'He won't listen to me, Don.' And she averted

her face and shut her eyes, seeing only the handsome young student on the university campus. Smiling at her, sharing his jokes with her. All the while betraying her. And their child.

The single solid shot reverberated back and forth along the upper storey of the building, the noise lingering, slowly dying as Don Trenchard pitched face forward into the debris on the floor.

McGirl kicked contemptuously at the body. 'The man had no dignity.'

Clodagh turned her face back to the scene; Muldoon and Doran looked, too, their outlines faint beside the windows.

'Give me a hand,' McGirl ordered. 'Leo, open a window at the front. Liam, give me a hand with the shite's corpse, lift it up to the sill. Careful!' he warned, crouching beside Doran as they reached up to tip the body over. 'Don't give them a target.'

Trenchard's body was hooked over the frame at the waist, the balance pivoting until McGirl gave one last push at the foot above his head. The shoe came away in his hand and the body disappeared. There was a mere split second's silence until they heard the thud as it hit the ground.

As if he thought it had been some last deliberate act of defiance by the dead man, McGirl threw the shoe contemptuously into the middle of the floor. He looked across to Clodagh: 'Now we'll see if they don't believe we mean business. Are all the explosives armed?'

She nodded, numb, aware that events had spiralled out of her control.

McGirl pushed his way into the office that served as their quarters. He picked up the slab of Semtex to which the small plywood ignition unit with its tail of aerial wire had been taped. He returned with it to the improvised cell and slid open the bolts.

Archie sat with his back against the radiator, upright and staring, his face a waxy white mask. 'Was that a shot?'

'Yes, that was a shot,' McGirl retorted, mimicking the boy's polite formality. 'And you'll be next, you little shite, if you don't behave.' He held up the bomb. 'Do you know what this is?'

'I think so, sir.'

'Explosive, right,' McGirl said, as he placed the contraption to one side before unlocking Archie's handcuffs. He then pulled over a straight-backed chair from the corner.

'What are you doing?'

'Shut up and sit. Arms by your side.'

Archie obeyed as McGirl began to unravel the parcel tape. He proceeded to bind the boy firmly to the chair back, unrolling the stuff tight around the small chest time and time again until he was satisfied it was secure.

'This charge is radio-controlled,' he said, taping the device beneath the chair. 'I've got the control switch. If anything happens, if the police or soldiers break in here, you do exactly what I say or you become so much instant mincemeat. Understand me?'

Archie's eyes were wide as he tried not to breathe. 'Excuse me, sir.'

McGirl stopped by the door. 'Yes?'

'I think you're a right bastard.'

22

'Trenchard is dead,' Maitland said.

Just minutes earlier the TO7 team had heard the conversation and the shot through the sensitive radio-relay microphone secreted in the land-line telephone.

Since last light the old brewery building had been flooded in invisible infrared light, allowing the surveillance teams to watch the scene through IR viewers. The falling body had been witnessed.

'Then I'm empowered by the Home Secretary to hand over to you, Major,' the Chief Constable said and leaned over the desk in Zulu Control to scrawl his elaborate signature on the form.

Major Miles Foxly, previously of the Coldstream Guards and now Commander of the Counter Terrorist Team, 22 Special Air Service Regiment, accepted the order. He turned to Colonel 'Taff' Lloyd-Williams. 'If your chaps are set, sir, then I think we're ready for the off.'

The colonel nodded. 'Just one thing. Don't mention this business about his son and the bomb to Harrison. The poor bugger's got enough on his plate. That aspect will be down to your boys, Major. There's not a damn thing he can do about it anyway.'

'And your Wheelbarrow team, sir? They're happy they can do the necessary?'

'Captain Heathcote and Corporal Clarke,' Lloyd-Williams replied. 'Our top Belfast team. Both recently worked with your people under Harrison when he was CO of 821 Squadron.'

Foxly gave one of his stiff, reserved smiles. 'Then, let's go!'

The signal was received by Captain Ran Reid and Sergeant Major 'Big Joe' Monk on the far bank of the Kennet. Six rubber

456

inflatables, earlier attached to guideropes spanning the river, began the process of ferrying the assault team, their equipment and expanding aluminium ladders. Under cover of darkness, they advanced in the predetermined blind spot at the rear of the building. Once Monk confirmed that the team was in position, the police negotiator rang through on the land-line. It was McGirl who answered.

'Good news from Dublin,' the officer said. 'They have agreed to receive you and agree to your conditions. As I speak, a helicopter is on its way. Therefore the police will need to illuminate the brewery precincts for it to make a safe landing. You should not be alarmed by these events.'

Meanwhile on the road outside the gates, Captain Heathcote, dressed in full bombsuit positioned two broad-band Lilliput jammers, one each at fifty metres on either side of the culvert where the radio-controlled bomb had been detected earlier. He began the return walk towards the bridge to be met by two Tactica trucks, one of which contained the Wheelbarrow.

'Gone active,' Corporal Clarke reported as the radio jammers began silently flooding the airwaves to break up any attempted triggering signal from the terrorists. This was a technical cat-and-mouse game that had become increasingly tricky of late as PIRA had refined the eight- or nine-pulse firing signal down to a mere two blips.

With the ECM established, the signalman radioed Zulu Control. In theory the culvert bomb was neutralised. But then who trusted theories? Minutes later they heard the approaching sound of the helicopter, the real purpose of which was to confuse the terrorists and disguise the noise of the robot.

The throbbing beat increased, hovering somewhere nearby, its flashing strobe the only indication of its presence against the backdrop of stars.

'Let's go,' Heathcote said.

Already, the ramps were down and Clarke had the Wheelbarrow down onto the tarmac in seconds, deftly playing with the joystick to swing it round and send it trundling alone towards the culvert in front of the gates.

Heathcote glanced at his watch. Dammit, they were late. Typical bloody police.

Even as the curse silently passed his lips, the Nitesuns sprang on, startling in their brilliance even behind the screening thicket. Most were angled to illuminate a patch of the concrete forecourt, but others had been directed at the building itself. Muldoon and Doran, who had been watching through their riflesights, would have been momentarily blinded, destroying their night vision.

The Wheelbarrow approached the culvert, wheezed to a halt, its mini-headlight on and telescopic arm extended to take the Pigstick into the small brickwork tunnel.

Both men studied the TV monitor. 'In position,' Clarke intoned.

Heathcote agreed. 'Fire.'

The loud crack of the exploding waterjet as it smashed into the radio-controlled power pack of the bomb was lost amid the rising crescendo of the helicopter.

'Looks good,' Clarke reported.

Heathcote grinned, snapped down his visor and began running awkwardly under the weight of the bombsuit. By the time he reached the culvert, Clarke had withdrawn the robot, allowing space for Heathcote to slide down into the ditch, inspect the damage and cut any remaining wires on the circuit. He raised his hand, thumb up.

Clarke immediately took control of the giant Attack Barrow that had been waiting in reserve. With a sudden jerk, it whined into life and began its determined way down the road towards the gates.

Muldoon raised the alarm and Clodagh rushed to join him at the window, the radio-signal transmitter in her hand. She pressed the button at the exact moment the robot crossed the culvert, shut her eyes in anticipation of the flash. Nothing happened.

Meanwhile Harrison sat with Sergeant Major Joe Monk in the black rubber inflatable as it was hauled across the river, secured by an overhead pulley line. The heavy bombsuit had been left behind, standing orders for once ignored. On an assault mission such as this, if anything went wrong, he would be killed regardless of any protection he wore. So, like Monk, he was dressed in black Panotex antiflash suit and hood with layered ceramic body armour and rubber respirator mask. He carried a Browning Hi-Power as his personal weapon and a canvas tool belt round his waist.

Monk would be his personal protector. His huge dark bulk and the doleful insect-eye lenses in the hood created an awesome spectacle like something from a science-fiction fantasy. He carried a 9mm MP5 Heckler & Koch sub-machine-gun clipped to his chest. Because the architecture of the building contained many open areas, he carried some of the most powerful Brock XFS-1 stun grenades along with CS gas containers.

While Heathcote and the Wheelbarrow teams made a noisy but powerful diversionary assault on the south side, Monk and Harrison would be making a silent approach at the north end.

This had been made necessary because earlier helicopter surveillance had detected what appeared to be antipersonnel devices in oil drums fitted to the roof. Experience of AIDAN suggested this was probably exactly what they were. Whilst casualties to assaulting soldiers were acceptable, the prospect of the old building collapsing entirely in the resulting explosions was not.

The alternative, and infinitely more stealthy approach, was decided on when architect's drawings became available which revealed the old water outfall system.

'*Zulu Control to Sunray*,' Harrison heard on the integral comms. '*Confirm Attack Barrow now entering factory gates and is in full view of hostiles . . . A shot has just been fired . . . Commence prelim EOD assault. Repeat. Commence prelim EOD assault.*'

Major Foxly's voice came on the net. '*Roger, Zulu. This is Sunray. EOD and 10 Troop . . . GO!*'

The inflatable nudged the far bank. In front of him, Monk's head nodded sideways, indicating the water. Harrison sensed the man was grinning as he rolled his large frame over the tubing gunwale and sank up to his waist in the black water that bubbled and foamed as he broke its flow.

Harrison followed, gasping inwardly as he sank into the cold liquid and felt it trickling down into his boots. He edged forward after Monk's dark shape, watching as the man found the rusted, half-submerged rim of the outfall pipe. Then he was gone, a duck dive; just a glimpse of a broad, black and dripping backside as Monk forced his way into the eighteen-inch-diameter pipe.

Earlier a recce team had removed the grille and checked t'viability of the access route. As Harrison stood shivering, wait for Monk to clear the entrance, he had his doubts. But then these men were the experts. The trouble was they expected everyone else to be equally fearless, regardless of any natural susceptibility to vertigo or claustrophobia. There was no time to linger. The rest of 10 Troop was closing up behind him, ready to follow.

Car bombs and derelicts, he thought, and the old black dog was back, snarling and snapping at his heels.

Taking a deep breath, he plunged face down into the murk. He opened his eyes but could see nothing. Although Monk had a torch with him ahead, the sergeant major's body virtually filled the tunnel allowing just a confusing glimmer to light Harrison's way. Cocooned in his respirator, he was aware of the filthy water at chest level, splashing over the eye lenses each time Monk moved forward. And he could sense rather than smell the rankness of stagnant water and rusted metal.

Slowly, painfully Harrison hauled himself along, his head brushing the curved arch above him, the pitted surface grinding on the flesh of his knees through the sodden trousers. Onwards, onwards. Only fifty metres, he knew, but it seemed like as many miles.

Oh, fuck, what was that?

Monk jerked suddenly, and let out an involuntary cry of surprise as Harrison glimpsed the flash of grey matted fur and long wormlike tail. Tiny claws scrabbled over his shoulders and down his back and disappeared to terrorise the rest of the SAS follow-on team.

Harrison shut his eyes. Bombs were one thing, rats were quite another. Monk was on the move again; Harrison wriggled on after him.

Meanwhile, four storeys above his head, the emergence of the Attack Barrow on the forecourt was causing continuing panic amongst the AIDAN team. McGirl was on the land-line.

He had to shout to be heard above the tumultuous roar of the helicopter outside. 'What's going on? Get that bloody robot out of here!'

The police negotiator was unmoved, his words silkily reassuring: 'It's purely routine. You've told us you've planted explosives on the door. The helicopter can't land in the vicinity until they've been cleared.'

'You lying bastard! You haven't agreed at all!' McGirl accused.

'Of course, if you're prepared to disarm the devices yourself . . .'

McGirl slammed down the handset. He was shaking with suppressed anger.

'What is it?' Clodagh demanded. The entire building appeared to be trembling in the downdraught of the helicopter's rotors.

'It's a trick. They're trying to break in at the south end.'

The sudden crack of a gunshot came from the window where Muldoon stood. 'Hit it!' he cried.

McGirl rushed to his side.

'Sod!' Muldoon said. 'It's still moving.'

Now the Attack Barrow was close in to the building, directly beneath them. It was impossible for Muldoon to fire from that angle without exposing himself to an army sniper round.

They heard the crack and fizzle of the cutting charge as it blasted a hole through the door. Then the mechanical wheeze was quite audible as the Attack Barrow edged forward like a curious animal, its TV camera nosing in for a closer look.

It had been assumed that the south end would be similarly rigged to the north end which Harrison had reported as being a horizontal Claymore device, a cut-off pressure gas cylinder, probably packed with nuts and bolts. It was, but where the north had been triggered with a light-sensitive cell, this one had been wired to an ultrasonic car alarm from an accessory shop.

Clodagh glanced at McGirl and shook her head.

The explosion rocked the entire building.

'CHR-I-I-ST!' Muldoon uttered as the remnants of the Attack Barrow blasted out across the forecourt, pieces of metal clanking discordantly onto the concrete.

There was a long moment of stunned relief, despite the continuing drone of the helicopter above their heads. Clodagh and McGirl joined Muldoon at the window with an exhilarating sense of triumph.

'Well done, Clodie,' McGirl said. 'That'll make them think.'

But it was a feeling of elation that was to be short-lived. The now familiar and irritating whir of mechanical defiance reached their ears again. Around the edge of the gate peered the Wheelbarrow that had taken out the culvert bomb, its disrupter recharged and looking for business.

In the outfall pipe, Harrison suddenly found his face next to Monk's enormous rubber-soled boots. The sergeant major was standing in the vertical brickwork shaft, his arms outstretched in order to grip the steel manhole plate and push it aside. In the confined space the grating sound as it slid over the concrete was deafening.

Then Monk was scrambling for a foothold, drawing up his full sixteen-stone bodyweight on his immense and powerful biceps. His hand reached down, offering a wrist-to-wrist fisherman's grip to pull Harrison out of the hole.

Breathless from the exertion, the SATO crouched, panting, until the next soldier was up, ready to repeat the process with those who followed. Looking around the deserted ground floor he could see the remnants of steel footings that had once bolted machinery to the floor, now covered in debris and accumulated rubbish from tramps, vandals and glue-sniffers over the years.

Monk indicated for the first man to wait, well clear, until the north-end stairwell had been cleared, then followed Harrison as he picked his way towards the inner door that opened onto the stairwell.

Harrison stopped there and, reaching out a hand, tapped the lens of the torch hooked to Monk's chest. The SAS soldier nodded and switched it off.

An Allen cold lamp would be used now, a small book-shaped container of grey enamel with a handle on top and a diffused fluorescent tube in the leading edge.

He closed his hand around the door handle and pulled gently.

It was locked. Monk saw the problem. The SATO couldn't use a small explosive charge because there was a light-sensitive bomb on the other side of the door. Monk delved into his pocket for his leather wallet of standard-issue lock-picking tools. Kneeling down in the light of Harrison's Allen lamp, he inserted one of the steel prongs and began to manipulate the tumblers.

Anxiously Harrison counted the seconds, his mind returning yet again to his son, sitting somewhere above their heads. And again he tried to push the picture from his mind.

Then from the far end of the building, they heard the sound of the second Wheelbarrow as its mechanical arm began ripping away the loose wreckage of the door to gain access.

Monk nudged him. Their inner door was now unlocked and Harrison slipped through, reaffirming as he did the positioning of the light-sensitive slave switch on the stairwell wall. He played the Allen lamp down over the bricks. There it was facing him, the blocked mouth of the cylinder, a thin crust of cement holding the lethal concoction of ironmongery and explosive. A sort of enormous and crude Claymore-type affair. A blunderbuss of horrendous destructive power, half buried in removed bricks, aimed straight at his groin as he reached up, feeling in the dim light for the linking wire.

Nothing. Just red dust crumbling under his fingertips. He spread his palms, probed around. He was starting to sweat, the lenses fugging and the smell of rubber from the respirator overpowering.

That was when he felt the tension, something rubbing against his knees. He went to kick away whatever was snagged in the material. Something stopped him. He directed the Allen lamp down his body. Half expecting a piece of old bedspring – there was a rotted mattress dumped in one corner of the entrance – his heart skidded as the light picked out the gleaming monofilament thread.

Christ, tripwire.

Monk heard the expletive in his earpiece, came forward.

'What is it, Tom?'

'By my knees, a wire.'

The sergeant major knelt, his face close to the transparent nylon thread, difficult to distinguish through the perspex goggles. As Harrison played the light, he traced it back to the source. One end of the wire had been wound around a small length of wooden dowel. It was held in position by a clothes peg, itself attached to a small power unit and a separate charge of Semtex which filled a hole where a brick had been at the bottom of the stairs. Had the dowel been pulled and the jaws of the peg closed, then the circuit would have been completed.

This second booby-trap device hadn't been in place when Harrison had left the building earlier.

'*Ease back,*' Monk instructed. '*Real slow.*'

Harrison moved one foot. The wire slacked. Then he shifted his second leg.

Monk's mouth was parched. '*You're clear.*'

Harrison crossed to the secondary device and, almost angrily, snipped the wire and shoved the dowel securely home. That would do no harm now; it would have to be fully disarmed later.

He turned to the light slave cell, traced the wire and cut it in two places. The Claymore device itself would have to be left until later; any antihandling mechanism might have been fitted, maybe a simple pressure switch or trembler that would trigger if disturbed. The battery power source itself was hidden somewhere within the brickwork.

Next Harrison inspected the outer doors themselves. Sure enough a simple contact-breaker had been fitted, a wire also leading . . . oh, God, no, only leading back to the Claymore – and the sodding thing was still live!

He swallowed hard and again cut the link.

Then he signalled to Monk that he wanted to speak to Zulu Control before going on. The SAS man settled on the steps, MP5 unclipped and at the ready, while Harrison pressed the send button. 'SATO to Zulu Control. I'm meeting with all manner of IEDs on this route. Suggest I investigate next floor before you tackle your end. Over.'

Taff Lloyd-Williams came on. '*Roger to that, SATO. We've just*

464

lost the Attack Barrow on the front door. The backup Mark 8 is in and starting to climb. Over.'

'Pull back,' Harrison advised. 'Tell them to check for a trip and a secondary. If they've got one it could well have survived the initial blast.'

'*Roger, SATO. Let us know what you find up there.*'

'Wilco and out.'

He joined Monk at the stairs and led the stealthy climb, using his Allen lamp and feeler-probe to check each step. Still no sound and no light came from above. No doubt the AIDAN team were confident that their defences were impregnable. Harrison had an increasingly uneasy feeling that they could well be right.

Their two heads peered over the top step of the landing, noses level with the floor. He lifted his Allen lamp and played it over the walls. The beam gleamed on the wet brickwork and the green fungal growth. Right-hand wall. Clear. Ahead. Clear. He wriggled forward on his stomach to see around the left wall of the stairwell to the far wall and the next flight.

And there it was.

The slab of plastic explosive, just a few ounces, had been tied with string which was fixed to a nail that had been hammered into the mortar. It was wrapped in parcel tape, three-inch galvanised bolts secured between the layers. Nasty. Enough to disembowel or castrate, maybe worse.

But how was it triggered?

The wire was black and difficult to identify at that distance, but he managed to trace it in the light from the Allen lamp down to the debris that littered the floor. Flattened cardboard boxes, sodden lengths of hardboard and yellowing newspapers. In fact quite a covering of junk.

Then he was back. Back in 1982, in the Ballymurphy derelict after the sniper. Just minutes before Don told him that Hughie Dougan had been caught.

Cars and derelicts.

Oh, shit!

He stared down at his elbows. They still rested on the hard

concrete. Half-an-inch in front of him was a flattened cardboard box that had once contained a refrigerator.

Somehow he just knew. What other tricks had Hughie Dougan taught his daughter?

Turning to Monk, he whispered into his mike: 'Get back down till I've cleared this.'

The SAS man nodded and slithered back down the steps to shield behind the wall on the lower stairwell. Confident that he was out of harm's way, Harrison switched on his standard right-angle chest torch, then stretched out his fingers to the edge of the cardboard. He eased one hand under and then the other. Gently, very gently, he began to lift. The light from his torch probed into the shadow. And there it was, the pressure mat.

It was a difficult manoeuvre, raising the large expanse of heavy cardboard clear. At one point an end flap dropped and swung perilously close to the surface of the mat. At last he was able to drop it behind him on the steps. Only then he realised that he'd been holding his breath during the entire operation.

Now he was able to identify the connecting wires and quickly snipped them before casting the mat aside.

He reported back to Zulu Control and told them what he'd found; the information was then passed on to the operators of the Wheelbarrow at the south end.

Monk was back at his side, anxious to get on, his team working up the steps behind him. But Harrison had to resist the temptation to cut too many corners, although the SAS man was clearly impatient for him to neutralise the nail bomb on the wall.

That done, they moved swiftly up the next flight, Harrison hopeful that they had cleared the last of Clodagh Dougan's defences. But, as they turned the next corner, he was confronted by a barricade. It was formed by an old iron bedstead frame with half its springs missing and held in place by crisscrossing spars of old rotten timber. In the middle of the obstacle sat a one-gallon motor-oil can, a battery taped to the outside and wires leading from the cap, slithering away to somewhere unseen amid the clutter.

'*Shit!*' Monk's voice was clear in Harrison's earpiece.

It didn't take a genius to work out that buried in the barricade were one or more tilt or pressure switches that would trigger the moment anything was disturbed.

Harrison shone his Allen lamp over the tangle of wood and metal, trying to work out its exact purpose. There had to be some logic in it, he told himself. But what?

'*There's one!*' Monk said.

The mercury tilt switch had been fitted to the underside, halfway along a length of timber that had been rested on the top edge of the blocking bedstead frame. Harrison shone his lamp along it. In total five wooden spars held the barricade upright, one other also with a switch. Both out of reach.

'If we can hold those two spars steady . . .' Harrison began.

Monk saw his point, beckoned up the next SAS soldier waiting below. The sergeant major pointed to the second spar. '*If you let it slip, we'll end up like paint on the walls!*'

The man grimaced in his respirator and set to the job in hand. Harrison crouched down and squinted into the lamp beam for a better view of the switches. The blobs of mercury were obviously at the bottom of the capsules, the contact points nearer to him. If the bedstead was pulled away, which would have been the most likely occurrence during a hasty assault, the spars would lower and allow the mercury to touch the contacts.

If they pushed, the spars might remain safely upright, but the bedstead would land on top of the bomb itself with unknown and probably horrendous consequences.

There was only one thing for it. He waved up more troops from below and told them to hold the bedstead firm. He then proceeded to treat it like a fence, mounting it one foot at a time until he could lift one leg over. His head cracked unexpectedly against the ceiling. Cursing, he looked up. Not the ceiling. It was the narrow conduit piping that had once carried power to the lights at each landing.

It gave him an idea. Feeling in his tool belt, he extracted a length of paracord, cut it and poked it through the small gap between the conduit and the surface of the ceiling. He tied a slipknot in one end and dropped it over the spar that Monk was supporting.

The SAS man nodded, obviously smiling inside his respirator as he saw Harrison pull on the loose end and the timber securely eased upwards and tied into the vertical position, the globule of mercury safely at the bottom of its capsule.

By the time he'd repeated the process with the second spar, the edge of the bedstead which he straddled was cutting painfully into his crotch. Cramp was beginning to set in.

Awkwardly he drew over his other leg and stepped down into the barricade, checking first that he wasn't placing his boot onto some nasty surprise. Now he could reach the oil can and swiftly cut the battery leads, then the wires to the tilt switches.

'Don't touch it or kick it,' Harrison warned. 'There could be an antilift device underneath it.'

As quickly as possible, without creating noise, the team carried away the bedstead frame and carefully removed the timber until they had a clear passage.

Harrison reported back to Zulu Control and advised that the oil can might still be active for the benefit of those following up.

Taff Lloyd-Williams informed him that the Wheelbarrow was making slow, but so far successful, progress at the south end and that still appeared to be the terrorists' chief concern. So far, so good. But two more landings to clear.

In fact the next landing was devoid of obstacles. But as Harrison used his feeler-probe on the last staircase, he found the tripwire, otherwise unseen in the lamplight. Letting them think they were nearly there, that they were over the worst, getting careless in their anxiety to get it over with, to get stuck in.

He traced the wire to the side wall where the old damp bricks had been chiselled out. The space was just deep enough to allow the Mk 15 to fit. A standard PIRA coffee-jar grenade. Filled with half a kilogram of Semtex and a metal fragmentation liner, a microswitch in the base that would be released when the glass shattered. If a careless foot had caught the wire, the jar would have toppled from its shelf. Crude but devastatingly effective.

Gingerly he twisted the jar round without lifting it, until he could get to the det and cut the leads.

Just a short distance to go now and they were entering Monk's domain. Now the SAS man took over the lead with his Number Two in support. With his back hard against the wall, he edged up the last few steps until his eyes were level with the floor of the top storey.

They'd discussed it earlier. On the south side, the stairwell came up on the right-hand side into a passage which was formed on the right by the building's outer wall and the thin brick wall of the first of the three offices on the left. That was the room the terrorists used most, where McGirl and Clodagh rested. The middle room was where Archie was held. Next was the office Muldoon and Doran used. The layout and approximate disposition of the hostiles had been worked out by the technical experts of SO7 and their thermal-imaging cameras designed for finding survivors in earthquake rubble.

Monk took the last few steps to bring him up into the passage. Ahead of him was a shut door. That led into the open space beyond. He had no doubt it would be wired. Very possibly to explosives hidden somewhere in the darkness of the stairwell. They had no way of knowing. So the door would not be their way in.

Instinctively Monk ran his free hand over the bricks of the partition wall on his left. It would take them straight into the first office where Trenchard had been instructed to leave the land-line telephone earlier.

He turned and beckoned the first men of the assault 'brick'. One dropped to his knee, covering the door with his Remington repeater shotgun. The next two carried the frame-charge between them, secured it to the partition wall and withdrew. Then Monk and the SAS trooper with the shotgun pulled back down the stairs.

Normally a frame-charge would not be used indoors because there was a good chance the reverberating overpressure of the explosion would bring the roof down on top of them. But there was an outside window across the top passage that should relieve the massive blast of displaced air. If the theory held good, it would be a damn sight faster than breaking through the wall with sledges.

The sergeant major spoke rapidly into his mike. 'Sunray to Zulu. In position. Request sitrep. Over.'

'*Roger, Sunray, McGirl has been told the helicopter is coming in to land.*' Diversion, get them to the windows, away from the boy. '*At present two hostiles by south stairwell – worried about Barrow – and one each on east and west sides, approx midway. Expect Armalites and sidearms. Three minutes okay? Over.*'

'Roger. Over.' Set.

'*Three minute countdown . . . now! Standby and off.*'

Monk pulled back further, to be well clear of the frame-charge blast. Glanced back at the stairway now filled with black figures, poised, sweating. Knew all had heard on the net. Safeties coming off. Tense, muscles like coiled springs.

Above their heads the ceiling began to shake as the helicopter came lower, swooping in for its final descent. Into the blaze of floodlights on the concrete apron at the front of the old brewery building.

Monk looked at Harrison, now drawn back against the wall to allow the others to pass, and gave him a thumbs-up sign of reassurance.

Get it right, Harrison thought savagely. I've got you this far, you big bastard, now you get it right for me. That's Archie in there. My son. Just through two thin partition walls. If he dies now, I'll even hear his screams. Get him killed, Sergeant Major Monk, and I'll fucking well kill *you*! So get it bloody right.

The sound outside was deafening now, the big Puma swaggering out of the night sky, its downdraught blasting away the rubbish on the forecourt, the building trembling to its foundations.

'*All hostiles moved to windows on east side,*' intoned the voice of the SO7 man with the thermal-imager over the net.

Nearly there, Harrison thought, looking at his watch. Thirty seconds to go . . . Too long, they should be going in now. McGirl and the others have seen the helicopter, will start thinking about leaving, collecting their weapons. Collecting their insurance. Archie. Go *now* for pity's sake!

The second hand dragged as though restrained by glue. 'Fifteen, fourteen . . .'

'*Standby, standby.*' Monk's voice in his ear. Patient. All the time in the bloody world.

'*One hostile leaving window for north end. SO7.*'

Sod! Which hostile coming towards us, towards Archie? No way of knowing.

Eight, seven . . .

How fast was the bastard walking? How long would it take him to get to Archie's cell?

Four, three . . .

C'mon, *c'mon*!

Two, one.

'*FIRE!*' Monk's voice yelled in his ear.

Leo Muldoon was halfway across the open space of the top floor, Armalite held loosely in his hand. There was a smile on his face. You had to hand it to Pat McGirl. Hard bastard, but he knew his stuff. Had got the Brits and Dublin by the short and curlies. A flight to freedom courtesy of the bloody Royal Air Force. Not bad that. Worth a few free beers down the Falls Road that . . .

All he saw was a sudden pulse of light ahead of him. It came from the open door of the office where McGirl and the Dougan woman had slept. The brilliance of the light blinded him, stopped him in his tracks. Almost simultaneously the rolling boom of the frame-charge hit him, making him jump.

He recovered quickly, bringing up his Armalite into the fire position, trying to focus, the afterimage of the explosion still etched in front of his eyes. Now the smoke, tumbling out of the open office door.

A thousand thoughts rushed through his mind. No one could have got through the north-end defences without them knowing. So it was some sort of grenade, lobbed from the outside . . . No, the land-line telephone. The bastards had filled it with explosive . . .

Outside, the floodlights died, pitching the place into utter darkness. It was followed by the crack of small-arms fire. He heard glass shattering, something falling onto the debris on the floor. The faint hiss and the acrid stench.

'GAS!' McGirl shrieked.

Muldoon dropped to his knees, threw down his Armalite and

grabbed at the army-surplus gas mask in the case attached to his belt. McGirl, you fucken genius, you think of everything.

The rubber strap was only halfway over his head when the first black shadow emerged from the haze of smoke, a starburst of light dazzling from the torch fitted over the barrel of the MP5. More shadows in the smoke, jostling for position.

His hand found the Armalite, began to lift it when the two rounds slammed into his chest. As he fell back, the air above his head was filled with a hail of fire passing in both directions.

Doran had opened up with half-a-magazine while Clodagh and McGirl were pulling on their gas masks. He saw the sinister dark figures in the smoke, tracked along as they tried to reach the second door where Archie was held. Then he aimed at the tell-tale positioning of their gun torches before they flicked off.

He saw two go down before the CS caught in his throat and eyes, his vision suddenly lost to the stinging gas.

'BASTARDS!' McGirl shouted, the voice muffled in the gas mask. With his left hand he reached into his pocket and pulled out the small cylindrical transmitter. His thumb found the power key, flipped it on.

Clodagh saw. 'No, Pat!' She stretched out her hand.

The surface of the wall beside them disintegrated, raked with fire from the intruders. Sprays of brick dust showered over them as they flung themselves down.

Clodagh levelled her Armalite, squeezed the trigger. The weapon trembled in her hands, the short burst whistling through the intervening space. She saw the phantom figures rolling left and right, parted by her aim. But she had no idea if she'd hit anyone.

Beside her, McGirl recovered the transmitter he had dropped in his moment of panic. Power on, he checked, his thumb moving to the red fire button.

Clodagh glimpsed what he was doing. 'Pat, for God's sake, not now! Not the boy!' Her words unheard.

Double-pulse, two blips.

The explosion appeared to rock the north end. For the first time, the door to the stairwell was blown open, triggering the booby trap. Another fizzling blue flash with a white core and an ear-splitting crack as the small charge was detonated. Then everything was lost in the tongue of flame and choking black smoke that tumbled out of the stairwell passage.

Harrison tried to pick himself off the floor. His ears were ringing, the excited voices in his earpiece strangely muted and echoing. Muffled words shouted into an iron pan. He knew then he was concussed. Where was he? What had he been doing? All was confusion, smoke and flame everywhere.

It started to come back, mental images, piece by piece like a cerebral jigsaw. He had been standing on the lower landing, keeping to one side. Saw the sheet of lightning as the frame-charge blew. Heard its blast and felt the heart-shaking kick of displaced air that blew the entire outside window and surrounding brick-work out into the factory yard. Saw Monk running up the stairs, through the ragged smoking hole and into the first office. Harrison standing, still tight against the wall, as the SAS figures, black and anonymous, rushed past him. Swarming like ants. More and more coming from below. Maybe only twenty, but seeming like hundreds.

Then down to the stragglers, the tail-end Charlies, and he had joined them then, no longer willing to wait. Anxious to grab his son, spirit him away as the second team rescued the boy and passed him back through the smouldering aperture.

There had suddenly been a lot of gunfire and he knew some-thing had gone wrong, sensed it. He wondered whether there had been a shortfall in CS gas. They'd discussed it earlier, how the mullioned steel windows would make a heli-assault difficult, even if the sills weren't rigged with explosive. How it would be difficult to fire in canister rounds from the outside through the small panes . . .

Harrison had recalled all this as he'd followed the charging SAS men into the first office. Through the open door, he heard the ear-splitting shriek and flashes of the stun grenades and saw muzzle flashes in the darkness. Had seen two bodies on the floor. Somehow knew, just *knew* that they were the men charged with getting into the second office and pulling out his son.

473

And that had been the moment the explosion had gone off! Now he realised where he was. He was sitting on the floor of the first office where he'd been blown, struck from behind by the mighty unseen hand. The stairwell. He knew it was the stairwell and, in confirmation, smoke came belching in from the passage with the flickering light of flame behind it.

He didn't need to be told what had happened. He knew. Maybe they'd forgotten or perhaps his warning message hadn't got through to everyone. But in the darkness and confusion and the scramble to get up the steps, someone had accidently kicked the oil-can bomb he'd been unable to defuse. It was no comfort now to learn that his hunch about the antilift device had been right.

His senses returning, he climbed to his feet. Gunfire was still crackling out in the main area, more stuns going off like mini-nukes in the blackness. He just knew it had all gone badly wrong.

A figure appeared at the frame-charge hole, his Panotex suit shredded, blood dripping from his arm. The man indicated back down the stairwell and shook his head.

No more explanation was necessary. Harrison could see the growing intensity of flickering orange light behind the wounded soldier. Could feel the rise in temperature already. All that rubbish on the stairs . . . the place would be an inferno in seconds. Tongues of flames greedily seeking the explosives he'd dismantled earlier.

Pitching onto all fours he wriggled across to the door that opened onto the main area. It was impossible to tell what was going on. Pitch black except for muzzle flashes, ribbons of smoke drifting through the torch beams scanning the void like search-lights. He crawled over the body of a soldier. Dead or dying, he couldn't tell. Then another, the man's hand reaching up, fingers around the handle of the second office door. The respirator had been shattered by the round that had smashed into his forehead and now the dead eyes stared at him. Sorry, mate, I did my best.

Harrison prised the fingers from the handle, feeling the bones resist, crackling as he tore them free.

Then the door swung open and he was in. 'ARCHIE!'

'Dad?' the voice was small and tremulous in the dark.

He switched on his chest torch.

His son was spotlit in the beam, lying on the floor, still strapped to a chair by parcel tape. Shaking uncontrollably like someone in a fever.

Then Harrison saw the bullet marks on the wall below the window and the torn holes in the radiator where the stray rounds had come through the door.

'I-I thought I-I'd b-better get down.'

Harrison grinned at his son as he knelt. 'Smart lad.' His voice muffled in the respirator.

'Careful, Dad, there's a bomb underneath the chair!'

He stared in disbelief. Who, in God's name could do such a thing? He reached forward, getting a better angle of light to it.

'I-t's radio-controlled.'

'I'm not sure, I can't see any aerial . . .'

'In my hand.'

What? Harrison stared. Archie's hands were strapped tight to his side, his fingertips barely below the seat on which he sat. Yet somehow he'd managed to stretch out beneath him, because now, between two fingers, was the little snake of aerial wire he'd torn away.

'It needs an aerial doesn't it, Dad? Like that model plane you made me?'

Harrison felt the relief ebb up inside him, couldn't stop the hot tears in his eyes. He looked again at the package beneath the chair, looked for and found the off-switch, then pulled out the detonator. Taking the craft knife from his tool belt, he sliced through the parcel tape that bound his son and helped him to his feet.

Then the door burst open behind him. The big hooded figure stared for a moment. It was Monk.

'*Is he all right, Tom?*' the voice said over Harrison's comms.

'He's safe.'

A nod of the head. '*What a fuck-up! Still, looks like it's over. We've identified three of the hostiles. Two dead, one wounded. I expect another body's out there somewhere, but there's so much smoke, it'll take a while to confirm.*'

'That explosion . . .?' Harrison began.

Monk shook his head. '*No details yet, but the stairs are burning like buggery. We'll have to exit out the south side.'* He turned to the dead soldier by the door and freed the spare respirator from the man's belt. It had been destined for Archie. *'Put this on the lad and come with me.'*

Harrison pulled the contraption over his son's head, gave him a thumbs-up and a smile of reassurance. Archie's eyes looked back nervously through the lenses.

'Keep close,' Monk said. *'We'll stay next to the wall.'*

Harrison put his arm round the boy's shoulders and followed Monk out of the office.

Flame was now licking out of the stairwell door like a dragon's tongue, the conflagration taking hold on the flimsy partitioning. The main area itself was now filled with dense, choking black smoke and clouds of cordite as Monk edged along the east wall, his Heckler at the ready.

The shooting had ceased, but amid the evil fog Harrison could see the sharp stabs of torchlight as SAS soldiers scoured the floor for signs of survivors, friendly or hostile.

They kept moving steadily, Monk arcing his MP5 left and right as they passed the halfway point. Harrison followed, a reassuring arm still hugging his son close to his side. Meanwhile the fire at the north end was sweeping through the office partitioning. The flame was almost white in its intensity, its heat like a furnace now, flickering sparks like fireflies drifting towards them, the force of the flames beginning to clear the smoke.

Harrison heard the sudden gunfire, saw Monk fall away, spinning as the shot tore into his shoulder. His weapon flew from his grasp.

Ahead the smoke parted momentarily and he glimpsed the south stairwell door. Just feet away stood Clodagh Dougan, light thrown by the raging fire dancing in the hair that swung around her shoulders. Armalite rising, aiming at anything that moved.

Saw him now. Not knowing who it was behind the respirator. Taking aim as she edged back towards the door and her escape route.

Harrison felt for the Browning in his holster, fumbling at the restraining strap, knowing he was going to be too late.

They all heard it then. The whirring motor and the sound of glass and debris crackling under its tiny caterpillar tracks. Clodagh Dougan turned towards the stairwell in surprise. Dazzled by the Wheelbarrow's mini-spotlight.

Was it Heathcote at the controls or the chubby corporal? Suddenly Harrison felt he knew. It was Clarke. In his element, a kid of the electronic age, wizard at Nintendo and the arcade computer games. Reflexes like lightning.

It must have been an instantaneous decision. Harrison heard the crack of the giant Hotrod disrupter as the waterjet fired, caught the glint of light on the plastic plug as it flashed through the blackness. Seven hundred metres a second.

She couldn't have seen it coming, smashing into her chest at that speed. It was as though she was struck by a thunderbolt from the gods. Didn't even scream. Was just hurtled backwards into the smoke and vanished from view.

Black-gloved hands came from nowhere. They grabbed Harrison and his son, propelled them forward, the boy's feet not even touching the ground.

Within seconds they were running down the stairs, past SAS troopers coming up. They passed Heathcote, in full bombsuit, making safe some device, but he was too busy to notice them.

Then they were out on the concrete apron beside the helicopter, respirators ripped off and gulping down fresh air. Harrison turned and glanced back. A trooper was helping Monk out of the doorway. The less fortunate were being half carried, half dragged.

Beyond the compound gates he saw the flashing lights of the ambulances pulling up. Soldiers and police officers were everywhere, stepping back as he and Archie came through.

Pippa appeared as though from nowhere in the crowd and swept her son into her arms.

Harrison looked on, feeling happy for his wife's relief and joy, yet feeling somehow apart. It was all different now.

'Tom, are you all right?'

It was Casey, standing and grinning at him stupidly, tears rolling down her cheeks.

'I'm fine. Archie's fine.'

She rushed to him, burying her head on his shoulder as he held her close. 'God, I can't tell you . . .'

'I love you.' Suddenly he felt elated, free.

She laughed. 'How much, bomb man?'

'Almost as much as I'd love a hamburger. I'm bloody starving!'

Epilogue

The senator was the last one to leave Trafalgar House. Most of the Unionist delegates, at least those who hadn't already stormed out in protest over one thing or another, had left on the Friday. A few who were working on the various subcommittees stayed on until the Saturday to complete their tasks.

But Abe Powers already knew what they optimistically refused to admit. The hopes and plans for a new Independent Ulster were dead in the water.

There may have been many small agreements, but the divisions on the bigger issues had become veritable chasms. Down to Bishop McLaverty's quiet sabotage, he suspected, but then perhaps the outcome had been inevitable anyway.

Further talks were scheduled but Powers knew they would come to nothing, just wither away. Soon they would be overshadowed by events at the United Nations as the American-led demands for a United Ireland grew. And it would be he, Senator Abe Powers III, who orchestrated them. Already he had a series of meetings lined up with the President for the following week to expand on his proposals. His grandmother would have been proud of him.

On the Sunday morning he rose early. After a shower and shave he breakfasted in his room and admired the view. The sun-drenched water meadows of the Avon and the distant spire of Salisbury Cathedral.

The newspaper he read was full of events which had culminated the previous weekend but had happened too late for the previous Sunday's editions. Now the newshounds had chapter and verse on the IRA abduction of a bomb-disposal expert and the siege of a derelict brewery building. With extra days to put together the reports, there were eye-witness accounts, photographs, detailed diagrams, profiles of the terrorists and the main players involved. Fascinating stuff. Two SAS soldiers dead and two seriously wounded, many with more minor injuries.

Maybe the Brits wouldn't be so keen to smirk now at the efforts of his own country's special forces.

And the terrorists. Two dead and the two leaders badly injured, the woman still in intensive care, her life hanging by a thread.

He couldn't agree with the endless speculation that had been in the press all week that there was some political motivation behind it – to put pressure on the government to agree to the rumoured new American initiative. Bishop McLaverty had assured him the IRA didn't do that sort of thing and he should know.

His breakfast eaten, Powers finished packing his suitcases and called down for his chauffeur to collect them. On his way out he thanked the SAS major in civvies who had been in charge of security.

'Just glad we had no problems, Senator.'

'All your lads gone home?'

'Left an hour ago. The locals will be pleased to have the road open again.'

'And you, Major, posted off to somewhere exotic now, I expect?'

A wry smile. 'Northern Ireland. Some things never change.'

Already the first of the removal vans had arrived to return the furniture, paintings and *objets d'art* to the government repositories. In a few hours Trafalgar House would be empty again.

The major watched from the top of the steps as the American's limo pulled smoothly away and disappeared down the drive towards the gatehouse. Heading for Alderbury on the edge of Salisbury, he knew, through a particularly beautiful and uninhabited stretch of countryside before taking the road towards Basingstoke and the M3 to London.

Sunlight warmed the soldier's face and momentarily he closed his eyes, enjoying its comfort. Hadn't seen much of this during the past few months. It had been another lousy English summer.

The explosion was unmistakable, even at that distance.

His eyes were open instantly, his hand moving to his shoulder holster. Below him on the drive the removal men were looking in the direction of the sound. One of them pointed. An oily cloud of smoke was mushrooming above the treeline.

But, even as the major ran towards his car, the man who had triggered the radio-controlled culvert bomb from a vantage point in the nearby copse was already on his motorcycle. The farmtrack would take him to the A36 in a few minutes.

Half-an-hour later Lewis Fawcett was in Southampton where he abandoned his machine in a back-street parking lot. He dumped his helmet and the overalls, which he had worn during his overnight vigil, in a large commercial dustbin before setting off on foot for the railway station.

There Fawcett bought a newspaper and drank a coffee while he waited for the train to take him to Waterloo. He took the Northern line to Euston, then bought a ticket to Stoke-on-Trent where he had left his car.

On the long and tedious journey, Fawcett thought how his life had changed since he'd left the Shankill as a young man to seek fame and fortune in Rhodesia as it was then. In fact he'd made neither as a special forces soldier. Not then, or even later when he switched allegiance to South Africa. Not now, after the second wind of change on the dark continent had persuaded him there was no future for his specialist skills under black majority rule.

Settle in Liverpool, old friends from Ulster advised him. Maybe we can put a little work your way. And from time to time they did. It helped to pay the mortgage on the little terraced house.

The train had completed over half the distance to Stoke when the young man entered the carriage and took the empty seat opposite him. A T-shirt beneath his leather jacket, the hair on his bullet head razored to a bloom, it was the same man he'd met on the journey down, who had handed him the first half of the money in one plastic bag and an explosive device in another.

'You've done us proud,' he said to Fawcett and slid another carrier across the table between them. 'With the compliments of Mr Jones. Go to the toilet if you want to count it.'

Fawcett noticed that the man had an initial tattooed on each knuckle of his right hand. PIKE – he couldn't quite see the thumb. 'I trust you. I'm back amongst friends. But you didn't have to supply the goods. I could have made my own.'

'No, you couldn't. Not a replica like that. It would have been the wrong signature.'

'Anyway it worked.' To Fawcett, a bomb was a bomb.

'One more thing.'

'The phone call?'

An envelope was passed between them. 'It's safe to ring – no trace. And try to remember your old Ulster accent.'

Fawcett nodded. 'I could do with more work.'

'Maybe, we'll see. This was a one-off. A sort of favour for a favour for old friends.'

'No surrender, eh?'

The young man's lips twitched in a half-smile. Then he was on his feet, sauntering away towards the next carriage.

Lewis Fawcett thumbed open the envelope and read what was typed on the sheet below the telephone number: *The Provisional IRA was responsible for the execution of Senator Abe Powers III this morning. This was punishment for his failure to admit an official representative of this movement to attend the Trafalgar House Talks. Signed: AIDAN.*

He had to smile.

It was one of those strange coincidence of events that so often seem to happen.

The following April, Clodagh Maria Dougan and Patrick McGirl were sent down for life at the Old Bailey on charges of murder and conspiracy to cause explosions.

That same Friday night the annual British Press Awards were being held at Grosvenor House. And Casey Mullins of the *Evening Standard* was on the shortlist for Feature Writer of the Year.

'Is it true you're being head-hunted by the *Sun*?' Eddie Mercs asked as the group made their way towards the tables. He didn't even pretend to keep the envy from his voice.

'Yeah,' she replied, clutching at Harrison's arm.

'You'd be a fool not to take it.'

She looked at the reporter and frowned. 'Listen, Eddie, rumour has it that one's IQ automatically drops twenty points when you join the *Sun* – I'm not sure I can afford to lose that many.' She glanced around her. 'Where's Candy got to?'

'Last I saw, she was with Hal,' Harrison said.

She shook her head. 'That girl's getting more like me every day. Still, who can resist those biker's leathers?'

'I'll get some,' Mercs said.

'Forget it, Eddie. I've moved on to bombsuits.'

Billy Billingham, the features editor, was waving frantically from their table, his carrot hair and multicoloured bow tie unmistakable.

'Does it revolve too?' Harrison whispered in her ear.

Casey giggled. 'And it squirts water.'

According to Mercs, the *Standard*'s proprietors had gone ape-shit. Twice the number of tables as usual had been booked and there had been no objections when Casey had asked for Harrison and her daughter to be allowed to join them. No problem, Billingham had said. He had the editor's ear and clearly the editor was certain that Casey had the title in the bag.

So she pushed her luck and added Midge Midgely and Al Pritchard to her list.

'Why don't you just invite every bomb-disposal man in the country?' had been the sardonic reply.

In the event Pritchard declined, but the blunt Yorkshireman accepted enthusiastically.

Harrison was pleased to have his old friend for company. Although he'd now come to know many of Casey's newspaper friends, he was still a little guarded in their company. Yet their cynicism and black humour, he came to realise, wasn't that different from that of the military. Not that he himself would be in the military much longer. In August he was due to leave to set up his own specialist consultancy. Someone had estimated that there were a hundred million antipersonnel mines left scattered around the world, claiming the lives of innocent civilians every day.

That alone would keep his company and others busy well into the next century.

But the really funny thing was, it had been Pippa's father who had put up the money for Harrison's new venture. After reading about events at the brewery, the old buffer had apparently decided that bomb disposal was 'proper soldierin' ' after all.

Pippa herself was now living with her PR boss, Jonathan Beazley, and had custody of Archie. It seemed the air was filled with flying cross-petitions and there'd be some messy legal battles to come. At least Archie was more than happy to spend most of his time at Hurlingham; he was now a total hero to his friends and was more determined than ever to be an ATO when he left school.

'Heard about Clodie Dougan, I suppose?' Midge said after the meal, as the compère from *UK Press Gazette* introduced the Heritage Minister who would present the awards.

Harrison nodded. 'Brought it all back today.'

Again he wondered about the culvert bomb that had killed Senator Abe Powers. It must have been planted by some other member of the AIDAN unit who was not at the brewery. Whoever was responsible, with the American dead there had been no more talk of a United Ireland. The US President seemed to have other things on his mind. However, shortly after Powers' murder, Britain had regained the initiative with the Downing Street Declaration. It invited the terrorists to lay down their arms and join the peace process.

'Wonder if Les has heard about the conviction,' Midge said. 'Seen him recently?'

'Not since Christmas. He was in rehab at Headley Court. He was still smarting over losing his second leg. Couldn't get the hang of his artificial ones. And he'd started drinking more than was good for him.'

Midge grinned. 'Bloody legless, was he?'

Casey was on Harrison's other side and heard the words. 'That wasn't . . .'

The Yorkshireman raised his hand. 'Sorry, sweetheart, bomb man's humour.'

It was then that the main award ceremony began in earnest. A

484

lot of bad in-jokes, clapping and thank you speeches. The audience drunk and happy, black ties askew.

'Now we come to the Feature Writer of the Year,' announced the compère. 'Stiff competition again, but we've a shortlist of six. Andy Dougall of *The Times* for his report on the Ethiopian famine. Bess Hartley of the *Daily Mail* for her series on the disabled living in modern society. Peter Bilton of *The Independent* for his Triad investigation. Casey Mullins of the *Evening Standard* for her highly personalised accounts of last year's IRA bombing campaign in London . . .'

The air was electric now. Casey's hand found Harrison's on the table and he squeezed it reassuringly. She looked at him and grinned. How radiant she looked tonight, he thought, eyes dancing with anticipation like a kid at Christmas. Body tense in the sequinned black number that showed shoulders sprinkled with freckles and hair up to reveal the hanging pearl drops on her ears.

'And the winner is . . .' the Heritage Minister began, fumbling with the envelope.

Harrison squeezed harder. Mercs and Billy Billingham winked across the table.

'Andy Dougall of *The Times*.'

The embarrassed, stuttering applause gradually built up as the journalist made his way towards the stage. No one had expected that. Casey's face crumpled as she brought her hands together.

'Sorry,' Harrison said and kissed her cheek.

'Outrageous,' Mercs grumbled. 'You was robbed.'

The ceremony moved laboriously on, but the magic spell had been broken. The glitz and glamour of it all now seeming self-indulgent and tiresome, even phoney.

'Just before we end tonight's proceedings,' the compère said, 'I have a special announcement to make. The judges have taken the decision to introduce a new award for first-hand account journalism which will be given in future only in the most exceptional circumstances. It will be named after its first recipient. The Casey Mullins Award.'

The hall exploded into applause. Casey was stunned, reeling

as Harrison and Mercs helped her to her feet and propelled her towards the stage.

'. . . And to present tonight's prize,' the compère continued, '. . . a very honoured special guest.'

As Casey mounted the steps, the curtains parted at the back of the stage. A tall, lean figure walked uncertainly forward.

Harrison's mouth dropped. He couldn't believe it.

Midgely stared. 'It's Les.'

'. . . Mr Leslie Appleyard of the Metropolitan Police Explosives Section,' the voice continued over the amplifier, 'the subject of one of Casey Mullins's most moving accounts of the Tick Tock Men – a term the nation now has taken to its heart.'

The embrace between Casey and Appleyard seemed to last for ever before the compère managed to prise her away and lead her to the microphone.

Tears were streaming down her cheeks as she gasped for breath. 'Ladies, gentlemen, I–I don't know what to say . . . To see Les here walking again is the greatest prize I could get . . . to win this award as well . . . it's too much!'

She looked back at the Expo and smiled. Then, regaining some composure, she continued: 'Hell, I'm going to be all-American and schmaltzy about this, I'm sorry. I just wrote about what other people did. This is *their* story. In particular it's Tom Harrison's story. Tom and I hope to marry later this year.' As the crescendo of cheers and wolf whistles rose, she squinted out beyond the spotlights. 'Tom, could I ask you to join me up here? My quiet hero . . .'

Midgely pushed his friend forward. 'Go on, you old bastard, it's your moment of glory. I'll never let you live it down.'

The applause had become a standing ovation by the time Harrison had reached the stage.

'I'd rather defuse a bomb than this,' he said hoarsely in her ear.

She laughed, holding her trophy high for everyone to see. 'Who needs a Pulitzer, Tom? I've got a Mullins.'

He kissed her cheek and looked out over the sea of cheering faces. From the corner of his mouth, he whispered: 'So have I.'